# THE RED FOX DIARIES

# THE RED FOX DIARIES

ENNES BASTIN

Published in 2026 by SilverWood Books

SilverWood Books Ltd
14 Small Street, Bristol, BS1 1DE, United Kingdom
www.silverwoodbooks.co.uk



ISBN 978-1-80042-322-0 (paperback)
Also available as an ebook

British Library Cataloguing in Publication Data
A CIP catalogue record for this book is available from the British Library

Page design and typesetting by SilverWood Books

# THE RED FOX DIARIES

# Prologue

"I'd like to make a withdrawal." The voice was soft, gentle, high-pitched and slightly reedy, with a clear twang of the north-west counties. It was also little more than a whisper, but projected with a clipped diction so as to be clear at the first time of hearing.

A wet Tuesday in central Shrewsbury was bad enough, but being assigned the lunchtime shift had just about capped it for Lowells Bank's most junior cashier. Lester Sweet was feeling sorry for himself. Fed up and irritated with the world, he couldn't even be bothered to look up at the new customer as he extended a limp hand for the anticipated withdrawal slip. There wasn't one. He raised his gaze a fraction and nearly choked. Although mostly concealed by the customer's coat sleeve, it was unmistakable even to the uninitiated: the so-called 'dangerous end' of a big black gun.

"Make n-no mistake, Lester," said the customer, bending slightly to read the cashier's plastic name tag. "I promise you I will shoot you if you do anything to draw attention to us."

The young cashier fought the urge to gag, swallowed hard, and nodded before finally raising his gaze to briefly look into the eyes of his nightmare. Using his facial expression alone, he showed just how exceedingly compliant he was about to be.

The creature staring straight back at him was not at all what Lester had imagined a bank robber would look like. But, then again, he'd never expected to ever meet one. The face, or what he could see of it set deep within the hood of a bulky grey overcoat, seemed absurdly small, its skin pale to almost white. The only visible colour was a bright ginger moustache that drooped down to the jawline on either side of a narrow, thin-lipped mouth. The eyes above were a soft watery grey, but still pierced directly into his soul as they peered out at him through circular wire-rimmed glasses, one arm of which was affixed to the frame with a thick pink-fabric sticking plaster.

Suddenly aware he was both shivering and sweating, Lester was also feeling more light-headed by the second, and a violent tremor was spreading down from his shoulders to his fingertips. He tried to mumble a plea for mercy, but nothing came free beyond the tiniest frog-like croak.

"Stay with me, Lester," cajoled the voice from beyond the counter, the words delivered in an absurd sing-song tone quite at odds with the scene being played out, "because if you don't do exactly what I ask, I will shoot you. And if you pretend to faint, I'll shoot you on the way down, just for messing me about. You see," the robber paused to slowly exhale through his nose, "there's n-nothing personal about this, Lester. It's just business. And it's n-not *your* money, so why take the risk of getting yourself hurt...or worse?"

The young man nodded, gulped in a short breath, and waited for the detailed instructions he instinctively knew would be coming.

"Fill this," said the robber, continuing to keep his voice steady and low as he used his gun-free hand to slide a folded Sainsbury's carrier bag across the countertop. "Only the n-notes, of course. And make sure n-nobody sees."

A soft double tap of the gun barrel tip on the counter surface made Lester flinch, but he was already hard at work, diligently emptying his cash drawer in double-quick time.

"N-now fold the bag top over and slide it back to me, slow and easy."

Lester did precisely as instructed, fighting to control the quaking in his upper body.

"Thank you, Lester, you've done very well. But n-now I've got one last little thing that I n-need you to do for me. Are you listening carefully?"

The distraught cashier nodded yet again, forcing himself not to faint and get shot, desperately listening to make sure he heard the robber's final instructions above the blood hammering in his ears.

"I'm going to walk out slowly and leave you to enjoy the rest of your day. But if you do anything, and I mean *anything*, to draw attention – raise the alarm, whatever – I will shoot the first person I see. I won't care if it's a man, a woman, or even a little kiddie – I will shoot them." The robber waited for the young man to look up and meet his eyes before finishing with a harshly whispered, "N-now, you wouldn't want that on your conscience, would you, eh, *Lester*?"

A silent wobble of the cashier's head was enough to confirm that the message had been received, understood, and would be complied with to the letter.

"So when I leave, you count slowly to fifty and then maybe take a n-nice long toilet break before you tell anybody about what's just happened here. Are we clear?"

Lester nodded. And he was still nodding several minutes after the grey-coated figure had turned away and calmly strolled off and out into the relentless Shropshire drizzle beyond the bank's front doors.

# Chapter 1

"Where've you been to this hour?"

It was always the first thing Roy said when she got home. And it was always called out from the armchair where he was always sitting. And it always had to be shouted above the blaring television that was always on and up loud. Somehow, 'always' had come to sum up life these last few years.

"Shrewsbury," she shouted back from the hall as she shrugged off her overcoat, at the same time slipping out of her shoes. "I told you this morning."

He used the remote to turn the telly volume down a few notches. "You didn't say you were going to be this late, though. I'm starving."

Carol bit her lip and just managed to stop herself speaking her thoughts aloud. You know where the bloody larder is, Roy. But, then again, maybe you've forgotten how your legs work since you retired. "Train was delayed," she said to the back of his head as she passed the open sitting-room door on her way to the kitchen. "Engineering works, so they told us. How was your bowling?"

"Rubbish," he grumped, adding an elongated growl to emphasise the single word. "Only managed five ends before it started chucking it down. And Cliff didn't even turn up. Prostate giving him grief, apparently. Funny how he only gets it bad when there's rain forecast."

Carol wasn't really listening. She'd only asked out of politeness. Just like she did every Tuesday and Thursday evening when he came home from the club. "I'll get the tea on straight away," she said, to make sure she didn't get the full commentary on the five ends they had managed. Or the medical reports from his other two ancient bowling mates. One or other of them always had some bloody ailment they thought worth discussing at length.

"What've we got?" he asked, still not moving from his chair or managing to tear his eyes from the box.

"I picked up some of those fat Cumberland sausages you like from Jenlow's on the way back from the station. So it's them with mash and a bit of broccoli. Alright?"

"Don't forget the gravy."

As if. After damned near fifty years cooking for him, she'd well and truly got the gravy message. *And* the very precise thickness of said delicacy as individually defined to match each different meal. "Fancy a cuppa while you're waiting?"

"Thought you'd never ask," came the reply, like she'd been holding back the offering for hours instead of the less than two minutes she'd been indoors.

There was no response necessary, so she simply took herself off into the kitchen to set about her evening routine of getting their meal, starting by putting the kettle on. As the tap ran to fill it, Carol stared at the reflection looking back at her from the kitchen window and chewed at the inside of her cheek. She often did that of late. The staring thing more than the cheek-chewing business. The window had become a good friend over the years, its age-deformed glass somehow managing to smooth out the deterioration that sixty-nine-and-a-bit years had wreaked upon her face, hiding the worst of the blemishes and firming the skin better than any expensive cream might. At times she could almost see the young woman she'd once been, and tonight her window was working its magic better than ever. She smiled and enjoyed the sight of her rejuvenated reflection grinning back.

She'd been not half bad looking as a teenager. Not a stunner, as they'd say, but definitely none too scabby. And she'd been the life and soul of the party back then. Always fun. The one all the other girls wanted to hang around with. Until she'd taken up with Roy, fallen proper in love and settled down.

Why did they call it 'settling down' and not 'giving up'? But had she? Really? Maybe, maybe not. She'd think about that one another day. Not now. No point in spoiling a damned good day out with too much soul-searching. Plus she was still enjoying the deep satisfaction of taking a little bit of happiness from doing solely what she alone had wanted to do without any other bugger demanding different. No husband, no kids, no grandkids. Not a soul expecting her to merrily fall into line with what they wanted while, all too often, making fun of her.

"Where's that brew?" came the 'nudge' shouted through from the sitting room, now above the familiar jingle of the early-evening news.

Lazy blighter, thought Carol. After all these years she didn't expect him to leap up to welcome her home. And she knew for sure he wouldn't even dream to ask her what she'd been doing all day. But, there again, if he did ask she probably wouldn't find the energy to tell him. He wouldn't listen anyway, and not in a million years would he believe that what she'd been doing could make anyone feel good. She began to chuckle, quickly suppressing it before he heard. Too late.

"What you laughing at?" came the shout from beyond.

At least his ears work, she thought. "Oh, it's nothing," she called back. "I just thought of something funny. Don't worry, dinner's on the go."

With the potatoes on the boil and the sausages sizzling in the pan, Carol took through his mug of tea, carefully putting it into his hands whilst making sure not to stand in front of the screen. He did say, "Thank you, love", but that was it, exactly as she'd come to expect. He was too engrossed in the news now. Something about China and computer hacking. Two places he'd never been and never would: China or computers.

For the next half-hour she busied herself getting their evening meal ready. They'd eat it off their laps in front of the telly, as always, watching whatever it was Roy wanted to watch. He usually said something like, "We'll enjoy this, love", but did he really know what his wife enjoyed any more? Carol knew not, but couldn't be bothered to make a fuss. To be fair, she didn't know either, so there was no point bringing it up. Just go along with it, like what most of the old wives she knew did. They grinned, they bore it, and then they moaned like hell about their husbands whenever they got together. To most of them, it eased the tedium. To Carol, it simply made it worse.

She was bloody bored most of the time and, although deep down she still loved her Roy and knew, deep down, that he loved her, she sometimes felt a bit like they'd both died and hadn't recognised it. They lived together, yes, but somehow they existed on parallel tracks, like passengers on two different trains running along side by side, the two of them merely looking across at each other through the windows and waving.

Somehow over the years her life had drifted from a small but mostly colourful garden to a barren terrain of endless grey. She'd first noticed it happening when Sarah and Paul had left home within a few weeks of each other, their daughter to a love-nest on the edge of town and their son to a shared student flat in Manchester. The gap they left behind was sudden and painful. 'Empty Nest Syndrome' they called it. No real sense of purpose any more. No value. Invisible until one or other of the fledglings was back wanting something: a few quid to tide them over to the end of the month, a free hot meal, a bit of washing and ironing done. And later, for Sarah anyway, she'd been back needing a babysitter and later a childminder. The granddaughters were a blessing, make no mistake, but now as young teenagers even they didn't hold back on making fun of silly old, boring old Grandma.

Roy retiring had pretty much capped it – cemented it, if you like. Locked in the hazy grey eternity of nothing. He wasn't one for travel, she'd known that. And money was and always had been tight, to say the least. So him having all day every day to do whatever he wanted, whilst actually doing bugger all apart from his two afternoons a week at the bowling club, had cast a brutal spotlight on the emptiness of her existence.

Her best friend had once asked her why she put up with it. The answer had been simple, even though it was delivered in the form of another question. "And do what?" she'd asked. It was the end of the discussion, and Janice had never raised it again.

In some twisted sort of way she was a lucky one, Janice. Her 'old man' had suddenly dropped dead six years since, and although she'd been genuinely grief-stricken at the time, it only took her a few months for the reality to dawn. She was free. On top of that, he'd left behind a bloody great big pot of money: a massive life insurance policy and all sorts of shares and savings she'd known absolutely nothing about while he'd been alive. And yet, despite all that, Janice didn't actually do anything different.

It wasn't until a few months back that she'd offered an explanation. Carol hadn't asked, but that afternoon, as the two of them sat having coffee and a slice of 'naughty cake' in Benjamin's, Janice had – suddenly and unprompted – laid it out. She may be going along the same old roads to the same old places, she'd said, but now it was because *she* wanted to. It was *her* who was picking the place, the day, the time, the route, and *she* was doing the steering rather than being a sack of spuds in the passenger seat. "A bloody attractive sack of spuds, mind you," she'd added, just getting the words out before bursting into her trademark cackling laugh that had all the other patrons in there turning around to stare.

Carol had joined in with the laughter. It had seemed the right thing to do. But what her friend had said set her thinking. She herself was more like a passenger in a car that was up on bricks. It never went anywhere. Of course leaving Roy was out of the question, and waiting for him to pop his clogs was something she refused even to think about. Besides, as and when he did go, there wasn't any money, she knew that. But Janice's revelation had delivered

Carol the jolt she needed to do something about her life. And on her short, solitary walk home that day she resolved that she would find something to do that was hers, something for her and her alone, something that would prove – to her at least – that she wasn't dull, boring and essentially pointless beyond housework. Yes indeed, she would come up with something that would make her feel better about herself and deliver a little bit of joy to her world.

The idea she'd eventually come up with still brought a smile to her face whenever she thought about it, and this evening was no different. She'd had a great day out, all by herself, simply doing solely what she alone wanted to do. And it had delivered wonderfully yet again. "Well done, you, Carol," she whispered to her younger self in the window glass. And with a small wink, she turned away and set about dishing up their tea.

Carrying her husband's tray through to him, she placed it carefully onto his lap like the perfect maid, before returning to the kitchen to fetch her own. A couple of minutes later and she was sat there beside him, as always in her separate armchair, her mind drifting away to nowhere.

Suddenly he shocked her nearly rigid by clicking the telly to mute. And then he spoke to her. He didn't actually turn his head to look at her as he did so but, then again, you can't have everything.

"Where was it you said you'd been today, love?" he asked.

"Shrewsbury," she replied, not knowing where he was going with the sudden and wholly unexpected interrogation. "Window-shopping," she added. "Oh, and don't worry, I didn't actually buy anything."

"Bloody hell. You weren't anywhere near Lowells Bank were you, in the centre?"

Carol gave herself a couple of seconds to think. "Yes, I was," she said. "Why?"

"That bank robber, the one with the ginger moustache, well, he did them over today. And it's his fourth, they reckon. Apparently walked in calm as you like and terrorised the cashier with a bloody great big gun. You could have got mixed up in that. I'm always telling you big cities are dangerous."

"Don't be so melodramatic, love." snorted Carol as she chewed on a piece of broccoli. "He didn't actually shoot anyone, did he? I mean, he never does, does he?"

"No, but he could have. You never know with these nutters."

"It's probably not even a real gun," she scoffed.

"The police seem to think it is. They're taking it very seriously."

"Okay, alright, you win. I won't go to the big city again if it worries you." She gave a snort of dry laughter. "As if Shrewsbury's a big city."

"I don't know why he does it," continued her husband, managing to somehow talk around a mouthful of sausage. "They said he only got away with six and a half grand. Hardly worth the risk, is it?"

"You wouldn't complain if six and a half thousand quid fell into your lap, would you? And if you're telling me this is his fifth, then..."

"Fourth," he corrected.

"Okay, his fourth, then he's up over twenty thousand. That's worth having."

"Yeah, I suppose you're right." It was a grudging concession, but he still wasn't ready to wrap up the discussion just yet. "The coppers reckon he gives it all away, you know. Like he's some sort of Shropshire Robin Hood."

"What makes them think that?" asked Carol, pausing her eating to ask.

"Apparently, every time he does a bank there's a mysterious donation to some charity or other within the next few days. Always in cash, and always the same amount as what he made off with from his last job."

"Coincidence?" she suggested.

"No," said Roy, shaking his head sagely as he assumed the role of armchair professor of criminology. "Last one he did, they had all the banknote numbers on file and managed to cross-check them with the bundle he left at some hospice in Church Stretton. Took the money back, they did. Confiscated the lot."

"That's ruddy mean," said Carol, turning her nose up in a show of disapproval.

"That is real life," corrected Roy, shaking his head again to emphasise his profound wisdom. "You can't have charities living off illegal profits," he added, now sounding both pompous and sanctimonious.

"Why ever not?" she challenged.

And that was the end of it. In a flash, the remote control was thumbed and the volume cranked back up to its customary brain-rattling level. He always did that. When he'd run out of ideas or simply couldn't be bothered to find one, he phased her out, cut her off, and metaphorically, like Elvis himself, left the building.

"Fancy some apple pie?" she asked when she could see they'd both finished their first plate. "I've got one in the freezer. Could have it ready in about twenty minutes."

Roy half turned his head and nodded. "A couple of scoops of soft ice cream would help it go down," he added, before returning his full attention to the weather forecast. Or was it the young bird doing it that demanded the sudden focus?

Carol got to her feet, collected her husband's plate onto her tray, and carried the whole lot through to the kitchen. She put the plates into the sink and ran the tap to bring the hot water through. The freezer was in the outhouse across the backyard, and she was wishing she hadn't mentioned the pie now. It was cold, dark and raining again out there, but she'd suggested it, and, besides, she needed to go anyway.

In the hall she slipped her shoes on, picked up her shoulder bag from under the pegs, and lugged it through to the kitchen, where she placed it gently on the table. Then she unzipped the top and reached inside.

The smile was already forming as she eased out the Sainsbury's carrier bag, unfolded it, and peeked inside. It certainly didn't look like six and a half thousand quid, but it would easily fit in the freezer. And tomorrow she could count it and decide which deserving souls were going to be helped out this time.

# Chapter 2

"Look busy! Shirley's on the way!"

The others looked up at their colleague and collectively jolted into action, choking down the last of their breakfasts, stuffing dirty plates into desk drawers, and launching themselves into theatrically conspicuous police activity: typing up statements, studying their notebooks, and shuffling files. In fact, doing everything and anything they could think of to make the squad room appear the hive of clinical, professional detective activity it was supposed to be on the morning after a major crime.

The office door burst open and Detective Inspector Graham Templeton strode in, as every day before, leaving it wide open behind him. And as ever before, he said not a word as he moved to position himself at the epicentre of their world, where he stood, shoulders back, chest forward, and feet wide apart, stretching himself to his full five feet and seven inches before rubbing his hands together for precisely the count of three. Then, also as every sodding morning since he'd become the great turd that had been dropped on them from upon high, he would speak aloud the selfsame bastard opening question. "Where are we?" He never said, "Good morning", never commented on the weather or his drive in, never asked how any of them were or if a beloved pet had been taken poorly overnight, just "Where are we?" To a man jack of them they wanted to shout back, "Fucking Ternbury fucking nick", but nobody ever did. The jumped-up little prick would have them all hanging from a lamppost outside the station front doors if they dared.

They knew his backstory in grimy detail, hearing about him through the grapevine well before he took the long and winding road up from London to mid Shropshire to cast his diminutive shadow across their door. A side-gate entry to the force, he'd been on the fast track up from day one. A few months here, a few months there, a quick tick in the appropriate box, and ever onwards and upwards. An assignment to the Fourshires Constabulary HQ at Attwood House and its cohabiting Ternbury Police Station maybe hadn't been high on his list of preferences, but here he now was, posing and pratting about under the protective wing of his doting uncle, who just happened to be the assistant chief constable. It was a connection he took every opportunity to 'let slip', just in case anybody dared to have a pop at him. So, all in all, a Teflon-coated pretend policeman, inexorably ascending to glorious magnificence, and perfectly content to use his colleagues' faces as footholds on the way up.

It didn't help that the team's chief inspector was off on long-term sick while his immediate superior, already a notorious time-server, now avoided any sort of proper work as he counted down his last few days to retirement. So between them they had unwittingly opened up a gaping void in the command structure that had delivered Templeton the blissful gift of direct access to the chief superintendent's backside, whereupon he kept his puckered lips seemingly permanently fixed.

All that said, and excruciating as it was to have to work under the heel of the man's always meticulously polished brogues, they all bit their tongues, put their shoulders to the wheel, and prayed that the harder they worked, the sooner he'd be whisked up the magic beanstalk and away into the clouds.

Turning slowly around in a far from elegant pirouette, Templeton surveyed his team, making no effort to hide how unimpressed he was by what he was seeing. He raked the spread fingers of one hand through his expensively coiffured blond curls, sucked in a dramatic breath of irritation, and lightly lowered his eyelids to block out the disappointment on view. "I asked," he repeated in his flat southern accent, eyes still closed as he spaced the words out with long gaps in between, "where are we? And when I ask a question I expect an answer, even if it turns out to be 'Fucking nowhere, sir.'" He snapped his eyes open and fluttered his lids for effect before staring directly at his second in command. "Why don't you give it a go, eh, Danny? Where are we?"

Detective Sergeant Danny Roberts had over twenty-five years of policing under his belt. From Special to PC and on into CID, he knew the ropes and had probably forgotten more than this little twerp of a boss would ever learn. He clenched his jaw and took a deep and stabilising 'do-not-slap-him-in-the-mouth' breath before getting to his feet to respond. "Lowells Bank, Shrewsbury centre. Just after noon yesterday. Ninety-nine percent certain it's the same bloke: general description, droopy ginger moustache, thick glasses with a broken frame, stammer, and his MO start to finish was exactly replicated. Apparently he stood in the queue, calm as you like, for twenty-odd minutes, then did the business in less than three and was gone. Melted away, same as always." Danny looked down at his notes for the exact number he'd written down when the bank had called it in the previous evening. "Six thousand four hundred and sixty quid, according to Lowells. All notes, of course, and nothing bigger than a fifty. Oh, and there was nothing clever about him not taking hundreds. The cashier didn't have any in his drawer at the time."

"Witnesses?" asked Templeton, holding his hands limply, palms up, like he was testing for rain. "Twenty minutes in a queue, somebody must have clocked him."

"We're working through them, sir." DC Jacquie Napier butted in to help her friendly sergeant escape the hotseat for a few moments of respite. She too stood up before continuing her contribution. "The bank have been through their records and supplied us the names of account holders they served in the half-hour up to the time of the robbery. There were a few more unidentified walk-ins who we can't—"

"CCTV?" snapped Templeton, as if it was a personally brilliant and insightful idea worthy of Sherlock Holmes himself. "Inside, outside?"

"That's me, sir," said the final member of their merry little band, raising a hand as he got to his feet to say his piece. This was Probationary Detective Constable Kevin Marsh's first assignment since getting out of uniform, and he was still very nervous around Templeton. For the first couple of weeks he'd thought he'd made a huge mistake in accepting the post, until Danny and Jacquie had managed to reassure him that the toxic puddle he'd plopped into was so far from the norm you'd need a telescope to see it. "I-I've got the b-bank's CCTV files," he began, fighting to get himself going. "Inside and outside. And I went into town yesterday evening to check out all the street cams and any other shop premises that might possibly have—"

"Bloody brilliant!" scoffed Templeton, clearly not meaning it, as he cut across the young DC. He gave a sigh of pantomime scorn before taking a deep breath that he held before exhaling loudly through his nose. "So, bottom line, we're fucking nowhere. Nowhere at all. Which means I have the sum total of sod all to tell our Lords and Masters. Am I right?"

"It's been less than twenty-four hours, boss," began Roberts. "We've—"

Templeton held up a flat hand to cut him off. "Yesterday was the fourth. Number four." He spread the fingers of his raised hand and sarcastically counted them off. "One, two, three, four. Four robberies, Detective Sergeant

Roberts. Four bank robberies. Four *armed* bank robberies. All identical. All on my patch. And all, it seems, a continuing great big fucking mystery to one and all."

"He's very clever," began Roberts in response, immediately wishing he hadn't started, but pressing on anyway. "He's in and out like a greased ferret. We never manage to get a good look at him on CCTV, and he—"

"Oh well, let's give up, then," sang a contemptuous Templeton. "Let's all pack up, leave this little bastard to do his thing while we go home to eat hot buttered muffins and watch daytime telly."

"Do you have any fresh ideas, sir?" It was Jacquie Napier again. The question could have been touching dangerously close to insubordination had it not been delivered with a face of intense subservience to a 'greater being'. Plus, as a woman, she had the added security of knowing Templeton's abject fear of even the hint of an 'inclusiveness violation' making a faint smudge on his gold-plated service record.

"I'm working on formulating a number of possible scenarios that could lead us forward," said Templeton, looking away and out of the window so none of them could see the 'bullshit' lamp flashing brightly in the middle of his forehead. "I'm intending to discuss a couple with the Super over lunch."

"Anything you could share with us now, sir?" asked Napier, forcing her voice to stay flat and businesslike. "To help us along, like?"

"Keep doing what you're doing," he replied, turning back to look at them. "But with a lot more speed, diligence and brainpower. Alright? Oh, and Danny?"

"Yes, boss?"

"Keep the whip in hand on this and make sure I'm kept updated on anything of value that I can safely share upstairs. Remember, team, when we win, we all win. And – heaven forbid – if we fail, then...well...you know." And with that stirring call to arms, Field Marshal Graham 'Shirley' Templeton turned his back on his troops to march off into his private office, slamming the door closed behind him.

"Twat!" breathed all three of the foot soldiers as one, the instant the door was closed.

"He hasn't got a single idea, has he?" said Jacquie to the ceiling. "Not one." She didn't need to look to see her colleagues nodding their agreement. "And that 'We're all in it together' crap was beyond contempt. If we do ever manage to crack this case, you can bet your pension he'll snaffle all the credit. Every last drop."

"And if we don't," added Danny, "he will flutter his angel wings and ascend unblemished to heaven whilst consigning our pathetic souls *alone* to hell."

"We'd better get on and bloomin' well solve it, then," said the youngest and newest of them with a strength and determination that surprised them all.

"You are so very right, Kevin, my stout and loyal yeoman," said their DS, walking across to pat the young man twice on his shoulder in a symbolic knighting. "So let us indeed get on with it like proper policemen rather than Mr Plastic Plod in there." He inclined his head towards Templeton's office door, beyond which they could hear muffled fawning as the man presumably telephoned 'upstairs' with an invented progress report. "The sooner we make him look wonderful," continued Danny, working towards his conclusion, "the sooner he'll be gone and the sooner we can get ourselves a decent gaffer. Agreed?"

"Agreed!" came the expected and forceful response.

"So, Kev, CCTV, all of it. Inside and outside the bank. Plus the council street cams and every one of those others you listed in your survey yesterday evening. And don't forget there may be some inside shops that could have an incidental view of the street through the window. Add in buses and taxis. Oh, and try to think of a way of collaring any private car dashcams, or cyclists with GoPro stuff. Maybe while you're looking through the street CCTV footage, see if you can spot any going past. Okay?"

"Got it," said Kevin, getting to his feet and setting off on his assigned task with a whole-body expression of bristling enthusiasm.

"Jacquie," continued Danny, "interviews. People in that queue. What did they see? Did any of them talk to our man, notice him? How did he behave? What was he wearing, *exactly*? What was he carrying? How did he walk? What did he bloody smell of? Anything. Anything at all. And get the photofit – or whatever they call it these days – bloke down to the bank to do what he can with the cashier. Alright?"

"Aye aye, Sarge." She play-saluted and winked at her friend and immediate superior.

"And, just in case you were wondering," added Danny, pausing for mildly humorous effect, "I shall be sat here, all alone but for the detached company of our pocket-sized but truly inspiring leader, and going back yet again through the files of the other three of this irritatingly clever little shit's bank jobs to see if we've missed anything. Somehow, in my ageing bones, I cannot help but feel there has to be something in there we're missing."

"Like what?" asked Kevin, already at the door with his coat on, but suddenly intrigued by the final musing of his experienced colleague.

Danny paused before replying, giving himself time to get his thoughts in a row. "Many, *many* years ago, a wise old copper told me to spend as much time looking at the gaps as the clues. Arthur, God rest his soul, was the best detective I ever worked with, bar none. And that bit of advice has stood me in good stead ever since."

"So, actually, you're going to be spending the day staring into space," said Jacquie, adding a playful giggle to show her DS she was pulling his leg.

"In a manner of speaking, yes," he replied. "Now, haven't you got work to do, you cheeky bloody monkey?"

# Chapter 3

As soon as Roy left for his afternoon's bowling, Carol made a pot of tea and sat herself down to decide where and how to pass on the proceeds from her latest 'day out', as she'd come to think of them. It had previously been a relatively straightforward task and one that she enjoyed, but this time was different. Having learned that the police had traced the last lot of donated cash and taken it back, she was in a jam. Of course she hadn't known the bank had recorded all the numbers. She hadn't even thought of it as a possibility. But the new-found knowledge and the problem it presented were sitting there like a massive boulder in the road. She had to think of a way around it.

Staring down at her shopping list pad on which she'd written out the five deserving causes, one of which could shortly become the recipient of an unexpected windfall, she groaned and cursed for the umpteenth time in the last five minutes. She was stuck and no mistake. Her first and simplest idea had been to break the donations down into smaller amounts to make it more difficult to trace. But that would take a lot more time and a lot more effort, as well as increasing the risk of somebody, somewhere spotting her, linking her to the handouts, and from there to the robberies. She could maybe do it in disguise, but she only had the one, and that would be even more daft, going out and about in her home town dressed up as the increasingly notorious bank robber. Her third thought was to launder the money. It was something that came up over and over again in just about every crime programme she watched these days, so it must work. The problem was that beyond the basic premise she had absolutely no idea whatsoever of how to do it. Another idea scratched off.

She leaned back in her chair and turned to look at her friendly kitchen window as if pleading for the currently absent reflection to offer her some inspiration. Unsurprisingly, it didn't, but the small break in mental focus allowed her mind to drift off, away from the problem in hand and back to the very beginning.

She was still amused, shocked, and not a little frightened by the thought that, from all the long list of potential activities and hobbies she'd considered as a way out of abject pensioner-housewife boredom, it was bank robbery that she'd ended up with. It had come to her in the middle of yet another sleepless night. Lying awake, staring at the ceiling as Roy snored contentedly beside her, she'd gone through and rejected the entire list of 'normal and appropriate' pastimes for elderly working-class women. Travel was out of the question due both to not having the money and Roy's flat refusal to go anywhere he couldn't walk to. Handicrafts were most definitely not her thing, as manifested by her innumerable failed attempts over the years to assist two generations of children with their homework craft projects. Painting a wall was the limit of her artistic ability, and she was tone-deaf and couldn't sing, so that killed anything musical stone dead. She could maybe heave the sewing machine out from the understairs cupboard, but for what? Yes, she'd run up a few pretty decent outfits in the past, but always from financial necessity rather than creative zeal. And now there was no point at all; she never went anywhere for it to be worth making something for herself, and the girls could buy whatever they fancied and better made for a fraction of the price in the high street.

Dead, dead, dead – the possibilities were killed off one after the other in double-quick time. Sport? Didn't even enjoy it as a youngster. Knitting? Hated it from the very first dropped stitch. Join a club, a society, the WI? Back-stabbing faux bonhomie. Not a chance. How about robbing a bank? Don't be bloody stupid.

It was the most idiotic, ridiculous, crazy-mad, daft, bonkers, numptyish idea, but one that simply would not go away. It kept swirling around and back like thin smoke, wrapping around her and tickling her senses. And she enjoyed the rush she got from the mere thought of it every time it wafted under her nose. So she started to pretend it was real: planning, preparing, imagining the moment she went in, how she would act, what she would say. Then, one afternoon, bored witless and the housework done, almost without any conscious pre-thought, she sat down and started designing her disguise and listing the props she'd need. Next it was practising her robbery lines in front of the bathroom mirror. The week after, while she was in town, idly mooching around window-shopping as she'd done a thousand times before, she found herself mentally mapping out CCTV cameras, their blind spots, and potential escape routes.

She couldn't actually remember the moment when fantasy had clicked over and engaged the first tooth on the ratchet that would crank her towards actually doing it. It was probably sparked by one or other granddaughter telling her how boring she was. Or maybe it had been her reflection in the kitchen window, the younger her, staring back and looking sadly at a life just dribbling away to nowhere. But whenever or whatever it had been, it really did...

Now here she was, sitting in her kitchen, trying desperately to work out how to give away a bundle of money that had just been illegally liberated from a Shrewsbury bank. Strange, isn't it? she thought. All those telly programmes, all those crime movies watched. Hours and hours of absorbing a criminal education, learning just about everything anyone needed to know about how to rob a bank, and yet sod all about how to safely and securely give the money away. She laughed aloud. And then laughed some more as she recalled that first moment of revelation – the morning after her first 'day out' – when it suddenly occurred to her that through all the weeks of preparation she had not once thought of anything at all beyond housework apart from doing the robbery.

She'd laughed until she nearly choked that morning, and had offered multiple thanks to some higher power or other that Roy had taken himself off down to the newsagents to pick up his bowling magazine and couldn't hear her. Looking back now, she could see that there'd been a fair bit of adrenaline overload breaking out at the time, but there was no doubt whatsoever in her mind that the primary cause of her hilarity was the sheer absurdity of it. The sudden realisation that in all probability the common-or-garden variety of bank robber started out from a position of wanting the money and then worked on how to get it. She'd done the complete opposite, dreaming only about the getting without any thought whatsoever of what to do with it once she'd got it.

The proceeds of that first time was a few quid under five and a half thousand. She'd kept it stashed in the freezer for nearly two weeks before she'd managed to come up with an idea of what to do with it. It just sat there, all that time, shivering away in a plastic container labelled 'tofu curry'. She'd tagged it as such because she knew Roy had never been able to come to terms with the concept of a meal not containing some sort of meat. To his mind, vegetarians were deviants, while vegans were the devil incarnate. So, in the extremely remote possibility that he went digging around in there, it was a nailed-on certainty he wouldn't open that one particular box. Actually, she was pretty sure he didn't know where the freezer was or how to open it, so her ill-gotten pot of money felt as safe in there as in Fort Knox. And for sure it was one hell of a lot more secure than the Ludlow bank she'd robbed to get it.

There were moments, real, genuine moments in those early days, when she'd thought about simply giving the money back. Like she'd taken her 'buzz' (as the granddaughters called it) from winning the game and so had no need of the trophy any more. And besides, she was under absolutely no illusion that what she'd done was anything other than wrong, and was sure both her parents were looking down disapprovingly from heaven. As a young girl, when her schoolmates were regularly shoplifting – nearly always in Woolworths on the High Street in town – she had resolutely refused to join in. To a large extent she was scared witless of getting caught and having to explain to her parents, but mostly it was a simple, old-fashioned sense of what was right and what was wrong. So giving the money back was probably the right and proper thing to do. But, before she managed to work out just how to do that, fate intervened and changed her mind.

It was a short item in the local evening news about an old people's home in Malpas, only twenty or so minutes away on the bus. The reporter told the story of how they were having to close down because the whole place needed completely rewiring and, even though a local firm had offered to do the work at cost price, the home still couldn't afford to have it done. Some of the residents had been there for donkey's years, and a couple of the frail old souls stammered and croaked their stories to the reporter, telling him how scared they were by the thought of having to leave their 'home'. Then the woman in charge, a lovely, soft-spoken, moon-faced lady with nicely cut blonde hair, came on to tearfully express her heartbreak at having to witness the anguish and distress in her elderly charges for the want of a mere five thousand pounds.

The news the following week was a whole lot brighter. The same boss lady was back on again, but now her moon-face was wreathed in smiles, thanks to the anonymous benefactor who'd posted a blank envelope through their letter box. In it she'd found five thousand four hundred pounds in cash. And that evening, as Carol sat wordlessly eating her tea and watching, with her unknowing husband doing the same beside her, she felt a warmth in her belly like she hadn't for as long as she could remember. The die was cast, so they say. She would rob another bank – just one more – but this time with the premeditated intention of donating the proceeds to another deserving cause. Have your fun and help some unfortunate souls into the bargain, she'd thought. Her old mum had always said a little bit of naughty does you good. She'd been right.

That second – and supposedly final – 'day out' had been even better than the first. Carol had been more confident, more in control, and had been able to actually feel the excitement while she was doing it rather than afterwards, like with her 'cherry pop'. In fact she'd been so high she'd had to remind herself not to skip as she'd casually sauntered off and away with a little over six thousand quid in her shoulder bag. It was also the death of any thoughts of giving it up. Why ever would she go back to endless greyness, merely 'waiting for God', as the saying goes, when she could fill what little was left of her active life with a blinding kaleidoscope of colour? And all for the price of a cheap day-return ticket on the train.

There was also another good reason for not packing it in after a mere two. Yes, the new activity she'd found and taken up delivered her a big slice of excitement and an entire cream gateau of joy, of that there was no doubt. But on top of that, it was proof perfect that she was not boring like most of her so-called friends were, and like pretty much her entire family thought she was. She would never be able to tell anyone, of course, but knowing it herself was more than enough to keep her grinning smugly inside, as and when the family started making fun of her.

What was more, she'd very quickly become aware of yet another important fact: robbing banks was actually something she was bloody good at. You may have left school with no more than two scraped CSEs, Carol, my girl, and you may not be able to answer a single question on *Mastermind* or get your granddaughters' jokes. But when it comes to robbery, you, Carol, are a genius. Varicose veins, haemorrhoids, occasional mild incontinence? Yes, yes and yes. Intellectually challenged, boring, incapable of anything beyond housework? No, no and bloody well no.

She'd also decided that what she was doing couldn't really be considered as simple, straightforward bank robbery. That bit was, after all, only a part of the overall operation now. And, knowing from the telly that every criminal activity, big or small, had to have an acronym, she'd come up with CFAP: criminally financed anonymous philanthropy. The label, to her mind, gave it a sort of validity in the world of crime, whilst lacing it through with a – alright, probably misplaced – sense of righteousness. But whatever, call it what you like, it was something she was good at and that was that. She was a natural.

The sound of a car pulling up out front blew away the warm fog of reminiscence, bringing her back to the harsh light of the here-and-now challenge. How was she going to give away this money without it being snatched back by cold-hearted coppers working their socks off for some greedy, rich bank? She had to find a way. There had to be a way.

"It's only me, Mum," came a call from the hall.

"I'm in the kitchen, chook," she called back, instantly recognising her daughter's voice.

Sarah appeared in the doorway. "As if you'd be anywhere else," she said, with a facial expression that silently said something along the lines of, 'My God, I hope I don't end up like you one day.'

Carol let the non-verbal slight waft over her head and away, getting to her feet to greet her elder child with a hug and a kiss on the cheek. "This is a nice surprise," she said, and meaning it. "Dad's out. He's—"

"Bowling. Yeah, I know. That's why I..." Sarah let the words trail off and looked away for a moment. "I don't suppose you could lend me a few quid, could you, Mum? The car needs a couple of new tyres and I..." She didn't need to finish.

Carol looked at her daughter with a mother's unbending love, and smiled. Yes, she could see the newly highlighted hair, the professionally done nails, and she was sure she'd not seen that pair of fancy high heels and matching handbag before, but, she knew, priorities were different these days. And Sarah was still her little girl, standing in the kitchen, asking if she could have some pennies for sweeties. "Fancy a cup of tea?" Carol asked.

"Sorry, no time. I need to get back before anybody important notices I'm missing."

"So you bunked off. Just like school."

Sarah dropped her head in play-acted contrition and nodded. "It's just..."

"How much do you need, chook?" Carol asked.

"It's not easy being a single mum, you know," said Sarah, not answering the question.

"I don't, thankfully," replied Carol, "but I can guess. And you're better off without Shithead, you know that."

"I know."

Carol was already across to the kitchen cupboard to take out the ancient Oxo tin that had been the Jackson's Bank of Housekeeping since the days when Roy had brought his wages home as cash sealed in a little cellophane envelope. "So, how much do you need?" she asked again, opening the tin lid to check how much was inside.

"I'll pay you back. I promise."

Carol knew it was a well-meaning but improbable promise, but didn't call it out. Instead she just tilted her head to one side and widened her eyes in lieu of repeating the question for a second time.

"The garage reckon they can do it for about eighty to ninety, with balancing and all."

"So a hundred, then," said Carol, "just to be sure it's covered." She counted out the required notes and held them out for her daughter to gently take from her fingers.

"Thanks, Mum," said Sarah in her best little-girl voice as she swiftly slid the money from view into her trouser pocket. "I love you."

"And I love you too, my baby girl. Just don't tell your dad I've bailed you out."

"Don't worry, I won't. I'm embarrassed enough as it is, asking you." Sarah blew her mother an air kiss and smiled. "Anyway, sorry, but I've gotta rush. Love to Dad." She leaned forward to give her mother a hug before heading for the doorway where she stopped and turned around. "Oh, I nearly forgot," she said in a voice that instantly betrayed that she'd done nothing of the sort. "Could you have the girls tonight? A bunch of workmates are going into Nantwich and they want me to go with them. Thursday is the new Friday, after all."

"Well..."

"Please." Sarah gave a small shrug. "I mean, it's not like you and Dad'll be going anywhere. You never..." She bit the rest of the thought off, not wanting to risk doing any more damage to her hope of a fun night out.

"Of course," said Carol, ignoring her daughter's rather-too-painful dig at her life, dipping back into the Oxo tin to extract a twenty-pound note. Again she held it out for her daughter to come and take. "Have a drink for me," she said softly, with a wink to show there were no hard feelings at what had been said. "Seeing as how having your girls will mean Dad and me will have to cancel our night of fine dining and dancing at the Casino Royale." She finished with a small laugh.

"As if," said Sarah, adding a snort of laughter as she took the offered note and tucked it away with the rest. "Thanks again, Mum." And with that, she was gone.

# Chapter 4

"No sign of Shirley yet, then," hissed Kevin as he entered the squad room. Being still only a few weeks into his probationary period, he still wasn't sure the 'powers that be' really couldn't hear all, like they pretended was the case.

"On a Monday morning?" replied his detective sergeant with a dry grunt of derision. "You must be bloody joking. He's never in until after ten on a Monday."

"Probably has a regular hair perm appointment," added Jacquie, setting the three of them laughing.

The problem was, they had very little to laugh about. It had been four days since the latest in their string of clearly connected bank robberies and they had made zero progress on tracking down the perpetrator. In fact, worse than that, although they had a mass of information, they had not one single what they would call 'solid' lead. And they ruddy well knew it; individually, collectively, and – worst of all – in the higher echelons above them.

"Right then," said their DS, clapping his hands to break through the almost tangible sense of hopelessness. "Let's we three sit down and go through it all again. Everything and anything we've got. Let's lay it all out, map it all, and have another look for the links, the patterns, and – dare I say it yet again – the gaps. Alright?"

With no other brilliant ideas, the other two nodded and dutifully scooted their chairs around to sit looking up at the whiteboard in front of which DS Danny Roberts was already standing. Taped onto the board was a map of Shropshire showing the robbery locations, and a detailed diagram for each one showing the bank and the robber's known direction of escape along with a timeline of the four events. They also had, in pride of place in the top middle of the board, the now all too familiar e-fit supposed likeness of their man.

"He still looks like ET with a moustache," said Jacquie. "Maybe that's our problem. He went home."

It was meant as a joke, but it somehow reinforced their sense of abject hopelessness.

"If he has gone home then at least we won't have another one to make us look even more hapless," said Danny, keeping his tone light-hearted but still professional. "However, I have a strong suspicion he hasn't either gone home or finished. He isn't going to stop now. Not after getting away with four. Mark my words, he is still around and, without a shadow of a doubt to my mind, working on another."

The others nodded their concurrence and prepared to offer what they had, even though they'd been over it more times than they cared to remember in the dozen or so weeks since the first robbery.

"Okay," said Danny, "let's kick off with last Thursday and cross-reference anything from that one to the previous three. Jacquie, interviews. The other punters in the bank at the time. Stood in a queue with our man for nigh on twenty minutes. Tell me somebody saw something. Please."

Jacquie shook her head before replying. "Nothing. Not a thing. Not one of them noticed anything at all. It was like he wasn't there."

"And the cashier?"

"Useless," continued Jacquie. "I won't put it in my report, of course, but Lester Sweet – and, yes, that really is his name – was a dopey twerp. More interested in me getting his name right than telling me what he'd seen. And, to tell it how it is, I reckon, at the time, he was so busy shitting his pants he actually didn't see anything worth telling."

"But he verified the e-fit, yeah?" pressed Danny.

"Yes, he did." Jacquie breathed out a long sigh of exasperation before continuing, speaking the words in a bored, flat sing-song, like she was being forced to recite a dull poem for the zillionth time. "Big droopy ginger moustache. Broken spectacles frame held together at the hinge with an Elastoplast. Dark, possibly grey hoodie. Brown gloves and huge black gun." She looked up and grimaced at her sergeant. "That's it. The lot. Same as all the others."

"Height? Weight? Approximate age?" pressed Danny.

"I had Dopey Bollocks sit on his seat behind the counter while I stood robber-side and stretched and crouched like an idiot kiddies' TV presenter, eventually getting him to guess around five seven. Weight, no idea. Too much coat. And as for age, well – and I could be indelicate here, but I'm not going to be – fucking no fucking idea. Or, to be clinically precise about it, somewhere between eighteen and sixty odd."

"Oh, come on," groaned Danny. "He must have—"

"He couldn't," cut in Jacquie, "or wouldn't look at the perp long enough to see anything worth remembering. Seems our favourite little shit-bag robber's face was deep inside the hoodie and the bits that did show were covered in ginger moustache and glasses. And he was wearing gloves, hence no chance of seeing the hands as an age indicator. So I reckon – he didn't say it outright, but I'm pretty certain – all he used to guess the age was the bloody voice."

"It was much the same with the others," butted in the team junior, flicking through one of a bunch of files he had on his knees and extracting a single page to read from. "'Thin and reedy' is the description that's pretty much common in all four statements, whatever descriptive words the witness actually used. Oh, and they all say the voice was higher pitched than what they'd have expected for a bank robber, not that any of them had any prior experience beyond the telly."

"And there's the stutter," added Jacquie. "All four of them said our man has a pronounced stutter on words beginning with 'N'. N-n-not that that helps a lot."

The joke brought a short, humourless laugh from the other two before the room fell silent and stayed that way for several seconds.

"So as far as age goes," continued Danny, speaking in a tone that underlined his sarcastic message, "our four eyewitnesses have successfully narrowed our robber's age down to somewhere between sixth-form college and an old people's home." He picked up his notebook to read. "Two and four had no proper idea at all, while one and three were very specific about it, but at opposite ends of the range, which means as far as age is concerned, we have absolutely no idea. Correct?"

"Correct," chorused the other two.

"There is one thing, though," offered Jacquie, "although in itself it's not a lot of use, but – like the stutter – it could be something if we ever do come up with a suspect. All four cashiers agree he's got a discernible northern accent. Cheshire, Shropshire, that sort of area. I know it's not much, but..."

"Right now I'd take anything at all," said Danny, feeling his earlier resolve to make some sort of progress draining away. He clapped his hands together again, to boost himself and hopefully re-energise the room. "Okay, Kev, you're up. CCTV."

Kevin shuffled his files, pulling the bottom one to the top, opening it, and pulling out an A4 photograph. He held it up for the others to see. It was a monochrome print from a CCTV camera, blurred and fuzzy from being blown up beyond the system's capability. "This is him inside the bank," said Kev, his downbeat tone giving away the paucity of information he was about to share. "It's the best I could get, by the way, so you can guess what the rest were like. Heavy dark-coloured hoodie-style overcoat, and that's about it."

"Nothing else?" asked Danny, trying to keep the pleading tone in his voice under control. "I can't put that up on the board, Kev. It's almost laughably pathetic. What about the counter camera? Tell me they have a counter camera."

"They do," replied Kev, looking down and away to avoid eye contact with his hugely more experienced boss. "It was even less help. Our man is a faceless, shapeless blob. That's it." He paused and took a deep breath before taking the risk of sharing his thoughts. "You know, I hate to say this, our man may look like a tramp but he's bloody good. I mean..." He stopped before he sounded too much in awe of the bad man he was supposed to be trying to catch and put in prison.

"Go on," prompted the other two as one.

"Well, he never – and I mean *never* – exposes anything to any CCTV camera, or not one that I can find. Inside the bank he's always facing away. At the desk he's head down, face deep inside the hood. And as for out on the street, well, that's not far short of masterful."

"Say more," prompted Danny.

"Okay, right," continued Kev, edging forward on his chair to deliver the rest. "He comes out of the bank and his head is already – yes, *already* – facing down and away from the street cams. He knows exactly where they all are, heights, angles, the lot. He then has less than fifty yards before the little side street he disappears down, but in that time he passes three shops, two of them with internal but pavement-facing CCTV. In both cases he is looking the other way as he goes past. He knows. He has to. I mean, he knows exactly what is where and how to avoid every freaking one of them."

"You said 'disappear'," said Danny, trying to pull his probationary DC away from full-scale adoration of a perceived criminal mastermind. "I hope you don't mean..."

"No, no," said Kev, shaking his head vigorously. "Not as in 'like a ghost'. No, he disappears from *view*. There are no cameras down that side street, but there are three at different angles and elevations in the square it comes out onto at the end: one a council job and the other two on private premises. Between them they fully cover the side-street exit, and he never appears. And before you ask, neither does he reappear back onto the main road where the bank is. He goes in, but he doesn't come out. Somewhere in that side street, to all intents and purposes, he disappears into thin air."

"What's along there?" asked Jacquie, trying to help, but realising as she listened to herself that she was doing little more than adding to the creeping sense of despair. She tried to recover it by launching into an energetic stream of possibilities. "More shops, alleyways off, a pub, a café, a public loo, a car park entrance, a..." Her voice trailed to silence as she recognised the forlorn look on her younger colleague's face.

"Nothing," said Kev, his one word like the tolling of an iron bell.

"At all?" asked a disbelieving Danny.

"At all," replied Kev. "A couple of shopfronts, places that have been closed down and boarded up for months if not years. And, yes, I did check. Got in touch with the property agents and had an inside look-see. No trace at all of anybody having been in or out since they were shut up. Beyond that, it's solid brick walls apart from a sort of a bit of an alcove thing that apparently used to be a back-access alley for the shops but got bricked up to eight feet or more high about five years ago."

"Over the wall?" asked Danny, more in hope than expectation.

"Razor wire all along the top. Bloody great bundles of it."

Danny clamped his jaw and breathed out long and slow through his nose, turning on his heels in a full circle as he did so, finally coming back around to look at his colleagues. "Don't tell me, either of you," he said softly, "because I know. I went back through the other three files over the weekend and it was exactly the bloody same in all three. This little toerag comes out of the bank, avoids every single bastard CCTV, slides down some back alley or whatever, and disappears." He paused, lightly closed his eyes, and put his two index fingers to his top lip for the slow count of three. Then he snapped his eyes open, glared at the others with an expression of intense frustration rather than hostility, and almost groaned out the words, "People do not disappear. There has to be an explanation. He went somewhere."

"But I—" began Kevin, only to be cut off by his DS.

"I can't believe I'm saying this, people," said Danny softly, a tinge of embarrassment in his tone, "but have we looked for secret passages: manhole covers, ladders," he paused as the seemingly hollow words drifted away to silence before finishing with, "or fucking bungees?"

The last suggestion broke the tension, and they all laughed. But this was no laughing matter. Not at all. They were nowhere and they knew it. And, worst of all for poor old Detective Sergeant Danny Roberts, he knew that sometime later that morning he was going to have to tell Shirley.

# Chapter 5

It had been an exhausting day out. Laundering money was not easy and, as Carol had come to realise, it was significantly more effort than robbing a bank.

After agonising for days, worrying that the money from her recent Shrewsbury 'day out' might be traced and snatched back by the police, she had sworn herself an oath that this would not happen. She would make the cash untraceable, and that was that. So for her the question had shifted from a hazy 'what' to a singularly focused 'how'.

A couple of days previously, whilst out food shopping, she'd nipped into the Civic Centre library to read up on the supposed answer to her prayer: money laundering. The visit had helped a bit, but not a great deal, truth be told. They only had the one book on the subject and it read like it had been written by somebody who didn't need to be taught anything. Agreed, it probably hadn't been the intention of the author to write an instruction manual, but that was beside the bloody point. The jargon was beyond her and – even as an avid and, more recently, very attentive crime-telly watcher – the concepts laid out were from another galaxy. It was, in short, ungraspable gobbledygook from about page three onwards, and she could feel the irritation building inside her as the words all too quickly began to float before her eyes.

She didn't even own a computer, let alone have the internet and hence access to all sorts of whatever beyond. And even if she had, acquiring the skill set necessary to use the blasted thing was a dream past reason. As she'd once told her best friend, her ancient mobile phone was the closest she'd ever get to NASA. Janice had laughed aloud for several seconds before asking what NASA was.

Interweb aside, Carol didn't have access to any of the other things that your average wannabe money launderer apparently needed to hand: no chain of cash-in-hand businesses, no casino, no second-hand car dealership, no offshore bank accounts, no real estate portfolio, nothing. And as she couldn't work out how those things operated anyway, she very soon came to the conclusion that she was wasting her time. It was a dead end. An absolute...

Hang on a mo. If she stripped away the fancy terminology and ignored the hundred and fifty or so pages after page three, there was one thing in there she could *maybe* use. Forget 'layering' and 'integration' – whatever they actually meant – and simply concentrate solely on Phase One from the money launderer's handbook: 'placement'. Split the money up into smaller amounts to get it somehow into the legitimate financial system undetected. That she could do. That she understood. That was and would be totally workable. She was up and she was running. Well, walking actually, given the state of her veins these days, but making progress, and that was the most important thing.

To be fair, it wasn't really money laundering in the complete and proper sense, but it still felt good in that it just about nailed on the certainty that the money would eventually get to where she wanted it to go without risk of it being spotted, identified, and snatched back. It would take time, delay the donation, but they didn't know they were going to get it anyway, so it didn't matter. It would also increase the gap between getting it and giving it away, which would be a spin-off benefit as the two events were less likely to be picked up and linked. So all she needed was a list of 'drop' accounts and the time to make it happen.

It was a week and a bit after when she got going. A Tuesday, late morning, and Roy was standing in the backyard, smiling up at a cloudless sky, dreaming of nought but an afternoon's bowling, when Carol pecked him a 'Have a good one, love' kiss on the cheek and set off for what she told him would be just another mooch around town for a spot of window-shopping.

The previous evening, while she'd been getting their tea, she'd defrosted the cash in the 'tofu curry' box and divided it into six polythene food bags, which she'd stuffed into the very bottom of her shoulder bag. She didn't know for sure but she guessed nine hundred quid wouldn't even raise an eyebrow at most banks, let alone bring down the SWAT team or whatever from the National Crime Agency. She'd written that last one down from the library book so she didn't forget it. She didn't actually need to remember it, but it made her feel good to have a real-life named adversary beyond 'the Bill'.

To test the water, she opted to start her 'placement' operation in Nantwich with its allegedly higher than average ratio of well-off folks. And if all went well there, she'd move on to Crewe. And, just as she'd hoped, the whole thing went like a dream: smooth, trouble-free, and – in places – downright enjoyable. Three building society accounts opened in Nantwich in less than an hour. Then on to Crewe for three more, before a self-congratulatory cup of tea in the station café there as she waited for the fourteen-o-nine back home to Whitchurch.

In each instance she had used her real name and address, opening the account with nine hundred and twenty pounds in cash. Only four of the banks enquired about why she was opening an account – mainly, it seemed, to find out why she had chosen them specifically and not a branch closer to home. Her prepared response was delivered with brilliantly acted mock embarrassment as she half-whispered that her husband was a lovely man, but just not good where money was concerned. If he found out she'd come into a windfall he'd...well, you know. Wink.

"Windfall?" asked two of them, clearly more out of polite curiosity rather than any policing of the system.

Prepared response number two, this time acted out with little shy smiles, a small giggle, and popping eyes of incredulity at the punchline. She'd sold some of her dear old mum's jewellery that had been cluttering up her dressing table drawer for years. Could not believe it when it turned out to be worth over nine hundred quid. And it had been sitting there all that time doing nothing.

As she sipped at her tea in the Crewe station café, she couldn't stop metaphorically slapping herself on the back and awarding herself an Oscar, a Golden Globe, a BAFTA, and one of the ones called after a famous old posh actor she couldn't remember the name of. Maybe acting was her thing after all. She was – she had to say – masterful at bank robbing, and she'd had them eating out of her hand this afternoon in each and every building society she'd been to. But, whatever you do, mind you don't get carried away, Carol, she told herself sternly. Every crime movie, every TV cop show and detective series she'd ever watched made that abundantly clear. If you get cocky, you get caught.

Caught? The word shocked her. She nearly dropped her teacup. It was the sudden and utterly chilling realisation that she had never once considered what would happen to her – or Roy – if she got caught. Did they lock up little old ladies? Yes, they most probably did. Oh gosh! A chill crept up her spine and back down again. How could she have managed to *not* consider the potential consequences? She must have, surely. Or maybe she had but had mentally snuffed it out so quickly it hadn't registered. Or could it perhaps even – somehow, somewhere deep, deep down in her subconscious – have been her true motivation? It was a scary thought, now it came to her. The idea that perhaps she wanted to be caught and exposed to friends, family, the world as *not* the dull, nothing-to-say, antique empty vessel they generally considered her to be. Wanting to show them in such a way that they couldn't wave it away. Wanting to have her day in court, to stand up and shout, "Guilty as charged for not being bloody boring." Could that be it? Really? The underlying reason why she…?

"Pah!" She almost spat the rejection aloud to the virtually empty café. And a whole host of far less ladylike words came to mind immediately after as she dismissed the idiot thought like she was shooing an angry wasp out of her kitchen. She didn't want to get caught. Of course she didn't. And she wasn't going to. So there!

With that minor tremor of confidence settled, she wandered out onto the platform to watch for her train coming in and use the change of scenery to get back to thinking only positive thoughts. The dirty cash had been 'placed', so all she had to do now was wait a few days or so and she could safely draw down the laundered money from her multiple building society accounts, bundle it up into the full amount again, and pass it on safely and securely to whoever she chose. Easy-peasy.

Only this time, though. Even as she'd been preparing it, she'd been well aware that her backstory would only work the once. She couldn't keep pretending she was selling more and more of her dear old mother's imagined jewellery. So what would it be next time? Car boot sale? Not really. She couldn't imagine they made that much money. Inheritance? She didn't look or sound like the sort of person who might have rich relatives, no matter how phenomenal her acting skills might be. So where could a woman like her suddenly come into several hundred pounds every few weeks?

The answer came at her in a roundabout way. She suddenly remembered the joke she'd made to Sarah the other day, about how having the granddaughters for the night meant she'd have to cancel her and Roy's night out at the Casino Royale. Quite obviously that place – wherever it was – remained as out of reach as if it had been on the moon. But the idea – the idea of gambling – that wasn't. More specifically, 'the horses' weren't.

Roy and her had never been ones for betting. What little money they'd had through life, they'd held onto. As he'd always said, "You never see a poor bookie." In other words, the punters always lost in the end. So collectively, the sum total of their family betting had been a quid on a picked-with-a-pin nag in the Grand National. All that said, she knew for a fact that there *were* times when you *could* win on the horses. She'd learned that the hard way, through her Sarah and the now gone-and-not-missed shithead of an ex-husband. He'd given Sarah two beautiful daughters but that had come with an abundance of grief and debt, mostly because of his inability to walk past a betting shop. On the infrequent occasions when he did win, it was a windfall that was there to be squandered as quickly and stupidly as possible. But on the many, many more occasions when he lost, it was first empty the housekeeping, second beg and cadge, and third start 'borrowing' stuff that wasn't his.

All that misery – leaving aside the massive family celebration they'd had when the divorce finally came through and Mick buggered off to who cared where – had at last delivered something positive. The germ that instantly grew into a solution. All she had to do was keep an eye on the racing and, every week or two, find a rank outsider who'd come in on huge odds. Then she could safely toddle into her gaggle of friendly building societies to bank her winnings. Six times. And if any or all of them asked, she would tell them, including the name of the horse, the course and race time where it had run, and the amazing odds she'd snaffled. So that was it. Fixed. Or was it signed, sealed, delivered, as the old Stevie Wonder song went?

As for pulling the nice clean cash out of its short-term hiding places, well, she had a whole host of good stories for that. Tyres for the (imaginary) car, replacing the old kitchen window (she would never do that!), the once-in-a-lifetime cruise (some hope!), a new big-screen telly (in their tiny sitting room?), de dah, de dah. And of course, there was always the need to cover her imaginary losses on the horses that *didn't* come in. Anyway, to most people, spending a few hundred quid wasn't even worth the breath to mention it. A few thousand, maybe, but nobody would ever know that her multiples of a few hundred would be put together and passed on. Nobody, that was, apart from her and whoever was lucky enough to get it.

As her train clattered into the station and groaned to a halt in front of her, Carol was smiling broadly. It had been a busy day, but a good one. A day that had got everything nicely set up, and a day that had also delivered a damned good plan for the future. And not only that, because, while she'd been out and about busily depositing money around Nantwich and Crewe, she simply had not been able to ignore the number of deliciously plump-looking banks just sitting there asking to be robbed. And so few CCTV cameras, she mused, as she settled down into her seat for the short ride home.

# Chapter 6

Detective Sergeant Danny Roberts was sat at his desk, shoulders hunched, staring intently at his computer screen, when the other two members of the team bundled into the squad room. They were chattering away, laughing about something or other, but stopped dead in their tracks when their leader swivelled in his chair to stare at them. His face was anything other than welcoming, and the two juniors stood and waited for whatever nasty was about to come their way.

Their leader's opening words were directed straight at the younger DC. "You told me he didn't come out of that side street, Kev. You said you were *certain*." The words were delivered with a cold control, making them somewhere between disappointed and plain bloody angry. Probationary DC Kevin Marsh knew exactly what his boss was referring to, and blanched, then reddened around his collar and stammered a response. "H-h-he didn't."

"Into the square at the far end, I'll grant you that," continued their DS, his delivery still harsh to the point of aggressive. "Assuming he didn't stay skulking in there for more than thirty minutes, I agree he didn't come out that way. But you also confirmed a hundred percent he didn't double back onto the main street, right?"

Kevin swallowed hard and nodded.

DC Jacquie Napier decided it was time to take a shot at lowering the tension a notch or two. "What's up, Sarge?" she asked. "I've never seen you like this before. What's—"

The DS slammed a flat palm down on the desktop, the noise of it echoing around the room. He waited for the silence that followed before continuing, flicking a disdainful hand at the monitor screen. "The bloody camera sweeps, Kev. It's not static. Not fixed on that side street."

Kevin was fighting to find words as he watched his superior officer lurch to his feet and begin striding around the room, growling like a wounded bear. At last words broke free. "I knew that, Sarge. About the camera sweeping. And I wasn't pretending otherwise. That's why I—"

"Why you what?" snapped Danny, turning to stare straight at his DC.

"Hey, come on, guys," said Jacquie, moving to position herself between the two men. "Let's calm it all down a bit, shall we? Behaving like this isn't going to do any of us any good. Danny, I can see you're pissed off but there has to be—"

The DS held up a hand for her to stop, and shook his head sadly. "I'm sorry," he breathed, clearly genuinely meaning it. "It's just this damned case. It's really getting to me. We are absolutely nowhere and bloody Shirley is doing my head in. Updates, updates, updates. That's all he ever does. Yatter, yatter, yatter. Offers sweet fuck nothing to help, but endlessly and incessantly demands I give him some sort of progress to report 'upstairs'. And there isn't any."

"We get it," said Jacquie. "But that's still no reason to start chewing our heads off."

Danny slumped back down into his chair and used only a slight inclination of his head towards the monitor screen to indicate the source of his ire. His explanation was delivered in a voice now more weary than angry. "The CCTV on the main street sweeps a hundred and eighty degrees roughly every fifteen minutes or so when it's on automatic. The operations room techie can control it and zoom in, but only when he or she spots something of concern and wants a closer look. We know our man is right on top of the whole CCTV coverage thing, so he could easily have timed it so that we see him going in, but don't see him coming out again. In short," he looked up at the ceiling and let loose a howl of frustration before finishing with, "we could have missed him."

"We didn't," said Kevin with a fortitude that took the other two by surprise.

"But we could have," repeated Danny, this time with understanding in his voice.

"I'm telling you we didn't. I didn't," replied Kevin. "Look..." Cautiously, he indicated his team leader should vacate the chair in front of the monitor and sat himself down, grabbed the mouse and, with a speed and dexterity to take the breath away, pulled up a menu, scrolling through to extract specific sub-files and bring them up on screen in a mosaic of overlays. His colleagues watched on in silent awe, waiting for the moment when all would be revealed.

When he had everything in place he began. "This is the primary feed from the council CCTV. Yes, it sweeps, I knew that. But at the moment when our man hits that side-street entrance, there he is, full on. Dark grey hoodie coat down to just above the ankles, shoulders hunched, looking down and away to make sure his face is completely hidden and, interestingly, as you can see, not carrying anything."

"Are you suggesting he's already handed the money off to an accomplice?" asked Jacquie, not really wanting to break her colleague's analytical discourse, but feeling the need to ask the question.

"Possibly, but unlikely," replied Kevin. "No time, too risky, and, besides, none of the CCTV footage – bank external or out in the street – shows anybody else near to our villain. My guess is that the money bag is inside the coat. It certainly looks bulky enough, but I'll come back to that in a minute, if that's okay."

"Carry on," prompted Danny.

"Right," said Kevin, re-running the clip of their man approaching the side street. "Look at his stature. Even with the heavy coat you can tell our guy is slight, small even. Plus," he ran the short clip yet again, but this time in super-slow motion, "the coat moves too much in my view. It's certainly not a tight fit, which is why I think the cash is hidden inside it along with the gun."

"Meaning our man is probably even smaller in stature than we first thought," said Jacquie, verbalising their collective thought.

"Correct," said Kevin firmly. "Height we've got, but weight, build, whatever, in my opinion is probably one helluvalot less than what we've been thinking."

"Anything else before we get to the punchline?" asked Danny, wanting to chivvy things along towards the explanation as to exactly why his earlier dismay and consequent anger were supposedly unfounded.

"Just the one thing," said Kevin. "Not that it's going to help us crack the case and find this little bastard, but interesting to my mind. Our man is most definitely far from what I would call," he paused to find the precise words, "the athletic type. His movement looks stiff, awkward, almost wooden. He may simply be concentrating on looking casual as he leaves the scene, but I don't think so. And he is most definitely limping." Kevin put the clip into slow motion again and played it backwards and forwards two or three times. "See?"

His colleagues nodded before realising he wasn't looking at them, so verbalised their agreement.

"Was he limping in the CCTV from the other jobs?" asked Danny.

"Yes," replied Kevin emphatically. "Same in all of the footage I've watched."

"So maybe a long-term injury of some sort," mused Jacquie aloud, knowing the possible implication.

"Make a note and follow it up," instructed Danny to nobody in particular. "Maybe do a sweep of hospitals, local area GPs, physios, whatever. A long shot, but at least it's something. Go on, Kev."

A quick clackety-clack of keyboard buttons, and a measuring grid suddenly appeared on screen, overlaying the shadowy figure of their focus. Danny had never seen such a thing before, but didn't let on.

"Using this," said Kevin, "I can gauge the rough height of our target, so..." he hot-keyed to another screen, this time looking up along the main street, "I can use the template to see if there's anybody in the crowd roughly the same size." He hot-keyed a second time and the new screen was looking down the main street in the opposite direction. He turned in his seat to look up at his DS. "Sarge," he said, his voice full of apology but bolstered by the strength of vindication, "I promise you there is not one potential target on that street for the next half-hour that fits the profile, and I have been through it twenty, thirty times or more."

The ensuing silence hung like wet washing for a few seconds before Danny snapped it. "He has to ditch the coat. That's the only thing that makes sense. And I reckon – always have – that the moustache is phoney and goes as well. Let's face it, a droopy bright ginger moustache would stick out like a sore thumb. It has to be fake. The glasses too, I wouldn't mind betting. All of it stashed somewhere, leaving him to walk away looking completely different."

"But where?" asked Jacquie. "I mean, he couldn't go leaving a pile of incriminating evidence down some side street, hoping nobody would touch it."

"Agreed," added Kevin. "And there was nowhere in that side street to hide anything. Plus this bloke is a tiddler, remember, so no way could he have thrown a bloody great coat over an eight-foot-high brick wall topped with bundles of razor wire."

"So maybe he—" began Danny, only to be cut off.

"I checked," said Kevin, adding another heavy sigh of frustration. "In the half-hour after the robbery there was nobody, not anywhere in the town centre area, who was carrying a big enough holdall, rucksack or whatever.

And I mean nobody. Shopping bags, yeah, loads of them, but nothing that I could see that could take the bulk of that hoodie coat."

"So...?" asked Jacquie, starting to voice but failing to complete the unformed question that was flying round them like a demented budgerigar.

"The only other thing I can offer," continued Kevin, working hard to rise above the sense of desperation, "is the only other thing I can actually see: his shoes. Flat black pumps of some sort, as far as I can make out. Like old-fashioned school plimsolls. But before you get all excited again, I have spent literally hours looking at every tape we've got and the only people on that street in the half-hour after the robbery wearing similar are all girls and all in their early teens. Oh, and none of them is toting a jumbo-sized rucksack, either."

"I've just had a nasty thought," said Jacquie, her tone reinforcing the full extent of the nastiness in her soon-to-be-shared revelation. "The hoodie coat is central to our man's disguise, right?"

The other two nodded silently and waited.

"It's April," she continued. "Universally shitty weather apart from the odd day of perishing cold sunshine, right again?"

More nodding, but this time with a slice of realisation as they guessed ahead.

"No way," said Jacquie, pressing on, "even in Shropshire, could our villain pitch up at a bank in mid-summer in a massive overcoat. Which means..."

"We've got a couple of months tops to catch him before he disappears off to a caravan in Rhyl or wherever for the summer," said Danny, finishing his DC's thought. "Then we'll be left high and dry, sitting around, twiddling our thumbs, waiting for the little bastard to come back all tanned and relaxed to start again in October. Shit! Shit! Shit!"

Before anybody could say another word, the phone on Jacquie's desk rang. She trotted across and answered. The other two watched as she made faces at them. It clearly was less-than-good news being imparted. She offered profuse thanks and gently replaced the receiver.

"That was Debs," she said, jabbing a thumb at the ceiling.

They all knew who Debs was: a close friend of Jacquie's and the frequently indiscreet PA/secretary to the chief superintendent.

"Sounds like right now," continued Jacquie, "Mister Potato Head is taking a rubber truncheon to our Shirley's bollocks, and Debs thought it might help if we knew so we had time to hide in a cupboard before our favourite DI comes down to pass on the brutality."

"I didn't know he was called Mister Potato Head," said Kevin.

"Have you not seen the size of the ears on our beloved chief super?" asked Danny, immediately breaking into snorting laughter.

He knew, they all knew, it was nervous laughter, because he knew, they all knew, they were in for a right royal hand-me-down thrashing in the very near future. And there was no escaping it. But at least they didn't have long to wait, as almost immediately the squad-room door crashed open and a scarlet-faced Detective Inspector Graham Templeton burst in, steam almost visibly coming out of his ears. He made a big point of ignoring them as he strode past to position himself less than two feet from the incident board, staring intently at the pride-of-place e-fit of 'ET with a droopy ginger moustache'.

Templeton held the pose for a slow count of ten, maybe fifteen, before he took a deep breath and went for his catchphrase opener, not turning to face them as he barked it out. Just as well, as the three stout foot-soldiers standing to attention behind him all silently mouthed the words along with their leader. "Where are we?"

Danny knew it was up to him to take the lead and, if necessary, the brunt of the heat. He also knew he had to make some sort of substance out of a few threads of gossamer. But before he could even begin he was cut off by Templeton – still not turning to face them – screaming at the top of his voice like an attention-deficit brat who'd recently overdosed on E-numbers.

"I don't like being criticised because my team are crap. I don't like having a new arsehole reamed because I'm forced to work with monkeys. And I particularly do not like my hitherto glittering career prospects being jeopardised by a fucking useless bunch of no-hopers who couldn't find a rhinoceros hiding in a refrigerator."

The three silently made bemused faces at each other and shrugged at the metaphor.

"Where are we, Detective Sergeant?" continued Templeton, his voice high and strained. "And do not dare to say, 'Nowhere, sir.'"

# Chapter 7

"What the flippin' heck d'you call this?" Carol had almost shouted the words down at her friend, who'd just skidded to a halt at the kerbside in a flashy bright red open-topped two-seater.

Janice twisted her neck around to peer out from under her baseball cap peak and grinned up at her lunch companion stood gawping on the pavement. "It's called a sports car, you dope. Come on, get in. Let's get this show on the road."

"What happened to the Jag?" asked Carol, still not moving.

"I'll tell you about it on the way. Come on, ruddy get in or the pub'll be overflowing with doddery old bastards and we won't get served till teatime."

Carol bent down to tug open the door and then had to suppress a grunt of discomfort as she was forced to twist a reluctant spine in order to manoeuvre herself into the very low bucket seat. She groaned again as she fought to reach for, grab, and then pull the door shut. "Where's the roof?" she asked.

"Down," said her friend, as if it was the most stupid question the world had ever heard. "That's what makes it a ruddy sports car."

"But it's April. It's cold, it's windy, and it will undoubtedly rain at some point."

"If you're going to keep complaining you can walk to the pub. So shut up and get with the programme. There's a spare cap on the floor down there somewhere, and the seats are heated. Feels like you've wet yourself, but once you get used to the sensation, it's more than a tad pleasant. So belt up and let's get going."

Before Carol could pull her seat belt across and click it into place, Janice crashed the car into gear and violently catapult-lurched away with a screech of spinning tyres. A few yards along the road a second ear-bruising cacophony of violated metal signalled Janice searching for and eventually finding second gear. The shift to third was even louder, although, mercifully, less viscerally jarring, while the grab at fourth was relatively approaching smooth.

"It's a bugger, this manual gearbox," shouted Janice above the whistling of the wind screaming over the windscreen top. "Lenny always had automatics, and anyway, he never let me drive no matter how pissed he was, so—"

"Watch that cyclist!" screamed Carol as a racing bike with a large elderly man in absurdly bright and tight clothing suddenly appeared front left.

Janice swerved around him, not slowing and if anything accelerating, shouting some garbled profanity at the man. "Bloody Lycra Lout," she continued to Carol. "They're a bloody curse, these silly old codgers on their fancy bikes. All over the shop, he was. What the hell was he doing?"

"Minding his own business, I think," said Carol. "Or trying to. How fast are we going? This is still a built-up area, you know."

"No idea about the speed," said Janice with a shrug. "There's too many dials on the dashboard and I haven't managed to work out what they all do yet. But I'm getting the hang of three pedals." To demonstrate her prowess she took a shot at another gear change, missing it horribly. She waited for the grating noises and the agonising banshee shriek of a violently over-revving engine to subside before opting for a return to the gear she'd been in before. "Almost had it that time," she added with another shrug of the shoulders.

At the junction with the bypass Janice must have decided it was easier to not slow down and be forced to try to change gear again, so simply put her foot down, shot across the stop line and careered onto the roundabout, slotting into a barely discernible gap between two articulated lorries before tyre-squealing right around the curve, then left off onto the bypass. "Neat!" she exclaimed, briefly letting go of the steering wheel with her right hand to fist-pump the air.

"Could we slow down a bit?" asked Carol.

"No chance," came the instant reply. "We're having fun, you old stick-in-the-mud."

"I'll be six feet under the ruddy mud if you keep driving like this. We both will."

"I've not hit a thing since I got her," said Janice, this time releasing her left hand from the wheel to gently pat the top of the dashboard.

"Which was when?" asked Carol, guessing the answer.

"Yesterday morning," replied Janice, immediately letting loose her customary cackling laugh that continued until the next roundabout loomed up ahead. At least this time she braked, in fact so hard they both lurched forward into their seat belts, before unleashing another deafening round of metal innards being tortured as she violated the gearbox yet again. They kangarooed around the junction and screamed away hard left, accelerating like a moon-shot blast-off but with the added accompaniment of crunch, graunch, crash as she got herself back up through the gears. "I think I'm finally mastering this whole stick-shift thing," screamed Janice, the manifest glee rippling through her voice.

"Have you actually got a driver's licence?" asked Carol, mostly in jest.

The answer was not what she wanted to hear. "Technically," said Janice.

"Meaning what, exactly?" pressed Carol.

"I applied for a provisional when I was seventeen, but by then I was already going out with Lenny and he insisted on doing all the driving. And I liked being driven around in his big old Wolseley, so I sort of, well, you know..."

"So you haven't," said Carol, just to be clear.

"Oh come on, Little Miss Goody Two Shoes," sang Janice in her best playful, taunting voice. "Just because you've never broken the law, not once in your entire life, doesn't mean we all have to be bloody nuns."

Carol bit her tongue, crossed her fingers, and kept her mouth shut for the remainder of the journey, hoping to all hopes that the 'Actually, I've robbed four banks' thought bubble wasn't as visible as she was worried it might be.

By the time they reached the country pub that Janice had chosen for this week's outing, the gear changes were only mildly excruciating and braking had become almost a thing of beauty. Parking, however, was still a little out of reach, thought Carol, as she looked back at Janice's little red sports car angled across two and a half spaces and with its nose deep into the hedge. Hopefully the journey back would be a little less fraught. But then again, if her friend insisted on her usual two large glasses of wine over lunch, maybe not. She'd have to worry about that as and when it happened. At least if she got stopped the police wouldn't be able to put any endorsements on Janice's licence; she didn't have one.

The two friends stood together at the bar to place their food orders and get drinks to carry to the table. As expected Janice opted for a large glass of the house red, while Carol, also as expected, went for her staple soda water with a slice of lemon. Janice gently pulled her leg about her abstinence, but she understood the real reason. Carol had told the sad story far too many times about what the menopause had done for her tolerance to alcohol. The fact that Janice had seemingly evaded that particular side-affliction was a minor source of irritation that Carol didn't allow to fester.

Once sat, without any prompting, Janice unloaded the story of the new car. For six years she'd been driving around in her Lenny's beloved big old Jag. She'd kept it out of some sort of absurd sense of loyalty to her late husband and his car that she'd never actually liked. "Who in their right mind buys a black car when you don't have to?" she'd scoffed. So, on a sudden whim on the sixth anniversary of his passing, she'd wandered down to the local garage, picked out something she liked the look of, and traded in "the bloody hearse" for a small slice of excitement. "You and Roy have never owned a car, have you?" asked Janice, making it more of a statement than a question.

"Never needed one," said Carol. "Roy always walked to work, he never wanted to go anywhere, and, to be blunt, we couldn't afford to have something we were never going to use sitting outside the house losing value."

"I couldn't be without my wheels," said Janice, her voice dancing like a girl fifty plus years her junior as she waved an arm around in excessively theatrical style. "Getting out, having that freedom, it's what life is all about and I love it. Hair in Chester on Tuesdays, manicure and facial in Tarporley every Thursday with a pedicure thrown in every second visit, zipping off to whatever pub I fancy whenever the mood takes me. There's nothing like it. And sometimes I just get in the car and drive around going nowhere in particular. Out of the house, on the open road, free as a bird, purely and simply because I bloody well can. And now, with my little red rocket," she paused to give Carol a huge pantomime wink, "it will be even more fun because I'll be doing it with the roof down, come rain, come shine." She finished with a beaming smile and a substantial slurp of wine.

Carol didn't really get it, but smiled politely.

Janice's response to her lack of response was a bit of a shock. The smile slowly faded as she gently placed her wine glass down on the table and gazed across at Carol with sadness in her eyes. "Who am I kidding, eh?" she asked, her previous tone of champagne bubbles replaced by flat beer. "It's all a load of bollocks."

"What do you mean?" asked Carol, somewhat disingenuously, having guessed ahead.

"It's total rubbish," said Janice, shaking her head. "All that 'merry widow' bullshit I just spouted. I'm not happy at all. Not a bit. In fact, I am bloody miserable most of the time and – truth be told – it makes me even more miserable when I pretend not to be."

"But—" began Carol.

"No, it's true," cut in Janice, not wanting her 'heartfelt share' to be interrupted. "I just can't see the point any more. Not any of it. I work so hard at filling my days with fluff when actually there is absolutely no point whatsoever. So why do I do it?"

Carol shook her head.

"You see," continued Janice, "you don't know either."

Carol shook her head again.

"Have you not noticed," said Janice, her tone now trending towards professorial, "that as men age, get old, they are considered sage, possessors of great knowledge, beings to be listened to and even revered. And the older and uglier they get, the more they come to resemble Yoda, the wiser they become in the eyes of society. But as women get old, lose their looks, their figure, their hair, we are generally considered useless, stupid, worthless. To the world at large, old women are pointless blobs of unsightly wrinkled flesh who do nothing more than clutter up the planet."

"Unless your husband needs a cooked meal or some clean clothes," added Carol, trying to steer the conversation back to a lighter, more humorous place.

Janice was having none of it. "At a certain age, we women simply disappear from the collective consciousness, become invisible. I used to like it when a man eyed me up and down or passed me in the street and then turned to have a second look. A wolf whistle was the ultimate badge of pride that I was happy to take and wear. A little bit of attention always did me the power of good. It proved to me that I existed."

Carol surprised herself by being able to remember that feeling, and gave her friend the knowing nod with a half smile for extra confirmation.

"But now, as I said, I'm invisible, *we're* invisible. Or worse still, we become this amorphous mass of indistinguishable old women. We're like the bloody Chinese."

"Now you've lost me," said Carol. "Who's like the Chinese?"

"We are. Old women. To most of the population we all look the same."

"I don't think you're allowed to say that any more," said Carol, shaking her head. "My granddaughters keep telling me that these days we can't—"

Janice cut her off with an elongated groan of frustration along with an exaggerated rolling of her eyes. "I know I'm not supposed to *say* it," she said, "but it doesn't change the fact of the matter. I can't tell them apart and it's the same for us old women. It doesn't matter a jot what *actual* size or shape we are, what colour we dye our hair, whatever, we all look the same in most people's eyes. For instance, I'd bet you a pound to a pinch of salt that lad who served us at the bar wouldn't be able to tell us apart." She paused before delivering the punchline. "Despite me being more glamorous, better dressed, more capricious, and looking at least ten years younger than you."

"What does 'capricious' mean?" asked Carol through the giggles.

"Absolutely no idea," snorted Janice. "But you get my point."

Carol did. Completely. It was a substantial part of her 'bank robbery escape' philosophy. Nobody would look twice at an old woman wandering away from a crime scene with a pistol and a few thousand stolen quid in her shoulder bag. And, even if they did, they would never remember what she actually looked like.

The laughter, sadly, was short-lived. "Do you know," said Janice, "day after day, night after night, I sit all by myself in that great big empty house and stare at the walls. Most nights I can't even be bothered to turn the telly on. I just sit there and stare at those perfectly decorated rooms with perfect carpets, perfect furniture, perfect bastard ornaments all clean and neat and polished and dusted, and I hate it. I hate the whole thing of it. Then I find myself hating Lenny for dropping dead and leaving me alone, and then I hate myself for hating him for dying." A small tear broke free from the corner of one eye and Janice angrily brushed it away with a knuckle. "Truth is, mate, when it comes down to it, bottom line, I am totally and absolutely fucking bored out of my fucking head."

Carol said nothing beyond a silent thank-you that Janice had muted the F-word – both times. But she knew exactly what her friend was going through. She'd been there herself until a few months previous. She nodded in a way that silently spoke volumes of understanding and empathy.

"You too," whispered Janice, nodding the confirmation.

"Oh yes," breathed Carol, sighing again to fill the space until she was ready to finish her say. "Not the bit about the perfect house and the polished ornaments. Or the bit about the dead husband. But with regards to the last of it, and – to risk stealing your words – being fucking bored doesn't even come close to it."

The bitter dark humour and the way Carol had delivered the line snapped the tension and both of them laughed aloud – maybe a little too loudly for what had triggered it, but the release provided was much needed. Carol pushed the humour on with a "Have you thought of taking up a hobby?" It was a sure-fire tickle of the ribs as, in the sixty-odd years she'd known Janice, Carol knew the closest her friend had ever got to a hobby was going out for lunch.

Janice knew it too. "You may laugh, you rotten excuse for a best friend, but actually I have been thinking about taking up a hobby."

Carol was shocked, and her whole body showed it. "What?" she asked.

"I'm thinking of taking up hooking," replied Janice, clearly fighting to deliver the word with mock seriousness of both voice and expression.

"Crochet?" asked Carol, struggling to keep her laughter in check.

"Walking the streets and doing the dirty for wads of cash, *actually*," replied Janice, with a head movement that would possibly have been described as coquettish. "I read in a magazine at the hair salon that quite a lot of young men these days like a bit of 'mature', so I should make a mint." She only just managed to get the last words out before the shaking giggles took possession.

"You know, I reckon you just might," said Carol, nodding sagely. "But..."

"No, no, I know what you're going to say," said Janice, fighting her words out through her laughter and holding up a flat palm to make sure Carol didn't say anything before she'd managed to finish. "Everybody round here knows me, so I'd have to go somewhere else, and that would make it all a bit too risky."

"You could stay here in town and wear a disguise," offered Carol, struggling to get the words out around her own choking giggles as tears ran down her cheeks.

"Great idea," said Janice, pretending to think about it, "but how many blokes are gonna pay to shag a pantomime horse?"

And with that, the two women collapsed into convulsions of laughter that continued unabated until a young waiter crept cautiously towards their table of maniacal hilarity to deliver their food.

They ate in silence for a few minutes before Janice rested her knife and fork down and spoke. "I do miss it, though," she said wistfully.

"What?" asked Carol, not being able to even guess what her friend was on about.

"Sex," said Janice.

Carol was majorly surprised by the sudden, flat, matter-of-fact way her friend said the word. It hadn't been a subject the two of them had ever touched on, pretty much since they'd been teenagers and talked about 'it' seemingly endlessly. And it wasn't something she herself even thought about much at all these days. Her and Roy hadn't done it for years. It had started to go off the boil when Roy had trouble managing it, and by then her workings were already on the blink, so it all became a bit of a rigmarole that very quickly dwindled away to nothing. Funny thing was neither of them seemed to have even noticed it had gone, let alone worried about it. And, to be brutally honest, although she sometimes thought about it in a sort of remote, cold, objective way, she couldn't say she actually felt like she was missing anything.

Janice picked up on her friend's lack of a response, but quickly glossed over it by pressing on with her own story. "Lenny and me were at it right up until he died, you know. Not every night of the week, but not far off. In fact he was on the job that night when his heart popped."

"Too much information," squealed Carol, happy that her prior period of introspection had passed. "Way too much."

"Oh come on. It's not like I'm going to describe it to you in mucky detail. But just in case you were thinking something dodgy was going on, I will confirm – simply for the record, you understand – it was straightforward, regular, routine missionary."

"Well, that's nice to hear," said Carol, not sparing the sarcasm.

"And I enjoyed it. Well, not that last time, of course, but all the times before. And I always had. Right from the very first time. The sense of being loved, being close to somebody, skin on skin, just the two of us together, where nothing else and nobody else mattered. You know, Lenny may have been a grumpy old sod a lot of the time, but he had a truly huge—"

"Enough!" shrieked Carol as loudly as she dared in a busy pub.

"I was going to say," said Janice, making a 'smutty you' face at her friend, "he had a truly huge sense of romance. You might not have seen it but he really was a sentimental old bugger when the mood took him. But that said, oh my God, when he got to it he was like a ruddy steam hammer."

"Another wine?" asked Carol as the only thing she could think of that might stop her friend talking about sex.

"Of course," replied Janice, immediately waving a hand at the young waiter to get his attention. "Another soda water?"

"If I have another I probably *will* pee myself on your heated seats, but you go ahead and I'll watch."

"Oh, you can watch, but only on condition you tell me. Tell me how *you* cope with the crushing, mind-numbing boredom," said Janice, tilting her head to one side, ready to receive. "For instance, say, what are you doing next week?"

"A bit of this and that," said Carol evasively. "Oh, and on Tuesday afternoon," she paused to smile, "I'm going to take the train into Nantwich."

Janice snorted derisively. "And that's going to get your blood pumping, is it?"

Carol made a 'probably not' face to her friend, whilst thinking, it damned well will when I stroll into a bank there with a gun up my coat sleeve.

# Chapter 8

"Have you two seen this?" were the first words Danny Roberts said as Jacquie and Kevin came back from lunch.

They stopped in their tracks and stared as their DS tossed the folded newspaper onto the desk in front of them. They took a synchronised step forward and bent at the waist as one to read the front page of the *Midwestern Echo*. First up was the two-inch headline that screamed, 'Police Flounder in Hunt for Red Fox'. It took less than a couple of seconds for the potentially obscure reference to make sense, but neither officer made a sound as they read the article below, both nodding gently as the story was told and the implications sank in. As they reached the end they stood upright and looked across at their immediate superior.

Jacquie spoke first. "Shirley's going to go apeshit." From the reaction of her colleagues she could tell she had succinctly summed up the collective wisdom of their merry little band.

"At least they didn't mention him by name," added Kevin with a face that said they needed to be thankful for small mercies.

"Or any of us," added Danny with a 'oh well, that's alright then' shrug, before adding, "but this Percy Walsh guy is too bloody accurate by half." He flicked a hand at the newspaper column journalist's by-line. "He's spot on when he says we have no leads and precious few clues. Spot on."

Jacquie was about to offer a protest but, realising how damnably weak it would be, thought better of it.

"The bit about our man disappearing without a trace is also mightily close to the truth," added Danny. "In fact, to be brutally honest, it *is* the truth."

"But how could Walsh know that?" asked Kevin. "I mean, well..."

"If you're suggesting somebody's been leaking," said Danny, "I don't think so. None of us would, and Shirley wouldn't for sure, 'cause it would make us – and, by association of *alleged* leadership, him – look like the hapless bunch we are. No, I reckon this Walsh bloke has simply looked at the nothingness we've put out there and guessed."

"Where does the 'Red Fox' thing come from?" asked Jacquie.

"Ginger moustache. It's obvious," replied Danny. "You know what the press are like. They have to make any story more melodramatic, big it up to sell more papers. And whether we like it or not, giving the new arch-criminal on the block a fancy Marvel Comics title is bound to work."

"But why *Red* Fox?" she pressed. "Why not *Ginger* Fox?"

"You can't call carrot-tops 'gingers' any more," butted in Kevin, fresh from his recent diversity and inclusivity training course. "It's gingist, apparently. One mention of 'Duracell' and they're all over you like a rash, screaming prejudice and discrimination. And they're organised these days, like some sort of Copper Nostra mafia, hiding away from bright sunlight but all just waiting for the opportunity to point their accusing white freckly fingers at any perceived offender."

"Thank you for that, Kevin, highly illuminating," said Danny, the sarcastic humour unmistakable in his tone. "And it sounds like that training course has really paid off," he added to complete the light-hearted rebuff.

"Sorry, Sarge," said Kevin, lowering his head in genuine apology. "I really am the prince of tolerance when it comes to race, religion, gender, disability, sexuality, you name it. It's just the bloody Swan Vestas that get up my—"

"Fox is a good one, though," said Jacquie, cutting across her colleague's continuing rant before he dug himself into an even deeper hole. "Our villain is in and out of the hen-house like greased lightning and then off away, back to his cosy den somewhere to count his chickens. Not a sight of his brush, not a trace of—"

"People!" snapped Danny, clapping his hands loudly, "this inaugural meeting of the Red Fox Appreciation Society is not getting us anywhere. It is our job to catch him, and what this admittedly insightful bastard Percy Walsh has put out there in stark and brutal black-and-white print for all to see is right on the money. Whatever fairy-tale title he might have bestowed on a miserable bank-robbing lowlife, his article reads very badly for us. He doesn't actually say it in as many words, but the whole piece screams something along the lines of 'Super-smart Red Fox running rings round the dopey policemen who remain utterly mystified to the point of catatonia by his predatory brilliance.'"

"That last paragraph doesn't read well either," added Jacquie. "Okay, Walsh doesn't risk sounding like he's condoning bank robbery to support needy charities, but he sure as heck makes a big thing about the Red Fox passing the money on to worthy causes. He's even managed to – albeit tenuously, I admit – link all four robberies to four big anonymous donations, and that's more than we managed to do."

"Even if we had, it wouldn't have helped any," said Danny. "Yes, we managed to get the Telford robbery cash back, but – and I hate to say this – even that made us look like the bad guys. Like we'd snatched an ice cream out of some little kiddie's hand. And, yet a-bloody-gain, even that small victory told us nothing. Nothing about the robber, nothing, nothing, nothing."

"He *will* make a mistake at some point," offered Jacquie, hearing her words sound vapour thin. "He'll cock one up, do something..."

"Jacquie," groaned Danny, shaking his head sadly. "Think about it. As you said the other day, we've probably only got a few weeks before he hangs up his hoodie coat and buggers off on holiday for the summer. But worse than that – far, far worse – never forget that he goes in there armed. If his next job did just happen to start going wrong, he might actually shoot somebody."

Jacquie could barely get the word out. "Sorry," she croaked.

"So," continued Danny, desperate to get the mood back up and brains running on positive power again, "to quote our glorious miniature and more-often-than-not-absent leader, where are we?"

The weak joke brought forth a burst of laughter that was almost immediately killed by the squad-room door crashing open. The bang was still echoing as DI Graham Templeton barrelled in like a curly blond Tasmanian devil. He took himself to the middle of the room before turning to scowl at his crew, his face as close to purple as feasible for a man not in the throes of severe cardiac arrest. A tightly rolled newspaper gripped in the white knuckles of his right hand was being smacked repeatedly into the open palm of his left. They didn't have to guess what paper it might be, and from there to what was almost certainly the trigger for this manifest anger.

Templeton stopped his palm bashing and extended his right arm, newspaper baton held steady and straight like a sword-fencer preparing to lunge, to point at his three team members one by one. Only when he'd completed the ritual in full did he speak, his voice contorted by barely restrained fury. "Right, which one of you has been gobbing off to the press?"

The three stood to attention and shook their heads in synchronised denial.

"So," Templeton stared at them, making eye contact with each in turn, "you're telling me this little fucker," he paused to stab an index finger three times hard at the rolled newspaper, "has some sort of mystical insight."

"He doesn't need to—" began Danny, only to be cut off.

"This says we are nowhere," continued Templeton, now waving the nasty, horrible, upsetting newspaper. "He says we know nothing, we have no leads, no clues, no ideas." His voice was rising with every phrase uttered. "He basically says we are fucking clue*less*. So which one of you has been giving him the inside run? Or is it all of you?" The final accusation was shouted in such a high register it risked bringing stray dogs a-running.

"Nobody in here," said Danny, almost firing the words out, stressing them hard, with spaces between, as he faced up to his petulant little shit of a boss. "Nobody in here has been talking to the press. *And*," he slammed the connecting word down to leave no room for an interruption, "there was no need to. We *don't* have any leads, and the mere fact that we have told the press absolutely nothing means this Percy Walsh git simply had to cock one ear, listen to the voices on the wind, hear sod all, and write a stunningly accurate piece saying we are nowhere."

As Jacquie and Kevin winced internally, waiting for the imminent backlash, Danny stood tall and proud at his defence of the team, allowing himself to muse on how his career had probably just cratered on the back of it. But what came next was a shock that took his breath away.

"You're right, Danny," said Templeton, leaning his head from side to side as he released the tension from his neck whilst also giving himself time to think. "We haven't told the press a thing, have we. And from that they would indeed quite naturally have assumed we are in possession of nothing to tell. Now, leaving aside the fact of the matter, maybe it *is* time for us to usher them into the fold."

The three foot-soldiers stood blank-faced and waited for the brilliant punchline.

"The Press – capital 'P' – are a resource," continued Templeton. "They can reach more people than we could ever hope to, what with budget cuts, manpower restrictions and so on. They can garner support, give us access to eyes and ears, spread the net, and help us to snare this Red Fox."

"Are you suggesting we—" began Danny, only to be abruptly stifled by his boss.

"From the geographic spread of the robberies and bank staff testimonies vis-à-vis our man's accent, it's a safe bet he is a local. So, even if the scumbag doesn't read this crappy local rag, he will almost certainly be living amongst people that do."

"So you—" Danny tried again, but got even fewer words out this time. Templeton was having his say and nobody was going to interrupt him.

"A few minutes ago I was all out to find a way to cut this Percy Walsh's bollocks off. But now, now I think about it, consider the broader picture, I have come to realise our paucity of communication has pretty much played into his hands. And this in turn leads me to a different conclusion, a different course of action."

Danny sort of remembered it was actually him who'd suggested that, but said nothing.

"Danny," snapped Templeton, pointing the rolled newspaper at his detective sergeant's face, "get in touch with the *Midwestern Echo* and get me a meeting with Walsh. I want him to come here for an exclusive interview with me as the Red Fox SIO. A one-on-one that will give me the opportunity to put the record straight and thereby get him and the *Midwestern* fucking *Echo* on our side."

"But, er, sir," began Danny, using the deferential title to hopefully save himself from a spell on the naughty step, "what *can* you tell him? We don't have anything. You know that. We..."

The sight of Templeton vigorously shaking his head was enough to get him to stop.

"There are a thousand ways to hide that fact," said Templeton, scratching lightly at his chin like a wise old Chinese monk, "and a thousand more to suggest we are making progress but cannot, at this stage in the investigation, risk releasing too much information for fear of spooking our Red Fox into going to ground."

The three silently glanced sideways at each other as they recognised how quickly and easily their leader had assimilated the criminal's new name tag.

"I was top of my class by a mile in interactional interview manipulation and influencing techniques at Hendon," continued the now irritatingly smug Templeton. He didn't exactly give himself a 'rah-rah' cheer, but damned nearly did. "So I can confidently assure you I will have our local hack eating out of my hand in minutes flat. And then, as he rolls over to have his tummy tickled, I will play him, use him, and tie him in knots to the point where he will be literally begging me to allow him to help us."

"And if he...?" asked Danny, his voice little more than a whisper.

Templeton made a face to say, 'Never going to happen', allowing it to hang there for the count of five, then slowly transforming it into the best look of evil a ten-year-old blond curly-haired Hollywood tap-dancer could manage before growling, "If he doesn't play ball then I will threaten the scabby little grunt with materially jeopardising a police inquiry, contempt of court, and, if necessary, the Official bloody Secrets Act, leaving him so shit-scared he won't want to risk writing another fucking word about the Red Fox case."

# Chapter 9

A late April sun was shining brightly in a clear blue sky promising warmth but delivering precious little as a bitterly cold wind sliced its way along the pedestrian precinct. What few hardy souls had decided to brave the numbing chill were all bundled into heavy coats with collars and hoods up, hats pulled down, and scarves tightly wrapped. It was a lousy day for window-shopping but a great one for bank robbery, as the diminutive figure in the heavy grey hoodie coat looked totally 'right' for the conditions. Carol knew she fitted in perfectly, and even allowed herself a small smile behind her fake moustache as she casually strolled towards her target.

This was her fourth visit to Nantwich in the last couple of weeks. The first had been to make her final bank selection, roughly map out the location and escape route, and spot primary CCTV cameras. The second had been to double-check and fill in any gaps, such as in-shop cameras and those linked to the many cafés and tea shops around the main square. And the third had been a dummy run, getting a feel for the bank itself: its internal configuration, security, and, importantly, the level of activity in the early afternoon of a typical Tuesday and hence how many cash desks were likely to be open. From there she had defined and fixed a 'hit time' that she would not allow herself to deviate from. She'd learned that lesson from an American TV cop show: deviation from the set plan introduces doubt that weakens emotional resolve and henceforth puts the perpetrator on a path to failure and ultimate capture. As the saying went – albeit from a completely different movie – the attack had to be executed with poise, precision and audacity.

Having lived her entire life surrounded by law-abiding folk, it was no surprise to Carol that she'd learned everything she knew about armed robbery from watching the telly: TV shows, movies, documentaries and, surprisingly, *Crimewatch*. And she found it mildly amusing that, in a bizarre twist, a programme designed specifically to catch villains had provided her, as a novice wannabe villain, with many of the essential tricks of the trade.

It was, however, the Americans who'd taught her the most. She could never remember the names of any of the programmes or movies and at times they sort of all melted into one but, oh my, what an education they delivered.

Lesson one: maintaining control at the scene of the robbery. Strong words delivered softly but with the maximum degree of intimidation. Threaten the ultimate in savagery from the outset. Start weak and you will fail. Make it brutally clear to the cashier from the very first phrase you utter that you are coldly prepared to kill indiscriminately if they even dare to think about not following your instructions. Show the weapon in a subtle way, leaving the victim to use their own imagination to maximise the horror. And never, ever, *ever* deviate from the prepared script. She'd practised her lines over and over in front of the bathroom mirror, editing and adjusting, getting every phrase, every intonation, every nuance pinpoint perfect. The way she spoke, too, was vitally important: clipped diction to make sure she didn't have to repeat herself, and all of it delivered in a harsh whisper that carried with it the maximum sense of terrifying menace.

Lesson two: witness misdirection. Apparently, or so she'd learned, witnesses notice very obvious markers to the exclusion of otherwise valuable detail. The bit of sticking plaster on the frame of the small round glasses, the bright ginger of the moustache, the fake stammer, the limp. All so obvious, and all there to draw attention away from what lay beneath and hence could be of use to the police. She often chuckled to herself when she recalled the night the stammer got folded into the blend of concealment. The late-night programme was a horribly wooden but fascinating 1970s true-crime docudrama. Roy was snoring gently in his armchair while a smartly uniformed, shiny-faced officer from the New York Police Department stared straight out from the screen to unwittingly deliver a masterclass in bank robbery to a fully alert and attentive sixty-something-year-old housewife, three thousand miles away across the Atlantic. "The accomplished bank robber will frequently embrace audible misdirection techniques," he'd intoned. "A fake distinctive marker that gives the 'teller' a focus of fixation such that, in later interviews, he or she will be unable to recall what the robber actually sounded like." Super-Cop had gone on to suggest a lisp but, next afternoon when Carol had given it a try, she'd quickly realised she sounded more like Daffy Duck than John Dillinger. Option two from the NYPD's expert had been a stammer, and here Carol had laughed herself to the point of asphyxiation as she tried and tried again to work it into her prepared robbery script. The 'f-f-f' made it f-f-flipping well impossible to threaten anyone, while the 'y-y-y' was equally y-y-useless. The 's-s-s' made her s-s-sound bloody s-s-soppy, and the 'w-w-w' she thought w-w-was downright hysterical. Luckily she still had the 'n-n-n' that worked n-n-nicely in every respect and was the n-n-no-contest winner and hence formally adopted.

Lesson three: the getaway car swap. She didn't have a car and, even if she had, she'd never learned to drive, but the principle was clear. You depart the scene of the crime in one 'vehicle' and then – at the first covert opportunity – switch to a different one. Her solution was as brilliant as it was simple, although the work that went into it was complex, technical and challenging. Getting it done didn't half cheer her, though.

Right from the beginning, when her new hobby had still been little more than a gaseous swirl of fantasy, she'd known that, as a short, light-framed and far from athletic 'woman of years', she would never be able to project the degree of fear-inducing power essential for getting the job done. Simple physicality was fact, and that was that. So, long before Janice's lecture on comparative social assessment and consequent societal reaction to aged persons of different genders, Carol had known she would have to disguise herself as a man. It was a straightforward decision, but one that immediately illuminated a number of key elements of the way ahead.

The harsh, whispery voice she'd settled on for controlling the crime scene did a good job at concealing the fact she was a woman, and the moustache was an obvious addition. The hood would hide her hair and the sides of her face, and the wire-rimmed glasses would further disrupt facial recognition as well as hide her thin grey but reasonably stylishly arched old lady's eyebrows. Gloves to conceal her hands (always a giveaway, apparently), and the flat black plimsolls and hoodie coat were about as gender neutral as was possible. But it was in the very last of these where lesson three kicked in and innovative brilliance delivered her crowning glory.

It had been a repeat episode of *Crimewatch*, enjoyed one morning while she was doing the ironing, that had highlighted the importance of drab clothing. Carol knew perfectly well that the programme's intention had been to demonstrate how it made identification infuriatingly more difficult for the forces of law and order, but to her it was informational gold in the opposite direction. The grainy CCTV clips of wholly anonymous villains in grey hoodies set the baseline. Leaving aside the impossibility of identifying who they were, the police couldn't even tell what gender or age they might be.

Admittedly, most of the footage had been captured at night under cover of darkness or at best partial artificial lighting, and high-street banks weren't open at night, but the central point was still valid. She needed a robbery costume that would allow her to walk in without arousing suspicion and out without being identifiable. That was the easy part. And the initial walk away from the bank wasn't a factor that could be manipulated either: CCTV cameras inside the bank would have her on tape anyway, so those covering the pavement outside would provide nothing extra, provided she kept her face turned away from all and any cameras. So it was the long yards beyond that posed the challenge, and that was when the trusty old Bernina sewing machine was dragged out from its resting place of many years to be pressed into action.

Roy had complained for hours about having to move everything away from the understairs cupboard door to heave it out. And then he'd grumbled like mad about how heavy it was and what it might do to his back or his bowling arm. But, after a lot of cajoling and the promise of toad-in-the-hole for tea, he finally did it. And he didn't once ask why she had so suddenly felt the need to start sewing again. He just stuck the machine up on the kitchen table and toddled off to the club for his Tuesday afternoon of woods chucking with his mates.

She'd already bought the material and hidden it in the back of the spare-bedroom wardrobe. And it only took her about four hours to draw up the pattern and cut out the pieces. She'd finished and tidied away well before Roy got home. His special dinner was already on the go, and he'd won his match, so he was happy as could be. And Carol was too, although she made a point of not smiling too widely. She saved that for her husband's Thursday afternoon out bowling as she set to and sewed the pieces together. And she'd actually done a little jig-dance when she'd tried on the finished article. A perfectly reversible overcoat.

Worn one way it was a drab grey hoodie coat with large side pockets that, having no lining, gave easy access to the inside, where she could hang her shoulder bag around her neck, all ready to receive cash, gun, glasses and moustache as she walked away from the bank. The instant she was in a CCTV blind zone, the hood was un-poppered and also stuffed into the bag. Then all she needed to do was step into a previously identified quiet, rarely occupied, and hence out-of-sight hideaway corner for the mere eight seconds it took her to – she'd timed herself as she practised and practised to get it down to the minimum – take the coat off and turn it inside out and into a reasonably stylish mustard yellow overcoat with grey edge piping that any woman of her age would be proud to wear. Another less than ten seconds to swap her black plimsolls for the coat-matching mustard yellow kitten heels in her bag, then casually sling said bag over her shoulder, and the 'getaway car swap' was complete. She could wander away as slowly as she liked, unnoticed and unhindered, back to the station to catch the train home in time to get the tea on.

And so here she was once again. A different town, but the same modus operandi. Fourteen forty-five on the dot, as decided and fixed in that last reconnaissance trip as she wandered into bank number five with the now familiar tingle already spreading deliciously through her veins as she took a place only two back in the queue for the next available cash desk.

What was it Janice said, teased her with? Something about an afternoon trip to Nantwich hardly being likely to raise the pulse rate? If only Carol could tell her friend the truth. But, no, that could never happen. Not a chance. Not in a—

Ooh, my turn already?

# Chapter 10

"You will not believe what I've just seen!" Kevin had come bundling into the squad room literally shaking with excitement, delivering his opening around a tumble of choking laughter.

Danny looked up from his computer screen to see his detective constable hopping from foot to foot whilst grinning like a demented Shropshire cat. He said nothing, just using his facial expression alone to say, 'Go on, then.'

Before Kevin could get out his revelation, Jacquie wandered in from the file room and stopped in her tracks when she saw her very clearly humorously agitated colleague. "What's going on?" she asked.

"You will not believe what I've just seen," repeated Kevin, now wildly rotating his clenched fists in small circles as he fought to control his excitement.

"Bloody get on with it," growled Danny as his impatience with the charade grew.

"You remember," began Kevin, "how Shirley was going to find a way to cut off Percy Walsh's bollocks?" He paused, pantomime-style, waiting for the audience response. He got a double nod and, deciding that was the best he was likely to get, pressed on with the rest of it. "Well, he'd have a job," squealed Kevin before stopping again.

"And why is that, Kevin?" asked a weary Danny.

The answer was all but shrieked. "Because *she* hasn't got any!"

Danny made a confused face, while Jacquie barked a single laugh.

"You mean..." she continued, leaving it at that.

"Correct-o," replied Kevin, spinning around on his heels in a little dance of glee. "Percy Walsh is a girl – I mean, a woman. And some bloomin' woman at that." He didn't wait for any more audience participation, crashing on ahead with the whole story spewed out at breakneck speed. "Late twenties, I'd guess. Brunette, slim, and tall as tall. Must be six foot at least, but six and a half with the spike heels she was wearing. Skin-tight black leather trousers and a bright red vest top with a neckline that, well, to say it plunged wouldn't do it justice. Oh em gee very, *very* tasty."

"Where did you—" asked Jacquie, before being cut off.

"In reception," continued Kevin. "I was just coming in, clocked Babelicious, couldn't help having a second look, then Shirley comes swaggering in to do the Big Boss-Man meet-and-greet thing."

"She could have been anybody," scoffed a disbelieving Danny.

"No, no, no," said Kevin, shaking his head. "It was her, I'm telling you. I checked the register and she is most definitely Percy Walsh of the *Midwestern Echo*. Signed in, ID checked and duly verified."

"How did Shirley react?" asked Danny, warming to the possibility that his boss would have found the gender surprise at the very least uncomfortable. "Please tell me you stayed to watch."

"Oh, I stayed, alright. Hung around for a chat with Sergeant Big Fat Bob on the front desk. He never misses an opportunity to bang on about Shrewsbury Town, so I set him running and left him to it while I watched the car crash. It was brilliant!"

"Tell," instructed Jacquie.

"Well," said Kevin, easing himself down into his desk chair to get nice and comfortable before story time. "Our Shirley has strode into reception, all assertive and authoritarian, looks around the half-dozen bods waiting there, doesn't spot anyone with a pad and pencil, so reckons his crack reporter hasn't shown up yet. Has a quick check with Big Fat Bob, who wordlessly points a sausage finger at Long Tall Percy. So Shirley adjusts his tie, brushes down the front of his jacket, checks his curls are in place, and does the strutting cockerel thing across to where she's sat. She looks up at him and he sticks out a welcome mitt, which she duly ignores. But then," Kevin started to giggle uncontrollably, "but then," the giggle morphed into a chortle, "but then..." He couldn't go on as the laughter took hold and tears ran down his cheeks.

"For glory's sake," sighed Danny, "bloody get on with it."

Kevin forced himself to pull it together, wiped his eyes, and finished. "Remember, Shirley is now standing up close and personal, no more than an arm's length away, waiting for a handshake that hasn't materialised. So when Ms Walsh suddenly gets to her feet, Shirley's nose is damned near nestling in her cleavage. I was choking at this point and Big Fat Bob's little piggy eyes nearly fell out of his massive swede."

"More, more," urged Jacquie, using wiggling fingers to give motion to the demand.

"Shirley stands there for about half a second," continued Kevin, "before he's reeling back and away like he's been electrocuted. His face – no, his *entire head* – is one big bright red pulsating blush, and he's stammering and jabbering away, trying to get across an apology and a welcome all at the same time. In the end the whole lot came out as a tangle of utter gibberish."

"And what was the goddess Percy doing at this point?" asked Danny.

"Just standing there," said Kevin, still chuckling. "Standing tall, cool, statuesque and stony-faced, watching half the Chuckle Brothers making an absolute tit of himself. If only I'd been able to film it on my mobile. I could have made a fortune."

"But he sorted it, right?" said Danny. "I mean, in the end, after he'd got his snout out from between her boobs, she went with him into the interview room?"

"Certainly looked that way," said Kevin with a shrug. "Although, to be fair, I had to leave before I totally cracked up and pissed myself."

"I've just remembered," said Jacquie, a wicked grin spreading across her face. "That bit our Lilliputian leader said about tying Percy Walsh in knots to the point where '*he*' would roll over to have his tummy tickled. Do you think...?"

"I am not allowing myself to even muse upon just how much fun that sounds for any normal bloke," said Kevin, shaking his head in a play-act of disappointment that he was not remotely likely to get the opportunity. "But for our Shirley, assuming he does remember those words, I most sincerely hope they have him writhing in agony."

For the next forty minutes or so the three troopers went about what had, of late, become their routine grind. Kevin went back yet again through the CCTV feeds collected from all four robberies, still trying to convince himself that there was a vital clue in there that he'd missed. Jacquie did much the same but with the witness statements, and Danny re-drew his timelines and known movements of the robber before and after each robbery. They didn't speak, didn't even look up as a dismal cloud of desperate dejection steadily formed above their heads as it had done day after day in the preceding weeks.

Nothing disturbed them until the office door swung open and Templeton breezed in. He was most definitely smirking like a fourteen-year-old who'd just managed to snaffle the seat next to his unrequited love-crush on the school bus home. Without addressing his team, he wafted across to the incident board where he casually, almost idly, fingered one or two of the exhibits hanging there.

Danny popped the balloon of pent-up expectancy with a "How was he, sir? The reporter bloke." It was a very deliberate use of the incorrect gender so as to not let on that they knew.

"*She*," replied Templeton in a strangely light to approaching ethereal tone, "was magnificent." He almost choked as he realised how the word could be misinterpreted, coughed, and ran a finger round the inside of his collar to loosen it a tad. "By which, er, I mean," he added, now using his 'ace detective inspector' voice, "Ms Walsh was professional, assiduous, diligent and conscientious. She pressed for answers without becoming aggressive, sought clarification on my key points without overstepping the boundaries of propriety, and fully understood and accepted the differentiation I insisted we establish between 'on the record' and 'off the record'."

"So you got her on our side, sir," said Jacquie, playing up to the boss.

"Indeed, yes, Jacquie. I did. Mission accomplished."

"So she's going to help," said Danny as a statement. "Or has she simply agreed to stop putting the boot in? To us, I mean."

"Both," replied Templeton with a smug grin. "However, best of all, I do believe I have established an ongoing working relationship where we can cooperate without losing sight of the fact that we, the police, must retain the controlling hand."

"Sounds good," said Danny, crossing his fingers under the desk so his superior officer couldn't see how little of what had been said he believed. "I can't wait to see what she writes next week," he added, this time not needing to cross his fingers.

"Same here," confirmed Templeton with a restrained air punch. "Now, as an early indication of our impending cooperation, Percy, er, Ms Walsh gave me a heads-up on something she picked up on the jungle telegraph just before leaving the office. Apparently there are rumours our Red Fox may have spread his wings."

The three dutiful sidekicks glossed over the flying fox image and pricked up their ears for something sensible.

"Meaning, sir?" asked Danny.

"There was a bank robbery reported in Nantwich yesterday afternoon. Early reports suggest the perpetrator was sporting a droopy ginger moustache. The local coppers are apparently currently dismissing it as a copycat *but* – or so Ms Walsh informed me – they are keeping an open mind. Therefore, just in case, we need to check. Danny?"

"Yes, sir?"

"Get onto Cheshire Constabulary. Find out who's in charge of the investigation and ask for a copy of their file. If it is our man then we need to be in pole position. Okay?"

"On it," said Danny, reaching for his telephone.

He'd barely touched the receiver when the air was cut through with the strains of 'I Like to Move It' coming from somewhere deep inside Templeton's jacket.

Templeton reached into his inside pocket, tugged out his mobile, and killed the ringtone by answering. "Detective Inspector Templeton." He listened to whoever was on the other end as his team watched on. The change in his facial expression was unmistakable and he most definitely was not liking what he was hearing. "No, you listen to me," he barked down the line, pausing before adding a wimpy, deferential, "sir." More listening, the occasional attempted interruption, and then a feeble "Yes, I understand", before pressing to end the call and slipping his phone back into his pocket. "Fucker," he breathed, more to himself than anybody who might be – or was – listening. "Fucking fucker."

"Not good, sir?" asked Danny, stating the bleedin' obvious.

Templeton took an age to answer, the muscles in his jaw rippling as he ground his teeth together. At last words came. "Some jumped-up arsehole chief inspector from Cheshire fucking Cheesehead fucking Constabulary says he's taking over the Red Fox case. Says he is convinced the Nantwich job was indeed the Red Fox, *and* as it was on his patch and hence under his jurisdiction, *and* as he is the senior officer between us, he gets to take it over. Oh, and he very gleefully pointed out that although we have had four robberies to his one, we have also had the better part of three months to investigate, wherein we have, in his words, 'got abso-fucking-lutely no-fucking-where'!"

"So...?" asked Danny, continuing in his role of designated team patsy.

"He wants all our files, witness statements, CCTV, the lot sent up to bloody Winsford by special courier to be on his desk before close of play this afternoon."

"Would you like me to arrange it?" asked Jacquie, forcing out the words around the clawing sense of humiliation and disappointment strangling her vocal cords.

"No," said Templeton in little more than a whisper. "Do nothing."

"But won't that...?" began Danny tentatively.

"Oh yes, indeed it will," replied Templeton, speaking the words into the air above his team members' heads. "It will most definitely royally piss off Chief Inspector fucking arse-wipe Overton. But I wouldn't mind betting he doesn't have the ear of his assistant chief constable to whisper into."

Danny, Jacquie and Kevin exchanged surreptitious sidelong glances. They all knew their ACC was Templeton's doting Uncle Gerry.

"So you're going to..." offered Danny, really getting the hang of the not-completing-his-sentences thing.

"I am going to nip upstairs for a little chinwag," replied Templeton in a light, airy, sing-song voice. He then pirouetted on his heels and jauntily strode out of the squad room to make his way up the golden stairway and into the Olympian clouds beyond.

# Chapter 11

"Have you heard from Paul recently?" asked Sarah. She'd just come into the kitchen where Carol was finishing up preparing Sunday dinner for the family. Sarah and the granddaughters never passed up the offer of one of Grandma's Sunday roasts, which always came with an excellent Yorkshire pudding, whatever the meat. And this week it was a special occasion, with Roy having celebrated his seventy-first birthday the previous Wednesday.

"He sent his dad a nice card," replied Carol, not looking round as she focused her attention on basting the roast potatoes. "And he'd put some money in with it, although what your dad's going to do with a Canadian fifty-dollar note I have no idea. I suspect they don't take them at the bowling club tea hatch."

Sarah laughed. "I'll take it and get it changed for him, if you like."

"Sounds like a good idea, thanks," said Carol, nudging the oven door shut with her knee. "Right, another ten minutes and we should be set to go."

"But have *you* heard from Paul?" pressed Sarah.

"Two or three weeks ago," replied Carol, making the infrequency of her son's communications sound inconsequential. "A nice long letter like always. Loads of stuff about the family, all the outdoorsy things they've been at, what he's been doing on the house, a bit about his work and so on. All in all, lots of lovely, well, you know."

Sarah did know. She also knew how much her mum missed her son, and, truth be told, she actually missed her annoying little brother as well. But at least she had the benefit of regular, albeit brief, message exchanges, meaning she didn't have to wait for weeks, sometimes months, between letters. "I'm trying to set up a video call with him next week," she said. "It's a bit of a sod, what with him being eight hours behind, but he's got the day off next Tuesday, so we're going to try to hook up late evening our time. Hey, Mum," she added, making it sound like it had been a sudden afterthought, "why don't you come round to ours and sit in? He'd love to see you and have a proper chat. And you could maybe see Mel and the kids."

"I'll think about it," said Carol evasively.

"Mum," said Sarah, moving to stand directly in her mother's line of vision, "why won't you let me fix you and Dad up with a computer so you could talk to Paul yourselves? I could get a really cheap second-hand one and show you how to—"

"We've been through this before, love. Your dad and me are both too long in the tooth to start learning fancy new stuff. And besides, who in their right mind would want to be looking at the two of us?"

"Paul would," replied Sarah emphatically. "You know he would."

And I'd like to see him, thought Carol, turning away from her daughter to stir the gravy whilst using it as an excuse to secretively chew at her bottom lip. She really would love to see him. But not on a screen in a little box. She wanted to see him in the flesh, to be able to hold him and feel him hugging her like he used to. The every-few-weeks letters were lovely but only the tiniest crumb of comfort for the ache in her heart. On the other hand – as she so frequently scolded herself – wanting him home was being bloody selfish. Her little boy was happy and doing very well for himself in his new life in Vancouver, and she needed to be happy for him.

"Or how about I get you a cheap-as-chips smartphone?" continued Sarah, not ready to give up quite yet. "Then you could WhatsApp him. It's a lot like chatting over the backyard fence once you get the hang of it. Plus you can send photos and do voice messaging and even set up live video—"

"Still too much," interrupted Carol. "Chook, it's taken me five years or more to come to terms with the phone I've got, and even there I keep forgetting how to answer the bloomin' thing. It would be a waste of money and bring nothing but more anxiety. Oh, and don't even think of suggesting it to your dad. He can barely operate the TV remote, let alone a *Star Trek* communicator."

That final jokey comment broke the mounting tension, and both women laughed.

Carol gave her daughter a quick hug before standing back a half-step to say, "You know how much I miss our Paul, and I really do appreciate you trying to help. But, truth be told, I prefer things the way they are. To see him and not be able to grab hold of the little blighter would hurt more than not seeing him at all. I get his letters, as regular as dodgy clockwork, and I really do enjoy writing mine back. I've never got anything interesting or different to say, mind, but I still manage to fill two or three pages every time."

"When's dinner ready?" demanded a pair of young voices from the doorway. "Grandad says his tummy thinks his throat's been cut," they added, before offering a synchronised "yeeuw, gross!" at the imagery.

Carol smiled adoringly at her granddaughters, who she loved almost more than life itself. Now both just into their teens, Lauren and Bethany were growing into very pretty young ladies. And most of the time they were well behaved and polite, thanks solely to their mum's constancy and strict hand. Carol dreaded the thought of how they might have grown up if their shithead of a father had stuck around, but he hadn't, so all was well that ended well. "Tell grumpy Grandpa to get himself sat up," said Carol, gently shooing the girls out of her kitchen before calling after them, "I'll be bringing it through directly." She stopped and looked at Sarah. "Please don't say anything about this to your dad, okay? He'll only get himself all wound up."

"Secrets are never a good thing," said Sarah, looking straight into her mum's eyes. "You know that, don't you? They always cause a lot more upset when they're found out."

"Sometimes the truth can do more harm than good," countered Carol.

"But you two shouldn't be keeping secrets from each other. Not after all this time."

Carol tilted her head to look sideways at her daughter. "Are you trying, in a roundabout way, to tell me your dad's hiding something?" she asked.

Sarah blew a soft raspberry and picked up two dishes of vegetables to carry through to the dining room. Carol watched her daughter disappear, then turned to quickly look at her reflection in the window. She gave it a single raised eyebrow. It did the same back.

Carol and Sarah shared the responsibility of dishing up, with only the application of gravy being left to the individual diners. Then they all politely waited for Grandpa to lift his knife and fork before digging in themselves.

They ate in silence for the first minute or so until Bethany looked across at her mum and asked, "Did she go for it?"

Sarah made a 'be quiet' face at her younger daughter.

"Did who go for what?" asked Carol.

"Oh, nothing," replied Bethany, her cheeks reddening as she quickly stared down at her plate and focused intently on cutting up a carrot.

"She meant," said Lauren, "did Grandma agree to getting a new phone so she can message with Uncle Paul?"

Sarah scowled ferociously at her elder daughter, but said nothing.

"No, she did not 'go for it'," said Carol, clipped and terse. "And neither is she getting a flippin' computer. 'Cause Grandma," she looked across at Roy who wasn't paying any attention to anything beyond his dinner, "*and* Grandpa are quite happy the way we are. There's a microwave oven in the kitchen – that, incidentally, I rarely if ever use – and that is as far as the modern world is going to invade this house. Alright?" It was a stern but still playfully delivered rebuke, topped off with a big pantomime wink that set both girls giggling.

Roy suddenly spoke up. He had been listening in after all. "If they did a steam-powered telly," he said, "we'd probably be onto that like a shot."

They all laughed this time, and Carol hoped that was the end of it, but Lauren wasn't about to let go.

"Is it because you can't understand new technology, Grandma?" she asked. "Or is it because you're scared of anything that's modern or different?"

This final challenge, even though it had been meant in a light-hearted way, had clearly, in Sarah's mind, crossed the line from playful to insolent, bringing Lauren a swift verbal clip round the ear from her mother. "Lauren! Behave yourself! And you apologise to your grandma. Right now!"

"It's alright," said Carol, her tone one of acceptance, understanding and appeasement. She put down her knife and fork and turned her head to look directly at her granddaughter. "It's a bit of both, I think, Lauren, love. As you grow up, for the first thirty or so years, you're always looking for the next new thing and you can barely wait for them to come along, and you grab as many of them as you can manage. But then, as the years pass, and especially when you get into your sixties and beyond, you find yourself starting to worry about what the next new thing might be, and if you'll have the brainpower or the courage to take it on."

"I'm sorry, Grandma," said Lauren, showing her best contrite smile. "I really am."

"That's okay, love," replied Carol. "Just remember what I've said. Okay?"

"But don't you get bored?" piped up Bethany. "I mean, always doing the same thing over and over every day. You never do anything new or different, Grandma. Surely that has to be boring even for old people."

Out of the mouths of babes and sucklings, thought Carol. If the girl had spoken those same words a few short months previous, their brutal accuracy would have brought Carol close to tears. Back then her life was even worse than unexciting. Back then she'd been precisely what Janice had so very delicately described as "fucking bored out of her fucking head". But not now. Not now she had her hobby. And, as a consequence, whatever her daughter, her granddaughters and probably her own husband thought of her, no matter how silly, how old-fashioned, how resistant to change and boring they thought her, *she* knew the reality. She was special. She did things – exciting things, things that put a tingle in her veins, things her family would not believe. Of course she could never tell them, but *she* knew, and that alone provided her with an impenetrable armour that protected her emotional core, whatever people thought or said. She allowed herself to enjoy the vibration of her secret reality for a few brief moments, then smiled at her patiently waiting granddaughter to reply. "There's always a way to find a little bit of excitement, Bethany, believe me. Ways that aren't always obvious to them as what's watching."

"When I grow up," said Lauren, "I'm not going to spend my life cooking and cleaning and washing and ironing for somebody else. I'm going to do real stuff, exciting stuff, things that I want to do and not what some stupid, stinky boy wants me to do."

"Well, that's a good start," said Carol, meaning it. "Boys are bad news. And they *are* stinky, that's for sure. So what's in this big personal plan of yours?"

"I'm going to travel," began Lauren, light dancing behind her eyes, "all over the world. I'm going to visit all of it, see new places, eat different foods, meet different people, and I'm going to try something new and different every single day."

"You'll need a good job to pay for all that," said Carol. "So I hope you're working hard at school."

Lauren's shoulders sagged. "I'm trying. I really am. But a lot of it's very hard."

"Life is hard," said Carol. "You just need to keep working at it."

Lauren nodded. "Anyway," she said, her earlier enthusiasm seemingly evaporated, "even if I don't earn enough money to see the *whole* world, I'm certainly going to make sure I don't end up rotting away in a poxy little terraced house in a tatty old nowhere town where..." She stopped dead and nearly swallowed her tongue as it suddenly dawned on her that – unintentional as it had been – she'd probably just horribly insulted both her grandparents and her mother.

Sarah made to retaliate, but Carol stopped her by reaching out a hand and gently touching her daughter's arm. She could feel the twinge of hurt from what had been said, but she knew it wasn't her granddaughter's fault.

"Times are different now, Lauren," she said softly. "When I was your age we girls weren't expected to do anything more than find a husband and have kids. Back then we didn't even get the same lessons as those stinky boys. While they were being taught things that would get them a job, we were being taught how to cook, sew, and clean house. Oh, we're all so high and mighty these days, ready to point the finger at other countries, saying how bad they are in the way they treat their women and how outrageous it is that they don't let their girls go to university and so on, but little more than fifty-odd years ago it wasn't that much different here. We girls, especially working-class lasses, weren't expected to have aspirations. And any that did were considered wrong 'uns. So, you see, you can't judge me or any women of my generation by your modern-day standards. You have access to pretty much everything, so it's up to you and nobody else to take advantage of opportunities that we never got." She snatched up her knife and fork and gave the whole audience a beaming broad smile before finishing with, "Here endeth the bloody lesson – excuse my French – so get on and eat up. There's a treacle pudding in the oven, and if we don't finish our firsts *tout suite* it'll be ruined."

They did as instructed, and it wasn't until all five plates were clean and the eating irons put down that anybody spoke again.

"Grandma," asked Bethany, her eyes wide and head tilted slightly, making her look even cuter, "if we go to Alton Towers again, would you and Grandpa like to come with us? So you can have some excitement."

Carol laughed. "Thank you for the invitation, pet, but I'd probably wee myself being chucked this way and that and flung upside down."

"I certainly would," chortled Roy, wiping a blob of escaped gravy from his chin. "No doubt about that. Last time we went to a funfair was here in town when we were first courting. It didn't go well. We were on the whirligig thing when I chucked up my entire fish-and-chip supper all over the—"

"That's enough, Dad, thank you," cut in Sarah. "We are eating, remember."

"She still went out with me again," said Roy, chuckling at the fond memory of youth.

"But surely," continued Lauren, ignoring the deviation as she took over the badgering from her sister. "*Surely* you must want to do at least one last little something a bit exciting before you..." She stopped and blushed beetroot red.

"Before we die?" said Roy, grinning as he finished the sentence. "Assuming that was what you were going to say, my little beauty, then the answer is no. You see, me and your grandma are very happy just jogging along as we are." He looked across at Carol and smiled. "We don't need excitement at our time of life, do we, love?"

Carol could see that her dear but deluded husband was reading her returned smile as concurrence. But, in reality, she was enjoying the thought of next Tuesday, when, bad weather permitting, she'd be donning her grey hoodie coat to go rob another bank.

# Chapter 12

"Maybe he's not so useless after all," offered Danny to his two CID colleagues. "Yes, I know he didn't actually do anything himself, but getting his dear old Uncle Gerry to snatch our case out of the grasping claws of the Cheshire bunch has to be a win."

"Only temporary, though," said Jacquie, raining on their parade.

"We've got a whole month," replied Danny, determined he was not going to let the mood puddle. "We don't have to even consider handing it over to the Winsford wankers until the end of May, and only then if we've not made any material progress. Plus, by then, as you so brilliantly pointed out the other day, Jacquie, the Red Fox will most probably be on an EasyJet flight to the Costa Blanca or wherever to enjoy his illegally earned summer break. No crappy weather means no hoodie coat to hide inside, meaning no robberies."

"So if we don't solve it in the next four-and-a-bit weeks," added Kevin, joining in as auxiliary cheerleader, "we hand over a case that simply stops dead in its tracks."

"If it hasn't already stopped by then," said Danny. "The weather forecast for the next few days is looking a little bit better, so maybe last Tuesday's job was his swansong for this season. Therefore," he stood up to deliver his rousing call to arms, "we need to bloody well get on and solve it. So come on, team, what have we got from the Nantwich job?"

"It was him," said Jacquie. "No doubt at all in my mind. Yeah, everybody knows about the ginger moustache, the glasses and the hoodie coat, but we've never publicised the stutter or the exact phrases he uses. I interviewed the Nantwich cashier and she recounted all of them, including a very precise identification of a north Shropshire accent. Turns out Miss," she paused to flick through her notebook, "Kathleen Duckworth is a self-professed expert on regional accent identification, and didn't she let me bloody know it." Jacquie made a face to suggest she was less than impressed.

"Anything else?" asked Danny, more in hope than expectation. "Anything new, anything different?"

Jacquie shook her head. "Same old, same old. Everything, start to finish. It's like our man is some sort of programmed robot fox. As far as Miss Bloody Smarty-Pants told me, what he said was, word for word, the same as all the others reported."

"Witnesses?" pressed Danny. "Inside the bank, in the queue? Outside on the street? Any-fucking-where?"

"Cheshire managed to trace a couple of people who were inside the bank around that time. Only one remembered a little guy in a big grey hoodie coat. Didn't get a look at his face. Didn't even register that he was worth looking at. As for outside, nothing at all as yet. Our guy's a ghost. Either by accident or – and to my mind this is far more likely – by design, he is very bloody clever."

"Kevin?" asked Danny, moving on from yet another round of Red Fox adoration.

"CCTV inside the bank, same as always. He knows where the cameras are – there's three, by the way – and manages to avoid all of them: head down and facing away. He also knows which hand to hold the gun in so that it can't be seen either on camera or by the other cashiers."

"And outside?" pressed Danny, becoming increasingly fed up with his team awarding multiple Oscars to a villain.

"Sad to say, and to repeat what Jacquie just said, same old, same old. Comes out of the bank, head down, facing away, strolls casually a hundred yards or so past a dozen shops and cafés before slipping down an alley and disappearing. In all that time he's in full view of two town cameras and passes five other private set-ups, but not a glimpse of his face. I've got all the feeds but I've only had time to watch the municipal tapes up to a half-hour after the hit and...well, you can guess."

"So no happy songs for our little Shirley to sing upstairs," said Danny, summing up whilst fighting to make it sound anything other than dismal.

"There is one thing," said Kevin, his tone tentative to the point of awkward.

The other two turned to look at him but said nothing, simply using their movement to press him into saying what was on his mind.

"The pattern of robberies," he said, still hesitant as he appeared to worry about sharing an idea. "I was wondering..."

"Go on," said Danny. "Anything. Anything at all that might help."

Kevin got up from his desk and walked across to the incident board to point a finger at the map on which they had marked each robbery with a red marker-pen cross. "Ludlow, Shrewsbury, Telford," he pointed at each as he called out the names, "Shrewsbury again, and now Nantwich."

"Yes," said the other two in unison, leaving the follow-up question unspoken.

"Nothing over here or here," said Kevin, using a rotating hand, palm flat on the map, to indicate the broad areas of country to the left and right of the marked robberies. "Just along here," he continued, now using a single finger to trace an imaginary snaking line that connected the red crosses.

"What are you getting at?" asked Jacquie, desperate to understand.

"They're all on the bloody train line!" shouted Danny, beating his newbie to the punch. "That is brilliant, Kevin. Bloody brilliant! Our Red Fox goes a-hunting on the chuffer. Has to be. Bloody buggering bravo, you!"

"Sorry to be the wet blanket, guys," said Jacquie, "but does this *actually* help any?"

"Yes and no," said Danny, now striding back and forth with renewed energy as he thought through the implications. "No, not in the bare informational sense, but yes from a number of other aspects. Like, if we can get CCTV from stations up and down the line, we just might catch sight of him getting onto a train somewhere on the way to a job. Then we'd know where he comes from and could narrow down the search area. Plus, if by some piece of magic we could catch the little sod getting off on his way back home, the same."

"And most trains have on-board CCTV," said Kevin, basking in the glow of his idea being picked up and run with so enthusiastically. "We might find him on the train, guard down – no pun intended – and revealing his face."

"Or, again, sorry to say this," said Jacquie, "it could be less of a Red Fox and more of a red herring that ends up distracting us and wasting precious time."

Danny looked at his DC and nodded. "You're quite right to look at this objectively, Jacquie, but it is a possibility, and – let's face it – it's the first fresh angle we've come up with since we started. We have to take it seriously and explore it until we can eliminate it. Okay?"

"Tell you what," said Jacquie, forcing herself to get with the programme, "how about we not only take it seriously, but go to the next level and set up a Fox trap?"

"Say more," said Danny, trying to guess ahead but deciding to give his previously negative colleague the space to redeem herself.

"We reckon," she began, "that with shitty weather quite the norm in May in Shropshire, there's a pretty good chance he'll knock over one or maybe even two more banks before his summer recess, right?"

The others nodded in a 'Get on with it' way.

"So what say," she continued, "we assume Kev is correct and Foxy does indeed travel by train. And let's also assume that the next job will again be somewhere along this particular railway line. So, for every stop along the way that has a bank within walking distance of the station, we set up some sort of rapid response arrangement." She paused for a moment to check her colleagues were still with her before pressing on to the end. "In the event there *is* another robbery, as soon as it's called in, we have the locals all primed and ready to get one of their lads or lassies down to the station in double-quick time to search all and anybody who fits the profile."

"Nice idea, but can we legally do that?" asked Kevin. "I mean, stop and search people only on the off chance we may find something?"

"Maybe not officially," replied Danny. "But there are ways around it. We could claim we were in possession of intelligence regarding a whatever."

"So?" asked Jacquie. "Do we...?"

"Let's set it up," replied Danny. "It's a long shot, I'll grant you. But right now it's something tangible and we don't have much if anything else."

"How far up and down the line should I go?" she asked.

Danny paused to think for a couple of moments before replying. "That, Jacquie, is a very good question. Until the Nantwich job I'd have said our man was sticking close to home, places he probably knows or could easily scout. So before last week I'd have said stick to Shropshire. But now we know he's expanding his hunting ground, we have to be ready for his next job being further afield."

"So," asked Jacquie, "what are we talking? Hereford to Stockport? Or further?"

Danny shook his head. "Shirley would string us up if he thought we were giving our brothers to the north even a sniff of a shot at snaring the notorious Red Fox on their turf, so the track effectively terminates at the

Cheshire border." He looked up to see the faces of his two colleagues looking silently very unsure of the stated position. "Yes, yes, I know we're supposed to be working together, and, yes, I know that if Foxy picks his next bank in their backyard we could miss him, but that is how it has to be. So keep it to Shropshire and Herefordshire for now, Jacquie, and let us all hope and pray our man's next outing is somewhere along our bit of—"

His final word was cut off by Templeton striding into the room, clapping his hands loudly. As usual, the three stood waiting for the customary opening catchphrase, and as one they were shocked when it didn't come.

Instead, Templeton started with, "Listen up, muppets."

Danny momentarily considered mentioning their possible breakthrough idea and the Fox trap follow-up plan but, thinking better of it, kept his mouth shut.

"In addition to successfully retaining control over the Red Fox case," crowed Templeton, "for which I know you are all extremely grateful to me," he paused to make eye contact with each of his team in turn, "I have been applying myself more fully to how I can move this investigation forward. As you lot collectively continue to deliver big fat zero in terms of meaningful progress using the old tried-and-tired methods, I have taken it on myself to personally do some modern-day detective work. And, I have to say, the top brass are mightily impressed by my initiative." In the absence of tumultuous applause, Templeton did one of his famous heel-spins, coming around to face his blank-faced congregation once more before continuing. "While you three have been lolling about in here, rowing up a gum tree without a paddle, I have been breaking the mould." He stopped and waited for a stooge to ask.

"And what did you do, sir?" asked Danny in the voice of a star-struck six-year-old.

"I took myself down to Aston University where I spent an utterly intriguing hour with a criminal psychology profiler." Templeton paused and then, strangely, clicked his tongue twice before finishing. "As a result, I can reveal to you that we now have in our possession a very precise profile of our wily Red Fox."

Three pairs of goggle eyes above three open mouths dutifully waited in less-than-enthusiastic expectation.

Templeton strung the pause out like a cheap magician building up to his big reveal, casually strolling across to the incident board, where he theatrically tore down the now notorious e-fit picture, holding it high before his captivated audience and flapping it gently a few times before finally speaking. "Apart from the obvious physical characteristics – white skin and short-arsed – along with our near certainty it's a local, I can now confirm that our villain is male and in his early to mid twenties. He is of above average academic qualification level, but below average on the sociability scale, meaning he will be working in a menial job far below his intellectual capability. He is single, incapable of forming a serious emotional relationship – so no wife or even proper girlfriend – and consequently he lives either alone or with his parents. Being scared of normal social interaction, he won't go out much and won't have many if any real live friends. Any interpersonal interaction he does have will be from behind a false identity, using a secure, private personal computer, on which he is a whizz."

"Impressive," said Danny, not meaning it but trying super-hard to conceal that fact in his tone and delivery. "Are you intending to share this with Percy Walsh, now you're on such good terms?"

"Absolutely not," retorted an indignant Templeton. "I'm not telling that woman anything I don't choose to. Of course I left her thinking we'd established a genuine two-way exchange but," he allowed himself a small, dastardly snigger at his brilliant sneakiness, "I played her, just like I told you I would, and hence she will do my bidding whilst I continue to give her nothing of any substance."

"But," began Danny, hesitating to consider his next words before continuing, "wouldn't it possibly help to put the profile out there? At least some of it? Get people thinking about whether they just might know the Red Fox? Your excellent character profile," he said, crossing his fingers again but this time behind his back, "is so detailed, so precise, it must surely narrow it down to only a handful of potential suspects. If we could get the public to recognise him and dob him in, we could—"

"A good idea but, sadly, not a great idea, Detective Sergeant," replied Templeton.

"Sir?"

"I do not want some pathetic, provincial trash-rag of a so-called newspaper taking the lead on this and possibly – no matter how remote that might be – coming up with something and snatching all the glory."

"Isn't that perhaps a little...?" began Danny. "I mean – how can I put it? – short-sighted?"

"That, Danny, is why I am a DI and you are – and will almost certainly henceforth remain – a DS. Strategic thinking," he continued, gently tapping an index finger on his temple. "Looking for the bigger picture, assessing the situation holistically rather than obsessing over little details and making mistakes. So, what say you keep doing what you're good at and leave the broader thinking and bigger decisions to me, okay, Detective Sergeant?" He didn't hang around for a reply.

# Chapter 13

Carol was inwardly smiling as she wandered slowly home from the station. It had been a most enjoyable afternoon out. With the sun regularly peeking out from behind cotton-wool clouds and barely a breath of wind, there was, perhaps, just a hint of summer in the air. She'd even gone without a coat for the first time this year, opting instead for the little brown jacket she'd had for seemingly a lifetime.

She'd enjoyed the feel of its familiarity the instant she'd put it on, and felt doubly good knowing she could still fit into her favourite old outfits when most of her friends of a similar age were – to put it politely – gently spreading. Janice, for example, had complained long and hard that some little bastard goblin had crept into her wardrobe one night and shrunk all her clothes. But then again, Janice had been a size eight, if that, all her life until her recent 'ballooning' to match Carol's comfortable twelve. According to Janice, her 'blubber' had started to appear almost from the day of her Lenny's funeral. She just hadn't been able to stop eating, and the bottle of wine most nights to help her get to sleep alone in that big empty bed hadn't helped. The abrupt termination of daily shags had probably been a contributory factor as well, thought Carol with a chuckle as she recalled her friend's account of the romantic steam hammer that had been her late husband.

Anyway, merrily dressed in her favourite jacket and a lightweight floral skirt, Carol had headed off to Crewe to deposit her recent bank haul, split evenly between her three building society accounts there. She'd given the Nantwich drops a miss this time, just in case – the extremely remote case – somebody there just happened to sense she was the bank robber of a few days previous.

It had been tremendous fun playing the part of the lucky punter with a story to tell. Every bit of it made up, of course, apart from the real facts – the venue, the date and race time, the name of the horse, and the odds – all of which she'd gleaned from Roy's newspaper. Who'd have thought a horse called Cuppa-Cha would romp home by four lengths at thirty-to-one in the three twenty race at Newmarket? And who in their right mind would have put fifty quid on said horse to win, simply because the name of it had made her laugh and it was its first time out in blinkers? As it turned out, only one of the three cashiers showed any interest at all in where the fifteen hundred quid had come from, and even he started yawning before the end of her tale. But she'd enjoyed it. Somehow, building a backstory had become part of the buzz. It was like a third life to add to her shady second.

The visit to Crewe had also delivered a spin-off benefit in definitively scratching it off the list of possible locations for her next 'day out'. Yes, there were a couple of ripe little banks there, all ready for the picking, but try as she might, she simply could not plot a sensibly secure escape and costume-change route. For a town often considered by many to be towards the lower end of the wealth scale, the security there was tight as tight. Bloody CCTV cameras seemingly everywhere on the main streets, and yet more keeping watch over smaller side streets and alleyways. There was a uniformed security bod in the shopping centre, and a couple of others here and there in certain shops. Even the bargain-price clothes shop that Carol popped into for a quick look around had an easy-to-spot plain-clothes store detective ready to pounce on anybody daft enough to try a bit of shoplifting. Maybe, she thought, the whole thing was that when you had not very much you hung on to it even tighter than if you had a lot.

Come to think of it, that was pretty much how her and Roy had been. Every penny he brought home was used sensibly where it delivered the most. They never went out to eat, drank very little, had not a single betting gene in their bodies, and never smoked beyond their teenage years when they did it mostly to fit in with the gang. Family holidays were always at home, with hot days spent on a picnic rug in the park, and the very occasional day trip on the train. So they got by on very little money, never feeling greatly deprived as there was always food on the table, clean clothes when any of them needed them, and a warm house to come home to in the winter.

The children had grown up happily accepting their life situation, helped by most of their school friends being in the same boat. And even now, with both of them having moved into comparatively well-paid jobs, they still spoke affectionately about their childhood and the times when the four of them faced down 'the cruel world'. And neither child ever even obliquely criticised their dad for not having earned enough money to buy them things they saw kids on the telly enjoying. He'd done what he could and he'd done it well, and they loved him all the more for it.

And she did too. Yes, her Roy could be a lazy so-and-so, although nothing like she remembered his father having been. And, yes, her Roy could be a bit grumpy at times, but – yet again – nowhere near as bad as that miserable old sod a generation up had been. And whereas Roy's mum was all too often seen about town with heavy make-up failing to conceal yet another black eye, Roy himself had never laid anything other than a loving finger on Carol in all the time they'd been together. It had been a good marriage and, boredom aside, not that bad of late. So why was she doing what she was doing and jeopardising what they had? The kids had never asked for more as youngsters, so why should she in her dotage? "Because you deserve it, Carol," she said aloud. "Roy has his bowling and you rob banks. Fair's fair, eh?"

With Crewe now scrubbed as an option, she'd have to choose somewhere else. A third bank in Shrewsbury was tempting but might be pushing the risk a bit, so it would have to be further down the line heading south. She'd been to Leominster a couple of times, years back, and remembered the town centre as quaint with lots of little side streets and back alleys. Could be perfect. So on Thursday she'd nip down for a look-see, then make a decision. And she'd have to get a move on. With the weather improving day by day, it was fast approaching a time when her brilliantly constructed reversible hoodie coat would have to be consigned to the spare-bedroom wardrobe along with all the other winter stuff. And that would be that. For now.

Then again, maybe that really *would* be that, she thought, pausing at her front gate to allow her brain cogs the time to properly grind through the possibility. By the time the cold and rain of the next autumn came around, might she find that she'd lost her nerve? Or got too stiff in her joints? Or maybe come to her ruddy senses? Ha! She barked a single, swiftly suppressed laugh to shoo away the thought. What had Lauren said about Grandma not doing anything exciting ever again until she died? If only the cheeky little imp knew the truth about her silly old, boring old grandma. Actually, if only *anybody* knew. But nobody could. Nobody must. And no bugger would, provided she was careful. Which meant so long as she could catch the train and walk to a bank, she wasn't going to give it up. Come the lousy weather that was autumn in Shropshire, she would dig out the special coat, stick on the ginger moustache, don the little round spectacles, and get back on her horse – figuratively speaking, of course.

Taking the few last paces to the front door, she keyed it open and stopped in her tracks. The telly wasn't on and blaring. She checked her watch. Five twenty-five. Roy was always home from bowling by now. A half-dozen possibilities flashed through her head, some harmless, most not. What had happened? She could feel her heart rate rising uncontrollably and a mild sweat of concern forming around her neck. She stepped inside and softly closed the front door, listening hard.

"Is that you, Carol?" came his voice, called out from the sitting room.

She breathed out the lungful she suddenly realised she'd been holding, and made her way inside, her pulse still too high as she knew something was up. At the sitting-room door she paused. "Are you alright, love?" she asked.

He didn't get up or turn to look at her. "Not really," he replied.

Carol slowly went in. Dropping her bag just inside the door, but not taking her jacket off, she went across to sit on the front edge of her armchair and look at her husband. His face was ashen white. She feared the worst. "What's wrong, love? Are you...?"

He forced a weak smile and shook his head. "Not me," he said. "Trev's missus."

Carol knew immediately who he was talking about. Trevor Knight was one of Roy's regular bowling buddies. His wife, Alice, had been in the same class as Carol at school. They'd never been close friends, but had always stopped for a few words if they'd passed in the street. Very obviously something horrible had happened to the poor woman, and Carol silently scolded herself for being grateful that it was Alice and not her Roy that had suffered something bad.

"We'd just started on the second end," began Roy, looking straight at Carol. "Trev gets a call on his mobile. It's supposed to be turned off once we step onto the green but just as well he'd forgotten. Anyway, we other three are stood there watching, irritated by Trev's bad form, and we see his face go white and his mouth fall open. We all think he's having a heart attack, especially when he starts staggering around. So me and Rainy grab hold of him while Cliff lifts the phone out of his hand and takes over the call." Roy stopped and wiped at his mouth with a knuckle.

Carol closed the distance between them by kneeling in front of him and resting her forearms on the tops of his legs.

"A neighbour had popped in for something," continued Roy, his voice cracking with emotion. "She found Alice laid unconscious on the kitchen floor. Dialled emergency and, as luck would have it, a paramedic had just been on a job in the same road and was there in minutes. He managed to get her stable, but..." He ran out of the strength necessary to complete the story.

Carol didn't know what to say, so merely reached out and waited for Roy to rest his hands in hers. She gripped them and held on. In the minute or more of silence that followed, she thought about Alice Knight but, strangely, not as she'd known her of late. All she could think of was the freckle-faced, gangly eleven-year-old Alice Yates with the sticky-out ears and the laugh that sounded like a suffocating pig. And there, stood next to her, was a scrawny eleven-year-old Carol Garton, the two of them swamped in their oversized school uniforms. It was always that way at the start of a new school year for children of parents who couldn't afford to buy two sets of uniform in a school year, so opted for buying a size up to accommodate several months of growth.

"They were supposed to be going on that fancy cruise next month," said Roy suddenly, breaking into Carol's reminisce and blowing away the more-than-half-a-century-old image. "Been planning it for years and saving up for about as long. We others felt like we'd already been on it, Trev has been banging on about it for so long. We were even pulling his leg about it when his mobile..."

"Where's Trevor now?" asked Carol in a whisper. "Is there somebody with him?"

"His sister and her husband are with him at the hospital. Cliff took him. The poor soul was in no fit state to drive himself. Rainy and me stayed on for a brew in the clubhouse and waited for some news. Just after four, Cliff phoned Rainy. Not good. She's on a life support machine and they've said they'll be surprised if she pulls through. I didn't know what to do after that, so brought myself home to wait for you."

"Can I get you anything?" asked Carol. "I think we've still got a bottle of stout in the pantry. Would you like that? Or something to eat? A snack before I get the tea on?"

Roy shook his head. "I can't stop thinking back to last Sunday. What our little girlies were saying about us being boring, not doing anything exciting. In fact, not doing anything at all. Just sitting here waiting to die."

"They were being young," said Carol. "What's that old saying about hiring a teenager while they know everything? They're at that age. The world looks simple and open for business. And they have no sense of time and no fear."

"Is that why we don't go anywhere?" asked Roy. "I mean, why *I* don't want to go anywhere? Is it because I'm frightened?"

"Roy, love," said Carol, leaning forward to rest a palm on his cheek. "Stop it. We do what we do and we do it together."

"But what if I wasn't here, love? Would you go off and do stuff? Go travelling, like Lauren says she's going to do? Or take up on some other secret wish you've got?"

"If I had a secret wish I'd keep it that way," said Carol, getting to her feet. "Either that or I'd get on and do it whatever."

"But—"

"Enough," said Carol firmly, putting her hands on her hips and looking down at her husband with a resolute firmness in her eyes. "It's one thing being upset about poor Alice Knight, but I am not having you getting all maudlin about what's not going to happen. So I'm going to get the tea on." She turned to leave the room, pausing in the doorway to look back at him, speaking sternly but with a crooked smile to show she wasn't being serious. "And if you want anything to eat tonight, you've got fifteen minutes to buck your ideas up."

In the hall she hung up her jacket before heading straight for the kitchen where she set about getting their evening meal. Yes, it was sad about Alice, but it wasn't her and it wasn't Roy. Them as was left behind had to carry on, keep going, or the whole world would come to a standstill. And all that nonsense about what she would do if he wasn't around was rubbish, plain and simple. He wasn't going anywhere, so she didn't need to give it brain space.

Although, now she came to think of it, a far more likely scenario was Roy being the one left behind alone. Not because she had any plans to pop off like it sounded Alice Knight was about to. No – facing the cold, harsh reality, it was what she was up to these days that could end up with Roy having the house to himself. If she did get caught they'd send her to prison for a very long time. And if that happened, what would he do? Sure as eggs were eggs, he wasn't going to up sticks and hightail it off to Las Vegas or Kathmandu. No, he'd more likely just sit in his armchair and starve to death waiting for somebody to cook his tea. That same old nagging question reared its ugly head again. Was she being selfish carrying on, risking getting caught and so chucking away what they both had? Was she thinking only about herself and not about her husband? Alice hadn't had to wrestle with any such question when she'd suddenly dropped down dead – or close – leaving her husband short of a cruise companion. So why did she herself have to spend so much time thinking about her Roy? She needed help.

Staring hard at her unblemished reflection in the kitchen window, Carol whispered a plea for guidance. "Tell me straight, Window – am I being selfish? Should I stop and go back to how it was before?"

She waited and watched as the face in front of her slowly contorted into the most delicious of 'naughty girl' smiles.

"Don't be silly, Carol," it whispered back. "Of course it isn't. And if by some rotten luck you did get caught, your Roy will just have to get out of his armchair and walk down to the bloody chippy!"

# Chapter 14

Danny Roberts sat with his head in his hands, not sure whether to scream or cry. Kevin had just delivered an abbreviated report on his task to assess railway station CCTV from each of the stations in the towns where a robbery had been committed, and on those specific days.

"Not a single frame?" asked Danny, not looking up.

"Not one, Sarge," replied Kevin.

"Or off the trains." This time Danny spoke it as a statement of fact.

"Correct," confirmed Kevin.

"Tell me why again," sighed Danny.

"The precise timing seems to vary from station to station, but in summary – and as far as our needs are concerned – none of them keep anything long enough to help us. It's all over-recorded every few days unless some authority or other files a specific request for it to be retained. And as for the trains themselves, well, so far as I could find out, some cameras are purely live feeds to give the driver and guard a sight into the carriages, while those that do have recording capability automatically over-record, sometimes in as little as the next journey."

Danny leaned back in his chair to stretch his neck muscles and sigh loudly at the ceiling. "Two days wasted," he groaned.

"Not necessarily," replied Kevin.

Danny used a raised eyebrow to ask him to explain.

Kevin got up and walked across to the incident board map, where now, in addition to the red crosses for the robberies, all the possible stations on the line within walking distance of a bank had been marked with a green cross. Pointing at each in turn, he explained. "We now know that all of our potential Red Fox transit stations from Hereford to Whitchurch have CCTV that records platform movement, even if they only keep those files for a day or two. We also know, and this is the important thing, we can get that footage retained if we submit a formal request in double-quick time. So—"

Danny butted in to complete the thought. "Even if our Fox trap doesn't work in real time, we can still get something to look at."

"Correct," said Kevin, snatching the ball back and running with it. "We still go ahead with the rapid response thing that Jacquie is setting up, getting a copper onto the platform to check out who might be passing through to catch a train home with a bundle of stolen cash in his knapsack. But, at the same time, we have everything ready here to immediately fire off a formal retention request into the station."

"Good thinking," said Danny, nodding appreciatively and feeling a tiny bit more positive than he had only seconds before. "Can you set that up?"

Kevin nodded. "I'll get onto it right away. Oh, and one other thing."

"Speak," said Danny.

"Jacquie and I were looking at the timing pattern of these robberies. They all happened on a Tuesday, apart from one that was a Thursday."

"So what?"

"So we can sensibly increase our alert level on those days. Plus," Kevin paused, "he always hits the bank early afternoon."

"And?" asked Danny.

"We were wondering if, where we get a bit of push-back from the locals, we could actually ask for a PC to be put in the station around those specific times on those particular days. Unless of course the weather is too nice for folk to be out and about in a heavy coat."

"Sounds good to me," said Danny. "Is Jacquie doing that?"

"Yes. We guessed you'd go for it. But the one thing where we do need guidance is the description we give to the rapid responders. I mean, how much of what we think we know do we tell them?"

"Not all of it, that's for sure," said Danny. "Just the physical, observable stuff, and only enough to narrow it down whilst not missing a possible catch. So," he got to his feet and started pacing the floor as he waited for Kevin to get pencil and paper ready, "height we reckon around five seven, and light build – we can't be any more specific than that given the baggy hoodie coat. Possible limp, but that could be put on. And I think we can all agree we can forget about the almost certainly fake moustache and glasses, so we leave them off."

"What about the voice and accent?" asked Kevin. "And the stutter? Should we include any of those?"

"No," replied Danny firmly. "Firstly, the stutter could be put on as a deliberate distraction, and if it isn't, it's something we can use if we ever get a suspect."

"What about Shirley's profile stuff?" asked Kevin. "Male, twenty to twenty-five years old, who's a socially inept intellectual genius and computer wizard?"

"Apart from 'male', I personally think the rest of it was a load of bollocks."

"You're not the only one," agreed Kevin with a wry smile. "Should I add the black plimsolls? I still reckon that's a marker."

"Add it, but not in the 'must have' column," said Danny. "Okay?"

"All good," said Kevin. "I'll get this typed up and pass it on to Jacquie. She's been doing all the legwork on getting the Fox trap set up, so only fair she gets to hand out the description, if you can call it—"

The crash of the squad-room door being violently swung open cut him off. The two men looked up to see Jacquie positioning herself square in the gap, feet spread wide for balance as she held high the latest issue of the *Midwestern Echo*. Neither man had to move from where they were to read the headline. 'Red Fox Running Rings Round Police'.

"Oh, bloody hell," groaned Danny, speaking aloud what all three of them were thinking. "Bloody, buggering, shitting hell."

Jacquie lowered the paper and moved into the room, kicking the door closed behind her and looking this way and that, checking to see if 'they-all-knew-who' was in attendance. He wasn't, and she gave an elongated sigh of relief. Danny made a grab for the paper to read more, but she snatched it away. She was going to read the lesson and they could sit in the pews and listen. She waited for them to get comfortable before coughing twice into a fist to add to the theatre, then, skilfully adopting the tone and intonation of a professional newsreader, she began.

*The notorious bank robber also known widely as The Red Fox continues to evade capture whilst expanding his territory north into Cheshire. His latest raid on the Counties Mutual Bank in Nantwich proves once again how this cunning local villain continues to bemuse and bewilder local police.*

"Bad, but not terrible," offered Danny weakly. "I mean, it's—"

He was stopped by the sight of Jacquie sadly shaking her head. She read on.

*Having been granted an exclusive interview with Detective Inspector Graham Templeton, senior investigating officer on this case, my eyes were well and truly opened as to just how easily the wily Red Fox has utterly and completely, dare I say, outfoxed the clay-footed police hunt.*

"Tell me it doesn't get any worse," pleaded Danny.

This time Jacquie didn't even bother to shake her head. She just used sad eyes to give a flavour of what was still to come.

*Despite his transparent efforts to obscure the reality of the situation and deflect my questions regarding progress, DI Templeton left me in absolutely no doubt whatsoever that the police investigation has made zero progress, even though there having now been five armed robberies. However, instead of sharing information in order to enlist the assistance of the always eager to help Midwestern Echo and its readership, all I was presented with was a smokescreen of evasive answers and hackneyed police clichés, all dished up with an unhealthy portion of patriarchal 'mansplaining'. In short, as DI Templeton essentially confirmed to me by omission, the police are nowhere: no clues, no leads, and – quite frankly – no ideas.*

"There can't be any more, surely," said Danny, his voice a thin whine, his head shaking sadly the whole time.

Jacquie's response was to fold the paper over to read the lower half of the page.

*As the latest robbery was in a neighbouring police authority, I followed up my wholly unedifying session of bluster with the head of the Fourshires Constabulary's crack detective team and placed a call to Cheshire Constabulary. In a terse but eye-popping few minutes with their Detective Chief Inspector Stephen Overton, I was given oblique confirmation that Templeton and his team have – and I quote – 'flat-lined'. Whilst Overton himself bluntly refused to share any details of the case, he did make extensive efforts to assert that he is waiting patiently in the wings to be called in to take over the investigation, as and when higher authorities deem it necessary.*

Danny slumped down into his chair and held out his hands, palms upwards, as if to say, 'Here I am, kill me now.'

"The next paragraph," said Jacquie, "just states the stuff we all know about the robberies, although, not surprisingly, nothing that could get the public to help us. So I'll skip to the darling Percy's sign-off." She lowered her eyes back down to the paper and read the last bit as if she was announcing the death of a beloved world leader.

*Being ineffective is not, in itself, a crime. Neither is being put into a position above your capability, for that is the fault of those who made the decision. However, pretending otherwise has to be taken seriously. Especially so when an armed robber is merrily wandering the western counties of middle England, terrorising bank staff and getting away with daylight robbery seemingly unchallenged. We, the good people of this area, deserve better.*

Jacquie slowly folded the newspaper and walked sombrely to her desk, where she plonked herself down into her chair. They sat for a long time in silent reflection before Danny spoke, his voice seeming to echo in the deathly hush.

"I suppose," he began, offering his words to the room space rather than the people there, "it was lucky our Shirley so brilliantly worked Walsh over, tied her in knots, tickled her tummy, and had her begging to do his bidding. Otherwise she might have written something nasty."

He'd barely got the last word out when all three of them collapsed into howling laughter. Even though the kicking had been received collectively, the majority of it had been directed at their pompous arse of a boss. And besides, what Percy Walsh had written was damned near factual. Or as accurate as it could be, given 'The Police' had strategically decided to tell her nothing.

"Lucky for us, Danny," said Jacquie, wiping the laughter tears from her cheeks, "you stuck to doing what you're good at doing and left the big-picture thinking to our leader. Without that holistic approach, we could be in the shit."

That set the three of them off howling again, until Jacquie's phone rang. She snatched it up and listened as another friendly warning came down from on high. She slapped the receiver down and looked across at her colleagues. "He's on his way down."

In seconds flat the hilarity was quenched, the newspaper hidden away in a desk drawer, and three police detectives were diligently hunched over their desks. None of them looked up as the squad-room door opened and Templeton entered. It wasn't his usual World Wrestling Entertainment mega-ego style fanfare entry. It wasn't even his cocky bantam strut to the middle of the room, ready to crow. No, it was definitely more of a wounded – and hence extremely dangerous – hyena's prowl to circle the room space with hackles raised as it sought the right moment to strike. None of the underlings dared make a sound. They could guess what was likely coming.

"You lot have let me down," he growled. "You've let yourselves down, this police force down, the people of the four shires whom we strive to serve down, and – to repeat – you have let me down. How many robberies is it? Let me tell you: it's five. How many weeks is it now? Let me tell you: too fucking many. How much progress have you lot made? Let me tell you: none." He stopped speaking to make another two slow laps of the available floor space, all the time breathing heavily through his nose. "To say the ACC is not amused with your performance would be an understatement of titanic proportions. Just be grateful that he doesn't have the time to bust your arses, because he's too busy in damage limitation regards the *Midwestern Echo*'s libellous insults to my integrity. Oh, I wouldn't want to be in Percy fucking Walsh's stiletto heels right now."

The image of Shirley in high heels could have been stomach-churning if the three under attack had allowed themselves a moment to think about it.

"The ACC," continued Templeton, still circling, "is also, as I speak, working to repel an aggressive attack from the Cheshire fucking Cheese-heads, who are all but demanding they be given the lead on this case. So, who among you is going to offer me and the man upstairs," he jabbed a thumb at the ceiling, "some tiny crumb of anything that he might use to fight back?"

Danny climbed to his feet like a sinner in an evangelist congregation standing to confess all and plead forgiveness. "We have made a breakthrough," he said softly.

Templeton stopped moving for the first time since he'd come in, stared directly at his DS, and cocked his head to one side like a partially deaf cockatoo waiting to pick up a distant mating call.

"From the pattern of robbery locations," continued Danny, "compared to the numerous other possible banks in the area that have not been attacked, we consider it a distinct possibility that the Red Fox is travelling to and from each robbery by train."

"Fuck off!" sneered Templeton. "Is that really the best you can offer?"

Undeterred, Danny marched across to the incident board map and replicated what Kevin had done when sharing his idea a few days before, complete with supporting explanatory gestures. All the while, he watched his boss carefully as the man followed the logic that led him from 'stupid idea' through 'potentially intriguing' and on to 'I could sell this upstairs'. Danny finished and held his breath as he waited.

"CCTV?" snapped Templeton.

"All wiped and gone," said Danny, quickly following the disappointing news with, "but we have a plan."

"Oh, good." Templeton even managed to make his faint praise sound sarcastic. "And are you going to share it with me, Detective Sergeant?"

"We're setting up a trap. To catch the Red Fox red-handed."

Danny could see that Templeton was very much hooked by the phrase. His eyes widened and he nodded a few times as he checked his watch, most probably thinking that if he got something good in the next few minutes he'd just about have time to trot it upstairs to the brass before they headed off out for lunch.

"Explain," commanded Templeton, circling an index finger to hurry things along.

Danny began his explanation with the team's collective certainty that another robbery would happen. He then ran through the mechanism of the rapid response, getting an officer to the relevant station, followed by the current status of its set-up. With no sign of any interim response from Templeton, he rounded his piece off with the prepared and ready formal 'request to retain' for the station CCTV. Three bodies waited, watching as Templeton allowed the whole 'wafer thin, but better than nothing' plan to percolate. Then he suddenly turned his back on the troops for a few seconds before spinning back to face them. He pointed a finger at Danny.

"Not brilliant, Danny," he said, "and full of holes as well as costly on manpower and provincial goodwill, but possibly just enough to keep you out of uniform, for the time being at least. And perhaps, just perhaps, by utilising the criminal profile I provided you with last week, you may strike lucky."

"Indeed, yes, sir," replied Danny, as so often these days crossing his fingers behind his back at the concealed reality: he was actually going to use hardly any of it.

Templeton checked his watch again. Probably had to get a move on if he was going to get his tongue into Uncle Gerry's arse crack before it left the building. "Good work, people. Carry on." And with that, he trotted off, out and up to share.

# Chapter 15

They'd opted for a corner table in the snug bar, which they had all to themselves. With the weather being mild and pleasant, the majority of patrons preferred to sit in the garden, where they could be pestered by flies and wasps as they breathed slurry fumes from the muck-spreading on an adjacent field. Janice had made it patently clear she didn't fancy joining in, and Carol was happy to go along.

Surprisingly, the drive to the pub had progressed in total silence beyond the initial greetings. Janice seemed unwilling to share the reason why they were once again travelling in her late husband's big black Jag, and Carol felt it unwise and un-best-friendly to mention it. She just sat back and enjoyed the near soundless gear changing of a prestige automatic gearbox.

With food ordered and drinks on the table in front of them, it was finally time to start chatting.

"How was your nerve-jangling, white-knuckled afternoon in Nantwich?" asked Janice, chuckling as she pulled her friend's leg over the outing she'd told her about during their last lunch date.

"Pulse-racing," replied Carol, adding her own little giggle.

"You were there the same day that Red Fox did his latest bank job, weren't you?" asked Janice. "That could have been something."

Carol instantly felt six inches taller at her friend's offhand mention of her newly bestowed supervillain title. She'd only heard of it a couple of days before in a local TV news item. Apparently some reporter at the *Midwestern Echo* had come up with it, and Carol liked it instantly. "Not sure," she replied vaguely. "Remind me, what day was it again?"

"I can barely remember what day it is today," replied Janice, "let alone what day the super-cunning Red Fox came a-creeping out from his lair to rob from the rich and give to the poor. You know, when it comes down to it, I'm rooting for Basil Brush and against the bloody rozzers. But it sounds like he's winning anyway without my support. You?"

Carol raised an eyebrow. "If you mean who am I supporting, then, yes, it has to be the Red Fox. He really does give the money away, you know."

"I do indeed," said Janice, nodding sagely. "That reporter bloke, Percy Walsh, tracked down where each bundle of money went. Luckily it was supposition rather than proof or the bastards would have snatched it all back, like they did those marked notes from that hospice or wherever it was."

"You seem to know an awful lot about it," said Carol. "I only heard about him – by name, that is – a few nights ago on *North West Tonight*."

"*Midwestern Echo* online," replied Janice, taking a gulp of red wine before continuing. "I used to skim it when it popped up on my news feed, but now I'm an avid reader. Well, the front page, that is. And I do believe I am ever so slightly in love with their star newshound. The way he absolutely stuck it to the dopey copper in charge of the investigation last week was bloody hilarious."

"Are you turning into an anarchist?" asked Carol jokily.

"Hardly," scoffed Janice. "But it's good to see somebody like the Red Fox trying to do something nice in this horrible world and getting away with it. And the police are all rotten. A bunch of corrupt bigots, they are. No wonder AC-12 is so busy." Janice could see Carol looking lost so explained. "Anti-Corruption Unit Twelve. *Line of Duty*. That tall Irish bloke with the absolutely massive conk."

At last Carol cottoned on. "Oh, the television series," she confirmed, nodding. "But that's not real life, is it?"

"Who cares?" said Janice with a huge shrug of the shoulders. "I still don't like them. And so I say, 'Go-go-go, Red Fox.'" She raised her glass in a toast before drinking deep again. "And, my furry hero, wherever you might be hiding, if you're ever up for a bit of hanky-panky with a mature but very well maintained admirer, then please, please, *please* look me up." With that she threw her head back and launched into a prolonged and far-too-loud round of the notorious Janice Worthington cackling laugh.

As much as Carol would have loved to bask in the warm glow of continued praise for her shadowy alter ego, she decided it was time to shift the topic of conversation. "How's Eddy?" she asked, referring to Janice's one and only child.

"You first," said Janice, turning the tables. "I've only got the one. You've got God knows how many. Plus," she paused and made a smug face, "I've got some special news to share, so I get to top the bill."

Carol accepted the logic, forced herself not to guess ahead to the 'special news' and set off. "Sarah and the girls are all doing well. Sarah's perpetually broke but managing, and she's hopeful of a promotion in the coming months. Granddaughters are beautiful and full of themselves, but doing okay at school. Lauren says she's struggling a bit, but she's so ambitious I think she'll work through it. And Roy is, well, Roy."

"And Paul?" asked Janice, satisfied with the update so far, but pouncing on the gap.

"Still in Vancouver, of course, and happy as a sandboy. Job's going well, and with his last letter he sent me some photos of the house and family. All gorgeous."

"How old is she again?" asked Janice, obviously referring to Paul's partner.

"Fifty-four this year," replied Carol. "And before you say anything, yes, I know, that puts her almost exactly midway between Paul and me. But she's fit as a fiddle, if that really is her in the photos, and worth a bob or two. And he really is in love with her. He even agreed to a quickie marriage so that he could legally adopt her kids."

"Shame you couldn't get across for the wedding," said Janice.

Carol nodded sadly and nudged things away from a touchy subject by demanding Janice take over. Irritatingly, the ruddy woman emptied her glass and insisted on getting a refill before telling any of it. The bar was busy by now, so the wait was interminable, and then, just as she got back, the food arrived.

"Don't think you're getting away with any more delay," said Carol. "You can talk with your mouth full if you want to, but get started. Right now!"

Janice very deliberately took a large mouthful of chicken Caesar salad and chewed for what seemed like an age before finally giving in to the intensely hostile stare being levelled at her from across the table. "My singular remaining immediate family member," she began, "continues to thrive under the hot Cypriot sun. I would say that 'happy' doesn't even come close to it. He damned near giggled throughout our entire video chat last night. Do you do WhatsApp with your—"

"No," snapped Carol, "and stop deviating."

"Business is booming, apparently," continued Janice. "They sold the entire first phase of six 'individual colonial-style bungalows' in less than a month. It was mostly Brits wanting to buy them, so he told me, but as they don't want to create a gin-and-tonic enclave, they set a rule of not selling more than two units to any single nationality. Sounds a bit like social engineering to me, but it seems to work for them. Anyway, with cash tumbling in they're already cracking on with the next wave. Eight of them this time. Four are already complete and the rest are due to be ready by September. The gardens look absolutely beautiful and the bungalows are grouped around a good-sized private pool. He sent me some pictures, and I have to say they look utterly divine." She stretched the final word out dramatically and chortled at the end.

"And the special news?" asked Carol. "Please tell me that wasn't it."

"Oh no," said Janice mysteriously, allowing the elongated pause to stretch. But, spotting that she was at risk of physical harm if she delayed any further, she finally coughed up the golden nugget. "Eddy and his business partner are now officially an item. And they are coming back to England at Christmas to tie the knot." She added a small 'ta-da' fanfare.

"Wow!" said Carol. "That really is fantastic news, even though you've never told me before that there *was* a business partner, let alone any romantic connection."

"Oh, Eddy's mentioned Robbie on and off over the past year or more and I'd noticed it was getting a bit more frequent of late, so last night I right-out asked him. And, yes, they've moved in together and set up home."

"Robbie, you say," said Carol. "I always liked girls with a shortened name that sounds like a boy."

"It's Robert," said Janice.

"Oh," said Carol, not sure exactly how to react.

"I always suspected," said Janice, pulling a knowing face. "Mothers can always spot it. Lenny would have been apoplectic, but I am truly and genuinely very happy for my little boy. And Robbie looks like a really nice chap from the photo Eddy sent. Cheered an old lady up, I can tell you, seeing a strapping young man with a ripped body standing there, all glistening in his swimmers. He's a big lad too, is our Robbie. Big in every way. Big shoulders, big arms, big beard and, from the look of his budgie smugglers, more than adequate in the—"

"Budgie smugglers?" asked Carol, genuinely not understanding.

"Tight little swimming trunks," said Janice, as if explaining the rudiments of swimwear terminology to a dullard. "They call them 'budgie smugglers' because it looks like there's a budgerigar—"

"Okay, okay, I get it," interrupted Carol.

"Although from what I could see," continued Janice, undeterred, "I'd say he's smuggling a sizeable parrot at the very least."

"Enough, please," groaned Carol.

"I'll tell you this for nothing," continued Janice the verbal juggernaut, "something that size has got to hurt. A lot! I mean, just the thought of it..."

"How much does he sell these bungalows for?" asked Carol, as the only thing she could think of to say that might stop her friend talking about the unimaginable.

"No idea. But Eddy says I could easily afford one." Janice's face became suddenly serious. She looked intently at Carol as if wanting to make sure she read her friend's reaction correctly when she next spoke. "He's pestering me to buy one and move out there full-time. He says I'd like it. The warm weather would be good for me, and he and Robbie could look after me when I get all frail and dribbly."

Carol bit her lip and hated that her immediate reaction to the news had been an intense wave of jealousy. Not jealousy that her friend had the money to seriously consider making the proposed move, but jealousy that she had the mental and emotional wherewithal to even consider such a huge life change. However, no sooner had that first knee-jerk emotion peaked than it was replaced by a second wave, this time of sadness approaching panic that her only really close friend might very soon be gone. "Are you going to?" she asked, trying her hardest to sound positive and encouraging rather than desperate and needy.

"It's tempting, I have to admit," said Janice. "All that sunshine, cheap booze and eye candy." She winked lasciviously. "But honestly, right now I just can't think. Everything I know, everything I've always known, is here in and around Whitchurch. It would be such a monumental change, and at my time of life, I..."

"You could go and have a look," said Carol, wanting to sound supportive.

"I could," said Janice, tapping a fingernail on her front teeth as she thought about it. "Hey, what say we both go? You and me. Road trip. Girls on tour. And don't you worry about the money. I'll pay."

Carol smiled, but shook her head. "Apart from not wanting to be a charity case, thank you very much, Rich Widow Lady, and apart from the fact I would almost certainly come back home to find a skeletal husband slumped in his armchair with the TV playing to his empty eye sockets, and apart from the heat that would do my veins absolutely no good at all, and—"

"Excuses, excuses, excuses," butted in Janice, waving her arms dismissively. "But not one solid reason why you can't come with me on a little—"

"I don't have a passport."

"It could be worked out. We could find a way. And timing isn't fixed, so even if it took an age to get a—"

"Why are you driving Lenny's old Jag again?" asked Carol, for the second time in not many more minutes deliberately asking an off-the-track question to radically change the subject. But, to be fair, this time it was a question that had been bothering her since the moment she'd first seen the familiar hulking black beast trundling towards their agreed pickup point.

Janice looked down and away, then sighed, letting her shoulders sag as she did so. After a few seconds of nothing, she looked up at Carol. There was sadness in her eyes. "Apart from not being able to master that little red bastard sports car's gearbox, it just felt all wrong, so I went and exchanged it back. The garage was very good about it. I didn't have to pay a penny."

"What do you mean, 'it felt wrong'?" asked Carol.

"It was more about me," said Janice. "*I* felt wrong – bad, I mean. You know, Lenny really did love that big old car, and by getting rid of it I felt like I was being unfaithful to him agai..."

The way her friend clipped off the last word, and what it was almost certainly going to be, jolted Carol as if she'd been electrocuted. She sat and said nothing, waiting. Janice could see from her friend's reaction that a dark secret she'd almost let slip had not gone unnoticed. She tried to cover it over by mumbling some nonsense about good memories being bound up in the car's metal, but it was no good. Tears were streaming down her cheeks, and she angrily snatched up her napkin to dab them away. Carol remained a statue, mute and immobile but watching every movement and facial expression change on the other side of the table.

At last Janice screwed the moist tissue into a tiny ball and tossed it dismissively onto the table. "My old mum," she began, "always told me the best way to keep a secret was never to have one."

"My mum," offered Carol in return, "told us that if you did have a secret then the only way to keep it was for nobody to know you had it."

"Wise women," said Janice, nodding gently, as much to herself as to Carol. "If only."

Again Carol played the wall: there to be bounced off or simply ignored.

"We'd been married twelve years when it happened," began Janice, her voice surprisingly steady, but low and breathy. It was as if, thought Carol later, her friend had been reading from a prepared and often-rehearsed script. A written confession that had been stored away, gathering dust in her brain, all ready and waiting for nigh on forty years to one day be brought out and read aloud. "Lenny was working all hours," continued Janice, still in the same flat monotone. "Early mornings, late nights, weekends. Eddy was away at boarding school, so I was on my own for hours and hours, day after day, night after night. I started feeling neglected, like I was a spare part to Lenny's machine. Yes, he was still affectionate when he was there, but that was infrequent to say the least."

Carol reached out a hand across the table to rest it on her friend's forearm. Janice looked down at it and smiled before pressing on with her big reveal.

"His name was Christoph," began Janice. "German. An engineer for some big company in Essen. Braithwaites had just bought some fancy new machinery from them and Christoph was sent over for a month to make sure it was installed properly. One weekend, Lenny asked me to show Christoph around some of north-west England's countryside, because he himself was too busy with the auditors up at the factory. It was fun. It was like being young again: mucking about, laughing, flirting. Christoph was a handsome man, vibrant, utterly charming, and *so very* attentive. He was everything I craved at that precise moment. And, yes, we ended up in bed together. In his room at the Hatford Park Hotel." She looked up at Carol, sadness and yet something approaching relief in her eyes. "Have you ever…?"

"No," said Carol. "Never been in that position. Roy was home every night at five twenty on the dot, expecting his tea on the table, so I never found myself alone." And I never got courted by a handsome German charmer either, thought Carol.

"I never saw him again after he went back to Germany. He was married too. With five kids. He told me that, right at the outset. And I understood. We both understood what it was we were doing and why we were doing it. Behaving like irresponsible kids, but with adult conscious brains. So we both knew full well it would end the instant he set off back home to his family. And that, in some ways, made it easier to do."

Carol nodded silently, sensing that, although the guts of the story had been relayed, there was still more Janice wanted to get off her chest.

"He sent me just one message afterwards," said Janice, a weak, lopsided smile now creasing her face. "It was a small card, addressed to me at home. It had a picture of a yacht on the front. And inside he hadn't put my name at the top or his at the bottom. It was just a handwritten note. 'Only look backwards to see what is in front of you.' I burned it in case Lenny found it, but I shall never forget those words. And he was right, wasn't he, Christoph?" As she spoke the name aloud for probably the last time ever, the tears flowed again.

Carol passed across her napkin for mopping duty and waited for whatever was to come next. Surprisingly, nothing did. Janice merely finished drying her eyes, sniffed loudly, and dug into her meal with the voraciousness of a starving animal. Carol played along, eating silently opposite the recently confessed.

"Thank you," whispered Janice suddenly. "I feel a lot better now."

Carol nodded, but still held her tongue. After all, what could she say?

"That's been eating away at me for a very long time," said Janice. "A very, very long time. And despite what our two wise mums might have told us about secrets, they never taught us how to cope with our feelings if we did have one. Especially if it carried a wagonload of guilt with it." She smiled weakly. "What about you?"

"If you mean do I have a secret," said Carol, "then the answer is yes. If you're asking me to share it, then the answer is most definitely no."

"Is it a guilty secret?" asked Janice, gradually recovering towards her usual teasing self.

"Yes, it is."

"And you won't share? Quid pro quo."

"No. And you wouldn't believe me even if I did tell you," said Carol, hoping that would be the end of it.

It wasn't. "Try me," prodded Janice. "And you know I can keep a secret. I kept that last bugger for damned near half a century, so..."

Being honest with herself, Carol knew she'd been working up to this moment for weeks. Somebody very clever on one crime programme or another that she'd watched had told the viewers that the only perfect crime was one that nobody knew had been committed. He'd then gone on to say that many *almost* perfect crimes were eventually exposed because the perpetrator simply could not resist telling somebody just how clever he or she had been in getting away with it. And this, Carol knew, was that moment for her. She took a deep breath and told.

# Chapter 16

Carol simply could not stop giggling as she bustled around the kitchen getting their tea on the go. Some of it was the direct result of the humorous content of her big reveal, but a lot more, she knew, was a nervous release of some sort. She'd finally told somebody her secret and it had felt wonderful, both from the sense of letting go but also because, possibly for the first time ever in her entire life, she'd blown her own trumpet. Yes, she had sat there across the table from her oldest and closest friend and crowed about what she had done, what Carol Jackson née Garton had done, what the invisible old lady, the silly old grandma, the dowdy old housewife had been out and about doing.

The genuinely funny bit, though, had been her friend's response to the revelation. Carol played it over in her head for the umpteenth time and, as on every previous occasion, laughed out loud as the scene ran through. Upon Carol revealing herself to be the Red Fox, her friend had remained stock still, thought about it for the slow count of probably nine, and then leaned forward across the table to reply in a hoarse whisper, "And I'm Angelina Jolie."

The conversation after that had been surreal, like a fuzzy, ungraspable dream, with questions and answers flying back and forth as a genuine nigh-on-seventy-year-old amateur supervillain tried but largely failed to convince her nigh-on-seventy-year-old best friend and very recently self-confessed adulterer that she was indeed the notorious Red Fox.

To be fair to Janice, her interrogation technique was sharp and jolly clever, dotting around this way and that, working to unpick the lock that would open the door to her friend's fantasy, while all the time trying to catch her out. She didn't, but on the other hand, try as she might, Carol could see she was never going to win. The only thing she could do was propose to the resolute disbeliever that she come round to her house the following Thursday afternoon when Roy was out bowling, whereupon she would exhibit the hard evidence necessary to prove it.

With Janice grudgingly accepting the invitation, Carol turned the tables. This one was a lot easier and it only took a handful of questions for Janice to admit she was not, in fact, Angelina Jolie. They'd left the pub together, arm in arm and in good spirits, both smiling without the burden of a dark secret locked away inside. And the drive back was good too, if a little strange as Janice, unusually, insisted on playing music in the car. Peter Gabriel wasn't exactly to Carol's taste, but apparently that particular cassette had been Lenny's favourite, which made it almost bearable. And then Janice started singing along loudly to a track called 'Sledgehammer'. It wasn't quite the 'steam hammer' of her friend's late husband's alleged bedroom performance, but it was jolly well close enough to set Carol grinning.

The sound of the front door opening drew her out into the hall to meet her returning husband. His facial expression gave away that the news was going to be bad.

"Alice didn't make it," he said, even before he'd put his bowling bag down. "She never regained consciousness. She died this morning."

Carol walked across to put her arms around her husband and hug him tight. "Poor Trevor," she whispered. "How's he coping?"

"Cliff called in on him this morning. His sister's staying with him for a bit, but her husband had to go back home to go to work. Cliff says Trev just sits there, staring at a little pile of stuff on the mantelpiece. It's the cruise tickets and their passports, all ready and waiting to go. Cliff said it damned near broke his heart. All that planning, all those dreams just gone to nothing in a flash."

"Hard for anyone to believe there's a God," said Carol. It was safe ground. Neither of them were believers. "If there is one, then he's got a shitty sense of timing."

"Apparently it was for the better," continued Roy, glossing over Carol's religious observation. "Cliff said the doctors told Trev she'd have been a vegetable if she had come round." He smiled crookedly. "I know that's not the right term, but..."

"Maybe if the ruddy medics spoke proper English more often we'd be able to understand them," offered Carol.

"You're not wrong," agreed Roy. "I can't understand a word. And they never seem to have the time to explain it in layman's... Anyway, enough of that."

"Get your coat off and come on through to the kitchen," said Carol, releasing her bear hug and heading back to her domain. "I'll get the kettle on."

When he came through as instructed, Roy seemed to have largely shrugged off his cape of doom and had a small smile on his lips. "With Trev and Cliff both missing, Rainy and me tried a couple of ends, but neither of us could concentrate on bowling, so we gave up and just sat in the clubhouse for a half-hour. That was when Rainy told me he's had a bit of fun with your mate Janice these last few days."

Carol nearly choked at the thought of the far-from-wholesome Colin 'Rainy' Day getting down and dirty with the always impeccably turned out, and all too frequently posh-above-her-station, Janice Worthington.

Roy could see his wife's expression and laughed. "No, not like that! Good heavens, he'd not get within sniffing distance of her even in his wildest dreams. And I doubt she'd touch that grease-covered so-and-so with a ten-foot barge pole."

Carol struck a silent 'Well, put me straight, then' pose.

"According to Rainy," began Roy, clearly enjoying his role as storyteller, "a couple of weeks ago, she just cruises into the garage in her Lenny's big old black Jag and, without a word to anyone, starts wandering around the yard, looking at what he's got on offer. In minutes flat she's spotted a little red Mazda open-top two-seater and less than half an hour later she's driving out in it, leaving Lenny's Jag in part exchange."

Carol knew the story behind it and the next episode in front, but said nothing. This was Roy's time. And besides, while he was talking about cars and Janice, he wasn't dwelling on the tragedy in the Knight household.

Roy chuckled again. "Rainy reckons she'd never driven a manual before. He said the noise when she drove off and tried to change gear damned near burst his eardrums. Said he'd tried to give her a few tips, but she wasn't having it. You know what she's like better than anyone."

Carol did. She nodded. "And then...?" she asked.

"Yesterday morning she's back at the garage," continued Roy, still speaking through little ripples of laughter. "Rainy says he is absolutely covered in oil – he'd been rebuilding a Transit gearbox, not that that matters – and she is dressed up like the Queen of Sheba. So they talk, negotiate, whatever, at a distance of about five yards apart, shouting to each other across the gap.

She says he can have the – and I quote Rainy on this – 'shitty little sports car' back and she wants her Lenny's Jag back."

"And?" asked Carol dutifully, despite already knowing the answer.

"What could he do?" asked Roy, not expecting his question to be answered. "She'd only had the Mazda a couple of weeks and he knew he was more likely to make money on that, even with a buggered gearbox, than he was with a twelve-year-old black Jag. So he did the paperwork in minutes flat – making sure to put an 'up yours' oil smudge across her copy – and she was gone. End of story."

Carol nodded without comment and set about getting their tea ready to dish up.

"You knew all that, didn't you?" said Roy to his wife's back.

"Most of it," replied Carol without turning around.

"Bit strange, though, isn't it?" pressed Roy.

"Not really," said Carol, turning back to face him. "She just changed her mind, that's all. Women do that. Especially when they're on their own. Especially when..." She stopped and shook her head sadly.

"You know, don't you?" said Roy. "I mean, you know the real reason she suddenly wants her old man's car back. It's a bloomin' horrible great tank of a thing."

"Let's eat in here tonight, love," said Carol. "Let's we two sit up at the kitchen table instead of slouching in front of the telly. We could pretend we're in a restaurant. And we can talk."

Roy visibly stiffened at the mention of 'we can talk'. Carol knew that phrase had carried a negative connotation for him right from back when, as a lad, it was the signal he was about to get a thrashing. "I haven't got much more to say," he offered weakly.

Carol ignored his pathetic effort at a get-out and set about laying the table. "Sit yourself down there, and when I've got our food on the table, *I* shall do the talking."

Roy did as he'd been told, and sat in silence until Carol had positioned herself opposite. But even with his plate under his nose, he didn't start to eat. "Is this something bad?" he asked.

Carol took a first mouthful and indicated he should do the same. "Did your mum ever say anything to you about keeping secrets?" she asked.

"Mum used to say we should all have one secret," he said, his voice wary as to why he'd been asked. "She said that was healthy. Any more was bad because the second secret always gave birth to a third, and from there on it was a race to disaster."

"Gosh," said Carol, impressed. "That's a whole lot more than my mum ever gave us kids. All she told us was that the only way to keep a secret was for nobody to know you had it."

"What are you getting at?" asked Roy, keeping his head down, focusing on his food.

"Janice confided in me today," said Carol, speaking the words slowly as she continued to debate in her head as to whether the information was hers to share. "She told me the real reason why she'd gone to get her Lenny's old car back..." She stopped again to give it one last consideration, tossed an imaginary coin in her head and, with it coming up 'heads', went for it. "Janice told me that getting rid of the car Lenny had loved so much was like being unfaithful to him," she paused for a deep breath and a slow exhale before finishing with, "again."

Carol had expected her husband to gawp, goggle-eyed, at the revelation. Or whoop and holler. Anything really, other than simply sit and nod like he was doing. "Are you not shocked?" she asked. "Even a little bit?"

Roy continued nodding. "Christoph Werner," he said softly.

Carol was shocked rigid for the second time in a single day. Janice hadn't mentioned her illicit lover's second name, but Christoph was most definitely the first.

"That was a very long time ago," said Roy, lightly and unemotionally, as if they were discussing an old brand of biscuits that they couldn't get any more.

"You knew?" asked Carol, unable to think of anything else to say.

"We all knew," replied Roy. "Probably the only person at the works who didn't know was Lenny himself. Christoph was a decent enough chap – for a German – and we pretty much guessed it was a mad fling that would end as soon as he went back home to his family, so..."

Carol was now aghast. "You never told me."

"Never told anybody," replied Roy. "None of us did. Didn't seem right. Lenny may have been senior management – operations director he was at the time – but he'd worked his way there and he was a good bloke. He remembered where he'd come from and he always treated us grease-monkeys on the shop floor like human beings. Never high and mighty like the other stuck-up prats on the board. He knew us all by name, all our wives' and kids' names, and he genuinely looked out for us every year at pay review time. So we agreed to look after him in return. You know, I genuinely believe he never found out to the day he died."

Carol was amazed. And whereas a few seconds earlier she'd expected her husband to be gawping in shock, she now realised it was her playing the codfish. "How did you know?" was all she could think of to ask.

"Piet Zielinski's missus worked part-time as a cleaner up at the Hatford Park Hotel. She knew Janice Worthington by sight from the works' summer parties, and recognised her going in, looking all furtive and whatnot. Saw 'Fritz', as she called him, coming and going at the same time, and put two and two together. It only went on for about a fortnight, and then it ended, like we always thought it would. He had a wife and five kids back home."

So everybody knew, thought Carol. The guilty secret that Janice had lugged around on her shoulders for forty-odd years. No, not everybody, she quickly corrected. Not Lenny. And, although Janice of course knew, she was thankfully never aware of how many others knew. And that was a double blessing for the Worthingtons. "Lenny never had an affair, did he?" asked Carol, bizarrely thinking that if he had, it would make Janice's guilt a little less barbed.

"Not that I know of," said Roy. "He was always working too ruddy hard. And before you ask, apart from a thoroughly mucky weekend with Raquel Welch back in the early '80s, neither have I."

"How was Raquel?" asked Carol, joining in with the joke and happy that the conversation was being led away from the shadows of genuine infidelity.

"Bloody gorgeous," replied Roy with a wicked grin. Then he slowly laid his knife and fork down on his plate to look across at his wife with unmistakable love in his eyes. "But nothing to compare with you, love," he said. "Not even in the same league. You are, and always have been, the one. The *only* one. From that first time I clapped my eyes on you sitting with your girlfriends on the park swings, pretending to smoke a ciggy to make yourself look hard, I knew you were the one for me."

It was the longest speech she'd heard him make for years, and the content had put a lump in her throat. Roy had never been one for great outpourings of emotion, and certainly not lovey-dovey stuff, but it had been wonderful to hear.

"I coughed my lungs up when I tried to inhale," she offered.

Roy laughed. "You were, what, fifteen?"

"Fourteen and three quarters," corrected Carol.

"Whatever, I knew right away. Didn't have the courage to do anything, but thought about nothing apart from you for days until...well, you know."

Carol nodded. Yes, she knew. "I clocked you too that evening, walking past with your mates, eyeing me up and down. I never for a minute thought I stood a chance. In fact I'd just about given up hope by the time you eventually got around to asking me out on a date."

"Date?" laughed Roy. "We walked down to the canal to look at the ducks."

"We held hands all the way there," said Carol. "And back. And you kissed me when we went under the bridge."

"We had to make sure your parents didn't find out for ages," said Roy.

"They'd have locked me in the house," said Carol. "What with you already being sixteen, not to mention being one of the notorious Meadow Close Jacksons."

"At least that was a nice secret," said Roy wistfully, picking up his knife and fork again to set about finishing his tea. "Most of them are rotten," he added around his chewing. "Secrets, that is. They sort of fester, don't they? Swell inside you, making them more and more difficult to get out, the longer they're kept caged up."

From romantic to philosopher in a heartbeat, thought Carol. Lovely, but unusual to say the least, on both counts. So what was it that had brought on this uncharacteristic spate of warm reminiscing and deep thinking? The sudden death of his friend's wife? A reaction to the story of Janice Worthington's infidelity and remembering how him and his workmates had all known but not told? Or had he maybe sensed a change in his wife's demeanour of late and felt like he needed to somehow tag along? She couldn't work it out, and so watched him clearing his plate, searching his every move for a clue of some sort. There was none.

When he'd finished and put his knife and fork down, he looked across at her, his expression serious. "Did you tell her *your* secret?" he asked.

Carol caught her breath and fiddled with her hair to both conceal her shock and buy time before answering. Had he guessed? What if he'd been rooting around looking for something and accidentally stumbled on her Red Fox disguise? Or somehow lined up the times and places of her days out with the sequence of bank robberies. She coughed to clear her throat. "And what secret might that be?" she asked.

Roy tilted his head forward and stared at her accusingly from under his brows. "You ate half of our little boy's Easter egg and told him the mice had had it away."

They laughed. Loudly. Together. Like they hadn't for far too long. A magical moment, two as one, loving and loved, joined inextricably by the multicoloured scenes of their years together. It was, thought Carol, the perfect icing on the layered cake of a strange yet amazing day. And was she really genuinely prepared to risk it all for the idiotic pursuit of a crazy-mad hobby? Yes, she was.

# Chapter 17

Detective Sergeant Danny Roberts stared out through the grimy squad-room window and growled at the blue sky beyond. He couldn't ever remember a time when he'd been depressed by good weather. But right now he was. Deeply.

It was the morning after a second Tuesday since the possible breakthrough regarding their bank robber travelling up and down the county by train, and the consequent plan to set a trap for the wily Red Fox. The effort needed to get it in place had been not inconsiderable, with active push-back from half the police stations contacted and grudging reluctance from the rest. Danny had hated himself for exploiting Templeton's widely known-about familial link to the ACC but, as he'd consoled himself, in troubled times, needs must. But no sooner had they finally managed to get the trap set up and primed ready to go than the bastard middle western shires of England went and delivered up the best sodding spring weather he could ever remember. And he knew all too painfully well that, as every week passed towards summer, the probability of 'heavy hoodie coat weather' cropping up again dwindled away yet further.

"Weather front supposedly coming in at the weekend," announced Jacquie, seeing her sergeant's slumped shoulders and offering good news of bad weather on the horizon in the hope of bucking him up. "Cold wind and chucking it down, by the sounds of it. Could last for a couple of weeks or more, so they're saying." She added a forced smile in the hope it would clinch the morale boost. It didn't.

"Nice try, Jacquie," said Danny, "but..." He paused to silently scream at the ceiling before looking back at her, shaking his head sadly. "I think he's finished for this year. Maybe forever."

"So we just...?"

"No! No, we don't!" snapped Danny, guessing ahead to what his DC was most probably about to say, and forcing himself to be positive. "We *have* to crack this bloody case in the next couple of weeks or risk Shirley missing out on his next promotion. And that would mean him not being..." He couldn't bring himself to say it. "We have to solve it, Jacquie, we *have* to. And although the train station trap is almost certainly our best bet, I simply cannot stop feeling that we ought to have enough information in our hands to track down this little shit."

"Danny," began Jacquie, her tone one of intense consolation, "we've been through everything a thousand times. You know that. If there was something in there – some missing link, some magical hidden clue, some trail of damned breadcrumbs to follow – one of us would have spotted it. Surely we would."

Before Danny could reply, Kevin burst into the squad room waving a rolled-up newspaper in his fist. The other two didn't need more than a single brain cell between them to guess what it was, and from there to the probable content. The only questions were how bad it was going to be and who was going to read it out.

Kevin didn't wait to be asked, planting his feet wide apart and flicking the paper out, all ready to read. He held it stiffly in front of his chest so that neither of the others could see the headline or chance an attempt to snatch it away from him. A single deep breath and he was off and running, delivering the headline like a town crier, but thankfully without the ringing handbell and the 'Hear ye, hear ye' at the beginning. "'Red Fox: Retired or Simply Relaxing?'" he intoned.

"It's a good question," said Danny. "Fair."

Kevin ignored the interruption and pressed on.

*With the unseasonably pleasant weather in the region, it looks like our Red Fox has hung up his trademark grey hoodie coat and headed off to the seaside for a spot of untroubled relaxation. Now, three weeks on from the last of his string of audacious bank robberies, everything points to his hunting season being over for this year.*

"Well, that's not too bad," offered Danny. "I mean, she could have..." He stopped speaking when he saw Kevin sadly shaking his head before resuming his reading.

*The Midwestern Echo is guessing that the deckchairs are also out on the sweeping lawns of the Fourshires Constabulary's Attwood House*

*HQ, so that Inspector Slow and the Sleepy Squad at Ternbury Police Station can comfortably snooze through these long, warm afternoons, much as they have been doing since the beginning of this poor excuse for a criminal investigation.*

"That bit's not so good," said Danny with a play-acted grimace. "Tell me she's had enough by this point, Kev. Please tell me she's not going to kick the poor, wounded little kitten when it's down."

Kevin didn't reply, merely reading on.

*Considering the number of robberies, the quantity of information widely available, and the vast range of technological tools they have in their possession, it seems inconceivable to the Midwestern Echo – and, we would guess, to most of our readership – that Fourshires Constabulary have made so little if any progress on this major case. Maybe they really are on holiday, as the vacuum of information would appear to suggest. Perhaps they're just too busy building sandcastles on the beach to set about developing any leads as to the perpetrator of this relentless series of armed robberies.*

"She's warming up, isn't she," groaned Danny, his whole bodily demeanour one of resignation. He knew there was worse to come, and braced himself to take it.

Kevin continued, still adopting his newsreader tone.

*So we at the Midwestern Echo think it is fair and reasonable to ask this question: is it time to call in the Famous Five, complete with picnic hamper filled to the brim with tomato sandwiches and home-made lemonade, to take over this investigation? It surely has to be worth a shot, not least because it seems to us that there is significantly more chance of their dog Timmy sniffing out the notorious Red Fox than leaving it to Inspector Templeton's tortoise.*

"Now that last paragraph was just plain mean," said Danny, not sparing the sarcasm.

He waited for a response, but none came. What could any of them say? Percy Walsh may have been relentlessly sticking it to them, and a long way off the mark with regards to their expended effort, but her conclusion, delivered in her particularly whimsical form of brutality, was pretty much the truth. They really were no further ahead, no closer to catching the bastard Red Fox, than they had been months before.

Kevin sombrely folded the newspaper like a reader at a funeral closing the book on his final passage, and sat at his desk to join in with the mourning of fine characters laid to rest. And there they sat, silent, in their own worlds of reflection, but collective in their dejection. Minute after long minute and nothing stirred, nobody made a sound.

Suddenly Danny lurched to his feet. "I've got an idea," he almost shouted, clapping his hands and moving to position himself midway between his two colleagues.

"Mass ritual suicide?" asked Jacquie.

At least that brought a laugh. Small and weak, but a fleeting moment of levity nonetheless.

"No," said Danny, seriousness in his tone, "but if it's not done right then we'll all be just as dead, effectively."

"Well, go on then," said Jacquie, desperately trying to summon up some enthusiasm. "We two aren't going anywhere urgent, so tell us."

"I read this Percy Walsh as a smart cookie," began Danny, making eye contact with his team members as he spoke. "She writes lightly and humorously between the bits where she takes a rubber truncheon to our institutional testicles, but there's solid substance underneath all of it."

Jacquie and Kevin used their expressions alone to show intrigue as to where their leader might be going.

"Whether she does or she doesn't, she writes like she *knows* stuff," he continued, "stuff she has no right to be able to work out. Yes, linking the hoodie coat to a restricted bad-weather hunting season is an easy one, but what if she's got more? What if by some magic she's seeing things from a distance that we three can't see because we're too effing close? And worst of all, what if she's got something up her sleeve for next week's *Echo* that... Well, it doesn't bear thinking about, does it?"

"She wouldn't, would she?" asked Kevin. "I mean..."

"Listen to yourself, Kevin," snapped Danny. "This woman's body may be in your dreams, but her spirit ought to be in your darkest nightmares. It's in mine."

"So come on then, Danny," said Jacquie. "Accepting everything you've just said, what *is* your big idea? I've got a sneaky feeling but I want to hear you say it out loud."

Danny perched himself on the edge of his desk before replying. "She managed – or so she says, and we've no reason to disbelieve her – to track down all the charitable recipients of the Red Fox robberies. Admittedly, we didn't really try to trace them because at the time it wasn't deemed of any value, but now we've got the railway link plotted on the map, what if we added the recipient locations? It could possibly, just possibly, give us a better image of the Red Fox's hunting patch, and from there maybe help us narrow down the possible location of his den."

Jacquie opened her mouth to speak, but was stopped by a gentle hand-wave and a shake of the head from her superior officer. Danny wanted to finish his piece before opening discussion to the floor.

"She never let on in her article who they were, who got the money, but what if she was prepared to tell us? And beyond that, what if we could somehow exploit her intellect, her insights, her detached view? As I was saying to you, Jacquie, before Kevin came in, we have been sitting here for weeks with a big and ever-growing pile of information pearls that, for whatever reason, we have spectacularly failed to string into a necklace. Now what if – just as a perhaps, a maybe – the delectable newsprint assassin Walsh could and would help us?" He finished his protracted speech only to find himself staring across at two shocked faces literally gawping back at him. He waited, listening to nothing beyond a resonating silence in the room, before pleading, "Somebody say something...please."

"Shirley would kill us," said Jacquie. "Dead."

"Not if he never finds out," said Danny, hearing his words as he spoke them and reflecting on how cheap and hollow they sounded. "And it *has* to be worth the risk."

Jacquie shrugged and made an 'on-your-head-be-it' face at her DS. "So, when are you planning on taking the cyanide pill?" she asked.

Danny winced. "I thought it would be better done woman-to-woman."

"Like fuck!" said Jacquie. "I'm not—"

"*Pleeease*," wheedled Danny. "For us."

"Okay, okay," sighed Jacquie. "If it saves us from having to see you on your knees and crying, I'll do it." She looked straight at her leader, making sure she had him locked eye to eye in full attention, before adding, "But you will owe me big time, Detective Sergeant Roberts. You do understand that, don't you?"

Danny nodded and put his hands together in a mock prayer of gratitude to the saint who might just help get them off the hook. "When can you...?"

"I know a friend of a friend who works there," said Jacquie. "I don't know her that well, but I could tap her up, maybe. She's only a junior accounts clerk but there's still a fair chance she could find out where our Percy goes for lunch, exercises, drinks, parties, whatever. Then all I'd have to do is just happen to be there around the same time and accidentally bump into her. And if that doesn't work, then it'll be up to you to submit a formal request for a completely informal meeting."

"If you do get to see her, are you going to do the same as Shirley?" asked Kevin with a salacious wink at his female colleague. "I mean, tie her in knots to the point where she rolls over so you can tickle her tummy?"

"Piss off, Kevin!"

# Chapter 18

Roy had nearly choked when Carol told him that this week her regular Thursday afternoon get-together with best friend Janice was to be at their house. Even though he knew full well that Carol and Janice had stayed close friends since their schooldays, through thick and thin, through highs and lows, not to mention their social-standing separation, he simply could not believe that 'The Big Boss's Wife', as he still thought of her, would 'slum it' round at theirs. "Wouldn't you be better off up at her place?" he'd asked, putting his tongue firmly in his cheek before adding, "drinking champagne and eating fish-egg canapés?"

Carol had let him have his fun, responding only with, "I'll try to make sure she doesn't leave a tiara down the back of the armchair when she leaves."

They'd laughed, and Roy was still chuckling as his wife stood on the front doorstep, waving him off to enjoy a 'thrill-packed' afternoon of bowling under a cloudless blue sky. Carol waited until he was well out of sight before scowling up at the relentlessly shining sun. She needed the weather to turn rotten again or she'd never get that Leominster bank done before summer set in.

She'd barely closed the front door when she heard a tap-tapping at the back. That was unusual, she thought. Nobody came to the house through the backyard, not even Sarah or the girls. With a frown furrowing her brow, she walked cautiously through to the kitchen and peered out through the back-door window. A face was pressed up close. It was Janice. At least, it looked a lot like Janice, but wearing a Zorro mask. Carol knew that because it had 'Zorro' written on it. She pulled the door open and stared quizzically at her visitor, who did a furtive look all around the tiny yard before lunging in through the door and slamming it shut behind her.

"That was close," breathed Janice dramatically.

"What the heck's going on?" asked Carol, standing away from her friend and planting her hands on her hips as she spoke.

"Can't be too careful," hissed Janice in a hoarse whisper. "The rozzers will be watching the front. Didn't want to compromise the Batcave security."

"I like the mask," said Carol with a smirk.

"Found it in Eddy's old toy box," said Janice, still hunching slightly and keeping her voice low. "Thought it would be a good idea," she added, lifting the bottom edge of the mask an inch or so to peep out before replacing it flush. "Didn't want my face on full show coming here. There's cameras everywhere these days."

"Is that because you're slumming it, coming down to the ghetto?"

"No, you dope, it's because I'm visiting a notorious supervillain."

"Are you taking the Michael?" asked Carol, adding a lopsided grin.

"Of course I bloody am," replied Janice, finally speaking in a normal voice as she theatrically ripped off the mask. "And don't you go getting all reverse-snobby on me, Carol Jackson. I was brought up only three doors down, remember. So don't get fooled by the dogs that I've got."

"Now you have lost me," said Carol.

"It's a line from the old Jennifer Lopez song. I think," said Janice. "Trouble is, Lenny always deliberately sang the wrong words and now I can't bloody remember the right ones. But no matter. The point is, chook, I'm still, I'm still Janice from the shop. Or was it block?"

"Have you been drinking?"

"Not yet," replied Janice, reaching into her bag to tug out a bottle of red wine. "Knew for a fact you wouldn't have bugger all in the house, so brought my own. It's a glass or two short of full, but it'll have to do. And if you haven't got a wine glass in the house, a coffee mug will suffice very nicely, thank you."

"Where's the car?" asked Carol as she retrieved a tumbler from the cupboard.

"Parked in Sainsbury's car park. Thought I could evade identification more easily on foot. And they use those number plate reader thingies, so..." She paused to wrench the screw cap off her bottle. "Thanks," she said as Carol handed her the glass that she immediately filled almost to the brim. "To the Red Fox, wherever he is," she toasted, raising her glass high before emptying half of it in a single glug.

"Now that last phrase," said Carol in a playful stern voice, "was downright rude. You know precisely where 'he' is. I told you on Tuesday."

"I have just two questions for you, my dearest and bestest friend," began Janice, taking a quick, reinforcing swig of wine. "Number one, when did you first invent this fantasy of yours, and, two, when did you actually start believing it?"

Carol got herself out another tumbler and filled it with water from the tap, using the space to get her thoughts in a row. This was going to be far more difficult than she'd thought. So was it perhaps better just to simply play it as a joke rather than…? No, it was not. She was not a joke and she was bloomin' well going to stand up for herself. "Come upstairs," she said, softly but firmly, "and do not spill red wine on the carpet."

"Are you taking me hostage?" asked Janice with a giggle.

"I am liable to clobber you with a frying pan if you don't give me at least a chance," said Carol. "So are you coming or not?"

Janice did a waggly-headed 'Okay, grouchy bear' sort of thing, and trotted on behind, climbing the stairs to the landing and following Carol into what had once been her Paul's bedroom. It always brought tears pressing at the back of Carol's eyes and a slight catch of her breath whenever she went in there. It hadn't been redecorated since her nineteen-year-old 'little boy' had left home to go off to university donkey's years ago. Even his posters of footballers long retired, forgotten rock bands, and now middle-aged TV chicks were still there where he'd tacked them up all those years ago. At first her and Roy had thought, and maybe even hoped, he'd come back home one day. He never had, of course, and she'd been idiotic to expect otherwise. He was grown up, living his own adult life on the other side of the world. She knew that. She understood the harsh reality of having babies and bringing them up only to have to hand them over to a future world of their own. But the sight, the feel, the smell of that cramped little room still cluttered with so many of his things always—

"Come on, then, Foxy," prodded Janice, topping her glass up from the bottle she'd brought with her. "Convert me. Make me a believer."

"If you don't want to play nice, you can—"

"Okay, okay, I'm sorry," sang Janice, waving both glass and bottle in an appeasing gesture. "It's just a lot to take in all of a sudden."

Carol smiled and nodded. "I have to pinch myself regularly to be able to believe it. There are times when it feels like I'm dreaming it. And before you say a word, I am absolutely bloody certain my marbles are not loose. I am not dreaming an alternative reality. I am living it. And you are the only person I was intending to share it with. So, do you want to see or not?"

Janice gave a minimalist double nod between two sips of wine.

Carol pulled open the middle drawer of her son's tiny dresser and reached deep into the back to extract a small cardboard box. She placed it onto the bed, took off the lid, and reached inside. "Exhibit A," said Carol, holding out an open palm with her false ginger moustache in its centre.

"A caterpillar," said Janice as she leaned forward to peer more closely at the item. "A ginger caterpillar. Or to be absolutely precise, a rather nasty *dead* ginger caterpillar."

"It's the Red Fox's trademark moustache," announced Carol, holding it up to her lip with a middle finger. "It's how he got his supervillain title," she added in a mumble around the finger.

"Is that it?" asked a disdainful Janice. "You hold a dead ginger caterpillar on your face for a couple of seconds and expect me to take that as proof you're a notorious serial bank robber? Give me a break."

Carol didn't reply, instead extracting the small round wire-rimmed glasses from her disguise box and putting them on.

"Donald Pleasence," said Janice, pointing at Carol with her bottle hand. "In *The Great Escape*." She shook her head sadly. "Blind as a bat, he was. Didn't know which way to run and got shot. They're not his, are they?"

Carol conspicuously ignored the entire comment, turning her back on her increasingly irritating guest to stash her props back into the cardboard box. With it safely re-hidden in the drawer, she wordlessly pushed past the disbeliever to get to Paul's three-quarter-height wardrobe. Opening one door, she extracted her reversible getaway coat, easing it on with the grey hoodie side out and pulling up the hood to peek out from its depths and scowl at her friend.

"You would not see me dead in that thing," scoffed Janice. "Sorry to say this out loud, Carol, but it is horrendous. Did you make it yourself?"

"I did," replied Carol proudly. "And the reason I did so is this." With as much of a flourish as the limited bedroom floor space would allow, she deftly transformed herself from a grey-hooded youth out for a day of armed bank robbery into a mustard yellow, smartly coated little old lady having an afternoon of genteel window-shopping. "My escape coat," she announced with a little verbalised fanfare to follow.

"Clever, very clever," cooed Janice appreciatively. "In fact I would have to say ingenious. But, sadly, still not what I would call proof. In fact, far from it. Reversible clothes were all the rage back in the '70s, and hence not that special. In fact I had one, a rather natty jacket that me and Lenny used to call my 'Gina Lollobrigida'. You see, whenever we went out to an Italian restaurant I always without fail managed to blob tomato something-or-other down my front. So before my profiteroles arrived I could flip 'Gina' inside out and look good as new. In fact, now I come to think of it, I might still have it somewhere at home. I could dig it out to see if it fits. It won't, of course, but I could maybe get it let out. Or even get a new one run up by..." She stopped abruptly and gurgled as her eyes suddenly focused on the big black gun now pointing straight at her forehead. "Was I not appreciative enough?" she croaked.

"Are you n-n-never going to stop yakking?" asked Carol in her very best menacing bank robber voice. "Your n-n-never-ending prattle is driving me n-n-nuts."

Janice moved her head to look at her friend around the unwavering dangerous end of the gun barrel. She then turned her head to one side to take a sip of wine before looking back at her friend. "Is it real?"

Carol laughed. "Of course not. It's what they call a replica – perfect in every visible detail and exactly the same weight as the real thing. The only difference is it can't shoot bullets."

"Where did you get it?" asked Janice, feeling a lot more relaxed as the gun was lowered away from her face.

"It's Paul's. He bought it when he was about fifteen. Saved for weeks to get it, he did. Spent every penny of his savings, pocket money, birthday money – the lot. Roy and me thought it was a waste of money but he wouldn't listen." Carol trotted out the story with enthusiastic relish as she remembered her son's quivering excitement as he ripped open the parcel when it finally arrived. "He was always playing with it, pretending, always the good guy, never the bad. We wouldn't let him take it outside the house, but in his bedroom he was Clint Eastwood, Bruce Willis, anyone tough and good. He even slept with the blasted thing under his pillow until he left home. Couldn't take it to university and certainly not to Canada," she continued, "so he left it here. It was originally a silvery colour but I didn't think it looked mean enough, so I sprayed it black. It's a Walther P88 in case you're interested. Nine millimetre. Bloody heavy but, hey-ho, that's bank robbery for you."

Janice had been listening attentively to the over-long and definitely over-excitable explanation, waiting patiently for Carol to finish before saying anything. But as she started to speak, she quickly decided better of whatever it was, and chose instead to refill her empty glass and amuse herself by sipping at it repeatedly. After what seemed like an age she found some words. "I have to say you are gradually swaying me towards believing you. But hell's teeth, Carol, you have to admit it's a big old leap of imagination to get all the way there."

Carol was already busy hiding away her 'paraphernalia of villainy', as she thought of them, but she was still listening to the wavering convert. "I wish I could show you the cash," she said casually over her shoulder, "but I've already given the last lot away. I keep it in the freezer between taking and giving. In a box marked 'tofu curry' in case Roy by some miracle decides to go digging around in there."

"That's convenient," said Janice, her conversion to the faith already slipping. "I mean, if you'd flashed a few grand's worth of frozen banknotes, that might just have tipped the balance."

"I'll remember that next time," said Carol as she shooed her friend out of her son's bedroom and back down the stairs and into the kitchen. "I'll hang on to it so that I can show it to Doubting bloody Thomasina. Okay?"

"Alright, alright," sang Janice, sitting herself down at the kitchen table. "Keep your ruddy tail on, *Foxy*."

There was something in the delivery of Janice's final word – the stress, the tone, the raised eyebrow as she spoke it – that Carol found disappointing to the point of infuriating. She'd opened up to her friend, shared the lot, everything, and yet still not managed to convince her that a damned-near-seventy-year-old working-class housewife, mother and grandmother could be anything other than...

"You don't believe me, do you?" she demanded, not able to hide the aggravation in her voice.

Janice focused on the wine bottle, holding it up to the light, and, seeing not much left, emptied the remainder into her glass. But this time she didn't drink. She just very slowly placed the empty bottle on the tabletop and looked up at her glowering friend with something akin to pity in her eyes. "I want to, chook," she said, shaking her head sadly. "I really do. The coat, the disguise, the bloody great big gun nearly, very nearly, got me there. But I've known you for sixty-odd years and...well, you know."

Carol sat down directly opposite her best friend and stared at her. She understood. And if their roles had been reversed, in all probability she would have been incapable of believing Janice. "I'll tell you what, Mrs

Worthington," she began, her voice soft and barely more than a whisper. "How about this? For now, for the next few days or so, you keep on believing that I'm a deluded old biddy with some particularly peculiar manifestation of dementia. Okay?"

"Okay," nodded Janice. "And then?"

"Then, if the weather turns nasty next week, as it is forecast to do, and there just happens to be an armed robbery at Bowlands Bank in Leominster at precisely two thirty on Tuesday afternoon..." She didn't finish the sentence. She could see in her friend's face that she didn't need to.

# Chapter 19

Danny and Kevin could barely contain themselves, fidgeting and repeatedly checking their watches as the time crept around to eight thirty and Jacquie's usual arrival time of a morning. They both knew where she'd been the previous evening and who with and the anticipation of what they might or might not be about to hear was crippling.

Jacquie's friend of a friend who worked in the accounts department at the *Midwestern Echo* offices had come up trumps. In only a couple of hours she'd found out damned near the entire daily schedule of the *Echo*'s star reporter. The key piece of information was that Walsh spent every Thursday evening without fail in a seven-thirty group class at the Yogamazing Studio in Shrewsbury. A quick and easy online registration and enrolment, a sixty quid up-front first session payment courtesy of Danny's personal credit card, and Jacquie was in. From there, all she'd had to do was pitch up at the right place and time, manoeuvre herself into position, and make contact with a hopefully receptive Percy Walsh.

Now, the morning after, Danny couldn't stop his stomach churning as he guessed ahead to what he might soon be hearing, the imagined result lurching back and forth between dazzling sunshine and darkest night. So much could have gone wrong. The least bad outcome would be a simple brush-off. The worst was a complaint that got back to Shirley. Everything in between was, well, in between. If nothing came of it the sixty quid would hurt too, as there was no way on earth he was going to submit an expenses claim and risk having Shirley spot it. They hadn't seen the man for the better part of two days, but that didn't mean he wasn't somewhere watching them.

The door swung open and Jacquie breezed in. Both men could see the smirk on her face as she strolled across the room, and Danny was sure he could hear her softly whistling. He held his breath and waited. And waited. And fucking waited as she ever so slowly took off her jacket, draped it with excessive care over the back of her chair, switched on her computer, sat herself at the desk, re-arranged her pencil and pad, had a rummage around in her desk drawer, opened her notebook, pulled a—

"Tell us!" shouted Danny. "For Pete's sake, Jacquie. Tell us what happened!"

She spun her chair around to face her colleagues, like Ernst Stavro Blofeld turning to face James Bond, and smiled superciliously. A gentle stroke of finger and thumb to her chin, then, "It was interesting," she purred, "very interesting."

"Please tell me it's interesting good," pleaded Danny, shuffling his chair across to be almost within touching distance of his extremely annoying DC.

"Don't you want to hear about how I did it? How I made contact?" asked Jacquie, now very deliberately stringing the whole thing out to its maximum.

Danny and Kevin quickly looked at each other, then looked back at her and nodded.

"Well, I didn't," said Jacquie with a sad face. "What I mean is, *I* didn't make contact with *her*. *She* made contact with *me*." She paused to check out the two faces staring back at her. Their expressions were nearly identical: a mix of intrigue, pleading, and bubbling infuriation at her games. "Alright, alright," she sang. "No more mucking about. Yes, I turned up as planned – yoga kitbag, clean leotard, the lot – but never made it out of the changing rooms before the damnable woman sniffed me out as a 'plant'. I won't tell you how much she *wasn't* wearing to spare Kevin's heart, but she simply strides across and asks me what the hell I'm doing there. Well, what could I say? I told her. Straight up. The whole scam. Thought I might as well fess up and get it over with. If she bummed me out I could go home without having to spend an hour breathing yoga farts."

"And?" croaked Danny, barely able to contain himself.

"I think I may be a little bit infatuated," said Jacquie. "She is absolutely brilliant. 'Fab' doesn't even come close. Insisted she do the class and I could either join in or shoot off down to the pub around the corner and wait for her there. I stayed. And, yes, it *was* an hour of breathing yoga farts, but it did feel somehow righteous."

Danny smiled at his star DC but said nothing, merely making a gentle 'Give it to me and get on with it' motion with a softly rotating hand.

"First off," said Jacquie, momentarily leaning back to smile at the ceiling, "Percy Walsh is an absolute darling. Too bloody fit and gorgeous by half, well dressed beyond my wildest imagination – the shoes alone were to die for – and beautifully turned out: hairdo, teeth, make-up. I felt like a scruffy frump in comparison, but I forgive her because she is also utterly charming, witty, smart as a button, and she absolutely detests Shirley."

"Because?" pressed Kevin, pulling his chair across the room to sit himself just on the shoulder of his DS. "I mean, why exactly does she detest Shirley? I can guess. I just want to hear it."

"I can't remember her precise words," replied Jacquie, "but something along the lines of him being an arrogant, none-too-bright, patronising, male-chauvinist knob who treated her most of the time like an addle-brained schoolgirl and the rest like a teenage boy might when coming face to face with his favourite centrefold wank-bunny. Her term, not mine. Anyway, she said that within half a minute of meeting him, her toes had started to curl up – metaphorically speaking, of course – with his cringe-worthy faux charm and pathetic attempts to make her think he was sharing when, in fact, he was doing nothing of the sort. Worst of all, she said, either he didn't have the guile to conceal that fact or he simply didn't deem it necessary, her being a woman and all."

"You see?" said Danny smugly. "I told you she was clever."

The three laughed together, long and loud, the two men stopping first as they desperately wanted to hear more of the story.

"You were right about more than that," said Jacquie, nodding. "She is damned near where we are investigation-wise and *she* got there without any access to all our witness statements or CCTV footage. She knows Foxy manages to effectively disappear, hence he has to somehow ditch his disguise somewhere along the line. She's pretty certain the ginger moustache and the glasses are props and, although the reported regional accent is probably real, the stutter probably isn't. She told me she'd researched a couple of old TV programmes – American, but still useful, so she said – and they explained a lot about the techniques of witness misdirection. She reckons the gun's a fake too, but that's just a hunch on her part. As is the feeling she's got in her waters that the Red Fox may eventually turn out to be the Red Vixen."

"What?" cried Danny. "A woman? Don't be daft! It's a man. Has to be."

Jacquie shrugged and made an 'I'm only telling you what she said' face.

"Didn't you tell her about the criminal psychology profile?" asked Danny.

"I told her, and her response was to blow a rather spectacular wet raspberry. Said most criminal profiles were laughably wrong and do more damage than good. Suggested we shred it before it pollutes our minds and buggers up the investigation even more than it already is. Oh, and she guessed the profile thing was Templeton's idea."

"Why a woman?" asked Kevin. "What makes her think...?"

"Nothing substantive. She was very up-front about it being a guess, like with the fake gun. She just *feels* there's something a bit 'off' with the whole thing. Of course she's not had access to our official witness statements, but she's read and analysed every bit of what little we've released, and watched and re-watched the TV interviews with the bank cashiers. And from that she reckons the Fox's broad MO, reported biometrics, small stature, and voice all tend to point away from the perp being male. Oh, and she said a fake moustache would be a slick disguise for a woman to quickly stick on and pull off before melting away into thin air."

"She happily shared all this?" asked Danny, his voice incredulous but tinged with a degree of wariness. "Simply sat there and laid it all out? Asked for nothing in return?"

"Said she wanted to help. Simple as that. Yes, of course she would appreciate an inside track – you know, first dibs on new information, or an early heads-up on the 'collar' as and when we get there. But beyond that she didn't ask for a thing, apart from never having to again experience that, quote, 'slimeball Templeton', unquote."

"Okay, go on," prodded Danny. "What about the good causes who received the money? Did she—"

"The full list," interrupted Jacquie, reaching into her shoulder bag to pull out a single folded sheet of paper. "She made it clear she can't actually prove any of them a hundred percent beyond the Church Stretton hospice, where the marked cash got taken back. Oh, and she wasn't too happy about that, so she only gave me the list on condition I don't use it to snatch back more of the money."

"You agreed to that?" asked Kevin.

"What do *you* think?" responded Jacquie, waving the list.

"Anything else?" asked Danny, perhaps more in hope than in expectation.

"First off," said Jacquie, clearly revelling in her position in the spotlight, "we already know from her last article that she'd worked out that the hoodie coat is fundamental to the Red Fox's concealment, and that it can only be deployed in poor weather. So either our man will have to change his MO or stop working in the summer." Jacquie paused for dramatic effect, looking at each of her colleagues in turn before finishing with, "But what we didn't know is that she has also worked out he's probably travelling to and from his robberies by train."

"Oh hell!" howled Danny, slapping a palm to his forehead. "That means..."

Jacquie held up a hand for him to wait a bit before he started sobbing. "She said she held it back from the last article because she could sense an approach was coming."

"Is this woman some kind of witch?" asked Danny.

Jacquie shrugged. "She could well be, but I think not. Otherwise she'd have simply told me who the Red Fox is and where to find him – or her. But anyway, that aside, she told me she was holding back on the train-travel thing because she knew if it was made public it really could hinder the investigation by sending the Fox to ground."

"So the ACC did get to her editor, then," said Danny with a grim chuckle. "Shirley told us, remember, that the old man was going to put the frighteners on them."

Jacquie's pealing laughter rang out around the squad room. It took her several seconds to recover her composure. "Percy told me about that," she said, forcing her words around her aftershock giggles. "She was in her boss's office when the call came in, and he put it on speaker so she could listen. It seems our top man came on all hard and heavy to the *Echo*'s top man, threatening him with all sorts if he continued printing 'libellous claptrap' and thereby 'recklessly undermining an ongoing police investigation'. Apparently he alluded to pretty much everything from 'aiding and abetting' to violating the Official Secrets Act and a lot more in between. Percy nearly choked laughing as she told me the *Midwestern Echo*'s editor-in-chief listened without a sound until the ACC had finished ranting, then politely enquired if the British police were 'formally attempting to constrain or curtail freedom of the press'. It brought, according to Percy, a very abrupt end to a hitherto beautiful conversation."

This time all three of them roared with laughter, Danny hugging his sides to stop them splitting, while Kevin dabbed at his streaming eyes with a handkerchief. But as the hilarity subsided, Danny looked across seriously at Jacquie.

"Is she going to publish it next week?" he asked. "The train-travel thing?"

Jacquie shook her head. "I told her about our trap. Yes, I know it was a risk, but by this time we were already well down our second bottle of very tasty rosé wine. The *Echo* paid for it, by the way," she added with a wink at her DS.

"And?" he asked, waving away her final comment.

"She understood. I didn't even need to spell it out. And she promised not to share anything about the train-travel – in print or verbally – before the end of May. By then she knows it'll be too warm for the Red Fox to go a-hunting, and, besides that, she told me that Chief Inspector Stephen Overbollocks from the Cheesehead Constabulary has already told her he'll be taking over the investigation from June first so she feels at that point she can do whatever she wants. Meantime, she's sworn a vow of secrecy and our trap can stay hidden. We just have to hope for bad weather to get one more shot."

"Brilliant, Jacquie," said Danny, getting to his feet and clapping applause. "Bloody brilliant. Better than I could have imagined, and sixty quid very well spent. I'm assuming that's all of it, yes?"

"Well, there is one small other thing, Sarge," said Jacquie, her face and delivery giving away that the impending revelation could be perhaps, possibly, maybe touching on awkward. "We were getting along so famously that I might just perhaps have let something slip."

"Such as what?" asked Danny.

"I think I may have mentioned Templeton's nickname."

# Chapter 20

Carol was sat at the kitchen table with a cup of tea when she heard the front door open. It could be only one person, and a smile came automatically to her lips as she waited for her daughter to appear. Softly closing the front door behind her, Sarah made her way across the hall, paused briefly to look in on her dad snoozing in the front room, and finally came into the kitchen, where she knew without a shadow of doubt her mum would be.

"He looks very comfortable," said Sarah softly, inclining her head towards the sitting room. "Does he do that every afternoon?"

"Has been for months," said Carol, getting up to greet her daughter with a hug and a peck on the cheek. "Has a good hour or more after his dinner and still sleeps right through the night. I think it's his age catching up with him. Tired all the time and off his food a bit lately too, come to think of it. He manages to get down the bowling club twice a week, although maybe he just goes down there and sleeps all afternoon."

"He ought to go for a check-up," said Sarah. "Just to make sure there's nothing..."

"My word, no," scoffed Carol. "You know what your dad's like with doctors. He could be on his last legs and he still wouldn't go near one. It's a man thing in general, but your dad manages to take it to the extreme." She added a little laugh at her husband's expense. "Anyway, what brings you here at this time on a Monday?"

"Don't worry," said Sarah, "I'm not on the beg again. And I still feel awful about having to ask that last time."

"Stop being silly," said Carol. "I'm always happy to help whenever I can. And it makes me feel good. I wish I could do more but, well, you know how it is."

Sarah nodded. Money had always been tight for her parents. They'd had to scrimp and save their entire lives. Even so, her and her brother's childhood had never felt poor or in any way disadvantaged. Most importantly, they'd always been loved unconditionally. And beyond that, they'd never gone hungry, the house had always been warm when needed, and they'd always had clean clothes for school. "You two should be looking after yourselves first, you and Dad," she said. "And I ought to be able to cope without sponging. It's just that—"

"Things cost more these days," butted in Carol. "And there are lots more *things* to spend money on. Me and your dad never had to worry about a car, mobile phones, big-screen telly, and the rest. You kids never pestered us for expensive fancy trainers or computer games. And we were happy to live simply. I didn't even get a proper washing machine until after you were born, and as for the microwave, well, that thing was a proper waste of money." She laughed at her often-repeated joke.

Sarah joined in. "You're the best mum ever," she said. "You always were. And the best grandma the girls could hope for. Dad the same, and I just wish I could do something special for you both. Especially now."

"What does that mean?" asked Carol, cocking her head to one side. "I mean, the 'especially now' bit?"

Sarah stumbled a little in the start to her reply, but finally managed to get it out. "You're not getting any younger, either of you," she said. "And let's face it, as the years pass you won't be getting any more sprightly. So what I meant was, I wish I could do something for you now, when you're still young and fit enough to enjoy it."

Carol waved the thought away like she was wafting a mildly unpleasant smell out from under her nose. "We've got everything we need, pet. Believe me. So don't you start fretting to the contrary."

"But say I won the lottery?" asked Sarah. "Say I won millions – what would you want? A big house? A fancy car? A round-the-world cruise?"

"Your dad wouldn't even go on the coach for a day trip to Rhyl, let alone go cruising around the ruddy world for weeks on end. *And* he got sick in a rowboat on the park boating lake, so there's no way you'd get him on an ocean. And who needs a great big house at our time of life? I'd spend all my time cleaning."

"You'd have a cleaner," said Sarah, playing out the fantasy. "And a gardener, a chauffeur for your Rolls-Royce, a cook, servants to bring you cups of tea."

"They'd get under my feet and irritate your dad, so don't even think about it."

Sarah leaned forward and hugged her mum again before disengaging to wander slowly around the small kitchen, breathing in the warm familiarity of it and all the little bits and bobs that had been there her whole life. "Did you never want anything more, Mum? Honestly."

"No," said Carol without a moment of hesitation. "I wanted your dad from the first time I clapped eyes on him, and all I'd ever dreamed of was a handsome husband, a little house we could call home, and a couple of kids to make us a family. That was it. The lot. And I got it all."

"But there must have been times you *dreamed* of something more. Surely."

This time Carol's response stuck in her throat. She *had* dreamed of more and she knew she felt guilty for having done it, like she was somehow being unfaithful to her Roy in not considering their life and what they had together to be enough.

"You *have*, haven't you?" said Sarah, pouncing on the absence of an instant response to her question, but adding a crooked smile to make her accusation less sharp.

"Not exactly," began Carol hesitantly, "but sort of."

"I thought so," said Sarah.

"Meaning what?" asked Carol.

"You've been different these last few months," said Sarah. "There's been a glint in your eye, like you've suddenly got thirty years younger." She stopped and pulled an exaggerated 'thinking' expression before whispering hoarsely, "You're not having an affair, are you?"

Carol laughed, struggling to stifle the noise so as not to wake her sleeping husband in the next room. "No, no," she finally managed to stammer out, shaking her head and dabbing at the tears of laughter with a small hankie. "Good heavens, no."

"So what is it, then?" pressed Sarah. "Drugs? Alcohol? Joined the circus?"

"You wouldn't believe me if I told you," said Carol, finally getting her giggles under control. "So I'm not going to."

"Oh, come on, Mum. You can't leave it like that."

"Let's just say I've started to allocate a bit of my time to me as me. Not me as housewife, cook, cleaner, shopper. Or me as Mum or Grandma."

"Doing what, exactly?" asked the now clearly intrigued daughter.

"Well," began Carol, leaving a long pause to wind up the anticipation, "when your dad goes out for his afternoon of bowling, I take myself off on the train."

"And do what?"

"Something and nothing," replied Carol obscurely. "But whatever it is, it's something *I* want to do and not what some other bugger wants me to do. On those afternoons out, for a few brief hours I am Carol. Not Mrs Jackson. Not Mum. And not Grandma."

"I think that's great," said Sarah, leaning back in her chair to applaud silently and beam a broad smile at her mum. "And it's about time too."

"Well, I'm glad you approve," said Carol.

"I do," confirmed Sarah. "But could you please be Grandma on Friday afternoon? I need the girls picking up from school."

# Chapter 21

Detective Sergeant Danny Roberts was staring through the squad-room window again, but this time smiling broadly at the utterly foul weather beyond. A lead-grey sky was lowering above a bitter wind that was dotted through with spits of icy rain. May in Shropshire at its evil worst, and absolutely perfect for a Red Fox to go a-hunting. "Has to be," thought Danny, clenching a fist as he whispered the words aloud. "Has to be. His swansong. His last outing before the summer holiday break. A day like this simply had to be too good for him to pass up."

"He won't be able to resist it, will he?" said Jacquie, echoing her leader's thoughts and not needing to say to who she was referring. "This weather is so flaming awful he has to go for one last hurrah. I know he will. I can feel it in my bones."

"Are we all set and ready?" asked Danny, turning to look at Kevin.

"Good to go, Captain," replied the probationary DC, tipping an imaginary cap. "Most of the stations are still griping about it, saying they're having to keep a man out of front-line duties, but they're going to do it, although a couple of them raised the legal question about random stop-and-search."

"It's not random," growled Danny. "It is targeted. They can see that from the profile we've sent out, plus the fact we're only asking them to do it after a robbery."

"Still random according to some," replied Kevin. "Just lucky our man's not an ethnic minority or we'd not stand a chance of getting—"

He was cut off by the crash of the squad-room door being all but kicked open. Templeton stormed into their midst, face red to purple, eyes blazing. "Fucking muppets! Fucking useless fucking muppets!"

There was nothing anyone could say in response to the opening salvo, so nobody tried. The three simply stood and waited for whatever was coming next.

"I find it inconceivable," continued Templeton, absurdly fluttering his eyelids like a flirtatious young girl, but probably doing it so that he didn't have to look at the trio of disappointment before him, "that just three individuals, insignificant individuals, could so royally piss off so many people – people that matter."

The 'insignificant ones' stoically maintained their blank expressions.

"First and foremost, the ACC has recently had a new arsehole reamed by the chief constable after he was shat upon by the Home Office – yes, the fucking Home Office – regarding the stories somebody down there has been reading in that filthy bastard trash-rag the *Midwestern Echo*. Stories about us not doing our job. And they – all of them, all the way right up to the Home Secretary herself – want it sorted. In short and brutal little words that even you lot should be able to understand, they want this Red Fox caught and hanged before that cow Walsh gets to type another word."

"Did the ACC talk to the *Echo*'s editor?" asked Danny, knowing the answer but obviously not letting on.

"No," snapped Templeton. "Decided it could be construed as tantamount to interference with Press freedom. He's going to have a quiet word with one of the paper's directors at their golf club over the weekend. But that doesn't change anything. He knows you've let him down, and he will make sure you pay for it if this whole bloody shambles doesn't get put to bed pretty damned quickly. And next," continued Templeton, before anybody could say anything, not that any of them was planning to, "expenditure." He flapped a single sheet of paper in the air as he spoke. "I have been going through the numbers and, 'Good Golly, Miss Molly'," he was using a sing-song sarcastic tone now, "what is it that jumps off the page at me?"

The three dutifully shook their heads.

"Not only me," he continued, shaking his head sadly. "The chief super clocked it as well. And he – of fucking course he did – dropped a lovely little memo to our glorious ACC to very helpfully bring it to *his* attention." Templeton held out the paper flat in front of him like a choirboy preparing to sing a solo. Luckily, though, he only read. "One hundred and eighty-six billable forensic services hours running fingerprint checks on the notes recovered from the St Thomas Hospice. One hundred and eighty-fucking-six billable hours. Do you have any idea how much that cost? Any at all?"

More dismal head shaking from the audience.

"It cost more than the money we recovered!" shouted Templeton. "So we get the stolen cash back and you lot spend even more than that wasting everybody's time fingerprinting it when dozens, hundreds, probably fucking thousands of random people have handled it. So, come on, then, share with Uncle: which one of you bumbling, brain-dead numbskulls set that running?"

"I thought," began Danny, taking a half-step forward to confess, "it would make sense for when we get a suspect in the frame."

"Well, you thought wrong, and you pissed off me and him," Templeton jabbed a thumb in the 'upstairs' direction, "more than you could ever imagine. And we together want this wild goose chase stopped before any more of our precious budget money gets pissed away."

"Too late," croaked Danny. "They finished last night. They're sending through the results later today."

Templeton quietly screamed at the ceiling and did one of his heel-turn pirouettes. "In that case, Detective Sergeant, you will forthwith write an official memo for the file accepting full personal responsibility for the abhorrent waste of money, and clarifying that you did it without – no, *in spite of* – my express instruction. And you will have that on my desk before you go home tonight. Right?"

Danny nodded and took the half-step back into line.

"Now, as we're all having so much jolly fun," went on Templeton, "let us move on to item number three on the agenda. The hitherto oft-mentioned ACC is also getting major grief from forces up and down the local railway track concerning your half-arsed so-called 'Fox trap'. He's been fielding call after call from all and sundry raising questions of cost, manpower and jurisdiction, not to mention legal concerns over random stop-and-search. He wants it shut down. The whole fucking thing."

"But—" began Danny, only to be cut off.

"I haven't finished," snarled Templeton. "He agreed it would be too embarrassing for him if we were to pull the plug right now as it would look like he could be pressured into changing tactics by mere underlings. He needs—"

Templeton was cut off by Danny's desk telephone ringing loudly. Danny made to go to answer it, only to be snapped at by Templeton.

"Leave it!"

They stood and waited for the ringing to stop before Templeton took up where he had left off. "The ACC cannot be seen to be bowing to subordinate pressure. He needs to maintain his air of command. And besides, we all know that our Fox is going to go to ground come summer. No hoodie coat means no disguise, means no bank jobs. So the ACC has given his approval for it to stay in place until the end of this week. Oh, and—"

Again he was cut off by the phone ringing. This time Danny ignored it without being told to, and they all once again waited in silence for it to stop.

"As I was saying," continued Templeton, irritation at the interruptions adding a cold edge to his tone, "you, Detective Sergeant Roberts," he pointed a stiff, damning finger straight at Danny's face, "will personally call each and every station chief and therein *personally* apologise to them for the annoyance and upset you have caused with your idiotic pantomime. Is that understood?"

Danny nodded and bit his tongue. Maybe, if he kept his mouth shut and his head down, when all this was over he might just still hang on to his sergeant's stripes.

"Oh, and one last thing," said Templeton, making it sound like he'd only just thought of it, when they could all tell it was his idea of a big finale. "Who sent out the Fox trap memo with the suspect profile?"

"That was me," croaked Kevin, feebly raising his hand as he spoke, like a seven-year-old answering a difficult question in class.

"Lucky for you I checked it," said Templeton. "At least my diligence saved us from yet more embarrassment."

"Was there something wrong with it?" asked Danny, as much to shield his DC as anything else.

"Wrong?" laughed Templeton mirthlessly. "Wrong? As the team's DS you should be checking everything and anything a wet-behind-the-ears probationary DC puts out. And if you had, you would have seen the glaring omission."

"Which was?" asked Danny, genuinely not knowing.

Templeton reached into his jacket inside pocket and pulled out a folded sheet of paper, taking an annoying age to unfold and scan it. "'Approximate height: five feet and seven inches. Light build.' The end."

"And?" asked Danny, shaking his head in incomprehension.

"Male, you idiot," snapped Templeton. "Our Fox is male, masculine, a man. The psych profile was explicit on that. Hundred percent. And you missed it. Just lucky for you I corrected it this morning and immediately sent out the proper—"

The phone started ringing again.

"For flying fuck's sake," howled Templeton, "will somebody fucking-well answer that fucking phone!"

Danny jogged across to his desk and snatched up the receiver, answering with his rank and name and then listening attentively. The others watched on as his facial expression went from listening, through interpretation of what he was hearing, and finally on to a broad grin. Gently he replaced the receiver. He didn't move back to where he'd been standing a few seconds earlier. He simply stood at his desk to make the announcement they'd all been hoping for. "Bowlands Bank, Leominster," he intoned, "and no doubt it was the Red Fox: hoodie, tache, the lot. The locals just confirmed they'll have a PC at the station within the next five minutes. This is it!"

# Chapter 22

Carol was all but floating back to the station. The whole thing had gone like a dream, better than ever. She'd been on top of her game, everything smooth and controlled, and she'd been in and out in double-quick time. Even the moment when the sweet young cashier girl had whispered, "You're the Red Fox, aren't you? I can't wait to tell my mates I've met you", Carol had handled with aplomb. A short nod of confirmation and that was that.

The morning itself hadn't started too well, though. Roy had been quiet and withdrawn to the point of barely talking to her. At first she'd thought it was the lousy weather wrecking his bowling afternoon, but then he'd reminded her it was Alice Knight's funeral and he'd promised Trevor faithfully he'd be there.

"I hate bloody funerals," he confided, not that Carol had ever been in any doubt about his feelings on that score. "Morbid affairs at the best of 'em," he continued, "and I can't stand all the religious mumbo-jumbo claptrap. When you go, you're gone. End of."

Carol agreed with him and told him so. At least she didn't know the Knights well enough to go along, and his half-hearted ask that she went with him for moral support was easily brushed away.

He'd kissed her cheek, said he understood, but then surprised her a little by getting her to promise there wouldn't be "any ruddy voodoo nonsense" at his "burning".

She'd promised, of course, but with an added, "Same for me if I beat you to the oven."

They'd hugged each other for an unusually long time after that, and it had felt good. Like the old days. Like when they'd been younger. Like when life had been bloody tough but they'd faced it together as one. Where had the time gone? So quickly rushing by like the countryside hurtling past a train window.

And now her work for the day was done, and done more wonderfully than any day's work before. Maybe that last hug had calmed her with its deep warmth spreading through her veins and into her muscles, freeing her brain to work like a well-oiled machine while her nervous system crackled and fired. Yes, it had been brilliant, absolutely brilliant. Even her transformation from grey hoodie-coated robber to thoroughly harmless mustard-coated little old lady had been slicker than ever before. She'd scoped the alley on her scouting missions and it had been as empty as a eunuch's underpants when the time had come for it to fulfil its function. Fifteen seconds, it had taken her, maybe even less. Then it was out and merrily on her way. She'd been so elated that, on the spur of the moment, she'd decided to break with protocol and stop for a quick cuppa on her way back to the station. Her train wasn't due for another half-hour, so better to wait in a warm and cosy café than sit on a ruddy windswept platform. And it gave her the opportunity to grab a delicious currant bun to go with the brew.

Giving herself ten minutes to make sure she got to the station and onto the right platform for the ride home, she paid up and set off. It was less than a couple of hundred yards and she was dawdling along, softly humming to herself and barely paying any attention to anything beyond her feelings of elation. In through the familiar station entrance, onto the familiar station platform and...her heart flipped.

Just inside the gate, a tall, uniformed policeman was quite obviously monitoring the people as they filed in. Carol stopped, quickly pretending to look for something important in her shoulder bag as the other passengers eased their way around her. She knew precisely what was in her bag, of course, but she needed to create a moment to pause, watch and think. Her heartbeat was already around double what it should have been, and a thin nervous sweat was forming around her neckline. The policeman, barely a dozen paces ahead of her, was ushering most people straight past, which was good news. But every now and then he would stop somebody and ask to see in their bag. A diminutive young man a mere five or six places ahead of her dutifully opened his rucksack, holding the neck wide for the policeman to delve inside and poke about. A few muttered words and the youth was shown on through. This was not good, thought Carol. Not good at all. In fact, this was bad. Time to turn and walk away. Far away. Back into town to wait for a later train. Or maybe get the bus home. Or...

She was still processing the options when she realised that all the other travellers had now passed through and she was standing alone, like a sore thumb, with the policeman staring directly at her. It wasn't an accusatory stare, more inquisitive, or bemused, even. But it was him looking straight at her nonetheless. Could he see into her mind, into her deviant soul? Did he already know what she was, what was concealed in her bag? And if she turned and walked away, would he chase her down? And when he caught her, as he inevitably would, would he swallow a story of a lost ticket, a suddenly remembered appointment in town, or a purse stupidly left in the café? The blood was pounding in her ears now as that sense of soaring euphoria from just a few seconds before was sucked down into a quagmire of blind terror. Do it, Carol. Walk away. Turn around and slowly walk. Walk. Walk away to—

"Excuse me, madam." The voice was deep and controlled, but gentle.

Carol turned to look up at the policeman slowly walking towards her.

He closed the distance before speaking again. "Are you intending to catch a train?"

"I, er, I, maybe," replied Carol, desperately trying to keep her frantic brain and consequently quavering voice in check. "I-I'm a little bit c-confused, that's all." Great work, she thought, play the dotty old woman. No way would he ask to look in Nutty Nora's handbag. No way.

"May I enquire as to your intended destination?" he asked, leaning forward to speak to her in a softer voice. "If you don't mind."

"Crewe, I think," she lied in her most frail and squiffy of voices.

"And may I also enquire as to what business you have had in town today?"

"A nice cup of tea and a currant bun," replied Carol, adding a dopey lopsided grin for good measure.

"That sounds nice," said the policeman, with a smile and a series of small nods.

"It was," confirmed Carol, keeping her fingers crossed in one coat pocket that her acting was easing open the gates to freedom.

"One last thing, if you would be so kind," said the policeman. "Might I have a quick peek inside that bag of yours?"

This is it, thought Carol. The end of a glittering if short criminal career. Shot down in flames on a bastard railway station platform in Leominster of all places. "Really?" she asked, giving it one last shot at avoiding disaster.

"I'm sorry," said the policeman, sounding like he really did mean it, "but..." He didn't finish. He didn't need to.

Carol eased the bag off her shoulder and handed it across, looping the strap over the officer's outstretched wrist.

"Blow me, that's heavy," he gasped. "I'm surprised you don't do yourself a mischief carrying this load about. But, then again, my old mum's just the same," he continued in a jocular, chummy fashion. "Carries the kitchen sink around with her, she does. Whatever you might need, she's always got it in there somewhere."

Carol smiled and silently nodded. Nice story, she thought. Before prison.

"I need to look inside, if that's alright," said the policeman, waiting for Carol's nod of approval. He placed the bag down on the floor and bent to unzip the top and ease the sides apart. The first thing he could see were the black plimsolls she always wore when 'doing' a bank. "Been to the gym, have we?" he asked, twisting his neck to look up at her and grin to show he was pulling her leg.

"New shoes," replied Carol, lifting one foot off the ground to indicate her mustard kitten heels. "Rubbing bad, they are. Brought the plimsolls along to change into if it got unbearable. Can't be doing with blisters at my age." Keep it chatty, she thought. Maybe, just maybe, he'll get fed up and tell me to get lost before he finds the money, the moustache and glasses, the gun.

"Is that a Sainsbury's bag underneath there?" he asked.

"Yes," she croaked. "Yes, it is."

"And may I ask what's in it?"

Before she could answer they were interrupted by another man's voice behind her calling out, "What the hell are you doing, Edrich?"

The policeman snapped upright from his crouched position over the bag and Carol turned to see a second policeman striding towards them, this one with sergeant's chevrons on his arm.

"I'm—" began the first policeman, before being snapped off by the second.

"Males!" barked the newly arrived sergeant. "The instructions said males."

"The set I got said all—" pleaded the constable, before being cut off again.

"That was superseded this morning. If you spent as much time reading the daily duty sheets as you do the..." He stopped, turned to face Carol directly, and smiled. It was forced and sickly, but three out of ten for effort.

Carol smiled back and crossed her fingers again behind her back.

"I am sorry, madam," said the sergeant in his very best oily voice, "that my officer has inconvenienced you. Please accept our sincere apologies."

"Of course," said Carol, trying not to whoop and holler in relief. "Think nothing of it. Just doing your job, I suppose."

The constable hastily bent down to re-zip Carol's bag and lifted it gently onto her shoulder. "I'm sorry," he said, and clearly genuinely meaning it. "My mistake. Anyway, you have a safe and comfortable journey back to Crewe, ma'am."

"Thank you, Officer," said Carol, turning to walk away.

"Oh, one last thing," said the policeman, calling after her. "What *have* you got in there that makes it so flippin' heavy?"

"A gun," replied Carol over her shoulder.

They both laughed.

# Chapter 23

Wednesday morning, and the mood inside the squad room was as dismal as the weather still was outside. The Fox trap had royally bombed. Despite getting an officer to Leominster Station within little more than fifteen minutes of the robbery at Bowlands Bank, the stop-and-search had turned up a big fat zero.

To make things even worse, the *Midwestern Echo* had somehow picked up the story in time for their weekly edition. Percy Walsh may have been Jacquie's superstar crush, and she may very well have kept her promise not to reveal the Red Fox train-travel link, but she still didn't hold back when it came to putting the boot into her friendly local police force. The banner headline of 'Fox 6 – Plod 0' was bad enough, but the 'Oh dear, Shirley' beneath it was plain cruel, even if very funny. At least she'd done a good job in concealing Jacquie's accidental leak by saying that Templeton had acquired the nickname at the very beginning of his police academy days, where his, quote, 'diminutive stature and curly blond hair had rekindled memories of the 1950s Hollywood child star Shirley Temple', unquote. The rest of the article was much as before, digging at police ineptitude when faced with an admittedly cunning but still merely provincial bank robber. However, as Danny and the others had sadly agreed, if the Home Office had done a big pile of doo-doos on the Fourshires Constabulary's top brass on account of the earlier stories, this one was going to bring forth gushing diarrhoea. And, as runny shit travels downhill very quickly, it was only a matter of time before it arrived in their laps.

That said, submersion in crap was a small negative compared to the massive sense of failure that had enveloped the three worthy foot soldiers. Twenty-four hours before, they really had thought they were on the way to laying fingers on their villain's collar, only for nothing whatsoever to materialise. At least they'd managed to quickly snaffle the CCTV tapes from Leominster Station, but that was all. Most of the trains stopping there in the three-hour window after the robbery weren't fitted with any recording devices at all, meaning if Mr Fox had indeed caught a train home, they were never going to know. It was a reality that only served to deepen the depression.

So there they sat, three lost souls cast adrift in a sea of despondency whilst desperately trying to keep busy to save themselves from collective suicide. Kevin, continuing his grind through the CCTV footage, had already done the tapes from inside and outside the bank, along with as much feed as he'd managed to collect from around town, and so was now down to the last of it from the station platform cameras. Jacquie was typing up her gathered witness statements from the day before, while Danny wrote and re-wrote his formal apology to the police forces he'd persuaded and/or coerced into helping set up the Fox trap, whilst confirming to them that the operation had henceforth been shelved indefinitely. He'd already written and filed his required memo to formally state that he alone had – without approval and in direct contradiction to the explicit orders of his superior officer – personally and recklessly authorised the budget spend on forensic analysis of the recovered stolen money. Templeton had drafted the key words for him to make sure none of the most damning adjectives, adverbs, and so on were in any way diluted or "euphemised", as Templeton had referred to it. And with the confession written and passed across, Shithead Shirley had added his confirmatory cover letter and clipped them both together into the official file. He'd been grinning as he'd done it, and took the time to suggest that Danny's sergeant's rank was hanging by a thread. All Danny could think of was hanging Shirley by his bollocks – if he had any.

"Anything?" asked Danny, looking across at Kevin hunched over his computer monitor. He wasn't expecting anything; he just needed a break.

"Nothing," replied Kevin, his voice heavy with weary frustration. "The usual stuff from the bank. Pitches up in the hoodie and ambles inside, where he never looks at the cameras. Then comes out, wanders slowly away until he slips into an alleyway and disappears. Poof! Just like that."

"Anything else around town?" asked Danny. "Before or after?"

"He definitely seems to be coming up from the station," sighed Kevin, "but after the alleyway, zilch. I've only just started on the station footage, and nought there either, so far. I'll keep going for another two hours after the robbery, and if there's no joy there I'll look back to earlier, just in case I can spot him coming in. But I don't hold out much hope, though. This guy's simply too good to foul up like that."

"It has to be a disguise," said Jacquie. "Like Percy said. The moustache and glasses, yes, that makes sense. But maybe the coat too. Maybe somehow he swaps coats on the way from the station to the bank and then again on the way back."

"So he'd have to have an accomplice," said Kevin. "That hoodie coat is too damned bulky to stash. We can all see that. In which case, the accomplice would have to carry it there and away, and I've not seen anything that would fit that scenario." He let loose an elongated animal howl of frustration. "Nothing at all."

"And I looked up and down the latest alley he disappeared into," added Jacquie. "Took a load of pics and a video on my phone if you want to see for yourself. There is nowhere down there he could have hidden anything. Just like all the others."

As if the day wasn't already bad enough, the door swung open and in breezed the short-arsed, curly-blond-haired personification of doom, snarling audibly as it made its way to the centre of the room. Two pirouettes for today, just in case the worms hadn't spotted it coming in, and then it spoke. "Righty-ho, okay, fuckwits," it began. "That is it. Time's up. You're done. Washed up. Finished."

The three sat or stood, wherever they were, whatever pose they'd been in when Templeton had entered, and stayed like it: a tableau frozen in time.

"You've had your chances, lots of them, and you have royally pissed them all away. Down the drain. Off and away to the sea. Gone. Never to return. And meanwhile, in the process, you have managed to get right up every senior officer's nose from the very north to the very south of our wonderful, mostly rural patch, whilst delivering – now, let me think for a moment..." He paused to theatrically count his fingers. "Oh yes: sweet fuck nothing."

Nobody said a word. Nobody moved.

"How's that cringing apology for wasting everybody's time setting up a hopeless, pathetic, pointless and laughter-inducing trap coming along, Detective Sergeant? I want it sent out before you even think about going home, and I want to see it before it gets sent. Understood?"

"Nearly there, sir," said Danny, forcing the words out between clenched teeth.

"And when you've done that, you can take this down." Templeton wafted a hand at the investigation board. "Get it all packaged up and sent up to Winsford. They're taking over as of next Monday, whereupon you shower will be reassigned as the chief superintendent sees fit. If I had my way, you'd all be stacking shelves in Aldi after this shambles of a nothing investigation, but, lucky for you, it's not up to me."

Still not a sound.

"So you've decided to play the silent card, eh?" said Templeton, nodding like a plastic dog on the rear shelf of a car as he gazed slowly around the room. "Probably for the best, actually, given the situation. Oh, and if I thought for one microsecond that it was one of you who had leaked the wholly inaccurate and quite frankly insulting nickname to the press, I would have your neck on the block faster than you could say 'blink'."

Funereal silence.

Templeton looked around the room one more time before sidling towards the door, where he suddenly stopped, held the pose for a second or two, before turning to face them. "I am going to have that bitch," he snarled, not needing to explain precisely to who he was referring. "She thinks she's so bloody clever, so smart, so fucking funny. She seems to think she can write insulting, libellous garbage week after week and get away with it. But, mark my words, she will rue the day she pissed on my shoes. One way or another, one day or another, I will have her." And with that, he was off and away.

The three waited in continued static silence until they were sure he was well out of earshot before releasing a loud collective exhale of held breaths.

"That went well," said Danny, bringing forth howls of gurgling choking laughter. "Time for the pub, I reckon," he added as soon as they'd calmed down a bit.

"Later," said Jacquie. "Right now we've got things that need doing. You have to get your – what was it? – cringing letter of apology written and I ought to set about getting the ruddy board taken down and boxed up, along with all the interview files."

"And I'd better get the CCTV videos boxed up," said Kevin. "Although to be honest, I'll be bloomin' glad to see the back of them. My girlfriend says I've been talking about them in my sleep."

"You're sleeping together?" said Danny in mock moral outrage.

Kevin ignored the jibe and sat himself back down at his computer screen, on which the Leominster Station CCTV footage was still running. He reached out a hand to kill the tape, but froze. Then he stared at the screen, shook his head, leaned forward, and stared again. "Hang on," he breathed, just loud enough for the other two to stop what they were doing and look at him. "Hang on a mo," he repeated, a little louder but with the same trance-like tone in his voice. He pressed pause on the player and stared closely at the image frozen static on the screen.

By now the others were already at his shoulders, one on either side, leaning in to look at the fuzzy black-and-white image on the screen. It was a tall police constable leaning over as he talked to what looked like a short, elderly lady swathed in a large overcoat and hat.

Kevin reached out a finger and tapped the screen lightly over the woman's image. "I've seen her before."

# Chapter 24

The questions came crashing in like a tidal wave around Kevin's ears: where, when, are you sure, what are you saying?

"I'm certain," said Kevin, waving his palms above his head in a plea for the interrogation to hang on a moment. "I have seen her before. And not just the once. I'm sure of it."

Again the avalanche of questions.

"Stop, please stop!" shouted Kevin. "I can't give you answers to most of what you're asking. All I can tell you is, this woman," he tapped a fingernail on the screen again, "or somebody who looks very like her, has been at more than one other robbery location on the day they went down. I told you, I've been dreaming – no, *nightmaring* – about these bastard videos, and I know I have seen her before."

"How quickly can you find her again?" asked Danny, gasping in his breaths to control the chest-constricting physical effect of sudden surging optimism. Forcing himself to calm down and try to stay professional, he added, "Are we talking hours or days?"

"Probably hours. Two, three, maybe four."

"And if we all look? Split the work up, share it out?"

"Less, but not hugely. I know how to run them, where to look, how to scan at a faster speed. Look, give me, say, two hours on my own in absolute peace and quiet, and I'll find you something. Alright?"

"You've got a deal," said Danny, patting his new superhero on the shoulder. He checked his watch. "Let's make it one o'clock to sit down together and hear what you've got – unless, of course, you crack the case before then. Meantime, grab me a screenshot of what you've got up there now, and I'll get onto Leominster and see if I can have a chat with that copper who was talking to her and find out what, if anything, he saw in her bag. And, fingers crossed, he ought to be able to give us a better description. He may even know where she was headed."

"If it is a 'she'," said Jacquie softly. "I mean, yes, Percy Walsh reckoned our Fox could be a Vixen, but what if it's the other way round? I mean, what if our man disguises himself as an old woman to melt away?"

"Good point," said Danny. "Very good point. But let's not jump the gun. For a start, until our Kev's done the hard graft, we don't have anything to show for sure that this person is there at multiple robbery events. And even then, if we do convince ourselves that he/she is there more than once, it could still be sheer coincidence, although I know none of us believe in that. But it still makes for nothing more than a lead. He/she could be an accomplice, our boy's mum, anything. So let's stay calm, stay focused, and do our job. Be excited, yes. Positive, definitely. But do not get carried away until we have something. Okay?"

"Got it!" came the shouted response.

It was nudging towards a quarter to one when Kevin stood up and announced to the room that he'd got enough. It was time to share. Danny and Jacquie dragged their chairs across to sit perched on either side of Kevin, ready for the big reveal.

He hot-keyed the screen to the picture they'd seen earlier. It was still fuzzy and the elderly woman was facing away from the camera, so no sign of any facial features. She also had her coat collar turned up and her hat pulled down to expose as little as possible. Not overly unreasonable given the weather that day, until one factored in the need to conceal of an escaping bank robber.

Kevin fast-spooled the video back to show their 'person of interest' entering the station, and then set it to real-life speed for them to watch what happened next. She came to the platform gate, then suddenly stopped, presumably when she noticed the crowd and/or the police constable. It was suspicious behaviour. They all knew it, but nobody made a sound. After stopping, she began rummaging in her shoulder bag as the other travellers moved around her and dispersed along the platform. Then the constable approached and engaged her. They talked for a few moments before he took her bag and began looking inside. Then another uniformed police officer, clearly identifiable as a sergeant, approached, words were exchanged between the two policemen, whereafter the woman was handed back her bag and waved on through to the body of the platform.

"What happened there?" asked Kevin, looking at Danny. "Did you manage to get hold of that Uniform?"

"I did indeed," replied Danny. "But I'll save my bit to last, assuming you have something more for us."

Kevin didn't respond, merely turning back to his computer and hot-keying to a new screen. "Shrewsbury, same date and approximate time of job two," he said, pointing at the screen and what looked clearly like the same elderly woman: same basic outline shape, same coat, same hat, same shoulder bag. Another hot key. "Telford, job three." There she was again. Another clack of the keyboard and, "Nantwich, job five."

"It's her," cooed Danny. "It's bloody her. Holy shit. She's there every time."

"Him or her," corrected Jacquie.

"There's more," said Kevin, now sounding just ever so slightly smug. "Are you ready for the big reveal?"

"Hit me," commanded Danny.

This time Kevin pulled up a new file. It was, he explained, an edited-together clip of extracts from several different CCTV feeds around the second Shrewsbury robbery. The two on his shoulders leaned in close to make sure they didn't miss a thing.

Kevin pressed play and then provided the voice-over commentary. "Here's our man, Mr Red Fox, coming out of the bank. He walks slowly down the street, making sure to keep his face turned away from all the many different cameras along the way, and there he goes into the alley. Tick-tock, tick-tock, and a mere twenty-four seconds later, who should come out of there but...?"

"Granny Fox," hissed Danny, clenching a fist into an understated pump. "Others?" he asked, not needing to lay out the question in full.

"Three so far," replied Kevin. "I thought that was enough to make the point and you'd prefer to hear sooner with less rather than later with a full house."

"And you were right," replied Danny. "So—"

"I've just had a thought," interrupted Jacquie. She leaned across Kevin to pull a sheet of blank paper onto his desk, snatched up a pencil, and started to sketch. "Basic shape of our Mr Fox," she said, drawing a vague outline of his hoodie coat. "And now," she continued, "the basic shape of our new movie star, *Granny* Fox."

The likeness was so remarkable that both of her male colleagues could instantly see what she was getting at, but the final link remained elusive until Jacquie explained.

"He flips the coat inside out."

"Stone me, yes," said Danny, slapping a flat palm on his forehead. "Of course."

"Shit!" cursed Kevin. "Why didn't I spot that before?"

"No reason you should," consoled Danny. "So don't beat yourself up about it. Just keep reminding yourself that it was you who spotted our missing link."

"Thanks, Sarge," said Kevin, turning around to face his leader. "Now, are you going to tell us what you got from Leominster Police?"

"PC Brian Edrich," began Danny, "sounded like a decent copper. Twenty-plus years and very happy doing what he does. Best of all, he remembered our granny, but I won't tell you why until the end. Okay?"

Two nodding heads told him to get on with it.

"He couldn't give me a physical description beyond 'little old lady' because, he said, they all look the same to him. And she was well wrapped up in her coat and hat and all. He said she was a bit odd, strange, 'kooky' was the exact word he used, but nice enough. No stammer that he recalled, which isn't really a big surprise, but definitely a local accent. And, yes, he did look inside her bag. Well, he *started to*, but then his sarge rolled up and gave him a dressing down for not having read the updated stop-and-search profile."

"What?" asked Jacquie.

"Seems he'd gone down there with Kev's first version," replied Danny, shaking his head sadly as he explained. "He hadn't picked up the new one that our Shirley had sent out saying that it was only males to be checked. He told me he'd just started looking inside the bag when he was told in no uncertain terms to stop it."

"Did he see anything at all?" asked Kevin.

"A pair of black plimsolls and a Sainsbury's plastic bag."

"Tick and tick," said Jacquie, air-gesturing the motion of putting two big ticks in two critical boxes.

"But he was certain it was a woman," said Kevin. "And an old woman at that."

"Yes and no," replied Danny. "Again he stressed she was all bundled up against the crappy weather. And the voice was thin and croaky. He was quite honest about it, saying he couldn't be one hundred percent certain about it being either a woman or an old one. He said his overall *impression* was 'little old lady', but he wouldn't swear to it. And besides that, he said her bag weighed a ton and he remembered being shocked that a little old lady could manage its weight."

"So we could still be looking at a little bloke of indeterminate age in a cunning disguise, right?" said Jacquie.

"Right," confirmed Danny.

"And are you now going to tell us the surprise ending?" she asked.

Danny laughed before responding. "When PC Edrich gave her back her bag, he jokingly asked her what she had in there that made it so flipping heavy. And do you know what she said? No, please don't guess, because I am going to tell you. Casually, over her shoulder as she wandered away, she said, 'A gun.'"

Kevin and Jacquie mirrored each other as their jaws sagged and they laughed dry, humourless laughter. Had they really been that close to snaring the Red Fox on what was probably – no, almost certainly – his last job for the season? Worse still, they all knew that if their Fox had been so close to capture, maybe it would send the clearest of messages that it was time to either move elsewhere or simply give up altogether. It had been a chance missed that they would, in all probability, never get again.

"I don't suppose he asked where she was going, did he?" asked Jacquie.

"He did," replied Danny, "and she said Crewe. But let's face it, if he/she had just robbed a bank and had a squeaky-bum narrow escape from The Law, would she tell him the truth? I think not. In fact, I know not."

"So we've got no way of knowing where he/she went," groaned Kevin. "One, we don't know for certain they got on a train, and two, none of the trains around that time had any CCTV recording equipment on board. Oh, and three, we're too late already to have any hope of getting CCTV from stations up and down the line to see where they got off. It will all have been overwritten by now."

"So basically, we're screwed," said Jacquie. "Yes, we've got what seems like a possible suspect in the frame. We might just have an idea of how he/she disappears by using a reversible coat, but we still don't know for sure gender or age, and we don't have a face either on film or from an eyewitness description. And to cap all that, we have no idea of where to start looking."

"Oh yes we do," said Danny mysteriously. "I know exactly where to look."

"How?" asked Kevin. "I mean, how could you know where Granny Fox got off the train, assuming she did get on one?"

"Remember I told you about a very wise old copper I worked with way back when, the best I ever knew?" asked Danny.

"Sort of," said Kevin.

"The 'Look for the Gaps' bloke?" asked Jacquie.

"Indeed, yes," said Danny, getting to his feet and walking across to the still-in-place investigation board. "Arthur told me over and over again, *ad nauseum*, that he'd solved as many if not more cases using the gaps in the evidence as he did *with* the evidence. And that, my dear friends, is the key."

"Oh, come on, get on with it," urged Jacquie. "Just tell us."

Danny raised a finger to point at the map. "Our train line," he said, tracing the marked railway line all the way from Crewe down to Hereford. "And the stops along the track at towns that have banks." He tapped a finger on each marked cross, one by one. "Now," he continued, very deliberately stringing it out, "here are the banks that Granny Fox has hit." Again he tapped the robbery crosses before turning to his enthralled but increasingly impatient audience and held his hands out. "Spot the gap."

"Whitchurch," said Jacquie.

"Correct!" exclaimed Danny. "Give the lady a prize. Whitchurch is the only town along this bit of railway line that has a bank but has not had a robbery. And what do we know about the hunting habits of foxes?" he asked.

It was Kevin's turn to answer. "They never hunt on their own doorstep."

# Chapter 25

Carol's insides were going up and down like a very small boat on a very rough sea. One minute she was high as could be, her blood surging with the rush of triumphant exhilaration from the previous day's oh-so-smooth and successful bank job in Leominster. But a moment later she was crashing down, almost literally quaking with fear as she relived her near-to-catastrophic brush with the policeman at the station. Then it was up, up, up again as she played back the fortuitous intervention that saved her bag full of incriminating evidence from being properly searched, and the way she'd walked away from the jaws of defeat, casually tossing the policeman a wickedly risky answer to his question as to why her bag was so heavy. She whispered the phrase aloud to her empty kitchen – "A gun" – and immediately burst into uncontrollable laughter.

"What are you laughing at in there?" asked Roy, calling the question through from the sitting room, where he'd taken himself off to read his latest copy of *Bowling Monthly*. "You're not going doolally, are you?" he added with a chuckle.

"I think I might be," she called back. "But don't worry. I'll still have your tea on the table at half past five."

"Good girl," he shouted back. "Nutty as a fruitcake, but still reliable."

Carol smiled at her other self in the kitchen window and the two winked knowingly at each other. They'd been doing that a lot lately: enjoying their shared secret. And she'd been talking to her reflection more frequently as well these days. Maybe she *had* gone doolally. Robbing banks? Taunting a police officer? No wholly sane old lady would be doing that, would she? And no wholly sane old lady would carry on robbing banks after such a close shave. Perhaps it *was* time to hang up the moustache and live out her days taking the odd slice of excitement just from the memory of it. The weather would be too good to be out and about in a hoodie coat anyway for the next few months, and by the time it got back to robbery weather she'd be seventy. Yes, it probably was time to stop. But then again, that Mary whatever-her-name-was on the telly baking programme was ninety-odd, so they said, and she hadn't stopped doing what she was good at. So, on second thoughts, Carol, don't make any rush decisions just yet. Wait until the lousy weather comes around again and see how you feel then. And for now, keep your options open.

Of course, she suddenly thought, she could give up the actual robbing and spend her time instead doing what all celebrities did, the famous and the notorious: write a book, a biography. Lay it all out: just how clever she'd been, how she'd fooled the police, and how she'd given the money away to good causes. It would make a good read. She'd have to do it anonymously, though. What did they call it? Ghost-writing? No, that would be if somebody else wrote it for her. Now that *was* a good idea. Get a professional writer to tell her story for her, all grammatically correct and spelled right. And she'd always been lousy at punctuation. *The Red Fox Diaries*, that's what they'd call it. Imagine walking past the bookshop in town and seeing it in the window. Better still would be when they made it into a movie. Then the whole world would be able to watch it and see that anyone – whatever sex, age or social background – could achieve something special if they put their minds to it. What a blast, as Bethany would say. Grandma up there on the big screen. She'd have to insist they picked someone glamorous to play her. But, then again, if she was still an unidentified villain at large, she wouldn't be able to—

The flowing fantasy was brutally cut short by an urgent tapping at the back-door window. Carol bent to get a good look. It was Janice again, thankfully not wearing the Zorro mask this time, but still there, hunched furtively at the back door, peering in through the window between swift, nervous glances to her left and right.

Carol opened the door just a crack. "Yes?" she asked, like a housemaid at a stately home cautiously enquiring of an unexpected visitor. "How may I help you?"

"Don't you ever answer your ruddy mobile phone?" hissed Janice.

"I can't remember where I left it," replied Carol honestly.

"Bloody hell! Get outside, now!" commanded Janice, still in her hissy snake voice.

"Wouldn't you rather come in?" asked Carol. "It's bloomin' cold out there."

"No. Your Roy's home. I know he is."

"What difference does that make?"

"He doesn't like me, and before you say, 'Nonsense', I know he doesn't. And anyway, I want to talk to you in private without the risk of him or anybody else overhearing."

Carol shrugged. "I'll get a jacket."

"Make it quick," demanded Janice.

Carol collected her jacket from the hall, and on the way back to the kitchen poked her head into the sitting room to let her husband know she was popping out to the shed to reorganise the freezer. His response of a single grunt was what she'd hoped for: he wouldn't be disturbing anyone for at least the next half-hour.

Stepping out into the backyard, she pulled the door softly closed behind her and stood, arms folded across her chest. "Well, go on, then," she said, knowing with a very high degree of certainty what it was that her friend was so agitated about.

"How did you know?" demanded Janice, still speaking in her ridiculous 'secret agent' hoarse whisper. "About the robbery in Leominster?"

Carol shrugged, made a face, and said nothing.

"You know him, don't you?" continued Janice, leaning up close so she could keep her voice low but still make her interrogation sound aggressive. "You have to."

Carol sighed, a mixture of infuriation and weary exasperation. "I told you, last Thursday afternoon. I showed you. I explained it all."

"But it was all dog shit," retorted Janice indelicately, adding a pig-snort of derision for good measure. "It had to be. Little old ladies don't rob banks."

"Who says?"

"The world says," snapped Janice, thankfully at last speaking in a normal voice. "It just doesn't happen. Ever! Little old ladies sit at home, drink tea, and knit between snoozes. Occasionally one of them might morph into an amateur sleuth, but they don't go roaming around the country robbing bloody banks."

"I did," said Carol with another shrug.

"You're nuts, bonkers, bananas."

"What, to do it?" asked Carol, a crooked grin on her face now as she sensed her friend's onslaught running out of steam.

"No," replied Janice, shaking her head wildly but beginning to also see the funny side of the exchange. "For believing it's actually you doing it."

"Do you want to see the money?" asked Carol casually.

"Piss off!"

"That's not very ladylike," sniffed Carol in her finest haughty tone.

"I don't feel very ladylike when my supposed best friend is taking the mick."

"Do you want to see it or not?"

"Aw, go on, then," sighed Janice. "And if it's play money – you know, fake like your gun and glasses and that horrible ginger dead caterpillar moustache thing – I shall never speak to you again. Ever."

"That could be a blessing," said Carol over her shoulder, chuckling as she led her friend the few short yards across to the lean-to shed and the freezer within. She unhooked the key from its hiding place on a nail around the side, unlocked the door, and switched on the light. "Are you sure you're ready for this?" she asked. "You know that once you've seen it, you're an accomplice."

"You're trying to scare me into saying I don't want to see it, because then you won't have to show me what isn't there. That's it, isn't it? Well, ha! No dice. Show me, and show me right now."

Carol reached into the freezer and extracted the tofu curry plastic box, holding it out in front of her like the third Wise Man presenting his myrrh. "Do you want to open it, or…?"

"Tofu sodding curry?" said Janice, twisting her face into an expression of absolute disgust. "That sounds utterly foul."

"It's meant to," said Carol. "That's the whole point of hiding something. Anybody who looked in here would see the label and probably gag rather than look inside. For sure my Roy wouldn't open it, but then again, I'm not totally certain he even knows where the freezer is. So, do you want to open it?"

"You do it," said Janice, the excitement now quite obviously bubbling inside her, but still with a hint of expecting to be proved right about it all being a hoax.

Carol duly clicked open the box and folded the lid back.

The response from Janice was near-as-damn-it instant, as she gasped in a huge lungful of air. She held it for a second or two before letting it go, taking a few short, gulped breaths and finally finding some words. "Fuck me! Fucking fuck. Oh fucking fuck, fuck. You…" She stopped speaking and stared open-mouthed at her friend, the now-confirmed bank robber.

"What a highly eloquent response, Miss Brontë," joked Carol sarcastically.

"You really are for fucking real," continued the goggle-eyed Janice, rapidly switching her gawping stare from the money to Carol and back again. "How much is it?"

"I haven't had the time to count it yet, but I reckon around five, maybe six."

"Thousand?" gasped Janice. "Pounds?"

Carol nodded. "I know it doesn't sound that much to a rich widow-woman like you, but five and a half is, apparently, the average take from a bank-cashier robbery in England. And so far I'm actually hitting a little bit above that."

"Now you're gloating," said Janice. "It doesn't become you."

"Sorry," said Carol. "I'll try to be better in future."

"That was the sixth yesterday, wasn't it," said Janice, speaking it as a statement of fact. "I read it on the *Midwestern Echo* website. 'Fox 6 – Plod 0' was the headline." She laughed, a short and thankfully suppressed cackle. "I really am in love with that Percy Walsh bloke who writes it. He gave the rozzer in charge another brilliantly savage kicking this week. He says this dopey detective inspector chappie is nicknamed 'Shirley', like, as in Shirley Temple."

Carol didn't know any of it, but it sounded amusing enough.

"And right now, at this moment," continued Janice, unfazed by the lack of any response from her friend, "I am exceedingly happy that he's a crap copper, because it means he won't catch my best mate, the notorious and brilliantly cunning Red Fox."

This time Carol smiled broadly at the praise being heaped upon her, but still said nothing as she made to tuck her money-safe back into its temporary hiding place.

"Ooh," squealed Janice, "before you do that, can I touch it?"

Carol laughed and held the box out for Janice to lightly rest the tips of two fingers on the uppermost note.

"You, Carol Jackson née Garton," said Janice, her voice quavering with emotion, "are one utterly amazing, brilliant, stupendous, fan-fucking-tastic piece of work, and I have never before, ever in my whole entire extended life, been so bloody, bastard proud of anyone I actually know, let alone am friends with."

"I thank you," replied Carol with a bobbed curtsy. "So in return, when they make the film of my life, I shall make sure that you get played by somebody super hot like, ooh, Julia Roberts or Scarlett Johansson or—"

"I'm more of a Halle Berry," said Janice, wobbling her head from side to side, fluttering her eyelids and pouting horribly.

"She's black," retorted Carol.

"Doesn't matter," scoffed Janice. "Not these days. And I rather fancy being portrayed as a gorgeous, super-hot black babe. And it would help to hide my true identity." She let the image float around her for a few glassy-eyed moments before looking at Carol. "Who's going to play you in this blockbuster?" she asked.

Carol ducked the question. "Fancy a cup of tea while you're here?" she asked, locking the shed door and re-hanging the key on its nail.

"Can't tempt you down the pub for a proper drink, then?" wheedled Janice. "I ruddy well need one after the last few minutes, and you could come along and watch."

"Thanks, but no," replied Carol. "I've got to spend some time thinking about who's going to be the lucky beneficiary this time. Giving money away is nowhere near as easy as most people would think."

"You really don't keep any of it, do you?" said Janice.

"No, I don't," replied Carol, shaking her head. "Not a penny."

"Why not?" asked Janice. "It's not as if you're well off. I mean, a few extra quid would make a big difference to you and Roy." The way she asked the question and the tone she used suggested she probably already knew the answer but needed to hear her friend say it.

"Because," said Carol, "keeping it would be dishonest."

# Chapter 26

Danny and Kevin were in the office and hard at it well before eight o'clock on the Thursday morning, despite all three colleagues having worked through, deep into the previous night. They'd divided up the mountain of collected CCTV recordings between them to speed up the search for more sightings of 'Granny Fox', as she'd now become known. Their primary aim was to show conclusively that she always appeared from the same point or close to where the Red Fox himself had disappeared moments before. And although they had agreed to keep an open mind on gender, the one thing they were absolutely certain of was that he or she escaped from the scene of the crime dressed as an elderly lady, complete with coat, hat, and, as Jacquie pointed out, low-heeled shoes.

Danny had ordered in fish and chips to keep them going, and the office lobby coffee machine took a hammering as they ground through the videos in near silence, apart from the occasional whoop of triumph at a new confirmed sighting. Each time one was found, Kevin took over to clip-copy the footage into a separate master file, making sure location, date and time stamps weren't compromised and the master file record was maintained so as to preserve each piece as presentable evidence.

The only disappointment had been their total inability to find any glimpse of Granny Fox's face. Not even a partial profile. The Fox was indeed not only a master of disguise and, they had to admit, an extremely proficient bank robber, but he/she was also quite brilliant at avoiding identification. There was no way it could have been by chance. No, this villain had scoped every job with a microscopic attention to detail that was utterly astounding, and Danny could feel a creeping sense of admiration for the predator he and the team were working so hard to capture and cage.

It was coming up midnight by the time the sixth and final 'Fox swap' had been nailed down, clipped and filed, and Danny formally called it a day. He would have liked to suggest a celebratory drink, but by that time everywhere was closed and he could see they were all on their chinstraps, so he merely sent them home with praise ringing in their ears and an exhortation to be revitalised and ready for a very special day ahead. They were, he'd told them, on the very brink.

Now refreshed after a surprisingly good night's sleep, and with his second coffee of the morning already inside him, Danny completed the typing up and filing of his interview with PC Edrich and the account of the constable's brush with their person of interest at Leominster Railway Station. He'd also earlier put in the file their current thinking on how the robber made his escape, including a pair of printed screenshots alongside Jacquie's sketches of the similarity in shape that had led her to guess at the reversible overcoat. Stretching in his chair to ease the tension in his upper back and neck, he glanced across at Kevin diligently re-checking the fruits of the previous evening's hard graft and making sure everything the Crown Prosecution Service might need was in order and ready for when they 'felt a collar'. It was coming, he was sure of that, and soon.

The phone on his desk rang and he snatched it up, hoping above all hopes it was what he'd been waiting for. It was. Jacquie was gushing down the line, the excitement in her voice making it near impossible for her to get the words out.

"You were right, Danny. Bloody hell, were you ever right!"

He'd known it was a longish shot but he'd been so sure that he'd asked Jacquie to head up to Whitchurch first thing to see if she could verify his hunch about it being Granny Fox's home destination. The previous afternoon, Kevin had quickly verified that there was no retained station platform CCTV, so it would be up to getting a person on the ground, looking for the evidence they needed.

"Calm down and tell me," instructed Danny, waving wildly at Kevin to come across and listen in. He switched the phone onto speaker just as Jacquie began.

"I took a guess that Granny Fox would be heading *into* town, so trawled the road in that direction, looking for cameras. First hit was an apartment block just down from the station. Six flats and a private car park out front that has a camera on it 24/7. I knocked up the janitor just after seven thirty – not a happy bunny – and very sweetly offered him the choice between giving me a quick look-see at the tapes or him making a visit to Ternbury Police Station within the next twenty-four hours. Easy choice, eh? Took me less than fifteen minutes to catch her walking past, heading into town."

"Did you keep the tape?" asked Danny.

"Yes, after a lot of hassle. Had to give him the cash to buy a new one. Arse."

"Great work, Jacquie. Any more?"

"You bet. There's an Indian restaurant on the corner at the crossroads and they've got more security cameras than Buckingham Palace. The owner was a real sweetie. Told me they'd had their front window smashed so many times the insurance company insisted they beef up their security. He said the police never follow it up but at least they know what the drunken bastards look like."

"And?" asked Danny, desperate to hear more good news.

"Have you ever had warm vegetable samosas and Darjeeling tea with a slice of lemon for breakfast? If not, you really should try it. It's amazing."

"Get on with it," growled Danny, being sure to make it sound playful.

"Granny Fox crosses at the lights and heads straight on towards the centre of town. And before you ask, she never faces the restaurant cameras, so still no sight of a face. That said, I've just walked down through town and it looks like a couple of the shops might have street-facing CCTV. No way to tell if they were working yesterday or at all, but I'm onto it. None of them open until nine-thirty or ten, so I'll have to hang around and you'll have to wait. I'll let you know as soon as I get anything. Oh, and is Kevin listening?"

"I'm here," said Kevin.

"There's what looks like a town CCTV camera covering the junction of Watergate and High Street. You might want to see if you can get hold of anything from it."

"Will do," said Kevin. "Great job, Jacq. And bring us back a samosa, will you?"

"Too late, mate. I ate them all. Speak later." She rang off before anybody could say another word.

"We need a street map of Whitchurch, Kev," said Danny, "to plot Foxy's route, camera by camera, street by street. Every sighting ought to narrow down his or her eventual destination. We just have to hope he doesn't do another one of his costume changes before he gets home."

"On it," said Kevin. "We're close, aren't we, Sarge."

"Very," purred Danny.

"This place stinks like a fucking chip shop." Templeton was suddenly in the room, nose wrinkled, sniffing at the air with a twisted look of intense distaste. It was as if he'd just popped up through a trapdoor like a pantomime villain, but there'd been no flash-bang and no cloud of smoke, so he must have walked in while they weren't watching.

"We did a late one last night," said Danny.

"And why is that still here?" snapped Templeton, totally ignoring his detective sergeant's words whilst jabbing a finger at the still laden investigation board. "I told you to get it all packed away and sent up to Winsford. And when I give an order, I expect it to be—"

"We made a breakthrough," interrupted Danny. "We're close to a—"

It was Templeton's turn to interrupt. "I thought I'd made it clear that 'upstairs' ordered we disengage from the case before you lot manage to transform a wretched disaster into an abject debacle. Did you not hear my explicit instructions, or did you simply not understand them?"

"We heard and we understood and we were on the point of complying when we – Kevin – spotted something that broke the case wide open. And I mean *wide* open."

Now that caught Templeton's attention. "Say more."

"Kevin was going through the Leominster Station CCTV and spotted a character he recognised from the other robbery locations. An elderly woman who—"

"Fuck...off!" sneered Templeton, spacing the two words far apart for maximum sarcastic effect. "You 'broke' the case?" He sang the phrase in a jokey little-girl voice. "You broke the case by spotting some old woman in a couple of the videos? Ha! Next thing you'll be telling me the Red Fox is..." He stopped dead, held the pause, then, "You're not going to, are you?"

"Not *exactly*," said Danny, refusing to back away despite feeling suddenly exposed. "But yes insofar as we've identified this same character at every robbery location."

"And it's an old lady, right?" Templeton was back to his sarcastic best. "Despite my university professor criminologist definitively stating our bank robber is a young male."

"He's *dressed up* as a little old lady," responded Danny. "It's a disguise." He decided it best not to add that they were still keeping an open mind as regards gender.

"And she's always there?" asked Templeton, intrigued now.

"Every time," replied Danny. "And Granny Fox, as we call her, always appears from the alley or side street where we lose sight of the Red Fox. So he goes in the alley and disappears, but a few seconds later Granny Fox suddenly pops out and toddles off to catch the train home."

"Show me," demanded Templeton.

Kevin was onto it like a flash, positioning himself at his desk monitor and pulling up one of his edited mash-up files. Templeton watched in silence as the robber strolled into the alleyway and precisely twenty-four seconds later an elderly woman with roughly the same silhouette wandered back out. Kevin stopped the video with Granny Fox stood static, mid freeze-frame.

"Zoom and enhance," commanded Templeton.

Kevin let loose a snort of laughter before choking it back.

"What?" demanded Templeton.

"That, er, 'zoom and enhance' thing," stumbled Kevin, "is, um, science fiction, sir. Yes, I know they do it in a lot of movies and TV shows, but you simply can't do it in real life. If I zoom in on this all I'll get is daubs. It's like looking at a close-up of the side of a Dalmatian dog."

Templeton forced a very obviously false laugh. "I knew that," he said. "Everybody knows that. Can't you spot a joke, Detective Constable?" He didn't wait for an answer, turning away from the insolent junior to look at Danny. "So you don't have a face, is that what you're saying?"

"Not yet," replied Danny. "But we could have very soon."

"And how, exactly, are you going to achieve this?" asked Templeton.

"We worked out that our person of interest took the train to Whitchurch after the robbery," said Danny, not bothering to try to explain how he'd arrived at that conclusion, "and we're currently working on the assumption that this is his home town. So DC Napier is up there now, tracing his footsteps from the station. Our hope is we'll be able to track him all the way to his lair."

"Den," corrected Templeton.

"And there's also a fair chance," continued Danny, ignoring his boss's pedantic and valueless interruption, "that at some point along the way, a hopefully increasingly relaxed Granny Fox may actually look at a ruddy camera and give us what we need."

"Good work, team," said Templeton for the first time ever. He glanced at his wristwatch. "Probably an appropriate moment for me to nip upstairs and share. Keep me informed every step of the way." He sailed across to the door before pausing to turn and look back at Danny. "How come your elaborately constructed trap didn't catch the little sod red-handed at Leominster Railway Station?"

Danny nearly bit through his tongue as he forced himself not to answer with the full story, saying only, "Our stop-and-search instructions said only males."

Templeton was away and gone before the answer had dissipated in the air, leaving the two other men alone in silence, staring at each other and making faces of disgust.

"Twat," breathed Danny.

Kevin nodded his agreement just as the phone rang. Danny snatched it up.

"Got her!" shrieked Jacquie down the line, almost before Danny had the receiver to his ear. He pressed it to loudspeaker just in time for Kevin to also catch the follow-up. "Got her, got her, got her, got her, got her!"

"Easy, tiger," pleaded Danny. "This old phone of mine won't last long if you keep screaming into it."

"Got her!" whispered Jacquie, but still with an exclamation mark.

"We're both listening," said Danny.

"A florist's shop on the road down into the centre had a street-facing CCTV and, yup, sure enough, there she goes: Granny Fox ambling happily past the window on her merry way home."

"And?" said Danny, knowing for sure there had to be more good news to come.

"Jenlow's the Butchers. Interior CCTV. Bullseye, jackpot," said Jacquie, the quaver in her voice giving away the imminent goal celebration.

"Tell," was all Danny could manage.

"The camera is only really there for the food hygiene inspectors so they can actually watch what goes on, but it also *incidentally* records customer activity, thereby also *incidentally* aiding a police officer with her inquiries."

"Go on. There's more, I know there is," said Danny, his voice half an octave higher than normal as the excitement gripped his larynx.

"Granny Fox – and I can now confirm it *is* she – just happens to pop in for a pound of Jenlow's prize-winning fat Cumberland sausages, a half-dozen rashers of excellent smoky back bacon, a slice of—"

"Get on with it," growled Danny.

"Not only does she look straight into the lovely, lovely camera," said Jacquie, struggling to hold it together long enough to deliver the punchline, "but Mr Jenlow, your friendly local quality butcher, personally knows her very well and has done for many years."

"So you...?" Danny couldn't get the question out. He didn't need to.

"Indeed I do," said Jacquie with a calmness belying her elation. "A face, a name and an address. So, assuming our Granny Fox really is the brilliantly transformed, notoriously cunning bank robber we have been chasing for months on end, I can now reveal that our Red Fox is none other than Mrs Carol Jackson of 5, Wharf Row Cottages, Whitchurch, Shropshire."

"Yes!" screamed Danny, punching the air with both fists.

"A very nice lady, according to the exceedingly helpful Mr Jenlow," continued Jacquie, the tone of her voice suggesting there was a cherry still to be put on top of this particular cake. "Oh, and my new favourite butcher also told me..." She stopped to wait for somebody to ask.

"What?" asked Danny dutifully.

Jacquie gave the smallest of chuckles before answering. "Next birthday, our Carol 'Red Fox' Jackson will be seventy years old."

# Chapter 27

With a name in the frame, so to speak, Danny and Kevin went into overdrive, accelerating towards the imminent arrest that they anticipated for sometime later that afternoon. First up was to verify that the given name linked up with the given address. It took Danny only minutes to confirm that Carol 'Granny Fox' Jackson did indeed live at 5, Wharf Row Cottages, the house she and her husband, Roy, had rented from the council for nigh on fifty years. A few minutes more and, with a little surprise, Danny discovered that Carol Jackson had no criminal record. The bigger surprise, given he had somehow subconsciously assumed that she'd been shown the ropes and maybe even put up to criminality by a close relative, was that her husband too had a squeaky-clean record.

It took the better part of an hour, with Kevin's help, to fill in more of the background. Roy and Carol Jackson had two adult children: a daughter living locally and a son who lived in Vancouver, Canada. Both of them had young families of their own and, again, neither had any history of lawbreaking. Carol had apparently not had a job since leaving school, while her husband had retired several years previously after working his entire adult life for the same engineering company in town. There was no record of either having applied for or used a credit card, and there was no sign of them ever having been in debt. The biggest shock to Danny, however, was that it appeared that neither of the Jacksons had ever possessed either a driving licence or a passport. All in all, the more they dug, the further their prime suspect shifted away from being a believable villain. There had to be something she or they were hiding, thought Danny. Nobody could be this off-grid and clean. He made a note to formally request access to their bank accounts and mobile telephone records, although he was beginning to think they might not have either.

Soon after one o'clock, Jacquie rolled triumphantly into the office to rapturous applause from her colleagues. She bowed and waved the two CCTV videos she'd collected like they were trophies at an awards ceremony.

Better still, she had in her possession – courtesy of the award-winning butcher's printer – a screenshot full-face picture of Granny Fox. It was the first time they'd come face to face with their robber, and it was something more than a shock.

"Doesn't exactly look a lot like a master criminal," said Danny, peering at the A4 sheet now taped, pride of place, in the centre of the investigation board.

"And this," said Kevin, pointing at his computer screen, "doesn't exactly look like the hideout for one either."

The others moved around to look at the Google Earth view of Wharf Row Cottages, with number 5 one from the end.

"So, what do we have?" asked Danny, as much to himself as to the others. "A sixty-nine-year-old, working-class wife, mother and grandmother with not even a hint of a criminal record living in a small rented cottage and with no car or passport."

"Has to be a front," said Jacquie. "I mean, she has to be living a second life somehow, somewhere. Right?" She looked pleadingly at her colleagues, hoping for them to back up her suggestion.

"Where?" asked Danny, holding his palms open to emphasise his question. "And how? There is nothing – and I repeat, nothing – anywhere that suggests she's anything other than what she looks like."

"Apart from," continued Kevin, "we know she most probably robs banks."

"And gives the money away," added Jacquie for completeness. "If I was genuinely living in that little cottage I'd keep at least some of it. Wouldn't you?"

"You'd think so," said Danny, "but who knows what's going on here? Everything else feels wrong, so why not that? We have pretty conclusive evidence it's her, but everything we know about her somehow points anywhere but her."

"So what do you suggest?" asked Jacquie.

"There's only one sensible thing we can do," said Danny. "We pull her in and question her."

And that was where the day hit the buffers. For although Danny's professional policeman brain was yelling at him to get mobile, get up there, and arrest the suspect before she had time to make a run for it, his self-preserving, hierarchically aware brain was telling him to get approval before he did anything. The problem was that none of them had any idea where Shirley was, and despite multiple calls to his mobile the little twerp never picked up. And if he wasn't answering his phone, then a text was pointless as well. Growling like a wounded bear as he paced up and down the length of the squad room, frustration and anger vying for supremacy, Danny finally decided he had to get things moving, which meant going over his unreachable boss's curly blond head. It was an idea instantly shot out of the sky by the mental image of an inevitably furious Shirley Templeton tap-dancing on his genitals as the prelude to ceremonially tearing off his sergeant's stripes.

"I'll call Debs," offered Jacquie, sensing the mounting rage in the office. "She might know where Shirley is. I doubt he'd risk going AWOL without letting the brass know where to find him."

The squad-room clock's second hand had barely completed a full sweep by the time the chief superintendent's utterly indiscreet PA/secretary had shared the full picture. Shirley was out playing golf with the 'Arse-Covering Cock' after which they were heading off together 'to get shit-faced pissed' at the latter's favourite 'tits-out club' in Wolverhampton. They would both have their mobiles switched off so that they didn't get disturbed drinking and drooling, plus nobody could track and trace them. Oh, and there was no point trying to get in touch with Mister Potato Head either, as the chief super was out buying saucy underwear for his grotesquely obese missus.

"'Arse-Covering Cock' is the assistant chief constable, right?" asked Kevin after Jacquie had recounted Debs' info verbatim to the team.

"It's only 'cock' when she's being polite," said Jacquie.

"But we are effectively screwed," said Kevin. "I mean, we can't do anything more until one or other of the three re-surfaces and signs off on the arrest."

"And it doesn't sound like it's going to be any time soon," added Jacquie. "In fact, in all probability it won't be until tomorrow."

Danny nodded. She was right, of course. He suddenly threw back his head and howled like a wolf who was sitting on a thorn. "This cannot be happening," he growled at the ceiling. "How can we run a shit-show like this? It's amateur hour." He shook his head sadly and looked at his colleagues. "You know, much as I hate to say this, our nemesis Percy Walsh isn't far off the..." He didn't bother to finish. He couldn't summon up the energy, and, besides, he didn't need to say out loud what they were all thinking. "Right, then," he said, forcing a smile onto his face, "everybody down the pub. This minute and no arguments."

There were none. And as files were locked away, computers shut down, and coats put on, Danny picked up his mobile and typed a simple three-word text to his absent twat of a detective inspector boss. 'Red Fox found.'

# Chapter 28

Templeton never replied to Danny's text. Worse still, he didn't breeze into the office until coming up eleven the next morning, and from his demeanour they could all see he was patently unaware that the bank robber they'd been chasing for months had been identified and located. It was only when he noticed the three expectant expressions staring at him that he reacted.

"What?"

"Did you not get my text, sir?" asked Danny, opting for the deferential.

Templeton grabbed his mobile from his inside jacket pocket and stared at it for a few seconds before turning it on. "Damned thing's been on the blink for days," he lied poorly. "Need to get a new one. Arrange it for me, please, Jacquie. So what did your message say exactly, Danny?"

"We've got the Red Fox. Name and address."

"Say again," said Templeton, looking up from his distracted scrolling through the messages he'd presumably missed since before teeing off the previous afternoon.

"We've got the Red Fox," repeated Danny, fighting to suppress his rising anger.

"You've got him?" replied an incredulous Templeton. "You've really got him?"

"Her," said Danny. "It's a *her*."

"Bollocks," replied Templeton. "I told you the profiler was very clear it's a—"

"He was wrong," snapped Danny, his irritation at the man leading to him taking a risk on both interrupting and contradicting all in one. "We have the evidence and it's a woman. Not only that, she's not young like the profile said. She's actually sixty-nine years old."

"In that case, double bollocks," retorted Templeton. "Are you seriously trying to tell me our six-times armed bank robber is some little, wizened, old, probably toothless and incontinent crone? Or is this some sort of jolly jest you're having before you all find yourselves back in uniform?"

Danny stood, arms by his sides, rocking gently back and forth, and said nothing, merely exhaling noisily through his nose.

"Oh, come on, then," sighed a clearly less-than-inspired Templeton. "Show me something that might possibly convince me."

It took less than ten minutes. Kevin had brilliantly supplemented what he'd shown to Templeton the previous day by splicing together all six post-robbery transformations into a summary highlights reel that required only minimal commentary. He'd also pulled out the freeze-frame of Granny Fox in Leominster, which linked seamlessly to Jacquie's Whitchurch 'follow-the-leader' videos and the ultimate 'bullseye' full-face shot. Danny took over with the silhouette sketches, explaining the probability of a reversible coat, and finally rounded off the mini presentation with the background checks and confirmation of the Fox's identity and place of residence. He very deliberately left out the rather large bundle of lifestyle information they'd assembled that had made it extremely difficult to envisage Mrs Carol Jackson of 5, Wharf Row Cottages being a serial armed bank robber.

Templeton stretched himself as tall as he could and puffed his chest out. "We've done a great job here, team. Great job." He coughed a small grunt of a laugh. "I didn't let on to you lot before, but I always knew that so-called criminologist's profile was crap. They usually are, you know. Just a shame the chief super pushed me into doing it."

"So can we pull her in?" asked Danny, glossing over the bullshit.

"Don't be daft, Detective Sergeant. We can't just wander up to the front door of an armed bank robber and ask him – sorry, I mean her – to pop down here for a cup of tea and a chat. An arrest of this ilk requires intricate planning, coordination, a strategy, not to mention an armed response team."

"She's a sixty-nine-year-old grandmother who can't weigh more than seven stones wet through," said Danny, exasperated.

"She's a cunning and ruthless armed bank robber," corrected Templeton.

"But she—" began Danny, only to be cut off by Templeton holding up a hand.

The three watched on in silence as their leader fell into an almost trance-like state, eyes half closed as he scratched at his jaw and gently nodded. They could almost see the idea fluttering around inside his head as it took shape, but had to wait for the slow count of seven before it landed and got shared.

"There's another good reason to hold fire on the arrest for a few more hours," said Templeton, an evil grin on his lips. "A very good reason indeed."

"Which is?" asked Danny on behalf of all three listeners.

"This is the chance I've been waiting for to stick a cactus up the arse of that vindictive cow Percy Walsh." Templeton waited for somebody to ask the obvious question but, as nobody did, he explained anyway. "Media people live for the exclusive, the stop-press, the 'breaking news' banner across the screen with their name on it. And what is it they hate more than anything? I shall tell you. When somebody else beats them to it."

"And this helps us how, exactly?" asked Danny.

"I am going to personally make sure," growled Templeton in his scariest supervillain voice, "that somebody else *does* get the exclusive and Walsh fucking doesn't. Ha ha, poor you, bitch!" He finished with an air punch to an imagined gut.

"Who?" asked Danny, not managing to summon up the energy for a longer question.

"It just so happens," began Templeton, doing yet another of his thoroughly irritating music-box-ballerina spins, "that yesterday afternoon I was in a meeting with the ACC and a dear friend of his who just happens to be the production director of our local television company. Fortuitously, as it now transpires, he offered us any help he could muster if we wanted to have a pop back at the hideous *Midwestern Echo*. He even gave me the personal number of their early-evening local magazine programme front-man, Leslie Isaacs. Have you seen him? *All Points West*? Six thirty every weekday? You really should give it a go," continued Templeton after observing three shaking heads. "It's rather good, actually. And even if you don't normally watch it, I would suggest you set the recorder for tonight's programme. It's going to be special."

Danny didn't like what he was hearing, but let it go. "What do you want us to do in the meantime regarding preparation, sir? Search warrant? Arrange back-up? Transport?"

"Paperwork, that'll do. Leave the rest to me," commanded the suddenly energised Templeton. "I'll get the armed response team signed off and set up and plan the approach. Oh, and as for the actual moment of arrest, I shall be doing that myself, personally. One-on-one. The hunter and the hunted."

Danny desperately wanted to ask Templeton if he would be wearing a pink jacket, blowing a horn, and shouting 'Tally-ho!', but thought better of it. "I assume you'll be wanting me along, sir."

"Let's talk about that later," replied Templeton. "I don't want a crowd milling around when I'm nabbing the villain. Anyway, for now there's lots to do, so get to it." He rubbed his hands together and shot off, leaving the others staring open-mouthed at his departing back.

Templeton didn't reappear until after five. He was smiling widely out from the neck hole of a far-too-large bulletproof vest, which made him look an even bigger small twat than usual. Or was that a smaller big twat? Who cared – either way, he looked utterly ridiculous.

"We go in at 18.45," barked Templeton, like some sort of miniature, low-budget movie commando.

"Why that exact time?" asked Danny. To him it was an obvious question.

"The precise mid-point of Leslie Isaacs' evening show," replied Templeton, as if it was the stupidest question the world had ever heard.

Danny shook his head in disbelief. "You mean you..." He tailed off, not wanting to actually say aloud the horror he was imagining.

"Live feed of the arrest," said Templeton, grinning and rubbing his hands together with glee. "That's what I've been setting up all afternoon. Scripting and choreographing in fine detail. Oh, and before you even think otherwise, it is all with the approval and blessing from 'on high'. The ACC is actually even more excited than I am about sticking one to Percy 'The Vindictive Cow' Walsh, and that's saying something. Plus, he reckons it will be excellent publicity for the Fourshires Constabulary, and help to counterbalance, if not swamp, all that negative shite the stinking *Echo* has been spewing out about us week after week."

"We don't actually know for sure," began Danny tentatively, "that Carol Jackson really *is* the Red Fox. Yes, I am – we are – ninety-nine percent certain, but it still could be a coincidence. Or, perhaps more likely, she could be an accomplice to the real—"

"Give me a break," snapped Templeton. "You convinced me and I sold it upstairs, so don't start back-tracking now. It's too late. Jackson *is* the Red Fox and we go in all guns blazing – metaphorically speaking, of course – to grab her, live on television. A Leslie Isaacs exclusive, and fuck nothing for Percy fucking Walsh." Luckily, he didn't end with a maniacal cackle, but his face did, silently.

Danny checked his watch. "I hope the search warrant gets here in time. I submitted the request but it seems like every magistrate in the county has taken Friday off."

"Ha!" retorted Templeton. "You need to go back to school, Detective Sergeant. 1984 Police and Criminal Evidence Act."

Danny shook his head. It didn't ring a bell even though it probably ought to.

"Section eighteen," continued a now gloating Templeton. "A search can be authorised by a police officer at or above the rank of inspector. And, oh my word, do we just happen to have one of those anywhere near?" He held his arms out wide to amplify his brilliant humour.

Danny felt a bit silly, then embarrassed, then murderous. Was it worth spending the rest of his useful life in prison for strangling this preening pile of crap? Not quite, but it was a very close thing. "Good news, then," he said.

"Indeed, yes," confirmed Templeton. "And fortunate. It would have been a great shame to have been forced to postpone the regional television event of the year just because *you* couldn't get the paperwork done in time, wouldn't it?"

"I've arranged transport," said Danny, rapidly moving on to something positive.

"Not required," scoffed Templeton. "I'll drive myself."

"But what about—" Danny was cut off before he could finish.

"We can't have a mob of extras cluttering up the screen and confusing the viewers. I shall be going up to the door solo," Templeton paused to pat his bulletproof vest, "to confront and apprehend the notorious Red Fox."

"So you don't want me or the others along?" asked a downcast Danny, sweeping an arm at the listening 'others'.

Templeton thought about it for a couple of seconds. "Those two can watch it at home," he said, dismissively waving a hand at Jacquie and Kevin. "You can tag along. But when I go a-knocking on her front door I want you hanging back, out of sight. This is my show now. Okay, Detective Sergeant?"

# Chapter 29

"Grandma," said Bethany, wandering into the kitchen, "you've got seventeen missed calls and thirteen unread texts on your phone. From four days ago."

Carol turned to look at the younger of her two granddaughters and smiled with love, as she always did when she caught sight of either of them. "Where did you find that, chook?" she asked. "It's been hiding for days."

"Down the back of the armchair seat cushion," replied Bethany as she tapped away at the mobile. "I was hoping to find some money, but..." She broke off. "You really ought to have a security pass-code on this, Grandma. Anyone could get in and look at your messages."

"I don't usually get any, and even if I did they wouldn't be anything worth keeping secret," replied Carol. "And besides, I'd never be able to remember a password code. I can barely remember how to answer the blinkin' phone."

"Who's Janice?" asked Bethany, now peering intently at the screen as she continued tapping and reading.

"My friend," said Carol. "Your grandpa used to work with her husband."

"She uses a lot of very bad language, doesn't she," said Bethany.

Carol made to take the phone, but her granddaughter was far too quick and jinked it out of reach.

"And what does she mean by 'You know Foxy, don't you'?" asked Bethany, before making a face and adding, "I didn't say out loud the very naughty word in the middle of that text."

"Oh, nothing," said Carol, finally managing to snatch the phone away. "My friend Janice thought I knew somebody famous, that's all."

"Somebody called Foxy?" asked Bethany.

"It's a nickname," said Carol. "Now, would you like to help me bake a cake for tomorrow?" she asked in an attempt to change the subject.

Bethany was not to be diverted. "Is Foxy a man or a woman?"

"Both," replied Carol.

"Like, as in a transgender person."

"No," corrected Carol, glossing over her surprise at her thirteen-year-old granddaughter's knowledge of such things. "As in, she's a woman who dresses up as a man sometimes."

"Oh," replied Bethany, nodding vigorously before exclaiming, "so she's a cross-dresser."

"No again," said Carol, becoming slightly flustered by both the interrogation and the youngster's seemingly encyclopaedic knowledge of... whatever it was called. "This woman only dresses as a man as a disguise. That's all. Like fancy dress."

"Cool," said Bethany, "but weird. And why the name Foxy? It sounds like it's meant to be sexy."

"It's nothing of the sort," said Carol, "and—"

The sound of the front door opening and Sarah calling out her sing-song "Hello" saved Carol from having to answer any more questions.

"Your mum's here for you now," she said, shooing the little'un out of the kitchen, "and I have to get on with tidying away the tea things."

As Sarah came into the kitchen, Bethany left it with the smallest of acknowledgements as they passed.

"And hello to you too, Daughter," said Sarah sarcastically. She looked at Carol. "Was I that bad at that age?"

"Not quite," said Carol with a grin. "But you had your moments, believe me."

Sarah went across and hugged her mother. "Thanks for helping me out this afternoon. The boss called a special Friday after-work glass of wine and nibbles – both of which were horrible, by the way – and there was no way I could get out of it without risking my promotion." She looked at her watch. "Bloomin' heck, twenty to seven – I am sorry, Mum, really sorry."

"Don't be," cooed Carol. "I'm happy to help, you know that. And the girls have been lovely. I haven't heard your dad chatting that much for ages."

"How is he?" asked Sarah.

"You keep on asking me that of late," said Carol. "Is there something going on I should know about?"

"No," said Sarah, stretching the word out to its maximum and shaking her head. "No, nothing," she added for confirmation. "But hey!" she said suddenly, with a loud single handclap as if to signal the need for a change of direction and tone. "There certainly *is* something going on down the road, though."

Carol didn't ask – she just made a 'tell me' face.

Sarah launched into it excitedly. "Well, for a start there's a TV truck parked up at the far end of the road. It's around the corner, so you won't be able to see it from the front garden, but there was a bloke there with a camera and another one talking into it. He looked sort of familiar but I couldn't place him."

"Is that all?" asked a wholly unimpressed Carol.

"No, that is not all," gushed Sarah. "Across the street from the telly van was a big black unmarked truck full of blokes all dressed up like soldiers."

"Maybe they're making a film," offered Carol.

"Surely they'd have to have loads of lights for the cameras to work, wouldn't they," replied Sarah. "And sound recording stuff and directors and—"

"Maybe it's a low-budget film," interrupted Carol.

"No," retorted Sarah emphatically, "it just doesn't make sense. No, I reckon they're on a job, getting ready to do a raid."

Carol was about to dismiss the idea when Roy called out from the sitting room.

"Hey, you two, get yourselves in here. Quick!"

The two women duly complied, trotting through to the sitting room, where Roy and both granddaughters were animatedly pointing at the television screen.

"That's just up the road," said Roy, his voice almost half an octave higher than usual with the excitement of it all.

"What is this?" asked Carol.

"It's *All Points West*," said Roy, not taking his eyes off the screen. "You know, the weeknight local thingy show. We usually watch it. It's got that bloke with the basset-hound eyes, Leslie something-or-other, on it."

"Isn't it usually in a studio?" said Carol. "He sits on a beige sofa, right?"

"Not tonight, by the sounds of it," said Roy. "He's just been on saying they're out on a mission, or something like that, and he's tagging along with the police to bring us exclusive live film of the action when it happens. Look, here he is now."

"That's him!" shrieked Sarah. "That's the man I saw talking to the camera up the road when I came past. I told you there was something going on."

"Who's that?" asked Lauren, pointing at a small blond man who'd just appeared on screen wearing what looked like a dark blue mattress on his chest.

"Turn the sound up a bit," instructed Sarah. "I want to hear what he says."

Roy obliged just in time for them to hear the interview, and the whole extended family listened in silence as the sub-captioned Detective Inspector Graham Templeton explained how they were about to witness the culmination of many months of intricate, exhausting but ultimately fruitful police work that he had personally led from start to finish. It was, he went on to say, a shining example of policing excellence from the highly proficient, committed, and investigatively unparalleled Fourshires Constabulary. When pressed by the interviewer for more detailed information, the detective inspector gave a coy smile and explained that he was unable to divulge at that moment the specifics around exactly what or who the target was, but assured the viewers – direct to camera – that all would become apparent within the next few minutes.

"Oh my goodness," exclaimed Roy. "This is proper exciting. And right up the road from us, too."

"Closer than that," said Bethany, again pointing at the screen as she moved to kneel down in front to watch even more closely. "Look, they're actually in your road now. See. Those houses are just up from here."

The camera was now following the striding detective, but slowing to pull back and increase the distance between them. For a moment it swung slightly to the side before quickly returning to focus on the detective's back.

"Who were they?" asked Roy, pointing at the screen where an instant before a pair of shadowy figures had briefly been in shot.

"That's those guys dressed like soldiers I told you about, Mum," said Sarah. "See, I told you they were for real."

"They had guns," said a knowing Lauren. "It's a SWAT team."

"That's only in America," said Bethany.

"No it's not!" snapped back Lauren.

"Tis so!" hissed Bethany.

"Girls!" shouted Sarah. "We're trying to watch this. If you want to argue, go somewhere else." She turned her attention back to the screen. "Oh, wow, that's Wharf Row Cottages. This must be going on right outside."

Bethany and Lauren jumped up and ran across to the front window where they both knelt to cautiously peer over the sill at what was going on out front.

"They're right outside," hissed Lauren in a hoarse whisper. "That little detective bloke and a bunch of commandos all dressed in black."

"And they *have* got guns!" added Bethany in the same tone.

"That's our front door," said Roy, who, along with his wife and daughter, was still watching the action on the television screen. "What on earth is going on?" he added in a tone of incredulity. "They must be having a laugh or—"

He was interrupted by a loud double knock on the front door. The sound resonated through the house. Everybody froze, apart from Roy, who quickly moved his thumb to mute the telly.

On screen, Carol could see her front door quite clearly in the illumination from the camera light, and in front of it, the rear view of a short man standing with his feet set wide apart. The sound of a repeat double knock echoed through the house a second or two before the muted on-screen man doing the knocking moved. "I'll get it," she said in a small voice.

She knew what it was about. It was that moment she'd hoped would never happen but always knew was a possibility. She'd even thought about it, imagined the scenario, like a movie in her head. It had been nothing like this, though. Not her walking through into the hall in her slippers to open the door to the police as her husband, daughter and two granddaughters crowded into the sitting-room doorway behind her to watch. In her imagination it had always been a private affair, one-on-one, just her and 'The Law'. Not at home. Not surrounded by her family.

With her heartbeat surprisingly steady, she unlatched the door and eased it open, flinching as the bright camera light hurt her eyes. A few blinks and she was able to make out the small man in a far-too-big-for-him bulletproof vest standing squarely on her doorstep. It was the detective she'd seen for the first time a few minutes prior, and she waited to hear the words she'd hoped she never would.

"Carol Jackson?" asked the detective.

"Yes," replied Carol, nodding. "Yes, that's me."

The detective turned his head to allow the camera behind to catch his full profile, and held the pose for the count of three before looking back at

Carol. He fixed her eye to eye, grinned, took a deep breath, and in a voice somewhere between a low growl and a whisper said, "You're nicked."

# Chapter 30

Carol found herself absurdly surprised by just how absurdly unsurprised she was on seeing the interview room. Bare grey walls, recessed ceiling lighting, single empty table with four upright chairs – two on either side – and, finally, the stack of recording equipment. It was as if all those hours spent watching television dramas of criminals being interrogated in such places had somehow been preparing her for this moment. What she hadn't been prepared for, however, was sometime before, being led out of her house in handcuffs, all of it broadcast live on the telly.

Worse than that, though, by a country mile, had been having to hear her family behind her as she went: Sarah screaming that there had to be some sort of mistake, the granddaughters sobbing with incomprehension, and her poor dear Roy asking over and over again, "What's going on? What's going on?" Carol herself had been ridiculously calm about it all inside, but the reactions of her nearest and dearest had torn her heart to shreds. And it was all down to her. Her and nobody else.

On the way out of the house, another man – older, taller, and a lot more portly than the first – had passed them going in. She'd assumed he was another detective, because he said something about supervising the search. It shouldn't have taken him long to find her robbery props. They weren't hidden very deeply at all. And her brilliantly constructed disguise coat was hanging plain as brass in Paul's little wardrobe. She just kept her fingers crossed that they wouldn't find the money. Somehow she still hoped to one day get it to somebody who needed it more than a ruddy bank did.

The boss detective, whose name she still couldn't get fixed in her head, was clearly very happy with his evening's work. He'd hummed softly to himself the whole hour or so of the car ride down to wherever they were now, whilst she sat handcuffed and silent in the back seat alongside a burly uniformed constable who'd kept falling asleep. She'd nudged him gently whenever he started snoring, but otherwise had no interaction with either of them.

At the police station she'd been checked in by an enormously fat police sergeant who everybody there called Bob. He'd very kindly offered her a cup of tea, but she'd politely declined. She didn't want a full bladder distracting her when it eventually came time to tell her story. And tell it she would. Start to finish. From that very first nagging worm of a dream that became a solidified idea. From the strategy, tactical planning, scoping, observation, preparation, and on to execution. Yes, she would tell them the lot, the whole shebang – everything apart from what she'd done with the money. No point having gone through all this if they were going to snatch it back, now, was there.

No sooner had she been shown into the interview room than Detective Short-and-Happy handed her over to a young and not unattractive woman before strutting out of the room like a bantam cockerel heading off to perch on a fence somewhere for a full-blown cock-a-doodle crow.

"Good evening, Mrs Jackson," said the young woman as soon as they were alone. She smiled and offered a hand to shake. "I'm Detective Constable Napier, and I am so pleased to finally meet you."

Carol took the hand and shook, adding a return smile for good measure. "Please call me Carol," she said. "'Mrs Jackson' always reminds me of my mother-in-law and, not to put too fine a point on it, she was just plain nasty."

"And I'm Jacquie," said the younger woman, giving a little chuckle at Carol's reminiscence. "But 'Detective Constable' when more important people are about," she added, looking in the direction in which her boss had just disappeared. "Now, we've got a few formalities to get out of the way before we get down to it, but is there anybody you need to let know where you are?"

"Oh, they know," said Carol, shaking her head sadly. "The whole family – apart from my son, who lives in Canada – were there when, well, you know." She held her arms out in front of her as if waiting for the handcuffs to go on again.

"But would you like to telephone somebody now to tell them you're okay?"

"We don't have a phone in the house and Roy, my husband, refuses point-blank to have a mobile. So it would have to be my daughter, Sarah, if anybody, and for the life of me I can never remember her number."

"Would you like me to get a message to her?" pressed Jacquie.

"That would be very nice of you," said Carol, smiling at the detective, who was probably, she thought, even younger than Sarah. "Make sure to tell her something simple. There was a lot of upset back at home this evening."

"I'll see to it," said Jacquie. "But first we need to get some routine procedural things out of the way."

Carol nodded her readiness to do whatever, and allowed herself to be led into a back room, where she was photographed and fingerprinted.

"Your first time, right?" asked Jacquie as Carol's fingerprints were taken.

"Yes," said Carol simply.

"Have you asked for a solicitor yet?"

"No," said Carol.

"Why ever not?"

"No point making a fuss," said Carol. "Dragging some poor soul out here at this time on a Friday evening, just to sit and listen to me confessing. I did it. All six of them. But then, you must know that or I wouldn't be here. So I really don't see any point in stringing it out."

Jacquie shrugged an 'on-your-head-be-it' gesture and led Carol back to the interview room to wait for whatever came next. After a few moments of silence Jacquie leaned forward across the table. "Me and my colleagues were dead impressed with the whole Red Fox thing," she said in a conspiratorial half-whisper. "It *was* a reversible coat that you used, wasn't it?"

Carol nodded. "I intend to tell you everything about how I did it, so there's no point trying to trick me."

"It's no trick," said Jacquie, making a disappointed face. "The tape recorder isn't on and there are no bugs in here, believe me." She put her head back and spoke to the ceiling in an overly loud voice. "Detective Inspector Templeton is a jumped-up little prick!" She looked back at Carol. "There, you see – I've just insulted my boss, and I wouldn't do that if he could hear, would I?" She laughed.

Carol joined in the laughter for a brief while. "I made it myself, you know – the coat. Pattern and all. Sewed it on my kitchen table while my Roy was out at his bowling club." She paused and half closed her eyes to imagine how clever she'd felt when she'd tried it on for the first time. "It takes me – sorry, *took* me – less than twelve seconds to switch from grey hoodie to mustard overcoat. Eight on a really good day."

"That really is truly brilliant!" said Jacquie, silently clapping her hands in a show of genuine admiration. "Where did you get the idea from?"

"Out of my head," replied Carol. "That's where all the ideas came from. The details of other stuff, though, I just got off the telly."

"Other stuff?"

"Yes – all the tactics, the methodology, the sort of words to use and so on. And spotting CCTV cameras is one of the most important things, along with knowing how to look the other way without making it look like that's what you're doing. Here, shouldn't you be writing all this down?"

"Oh no," said Jacquie. "Templeton and my DS will be doing the formal interview. This is just more of a fan's forum." She winked theatrically. "I think you're fab, and now, having met you in person, I'm even more disappointed that we caught you. Were you going to start again next autumn?"

Carol chuckled. It was obvious they would have guessed she could only use the hoodie coat disguise in rotten weather. "I was thinking about giving up," she replied. "Especially when I nearly got nabbed at Leominster Station. But then I was thinking about that Mary what's-her-name who does the baking thing on the telly, and if she can keep going till she's a hundred, then why not me? And, between you and me, robbing banks is just about the only thing I've ever been good at, beyond raising a family and keeping house. So I ask you: would *you* stop doing something you were special at?"

Jacquie shook her head. "I understand, Carol. All too well. Do you know, there's still too many men who think women should only be allowed in the police force to type and make the tea. Luckily, I'm a pretty good copper, because I'm lousy at both the other things." She smiled before flicking her face to a serious expression. "Please let me get you a solicitor. It's completely free. You wouldn't have to pay a penny, and they could really help."

Carol smiled at her friendly detective and deployed the phrase she'd always used when not wanting to say a straight no. "Let me have a think about—"

She was cut off by the interview-room door swinging open and Detective Templeton strutting in, clapping his hands. The other man she'd seen at her house was trailing in his wake.

"Thank you, DC Napier," snapped Templeton. "That'll be all."

Without a word, Jacquie left the room, closing the door behind her, while Templeton and the other one sat themselves down across the table from Carol. Templeton glowered at her, all bristle and pathetically poor play-acted menace. Number Two gave her a surreptitious smile and half a wink. Templeton clacked down the recording equipment starter keys and announced the date and time, Carol's full name and address, and himself and Detective Sergeant Roberts as being present. Carol sat and waited.

Templeton fixed her with an intense stare that might have been unsettling if it had been coming from a bigger and less blond and curly man. "Five to ten," he growled at her in a threatening tone that was made not scary at all by the awfulness of the wannabe bully's acting.

Carol couldn't resist the opportunity for a bit of naughtiness with this horrible little man. She looked back at him quizzically. "You just told that recording machine it was eight forty-seven."

Templeton was momentarily knocked out of his stride as he worked out what his suspect had just said. "No," he came back eventually, "you are looking at five to ten years in prison. *Five to ten*. But maybe a lot less if you cooperate."

"I mean to cooperate," said Carol, making sure to not show him that she'd spotted his sidekick suppressing a grin.

"We have photographic evidence," continued Templeton, blustering on, having clearly not registered Carol's words, "that places you at the crime scenes – all six of them. In addition to which, we now have – by virtue of a lawful search of your place of residence – material evidence of your involvement: to wit a false ginger moustache, a handgun of the type reported by eyewitnesses to have been used in said robberies, and a reversible hoodie coat seen and documented at each of the *six* robbery locations." He gasped in a breath at the end of the longest single sentence Carol had probably ever heard. Her Roy barely managed five words without needing a lie-down.

"Didn't you find the glasses?" asked Carol, still feeling the uncontrollable urge to tease. "They were part of the disguise too, you know."

"A-ha!" said Templeton, like he'd just cracked a hard-nut supervillain with his brilliant interrogation technique. "So you admit to carrying out these *armed* robberies and, in the process, stealing significant sums of money." He most definitely stressed the word 'armed'.

"The robberies, yes," said Carol, nodding. "But I didn't *steal* the money." It was her turn to emphasise a keyword.

"How does that work?" asked an obviously confused Templeton.

"I didn't keep it," said Carol, "so I didn't actually steal it. I merely relocated it. I'm like a sort of – what do you fancy people call them? – like a wealth manager."

"Okay, right," said Templeton, saying both words in a childishly sarcastic voice before reassuming his pathetic hard-cop act. "Whatever you might call it, Mrs Jackson, however you may want to dress it up, you *did* walk into six banks with a gun, you *did* threaten those cashiers in the most frightening way possible, and you *did* force them to put money into a bag that you then *did* subsequently remove from the premises. Correct?"

"In a way," replied Carol.

"Meaning what this time?" sighed Templeton.

"It was only a toy gun."

"They didn't know that!" snapped an increasingly flustered Templeton.

"Of course not," scoffed Carol. "Otherwise, I might as well have used a banana."

This time, Detective Two failed to prevent a brief snort of laughter from escaping.

His boss swung his head around to momentarily glower at him before turning back to re-fix Carol with a full-on, full-force stare. "I am not going to sit here and play word games," he hissed. "I know you did it. I have all the evidence I need to send you down for a very long time. So why are you playing games, eh?" he demanded.

"I'm not," she said in her sweetest little-old-lady voice. "You are."

"Meaning what now?" demanded Templeton, leaning back in his chair.

"It's you who's doing all the play-acting: the cheap TV cop routine, some sort of *Sweeney* tribute act. And, quite frankly, none of it was necessary. I told you right at the beginning – if you'd have bothered to listen – that I was going to tell you everything."

Templeton did the best he could to keep a straight face, having been scolded, and casually got to his feet to look down at his sidekick. "You can take it from here, Detective Sergeant Roberts," he said in a tone of feigned weariness. "Take Mrs Jackson's full statement and call me when she's ready to sign it so that I can personally charge her." He didn't wait for an answer, instead flamboyantly stopping the interview tape and breezing out of the room.

Unlike his boss, Detective Sergeant Roberts was a very nice man. He insisted she call him Danny, and told her, like his friend and colleague Jacquie had before him, that they were very pleased to finally meet the robber they'd been chasing down for months. He made sure to keep the statement-taking process businesslike but light and friendly, gently asking for clarification around certain key details and occasionally re-checking the times and dates, but largely leaving it to Carol to tell her story the way she wanted to tell it. And, truth be told, she enjoyed blowing her own trumpet for only the second time in her life, after her very recent reveal to Janice. It felt good, as did finally getting the weight of her secret other life off her chest.

"I have to tell you, Mrs Jackson," said Danny, "I—"

"Carol," she corrected.

He smiled the smile of a nine-year-old in a big man's body. "I have to tell you, *Carol* – and I probably shouldn't – that I was really, seriously impressed by the Red Fox's robbery craft. We all were. The speed, the precision, the audacity, the simple yet effective facial disguise, the CCTV awareness. Everything about it was top-notch, right up there with the very best. Oh, and the reversible coat, well, that was just a stroke of pure genius. Kept us guessing right up to jolly nearly the end."

Carol smiled.

"And I've a confession to make," added Danny, now in a whisper, "that for the very first time in all my far-too-many years of policing, I actually felt sad about catching the perpetrator. Even more so now that I've met you."

Carol was basking in the warmth of his glowing praise, but still managed to wave away his last comment with a "You were only doing your job, Danny."

He gave her a wink of thanks and changed tack. "Why haven't you got a solicitor? He's free, you know, if that's what you're worried about."

Carol sighed. "I've been through it with your Jacquie," she said. "Even with a free one, I'd still be wasting his time. Look," she said, waving a weary finger at the confession statement, all written out in black and white and now merely waiting for her to sign. "With that all down there what is the point?"

Danny shook his head. "A solicitor could still—" he began, only for Carol to cut across him.

"Shall we get this over with?" she asked, using her facial expression as an apology for interrupting. "Before it gets too late for everyone?"

The big man shrugged a sad 'at least I tried' and called Templeton to come down for the formal signing of the confession. He was there in what to

Carol seemed so short a time that she wondered if he'd been sat outside the interview-room door the whole time.

"All set, Detective Sergeant Roberts?" asked Templeton as he swept in. "No surprises, no hiccups, no more ruddy word games?"

"None, sir," responded the now standing Danny.

"And you, Mrs Jackson – everything here, all fessed up and clean of soul?"

She wanted to say there was no such thing as a soul, plus a whole host of rude stuff, but bit back on it and swallowed. A single nod was all she offered in place of words. Templeton used a theatrical flourish to produce a swanky biro from his inside jacket pocket and presented it to Carol. She took it and signed her name across the bottom of the page, handing the pen back to its owner for him to countersign. He was grinning like a cat that had just consumed a week's worth of cream as he got to his feet to look down at her.

"Carol Jackson," he began, using what Carol guessed was his best 'official police business' voice, "I am hereby formally charging you with six counts of—"

He stopped dead as the door opened without a preceding knock, and swung around to glare at whoever had had the temerity to interrupt his performance. Standing half inside the doorway was a petite, immaculately dressed, and undeniably beautiful young Indian-looking woman.

"Who the hell are you?" snarled Templeton. "And what the hell do you—"

"Good evening," she interrupted, her voice soft but firm, the accent what they used to call 'BBC English'. "My name is Sonia Patel and I am Mrs Jackson's solicitor."

# Chapter 31

Templeton, already on his feet, took two overly aggressive paces towards the interloper, who didn't bat an eyelid, let alone flinch. He tried to stretch himself tall so he could look down on her but, being only maybe two inches at most taller than her, the whole charade was more funny than intimidating to Carol's eye. And it seemed from her demeanour that the solicitor lady was no less underwhelmed.

"She...she," stammered a clearly furious Templeton, angrily stabbing a finger in Carol's direction, "waived her right to a solicitor."

The young woman calmly pulled a slip of paper from the outside pocket of her briefcase and peered at it for a few seconds. "As a matter of fact, Detective," she said softly, looking up to meet Templeton's hostile gaze full on, "Mrs Jackson requested a DC Napier – I do hope that is the correct name and title – to summon me."

Templeton swung around to glower at Carol. "You did what?"

Carol just had time to glance over Templeton's shoulder and see the solicitor's half-wink and nod at her before she upset the apple cart. "Exactly that," she said.

"You said you didn't want one," blustered Templeton. "You told me you—"

"I changed my mind," said Carol. "I can, can't I?" she asked, playing the ignorant.

Templeton gave a loud harrumph before snarling, "It makes no difference. You confessed in writing and you signed it. So, despite this irritating but nonetheless pointless interruption," he paused to rotate the tension out of his shoulders, "I am charging you. So, here we go." He stood to attention and used his special charging voice to do the full official speech. "There!" He almost spat the word at the solicitor. "Now you can do what you want. She," he jabbed an angry finger at Carol, "is going nowhere, so don't even think about asking for bail." Turning his attention to the lovely man

Danny, he barked a command. "I want you and Napier in my office, now!" And with that, he stormed out.

Danny duly followed on, but not before turning to give Carol a shy wink and a hunched-shoulders thumbs-up.

"Well, that was jolly unpleasant," said the solicitor in a light sing-song as she strolled across to softly close the still-open door.

"Sorry," said Carol, "but I'm more than a bit confused about what's going on here."

"Firstly, Mrs Jackson, kindly let me introduce myself properly. My name is Sonia Patel, Sonia to you from now on, and I am currently on call as what they term the police station duty solicitor for this area. As such, I am here now in the capacity of your legal counsel." She held out a slender hand for a shake.

Carol got to her feet to take the hand and was impressed by the firmness of its grip for such a petite young woman who looked more like a smart-suited schoolgirl than a presumably qualified lawyer. "Please call me Carol," she said, before shaking her head. "I still don't understand. I really did tell them I didn't want a lawyer. I didn't want to make a fuss or waste anybody's time."

Sonia indicated with a wave of one hand that they should sit, and waited until Carol had done so before taking a chair across the table from her. She smiled again. "A guardian angel was concerned that you might not be fully aware of the true complexity of the situation you find yourself in. She called and asked that I talk with you before you cement your determination to proceed without legal advice."

"Jacquie?" asked Carol.

"Yes indeed," replied Sonia, nodding. "And thank you for playing along with the subterfuge earlier. What she did, for all the right reasons, is counter to protocol. I assume Detective Inspector Templeton did formally offer you access to legal advice?"

"Not exactly," replied Carol. "I think I rather jumped the gun by wanting to confess. Get it over and done with. But the other two detectives certainly did offer. In fact they both tried to persuade me to have a solicitor. So, overall, I'd say the police as a whole probably did."

"And your reluctance?" asked Sonia, not feeling the need to ask the question in full. "You realise I do this for free as far as you are concerned?"

"Oh yes," said Carol. "Both Jacquie and Danny told me I wouldn't have to pay. It's just that I did do them – the robberies, that is – and I'd always told myself I'd confess if I got caught. So it seemed to me like getting anybody else involved would be plain silly and a waste of everybody's time."

"And that is where DC Napier and I hold a different view from yours," replied Sonia. "My primary role here right now is to help you navigate safely through the process, to ensure you are treated fairly and correctly and that your legal entitlements are both offered and delivered. I can also act as the lever to make sure you get the external contact – the visits – you need, and that you are comfortable for as long as you are required to be here."

"How long *will* I be here?" asked Carol. "As in, here in this police station?"

"I suspect until Monday," replied Sonia. "It's usually best not to get arrested on a Friday evening." She gave a wry smile. "But hopefully on Monday we can get you bailed so you can be at home with your loved ones until...well, you know."

"Talking of prison," said Carol, "which I assume is that last bit you didn't actually say, that nasty Detective Templeton told me I should expect between five and ten years inside, but it could be a lot less if I gave him a quick confession." Carol gave herself a short pause to reflect on how matter-of-fact she'd been when talking about prolonged incarceration, before finishing with, "Is that really true?"

Sonia made a 'yes and no' face. "I obviously haven't had the time to look at your case in any detail, but hearing the charge he read out just now, and assuming nobody actually got hurt," she paused to wait for Carol's confirmatory nod before continuing, "the sentence ought to be no more than five years. Now, that can be increased to an extent on the back of multiple offences, and/or if you laundered the proceeds."

"And on the reduction side?" pressed Carol. "I mean, the quick confession bit?"

"Usually, yes," said Sonia, her face showing that there was a 'but' to come, and it quickly did. "*But* less likely if there are aggravating factors."

"Such as?" asked Carol, not really wanting to hear, but needing to.

"Again, multiplicity of offences," said Sonia, counting the factors off on her fingers as she went, "refusal to cooperate in retrieval of the proceeds of said crime or crimes, non-disclosure of key accomplices, and sometimes, usually only in exceptional cases that have received high levels of negative publicity regarding the police, the Home Office may pressure the Attorney General into suggesting to the – of course, wholly independent – judiciary that sentencing leniency is not in the best public interest."

Carol sat back in her chair and cocked her head to one side before replying. "Not looking good, then," she said with a lopsided grin.

"Now *you* have to explain to *me*," said Sonia, leaning forward in anticipation.

"First off, I'm not going to help them snatch the money back from people who need it a heck of a lot more than the banks do," said Carol. "Plus, I did it all myself so there are no accomplices, I did six banks so that's a whatever-you-called-it, I did launder the money, and, from what I've heard from my best friend, the *Midwestern Echo* has been stirring up negative publicity for the police right from the start. So I make that four or maybe even five black marks in a row."

Sonia nodded. "In that case, you need me more than I thought. If I could find a hole in their case, some sort of doubt or procedural—"

"Sorry to interrupt the thought," said Carol, "but I don't think so. You saw the confession. It's all down in black and white. I told them everything from start to finish, and I signed it. So when they ask me, I'll plead guilty, quite simply because I am."

"Could I maybe still come to court with you to make sure you get bail?" asked Sonia, her voice reminding Carol of when Sarah was seven years old and pleading with Mummy for them to do some cake baking together.

"Do you really want to waste your time on me?" asked Carol. "I mean, haven't you got lots of other more important..." She stopped as she saw disappointment in the young solicitor's beautiful big brown eyes. "What's up, pet?" she asked.

Sonia looked across and smiled. "I don't think anybody has ever called me 'pet' before."

"Not even your mum and dad?"

"No." Sonia laughed. "They call me '*golu*'. It's a Hindi word that loosely translates to 'chubby'. Apparently I was a bit that way as a newborn and it somehow stuck."

"You're certainly not chubby now," said Carol. "There's not an ounce of spare flesh on you. In fact I'd say you're as close to perfect as could be."

"Thank you, Carol."

"Where are you from, pet? India, Pakistan?"

"Cheltenham, actually," said Sonia. "Yes, my parents were both originally from India, but I was born here. So I am officially as English as warm, flat beer and heavy dessert puddings – the former I detest, by the way, and the latter I simply cannot resist, which will inevitably lead to my physical decline and downfall." She laughed again.

"If I wasn't going to prison," said Carol softly, "I'd make you one of my steamed spotted dicks. They're something close to legendary in our family."

"Now that is a big incentive to get you home as quickly as possible," said Sonia with a chuckle. "If you will give me the opportunity to try."

"You changed the subject," said Carol, fixing Sonia with a firm stare, the sort she'd used to get her kids to confess to some naughtiness or other.

"When?" asked Sonia, clearly knowing but being evasive.

"When I suggested I'd be a poor use of your time," said Carol. "So go on, tell me."

"This is not about me," said Sonia, looking away briefly before returning to make eye contact. "This is about what *you* want, Carol. Nothing more."

"Tell me," insisted Carol.

Sonia sighed heavily. "I've been working for this same legal firm for more than two years. I work harder and I'm smarter than most of the men, but they never give me a proper chance to prove how good I am. I get allocated this duty solicitor role more often than the others and given just enough court time to retain my accreditation, but if anything juicy crops up then one of the partners, both men, always takes over. So I get to spend my talents representing lowlife repeat offenders – bicycle thieves, vandals, shoplifters and the like – helping them to bargain their way to a community service order so that they can get back out on the streets and carry on as before. Some of them I get to see more frequently than I do my family."

"So you fancied having a trip to court with a six-times bank robber?" asked Carol. "Merely to sit and hear her plead guilty as charged?"

"And to try to argue down your length of sentence," said Sonia.

"In that case, pet," said Carol, "I would be delighted to have you tag along."

# Chapter 32

Monday morning and Carol was awake early and, amazingly, feeling a great deal better than good. For her two-and-a-bit days in custody she had been pampered and spoiled like she could never remember before. No cooking, no cleaning, no shopping, no childcare, warm and comfy with a single bed that didn't have anybody snoring all night alongside her. She'd also been well fed with reasonable-quality meals, along with seemingly endless cups of tea brought to her by the very friendly desk sergeant Big Fat Bob, as she now knew him. Jacquie and Danny had looked in on her regularly to make sure there was nothing she was wanting for, and, best of all, Sonia Patel, the little darling, had been going through her story in fine detail, searching for any angle or crack she could use to reduce the inevitable prison sentence.

The only disappointment of the weekend had been that her Roy had not been allowed to visit. She knew it would be a tough first meeting with him but had hoped to get it over and done with quickly. She felt utterly awful about it all, but still hoped to be able to explain without upsetting him further by saying it had all come about because she'd been bored. She'd spent hour after hour going through multiple scenarios in her head, and had just about settled on one when Sonia let her know it wouldn't be happening. The good news, however, was that Sonia also felt it was a near nailed-on certainty that after Monday morning's preliminary hearing in court Carol would be bailed and so able to go home and explain everything to her husband without the pressure of time or other people hanging around.

A more upsetting moment had been Jacquie's recounting of her brief telephone conversation with Sarah. Apparently Carol's daughter had been brusque and snappy, saying she didn't want to speak to her mother, the 'family-destroying thief' who had left them all traumatised, embarrassed and 'downright fucking furious'.

"She'll come around," said Jacquie, holding Carol's hand to help quell the shakes of disappointment. "It's just a bit of a shock right now, that's all."

A private security company transported her to Shrewsbury Crown Court, as that function, she was told, had been third-party outsourced – whatever that meant – to save money. So it was a pair of scruffy, unshaven young men in ill-fitting uniforms who'd driven her there, sat in the back of a tatty old van that smelled of urine. It was, she thought, without doubt the very worst part of her entire experience so far as a soon-to-be-convicted bank robber.

The Crown Court building was, to say the very least, uninspiring on the outside from what Carol could see of it through the van window as they passed, and the interior was only marginally less so. But, as with the interview room before, Carol's hours of telly watching had prepared her to the point that she felt completely at ease in her new surroundings. And seeing Sonia standing waiting for her at the entrance to the holding cell made Carol smile. The young solicitor returned the grin, telling Carol how amazed and impressed she was by her client's calmness, verging on serenity. Carol's explanation made her laugh, but almost immediately Sonia's face turned serious.

"I've just heard we've drawn Judge Vivian Dickens," she said, adding a little "eek!" as an exclamation mark.

Carol's look of total incomprehension compelled Sonia to explain.

"She's notoriously tough, hard-nosed, no-nonsense, and apparently an absolute stinker. Luckily for me, I've never crossed her path before but..."

"You'll be alright, pet," said Carol, patting her solicitor gently on the arm. "Just try to enjoy yourself."

"It's not me I'm worried about," said Sonia. "Dickens is like a modern-day Judge Jeffreys. She may not have you hanged, but she doesn't do lenient."

"I have absolutely no idea who Judge Jeffreys was, but I'm sure you'll see me right," said Carol, adding an encouraging smile and a stage wink for good measure. "And it's only for a few minutes, so as I said, try to enjoy your moment in court with a notorious multiple bank robber."

"I just wish we could give it a go," said Sonia. "I've been sifting back through everything you told me and all the files as far as I've been allowed to see them, and I really do think we could have a..." She stopped as she saw Carol's facial expression. "Okay okay," she said, waving her hands in appeasement, "I know. You want this all done and dusted as quickly as possible. It's just that I was hoping for..."

"A moment in the sun," said Carol, finishing Sonia's sentence for her. "And I am truly sorry that I'm not up for it."

The rest of any potential discussion was cut off by the call for them to go in. The court was ready and Judge Vivian Dickens was not a woman to be kept waiting.

As Carol emerged into the dock, the surrounding courtroom looked to her – yet a-ruddy-gain! – completely familiar. A modern version, for sure, but still exactly as they looked on the telly. A good squint around, and all the usual bits and pieces were there, including a public viewing gallery jam-packed with people wanting a personal look at the notorious Red Fox, recently arrested on live television. Carol, though, had her eyes fixed on the hatchet-faced old woman perching on the high seat like a malevolent crow. Not a pretty sight on any count.

Sonia had now popped up down below, also in her legal costume, and turned to give Carol a small and possibly slightly nervous smile. Carol smiled back before looking across at 'the opposition', as she thought him, a small, hunched vole of a man who was repeatedly sniffing at some sort of nasal inhaler thing. He didn't look like much of an adversary, but then again, it didn't really matter a jot. In a few minutes—

The thought was snapped off by the usher chappie bellowing out the case reference. Almost as quickly, Judge Dickens fixed Carol with an icy scowl and demanded she tell the court how she would plead to the charges as brought.

Carol made to say 'Guilty', but the word stuck in her throat before she could shake it free. She glanced down at Sonia, who was expectantly staring up at her with those beautiful big brown eyes. So petite, so gorgeous and so badly treated by the apparently horrible and patronising men at her law firm. A truly lovely Cheltenham – wherever that was – young woman desperate to have her day in court with a proper case in place of her usual allocation of lowlife repeat offenders. So sure that she might have found some weaknesses in the case against Carol, along with an equally firm certainty that the end result couldn't be any worse, whatever they did. And besides all that, thought Carol, maybe it was simply too soon to end her journey here. All that effort, all that planning. And all that praise from the detectives who'd tracked her down – praise bordering on hero worship. While on the other side of that particular coin, the nasty little so-and-so Templeton, gloating at her capitulation and all but dancing on her metaphorical grave. She took a deep breath, put her shoulders back and spoke the words loud and clear. "Not guilty."

What followed was unexpected by Carol. The vole man was on his feet, protesting loudly about something or other. Sonia was all but doing a merry jig as she turned to grin and wave at Carol, and the crowd in the public gallery were slowly breaking into applause as the Wicked Judge of the West shouted, "Be quiet! Everybody! I will not tolerate this pantomime in my court!"

"Your Honour," said the vole between sniffs.

"What, Mr Stubbs?" snapped the judge.

"This is ludicrous. The accused is pleading not guilty after signing a full confession. It makes no sense. It cannot be—"

"Your Honour," cut in Sonia, on her feet and waving a hand.

"I am not a request-stop bus, Ms Patel," snarled the judge. "Kindly refrain from waving at me. Instead explain to me what is going on here."

"Your Honour," began Sonia, giving a small nod of apology for her waving transgression, "my client and I believe there are certain weaknesses to the prosecution's case, and as such—"

"She signed a confession, Ms Patel," interrupted the judge.

"There are – *were* – possible—"

"Ms Patel." Judge Dickens cracked the words out like gunfire, then held the pause for the echoing ricochets to pass before finishing. "If you are intending to play games, to make a mockery of my court, you will be embarking upon a huge and career-destroying mistake. You do understand that, don't you?"

"I do, Your Honour. But it is the express wish of my client, who—"

"Enough!" cut in the judge. "Save it for the trial."

"Your Honour," said the vole, now on his feet. "This is nonsensical. We have a signed confession. So how can—"

"She can, Mr Stubbs," snapped the judge, "and that is that. If you have what you say and it is indeed all tickety-boo, then it ought to make your life at trial very easy, oughtn't it? So kindly stop bleating and let us move on. Bail?"

"We request unconditional," said Sonia immediately.

"Mr Stubbs?" asked the judge.

"We oppose bail, Your Honour," he responded in a flash.

"On what grounds?"

"Flight risk, Your Honour."

"My client is a sixty-nine-year-old woman," butted in Sonia, on her feet again, "with no passport and no driving licence. She cannot be considered a—"

"She has shown herself," interrupted Stubbs, "to be a devious and cunning operator who is a master of disguise. This alone would make her a flight risk. However, the critical concern underpinning the Crown's objection to bail is that we believe the defendant to have not acted alone. We believe that there is an accomplice who remains at large and who could effect an extraction, so as to evade justice."

"An accomplice?" demanded Sonia. "My client has been explicit in stating that she worked alone. From where have you conjured up an accomplice?"

"It is the Crown's considered opinion," said Stubbs, "that the defendant's profile – her background, education, absence of prior criminal history – is at extreme odds with the crimes as committed. The likelihood of the accused having the intellectual or experiential wherewithal to have committed these robberies with such a high level of sophistication and prowess is, in the Crown's view, improbable, trending impossible."

"This is pure fantasy, Your Honour," howled Sonia. "Insulting fantasy. Moreover, the prosecution is saying my client is at once too ignorant to have worked alone, and yet too intelligent to be granted bail."

"Stop!" barked the judge. "I will have no more of this bickering. Mr Stubbs, kindly temper your choice of words. I will not have you insulting the personal attributes of the defendant. Character, yes, but personal attributes absolutely not. Mrs Jackson is entitled to civility and you will act accordingly. Do I make myself clear?"

Stubbs gave a nod and mumbled a clearly-not-heartfelt apology.

"Thank you, Mr Stubbs," said the judge. "Now, after due consideration, bail denied. The defendant will remain in custody until trial."

"Your Honour—" Sonia was on her feet again.

"Enough from you as well, Ms Patel," snapped the judge, cutting across her. "I have made my decision, so that is that. However, I can offer you some good news. I have just this morning had a case cancelled from my schedule, meaning I have a window of opportunity to take this case to trial a week on Tuesday. Can you be ready in time for that, Mr Stubbs?"

"This afternoon would be good for us."

"That is not what I asked, Mr Stubbs."

"A week on Tuesday will be perfectly acceptable, Your Honour."

"Ms Patel?"

"Tough, but probably just about achievable, Your Honour," replied Sonia.

Judge Dickens gave the court a milk-curdling smile of the thin-lipped, no-teeth-showing variety. "Very good," she purred. "And just so the both of you know, I want this whole case wrapped up quickly and without shenanigans. Your verbal ping-pong of this morning, although thankfully curtailed, was nonetheless irritating. I want none of that next time I see you. I also need to warn you that I have been made painfully aware by 'the powers that be' of the press interest in this case, and I will not, under any circumstance, tolerate even the merest hint of a media circus polluting my courtroom. As a mark of my position, let me issue this warning: if either of you so much as alludes to the idiotic and quite frankly puerile appellation 'Red Fox', you will instantly incur my merciless wrath."

# Chapter 33

It had been an interesting day, one that had started badly and finished well with a large slice of something in between in the middle. But then again, life of late had been rather full of ups and downs. It was as if Carol's previous steady, flat, grey existence had been catapulted into the middle of Chinese New Year fireworks. In many ways, that was good. It was, however, utterly exhausting.

Almost since the moment of her not guilty plea on Monday morning, her world had been a blur. Within hours she'd been requested to appear in not one but two identity parades, around which Nasty Little Templeton had interviewed her again, this time pressing for her to reveal the identity of her non-existent accomplice. And no matter how many times she told him there was none, he stubbornly refused to hear her. It was only the threat of a formal police harassment complaint from Sonia, who'd sat at Carol's side throughout, that made Templeton back off. He clearly wasn't happy about the not guilty plea, but seemed to gain some degree of malicious solace from his suspect being retained in custody. On the good side of the whole 'being with the police again' thing, Lovely Danny had bought her a Danish pastry that he surreptitiously handed across when he was sure his boss wasn't looking.

The rest of that day and the one after, Sonia had painstakingly gone back and forth, over and over again, every fine detail of the robberies and the events surrounding the arrest and subsequent interviews. Carol sensed there was some sort of strategy being formed behind the young woman's beautiful eyes, but didn't ask and an explanation wasn't offered.

The one thing Sonia did share and apologise for, even though it wasn't really under her control, was her inability to arrange a visit from Roy until the Wednesday. Yes, she'd assured Carol, she was legally entitled to seven visits each week, but for one reason or another it was taking longer to set up than they'd hoped. And anyway, as Sonia had heard from Sarah, Roy was finding it difficult to get to the prison. With no car and far too long a walk from the railway station, he was at the mercy of having to cadge a lift. Carol wasn't too upset. Of course she wanted to see her Roy, to have the opportunity to try to explain to him face to face, but at the same time, the delay gave her the breathing space to spend yet more time on going over how she could tell him in such a way as to not upset him still further.

But here she was now, Wednesday morning with a good breakfast inside her, washed and hair brushed, sitting comfortably in her private little cell, all ready and waiting for eleven o'clock and the meeting with her probably angry, certainly disappointed, and most likely badly hurt husband. It was an hour away, but that wasn't a problem. Time could tick around to it and she could go through her planned script for the umpteenth time.

The door opened and the skinny warder with the bad teeth and huge hairy mole on her top lip told Carol she had a visitor. Carol said nothing, assumed Roy had arrived early, got to her feet, and silently followed in the wake of the guard's choking body odour. A half-minute later and, instead of her expected destination of the visitor meeting area, she was shown the door of an interview room. Oh no, not ruddy Templeton again, she thought.

It wasn't. The man inside was probably in his late fifties, pudgy and pale with a roll of neck fat tumbling over his admittedly crisp white shirt collar. The suit too was fancy. Carol was no expert on such things, but it looked expensive. Just a shame, she thought, the man hadn't bought one a size larger so it didn't stretch so tight across his belly. He held out a meaty palm for a shake.

"Mrs Jackson," he said, the accent affecting posh but a good bit short of it. "Miles Mallins. Pleased to meet you."

Carol took the hand out of politeness, instantly wishing she hadn't as its clammy chill enveloped hers. "And you are?" she asked pointedly.

"Senior partner, Mallins and Chard," he crooned, as if merely saying the name was something magical. He produced a business card seemingly from thin air and thrust it into Carol's now-moist hand. "We have the honour of representing you at trial."

"Where's Sonia?" asked Carol. "Sonia Patel?"

"Ah..." mused the blob. "As your case is likely to attract a good deal of publicity, we, the partners, considered it politic to assign you a more senior—"

"No!" said Carol, firmly but still managing to keep it the right side of shouting.

"Mrs Jackson – may I call you Carol? – you must see—"

"No, you may not call me Carol," she said, cutting across him. "And I see very well, thank you. And I do not like what I see."

Mallins turned away, presumably to maintain his composure. When he turned back there was a horrible false smile stuck across his blubbery chops. "It is with your best interests at heart that we—"

"I don't want to sound unladylike," said Carol, looking down at the business card before snapping her gaze up to lock eyes with the man, "but you can bugger off."

"That, er, that... I mean, you—" stammered Mallins.

"Either you put Sonia Patel back on my case or..." Carol wasn't quite sure how to finish her wafer-thin threat, so decided to leave the unvoiced end to speak for her.

"Not an option," snapped Mallins.

Carol waved the business card in his direction. "Then I shall have to tell the press what a bunch of useless toads you are at Mallins and Chard. How does that sound?" She could feel her heart thumping in her chest. She'd never confronted anybody like this since back-chatting a bully in the school playground. She'd got a proper slapping for that back then, but this was different. Why the heck should she kowtow to this lump of lard? And why should poor Sonia get heaved aside by him just because her case was likely to grab a bit of publicity? "Your choice, Mr Mallins."

"And your mistake, Mrs Jackson," harrumphed the snotty kid grown old and fat.

"Thank you for your visit," called out Carol sarcastically to the man's disappearing back as he flounced out, leaving the interview-room door open wide.

At two minutes before eleven, Carol was shown into the visiting room. It wasn't huge, but was still big enough for half a dozen well-spaced table-and-chair sets. The prisoner access door was on one side and the visitor entrance on the opposite. Carol deliberately chose the table furthest from where Roy would be shown in so that she could look at him on his way across and hopefully convey a lot of what she needed to say by her facial expression before he got to her. And she was feeling surprisingly good: calm and strong. The earlier altercation with Miles Mallins had unexpectedly helped a great deal by giving her an adrenaline rush that had now stabilised, filling her with inner steel. So she sat, serene and ready, hands loosely in her lap, breathing steady, with her gaze fixed firmly on the door.

The instant she saw him, uncontrollable tears formed in the corners of her eyes. He was the only man she had ever loved. All those many years together, all those struggles to raise a family and have a life, a good life and most of the time a fun life, a lifetime she'd just gone and punched in the face and trashed, all for some crazy, mad, selfish whatever. "How could you have done it, Carol?" she asked herself under her breath. "How could you have?"

She couldn't read her Roy's expression when he first clapped eyes on her. She was an easy spot, being the sole occupant of the room beyond the uniformed warder, but he still paused just inside the door and looked at her, fixed her with his eyes, his face as blank as a professional poker player's. All those hours she'd spent preparing for this moment, all those rehearsed scenarios, simply evaporated from her mind like early-morning mist under a rising summer sun. He walked slowly over and sat himself down opposite her. His eyes were lowered, but slowly came up to meet hers. They looked across at each other for what was probably no more than ten seconds, but it felt to Carol like an eternity. Thoughts and emotions were silently firing back and forth along their sight line. Then, suddenly, they both started speaking at the same time, Roy asking, "Why?" as Carol began with, "I'm sorry." As instantly as they'd started, they both stopped. She nodded at him to go ahead. He nodded back that it was her who should start.

"I'm sorry, love," she whispered. "I truly am."

Roy pursed his lips and nodded slowly a few times. "So it is true, then," he said, "what they're saying. You did do it."

"Yes," she replied, still in a whisper. "Hard to believe, eh?"

This time he grunted a tiny, non-humorous laugh. "That's an understatement if ever I heard one."

Carol couldn't think how to respond, so didn't try.

"Why?" he asked, using a single word to puncture the suffocating silence.

Now this bit she had prepared. "I needed something. Something that was me. Something that..." She couldn't go on, as the many-times-rehearsed script warped and buckled inside her head. She couldn't remember it, couldn't see it. "I..." she restarted, only to choke again.

"Take your time," he said, reaching a hand across the table towards her. "Are we allowed to touch in here?" he asked, suddenly practical.

Carol shook her head to show she neither knew nor cared, and extended an arm to allow Roy to encircle her hand with his.

"Go on," he said softly.

"It was nothing to do with you, love, nothing. It was all me. Only me."

"And?" he asked.

With a long sigh, she began. This time not from the prepared script, instead simply allowing the words to flow out straight from her heart. "I felt old and I felt somehow pointless. Like I'd done all of what I was supposed to do on this earth, and that was that. Over and finished. All that was left, as far as I could see, was a long grey drift to the end. And when I looked at you and Sarah and her beautiful girls, I saw you all looking back at a shadow, something here but not here." She coughed to shake her next words free. "There was no *me* any more. No substance, no person, no Carol. There was a wife, a mother, a grandmother, yes, but no *me*. I'd become empty, like one of those Christmas tree decorations: shiny foil on the outside but hollow on the inside. Oh, it was my fault, I know that. I'd allowed it to happen. I'd let *me* dissolve away to nothing. I know I'm not clever, I don't have anything interesting to talk about, I can't understand new technology, and I don't get ruddy jokes. But I'm still a person, or at least I was. And doing what I did these last few months filled all those gaps and helped to make me..." She left it there, unfinished but complete.

"I'm sorry," he said softly, squeezing her hand.

"I told you, love, it's not your fault," she said, her voice firm. "It was me. I let it happen. And then I set about doing something to fix it. What I chose – yes, *I chose* – to do about it wasn't your fault either. Making the choice was part of Carol being reborn as much as actually doing it was. And do you know what?" She coughed a small, dry laugh at the irony. "Taking the blame now feels nearly as good as doing it. Somehow this is rock-hard proof that I really did do something extraordinary."

"Sarah said she'd noticed a change in you of late," said Roy. "A few weeks back, it was, when she told me there was an extra sparkle in your eyes that gave away something was going on. But, blow me, didn't she ever guess wrong what it was."

Carol didn't ask the obvious question, instead opting for, "How is she?"

Roy gave a lopsided grin. "To say she's furious wouldn't even get close. I think it's embarrassment more than anything, though. You know what a control freak she is. And this came at her from so far out of the blue, she never had an inkling. She'll come around eventually, but right now she won't be coming anywhere near you."

"So how did you get here?" asked Carol, deliberately steering the conversation to lighter things. "I'd sort of guessed Sarah would have driven you."

"Trevor brought me down. He offered. He hasn't hardly been out of the house since his Alice's funeral. Only comes bowling once a week now as well. Anyway, he'd watched it on *All Points West* and turned up on the doorstep Saturday morning, asking if he could do anything to help." Roy gave another small laugh, this time at the thought of something funny. "He told me his Alice would be cheering you on from heaven. Said she'd always wanted to do something really bad, but had never had the nerve. Apparently once upon a time she'd told Trevor he was 'fucking boring'. Bit rich, that, eh, him being an insurance salesman and all." Roy laughed properly this time. "By heck, that felt good," he said when he'd finished.

"It sounded good too," said Carol. "And say thank you from me to Trevor."

"Will do."

"And what about you yourself?" she asked. "How are you keeping? Without your adoring cook and bottle-washer, I mean?"

"Sarah's been feeding me. It seems like it's her mission to make me fat. But she's been really supportive – of me, that is. And she set up a video link thing to our Paul."

It was the thorn that had to inevitably prick the skin at some time. It still hurt, though. She waited to hear how her son had taken the news of his mother being an alleged serial bank robber who'd been arrested live on television.

"He wanted to come straight over," said Roy. "I told him it was bloomin' daft as there was nothing he could do. Best he stays where he is, and once it's all sorted and the dust has settled, he can make a sensible decision."

"You told him all that?" asked Carol. "Straight?"

Roy looked a little sheepish. "Sarah did. I just agreed." He chortled again. "My word, here's me laughing my flamin' head off and holding hands with an – I have to say, utterly delectable – arch-criminal who is most likely going to prison for a very long time when..." He stopped absolutely dead and his face blanched.

"When what?" asked Carol, leaning forward across the table to be able to look more directly into her husband's downcast eyes.

"Secrets," he whispered. "What is it about blasted secrets? Why are they so difficult to keep and yet still so difficult to share?"

"I'm sorry," she said. "I couldn't tell you. I didn't dare. I often thought about it, but I knew you'd talk me out of it, or lock me up so I couldn't carry on. And I didn't want to stop. It made me feel like I could fly. And besides that, I was really good at it."

"That's what the news people are saying. A lot of them sound more like fans than...whatever the opposite is. But no matter how good you were, you still got caught."

"In the end, yes, I did," said Carol. "I most certainly did."

They spent the remainder of their allotted time together holding hands across the table and very deliberately talking about anything apart from robbery and imprisonment. Carol reflected later on how little they'd talked, really talked, when they'd been at home together in what would be termed a normal life. Maybe this was what she'd been driven towards: reopening a communication channel. Or was it that she finally had something worth talking about, even though they'd glossed over the details? Whatever it was, that morning she'd felt closer to her husband of nigh-on fifty years than she had done for ages. The downside of that was she felt even worse about being the cause of their imminent long-term enforced separation.

She spent the afternoon by herself back in the now familiar comfort of her remand cell with a cup of tea and an afternoon custard cream, doing nothing but letting things mull over inside her head. She'd never been a reader – books or newspapers. The occasional flick through a magazine was the most she ever went for, but even there, the swathes of glossy adverts for things she didn't need and couldn't afford anyway always put her off. She enjoyed watching the telly but could see, now that she had the time to think about it, how she'd often drifted away into her own thoughts, despite her eyes being on the screen. Maybe that was why Roy always had to explain to her what was going on and who was who.

She didn't know precisely what time it was when a gentle knock on the door preceded it opening to reveal her Angel of Cheltenham. Sonia beamed a smile at her.

"You really stirred the pot today, Carol," she said, her normally flat, controlled tone quavering with emotion. "I thought Miles Mallins was going to explode when he came back. He didn't say a word to me, though. He just stormed along the corridor and into his private office, slamming the door shut so hard a piece of my office ceiling fell down." She gave a short snuffle of a laugh. "He sent a flunky down to tell me the case was mine, but then followed it up with a personal e-mail telling me if I mess up I shall be fired without compensation."

"I'm sorry, pet," said Carol.

"What?" exclaimed Sonia. "It's brilliant and I utterly adore you. Not only do I now get this case – a real, meaningful case – but I am also now in a totally win-win situation."

"Meaning what, exactly?" asked Carol.

"If I do well I get exposure and the chance to move on and up somewhere other than my current employers. While, on the other hand, if I do less well, I will be freed from the shackles of the disgusting Miles Mallins and his equally awful partner without having to make that leap off my own bat. Win-win! So come on, let's go through everything one more time."

# Chapter 34

It was five days after Roy had been to see her when Carol had a visit from somebody other than Sonia. The adorable young solicitor had popped in every day at some time or other, fitting the call in between her other responsibilities. She assured Carol that she was confident she had done as much as she possibly could in preparation for the trial, so she was only looking in to make sure her favourite client of all time was being well looked after. Carol told her over and over that she was more worried about her and how she was being treated by her quite disgusting employer. 'Frostily' had been the solicitor's reply; but nothing worse than that, and pretty much how it had always been since they'd hired their token 'not white, not male' tick in the box.

Roy had promised Carol he would find a way to get down to see her regularly – even if he had to learn how to drive, he'd joked. It would, he'd said, be more enjoyable than being sat at home, where he felt more of a prisoner than she probably did, given the press had been virtually camped outside their house. Every time he'd tried to go out, they'd all scrummed around him, hurling questions and snapping photos. There'd been a TV van out there too for the first day and a bit, but they'd soon gone off somewhere more interesting. So he'd taken to sneaking out through the backyard to go bowling, but they'd spotted him and followed, which didn't go down well with the other club members at all. Talking of bowling, all three of his best mates had offered to help out if they could, but he didn't want them to feel like he was taking advantage. Rainy was still working full-time at the garage, Trev was keen to help but was a scary dreadful driver, and Cliff was having issues with his missus and her 'condition', whatever that was. So he'd said thank you and promised to ask for a lift when he needed one, most probably when the trial started. But one thing was for sure, he'd told her, to a man jack of them they were rooting for her, whatever she'd done.

So all in all, it was something of a surprise when, early afternoon on the Monday, the day before the trial was due to start, she was roused from a delicious early-afternoon snooze by the warder telling her she had a visitor. Intrigued, she shook herself fully awake and trotted on behind to the visiting area.

There was not a soul in there when she arrived and, thinking it had to be some sort of mistake, she stayed standing, watching the visitors' entrance door and waiting. When it did finally open, the sight was something to behold. Dressed from head to toe in black, veiled hat and all, was Janice.

Carol couldn't help but laugh as her friend swept across the intervening space and offered a husky, sepulchral, "Hello, Carol."

"This is a prison, Janice, not a ruddy funeral parlour."

Janice snorted a laugh. "I just felt wrong wearing colours. I thought it would be out of keeping with the situation."

"But the veil?" asked Carol. "Seriously?"

"It's the only black hat I've got," retorted Janice. "I bought it to wear at my Lenny's funeral and didn't want to rip off the veil just for today's visit in case another burning comes along sometime soon."

"Got anyone in mind?" asked Carol. "I'm hoping to avoid the death penalty."

Both women laughed and embraced.

"Are we allowed to do this?" hissed Janice in Carol's ear. "I thought touching was forbidden in case I'm passing you the drugs I've got hidden up my bum."

"If you have, I'm not taking them."

"What about the mobile phone?" asked Janice, struggling to get the words out between convulsive giggles. "Do you not want that either?"

Carol snorted. "Only if you've got a spare battery charger up there too."

They laughed long and hard after that, Carol quickly checking over her shoulder to see the reaction of the onlooking warder. There was none. But the laughter had been a blessed release of tension for Carol, and it looked like the same was true for Janice.

"Sit down and chat," commanded Carol. "Tell me something, anything that isn't about robbery, police, courts or prison."

"You're not getting off that easy," scoffed Janice. "You have to tell me about all those things you've just listed. Apart from the robbery, 'cause you've already told me about that. Start with the rozzers. What have they been like? Did they good-cop-bad-cop you? Rough you up?"

"No, none of that," said Carol, shaking her head. "The lead detective is a nasty little worm of a man called Templeton."

"Shirley," said Janice, nodding sagely. "That's Shirley as in Shirley Templeton. Little bloke, blond curly hair, tap-dances. Oh, and I made the last bit up." She laughed again, and Carol joined her.

"But the other two have been really nice," continued Carol. "They're like a mini Red Fox fan club. Keep telling me how impressed they were with my robbery craft. The more senior one, Danny, even told me he was sad he'd caught me. Brought me in a Danish pastry last week and all."

"Oooh, so it's Danny. First-name terms with the fuzz, then," cooed Janice. "I am impressed. And what about your weasel?"

"My what?"

"Weasel, brief, lawyer," said Janice, as if speaking to a dullard. "Come on, girl, you need to get up to speed with the chokey lingo."

"My solicitor is beautiful and a truly lovely girl – young, enthusiastic, and very smart," said Carol, smiling to herself as she thought of Sonia Patel.

"Good track record?" asked Janice.

"Not yet," replied Carol. "But she will have very soon. Will you be coming along to watch tomorrow?"

"I'm having my hair and nails done in the morning and I've got a facial booked for the afternoon, so probably not," said Janice nonchalantly. "But I'll do my best to get down for Wednesday."

"Wear something different," said Carol with a wink.

"Message received," said Janice with a return wink. "Anyway, how is it in here?" She looked around at the visitor room and sniffed. "Have you joined a gang yet? Got in with the kingpin? Started getting your prison tats?"

"No, no and no," said Carol, grinning at the dark humour. "I keep pretty much to myself, but there is a fearsome large woman they call Tinkerbell who must be eighteen stones if she's an ounce, and she's a Red Fox super-fan. Told me that if I get any aggro from anyone to let her know and she'll 'do' them. She would, too. She's in here for stabbing her husband and mother-in-law, the latter twenty-seven times, apparently. Oh, and her real name's Fleur, by the way."

"Nice," said Janice with a wince of a grin. "Very nice. And to think I was going to bust you out of here. Doesn't seem any point now you've got a bitch."

"Bust me out?" asked Carol. "How?"

"For some reason I imagined they'd let me drive Lenny's car into the exercise yard. Then I'd distract the screws while you climbed into the boot."

"You didn't really imagine this, did you?" asked Carol.

Janice shook her head and let loose one of her cackling laughs, although thankfully moderated to suit the institutional situation. "Would have been good, though, eh? We could have smashed out through the gates and driven off into the sunset like Thelma and Louise."

"They both died in the end," said Carol. "Drove over a cliff, as I remember."

"Good point," said Janice. "Back to the drawing board."

"There is one thing you could do for me," said Carol in a whisper, checking again over her shoulder that the 'screw' was still paying them zero attention. "The police didn't find the tofu curry."

"Lucky them," said Janice with a sniff.

"No, you dope," said Carol, exaggeratedly mouthing the words as she whispered, "*the tofu curry.*"

The penny dropped. "Oh," said Janice, doing the same rubber-faced mouthing as she whispered back, "*the tofu curry.*"

"I don't suppose you'd mind dropping it off somewhere deserving, would you."

"Think of it as my singular contribution to criminality," said Janice. "Did you have anywhere specific in mind?"

"You choose," said Carol, before clapping her hands to signal a change of subject. "So come on," she chirped. "Your turn. Did you buy one of your Eddy's bungalows in Cyprus?"

She'd been expecting a straight negative response, but instead got a look somewhere between embarrassed and guilty-sad.

"You did, didn't you." Carol spoke it as a statement of fact.

Janice nodded. "I'm not going to live there," she said. "Not permanently. I just...well...I...oh heck, he was very persuasive, Carol. Both of them were. My Eddy and his paramour, Robbie the Parrot Smuggler."

The last phrase cracked the tension, and both women again dissolved into fits of laughter.

"I'm pleased for you, Janice," said Carol. "I really am. And it's not as if I'm going to be very good company for the next few years at least. Not unless you do something equally outrageous and we end up sharing a cell."

"How long do you expect to get?" asked Janice, suddenly serious.

“Five-and-a-bit,” said Carol. “Years, that is. Could be more, could be less, but that’s about it. And if I behave myself – don’t start too many riots, dig a tunnel, or stab another inmate with a sharpened toothbrush – I could be home in less than three.”

“Was it really worth it, chook?” asked Janice.

“Yes,” said Carol, nodding. “Yes, it was.”

# Chapter 35

The same security company transported her to the courthouse in the same smelly van. The guards were different from the first time, but no less scruffy and generally unkempt. At the entrance they handed their charge over to the court security, who signed the transfer papers and waved them off for a nice day somewhere else.

Sonia, already robed and wigged, was waiting for Carol at the holding cells. She didn't look as happy as she usually did.

"What's up, pet?" asked Carol. "You look a bit down in the dumps."

"They've brought in a big hitter from down south," groaned Sonia. "Stubbs has been ditched. Looks like somebody somewhere high up has decided there are to be no chances with getting you convicted and sentenced hard. It has to be about those stories in the blasted *Midwestern Echo* giving the police a kicking week after week. Somebody wants to redress the balance and make you an example into the bargain."

"Calm down, calm down," cooed Carol. "The bigger they are, the harder they fall. Or, to put it another way, if you give some superstar legal a run for his money, then think how much better that will make you look."

Sonia smiled a big thank-you. "At least I'll know what he's going to do."

"How does that work?" asked Carol.

"We studied the court cases of half a dozen well-known barristers at university, and Quentin Bellinger was one of them. He runs the same game pattern every time. There are rumours he takes bets with his cronies to see how quickly he can get a conviction and how few witnesses he has to call to get there."

"I'm still a bit lost," said Carol. "Same game pattern?"

"Do you play chess, Carol?"

"No."

"Understand the rules?"

"No."

"Okay," said Sonia, "so no chess analogies. Let's just say, in simple terms, he will start with a few low-grade witnesses that he knows can be torn to shreds by even a half-decent defence. They're sacrificed to the greater good, because from the opening exchanges he will be able to see how capable or poor his opponent is."

"Got it so far," said Carol. "And then?"

"Then he brings out his star witness," continued Sonia. "This is the one that will wow the jury and allow him to paint his portrait of an undeniably guilty defendant, a picture that will sit fixed at the very forefront of the jurors' minds."

"Makes sense," said Carol, "but I've got a feeling that's not the end of it."

"He always," continued Sonia, "always, always, always holds something back, like a secret weapon, a doomsday bomb, something he keeps hidden in the shadows, only to be unleashed if he feels he is at risk of losing. It's like his trump card up the sleeve that he won't pull out and play if he can win the hand without."

"Any idea what it might be?" asked Carol.

"Not yet," replied Sonia, "but I shall be looking for it, I promise you that."

"You'll be great," said Carol, patting her young solicitor on the arm. "I know you will. Now, isn't that my case I just heard them call?"

As Carol came up the stairs into the dock, the courtroom was the same as last time, but also very different in that it was full to bursting. There were significantly more people down in the body of the room, a jury was already sitting there staring at her, and the public gallery was once again crammed with people she didn't know. Sonia looked up at her and gave a tiny wave and a nervous smile, and Carol responded like for like. Sonia inclined her head ever so slightly in the direction of a very tall, slim man who looked like he'd been born to wear a wig and gown. It had to be the Bellinger bloke she'd spoken about, the big hitter from down south, the man she'd studied at university, the man with the predictable pattern. Carol looked back at Sonia and winked a 'you go get him'.

The only thing missing to complete the scene was a judge, and right on cue, the wicked witch floated in and perched, immediately scanning the assembly with the eyes of a hawk. "Ah, Mr Bellinger," she intoned, "I'd heard you were heading north for some purpose other than blasting poor dear game birds out of the sky. And here you are in *my* courtroom. Without giving away any trade secrets, would you care to give me a hint as to why the perfectly adequate Mr Stubbs is no longer with us?"

Bellinger, already standing, stood even taller to address the judge in a voice that sounded somehow perfectly tuned to the setting in both volume and tone. His words were spoken with a precision and delivery that left them clear and resonating with positive purpose – like a supreme actor, thought Carol. "Powers greater than I, Your Honour, considered it essential that this particular case be pursued to its necessary conclusion *sine periculo*, and—"

"There will be no Latin in my court, Mr Bellinger," snapped the judge, cutting across the barrister's speech. "Save it for your boys' club dinners. English only, please. Now finish what you were saying so we can get along."

Bellinger seemed totally unfazed by the rebuke, and merely took up where he'd left off. "The Crown desires a rapid conviction without risk of anything that might lead to either an appeal or an absurdly lenient sentence, Your Honour. And I was considered to be, in simple terms, the man for the job."

Judge Dickens raised a single eyebrow half an inch. "Well, we are indeed honoured by your esteemed presence, Mr Bellinger. However, be aware, I will not tolerate any of your Old Bailey flash-powder theatrics. So keep it simple, keep it short, succinct, and always in plain English. If you can manage all that, I'm sure we shall get along merrily. Understood?"

"Indeed I do, Your Honour."

"Now to you, Ms Patel," said the judge, turning her fearsome gaze onto Sonia. "I must tell you I am more than a little surprised to see you here this morning. Messrs Mallins and Chard off playing golf, are they? It's not like those two to miss an opportunity like this for getting their names in the paper."

Sonia got to her feet and coughed lightly into a fist before answering. "I was selected to take this case, Your Honour," she said, keeping it super-simple and short.

"Well, let us hope for your client's sake that you're up to it, Ms Patel. Mr Bellinger here takes no prisoners and I certainly shall not be bailing you out if you get into difficulties. Right, with the pleasantries done, let's get cracking, shall we? Mr Bellinger, the floor is yours. Opening statement. Short and sweet, please."

The man stood and fluffed his robe – like a raven preparing to fly, thought Carol as she watched him from her privileged observation post. He turned his entire body so as to be front-on facing the jury and paused for a second or two before launching into it. He was good. Very good. Of all the many court case speeches Carol had heard on the telly over the years, this man was as good as any and better than most. He laid out her crimes without getting too deeply into detail, actually spending more time on stressing, in a genuinely blood-chilling tone of voice, how she had terrorised the poor cashiers with threats of indiscriminate violence. The money laundering was a throwaway point, the calm before the finale where he rhythmically boomed out the multiple offences, the flat refusal to aid in the recovery of the stolen moneys, and worst of all, her continued concealment of the undoubted accomplice, the true brains behind the catalogue of villainy.

Carol was shocked and angry, just as she had been when Templeton had been banging on about it. And Stubbs the solicitor vole, he'd been the same. It was the main reason why they'd blocked her release on bail. So what was it with these people, these men? She wanted to stand up and shout at them, but... Just sit, Carol, bite your tongue. You know the truth. They don't.

She'd been so caught up in her internalised rage that she'd not noticed that Sonia was now on her feet. She looked so small compared to her adversary, but her voice when it came was crystal clear, powerful, modulated, and gently assertive. The case was flawed, she told the court, from start to finish. Corners had been cut and mistakes had been made. Every shred of evidence the police had was either circumstantial or coincidental. There was not one single iota of factual forensic evidence linking her client to these crimes, and as such, the shadow of doubt did not merely hang over the prosecution's case – no, the shadow of doubt was in fact the predominant element.

Carol wanted to applaud. It was a brilliant speech delivered brilliantly. So much so she could almost have believed herself that she didn't do it, if she hadn't known better. But there was no time to dwell – the first witness was being called, a young man she'd met once before, across a bank counter. And she guessed he'd probably seen her a second time, but from behind a two-way mirror in one of the identity parades she'd been called to.

Lester Sweet looked uncomfortable wearing a suit with no plastic name badge on the pocket, and kept touching at the place where it ought to be. Sworn in, he sat fidgeting in a manner like what Carol used to call having ants in his pants.

"Mr Sweet," said Bellinger in a nicey-nice, congenial-old-uncle voice, "would you kindly tell the court what happened on that fateful day when you came face to face with your first – and hopefully your last – armed bank robber?"

Sweet touched at his hair, the corner of his mouth, his tie knot, his absent badge, and his hair again. "It was horrible, sir," he said in a barely audible whisper.

"Speak up, Mr Sweet," demanded the judge.

"S-sorry, Your Worship," said Sweet, drawing a scowl of exasperated dismay from the judge at his ludicrous error of title. "It was horrible," he repeated, now almost shouting. "She threatened to shoot me and everybody else if I didn't do what she told me. Said she didn't care if it was a man, a woman or even a little kiddie."

"She," said Bellinger, making it neither a question nor a statement.

"Y-yes," stammered Sweet.

"It must have been terrifying for you," said Bellinger.

"It was," said Sweet with a vigorous series of nods.

"And the gun?" asked Bellinger. "The handgun she used to terrorise you? I understand you managed to identify it."

"The police showed me and I instantly recognised it. A Walther P88."

"This was the weapon recovered from the defendant's dwelling," said Bellinger to no-one in particular. "I understand you also identified the fake moustache and hoodie coat found in the defendant's possession. Am I correct?"

"Y-yes."

"And you identified the defendant," Bellinger swung around to point a lazy finger at Carol, "in an identity parade line-up from amongst six persons, correct?"

"I did," said Sweet, more strongly as he relaxed into his imagined star witness role.

"Thank you, Mr Sweet," said Bellinger, immediately turning his back on the young man and sitting himself down.

Sonia was on her feet in a flash, a bundle of nervous energy. "Mr Sweet, or may I call you Lester?" she asked.

"Lester's good," he answered.

"I'd like to say I sympathise with you having to go through such a horrific ordeal. You were very brave to come here to re-live it. And to aid the police in their investigation."

"It's my duty," said a now-glowing-with-praise Lester Sweet.

"However," said Sonia, having built the witness up only to knock him down, "just now you referred to the robber as 'she'." The sentence had been couched as a statement, leaving Lester to turn it into a question in his mind.

"I did."

"And yet, in your initial statement to the police you referred to the robber as a young male." Sonia paused to make a confused face, and turned to show it to the jury. "Can you help me to understand how 'young male' translates to the accused, a sixty-nine-year-old woman?"

"I made a mistake," said Lester, swallowing hard. "I was in shock when they took the first statement. Once I'd calmed down and had time to think it over in my head, I went back to the police and corrected myself."

Sonia lifted a sheet of paper from her table and looked for something, even though to Carol's eyes she didn't need to. "Ten weeks later," she said. "And, strangely, on the same day as the identity parade. Something of a coincidence, don't you think?"

"I-I-I wanted to save on the travelling expenses. Doing both at the same time."

"But the two were not in any way linked," continued Sonia. "The identity parade and your sudden epiphany – or, to put it into more simple English, your moment of, shall we say, delayed recall?"

"N-no."

"That's good. That sets my mind at rest." She spoke the words in a tone that left no doubt that it had done anything but. "Oh, and purely out of interest, were they all mature women in this line-up, or was there a mix of gender and age?"

"All little old ladies," said Lester.

"Despite you having previously identified the robber – *your* robber – as a young man."

"I didn't make the rules," he grouched, a hint of petulance creeping into his voice as he felt the heat. "I just went and did what I had to do as a good, honest citizen."

"Admirable, Lester. And thank you from all of us. Now, the gun. It sounded to me like you're something of an expert in this area. Military service?"

"*Call of Duty*," replied Lester, sounding more self-assured than at any time before. "Mostly. But a few others as well."

"Computer games?"

"Yes."

"And you managed to identify the gun based on that. How very clever of you."

"Thank you."

"Especially so," continued Sonia, again pretending to read from the sheet of paper in her hand, "when your initial police statement said no more than '*He* had a gun. About an inch of it was poking out of *his* coat sleeve. It was heavy. I could tell by the sound it made when *he* tapped it on my countertop.' *He*, *his*, *he*. Gendered pronouns aside, Lester, was this another delayed memory surge, identifying precisely the make and model of gun from a mere inch of visible barrel?" Sonia didn't wait for him to reply. "No further questions, Your Honour."

Carol fought to suppress the urge to cheer. Then she remembered what Sonia had told her. Bellinger always put up some sacrificial lambs at the start, witnesses he would expect to be torn apart by even a half-competent solicitor to see what he was up against. No matter. Sonia had ripped that one to shreds right enough. Game on.

Next up was a white dumpling of a middle-aged woman in a too-tight navy-blue Crimplene suit, who was introduced as Kathleen Duckworth from the Counties Mutual Bank in Nantwich. Unlike Lester, this woman looked completely at ease and full of herself, sitting as if perched like a very large songbird getting ready to warble. Carol expected her testimony to be more of the same, but it wasn't.

"Ms Duckworth," began Bellinger, swaying gently as he asked the question, "you came face to face with the defendant, correct?"

"I did," replied the woman confidently. "Although she was wearing a disguise."

"Ah, so you saw through it," said Bellinger, pretending to be impressed.

"More around it," said Duckworth.

It was Bellinger's turn to pull a confused face now, and he swivelled the best part of a full circle so the whole court could see it. "Could you please explain to the court?"

"I did it by voice."

"By voice?" enquired Bellinger, now acting so very intrigued.

Kathleen Duckworth shifted in her seat to face the jury as she answered. "I am a recognised and accepted expert in the identification of regional accents, especially sub-regional accent variations in the north-west of England, and—"

"Thank you, Miss Duckworth," said Bellinger, "we get the gist. You are an expert in the science of accents. So, now, please tell the court about your encounter with and subsequent identification of the defendant."

"The robber had a very particular central north Shropshire accent that is characterised by clipping certain aspirates whilst elongating elements of—"

"And the identification parade?" interrupted Bellinger. "Which I understand was conducted in the 'blind – vocals only' format."

"Correct. And it was very straightforward, a super-simple spot," chirruped the dumpling-bird. "There was absolutely no doubt whatsoever the robber was the person I picked out of the line-up the instant they spoke." She finished with a wide grin, leaving Bellinger to silently return to his chair.

"In your statement to the police," said Sonia, already on her feet and looking straight at the witness, "immediately after your encounter, you said you were *certain* the robber was a man in his early twenties. Is that correct, Ms Duckworth?"

Duckworth twitched and squirmed a little in her chair. "The voice was husky and high-pitched. I told them it could be a young man or an elderly woman."

"But the second half of that comment does not appear in your statement," said Sonia, speaking in a soft, non-accusatory way whilst turning the sheet of paper this way and that in her hand.

"It must have been missed off," said Duckworth. "I definitely said it."

Sonia wagged her head from side to side in a 'That's what you say' sort of gesture, making sure she left doubt in the minds of the jury members without having to hammer the point. "And so you used your special skill to pick out the defendant's voice from among the other five in the audio identity parade."

"I did. There was no doubt at all. Not a shred."

"Thank you," said Sonia, making to sit before suddenly popping back upright. "Oh, one last thing, Ms Duckworth. Just as a matter of interest, how were the other five in the line-up? Easy to pigeonhole?"

"Oh, easy-peasy," said a smug-sounding Duckworth, counting them off on her fingers. "A south-west Wirral, a Shrewsbury central, a north-east Worcestershire, a Staffordshire border, and a Chirk, although I couldn't quite tell which side of the Welsh border she was from. It gets a bit difficult around that area."

"So only one – what did you call it? – central north Shropshire?"

"Yes, just the one." The instant she said the words, Kathleen Duckworth's face fell as she realised that she'd walked straight into a trap.

"So," said Sonia, bouncing her gaze between the witness and the jury, "with your accent recognition skill you picked out the only one of the six who had the accent you had originally reported. I would say that in many ways that would be like my client being black and standing in a line with five white alternatives." She didn't expect a response, and didn't give the witness time to offer one. "No further questions."

Carol was musing over how much fun this would have been if it hadn't been her sitting in the dock, when the judge broke into her reverie.

"One more before lunch, Mr Bellinger, and for the love of Eve, kindly try to make it a little more challenging for the defence."

Bellinger nodded, and called his third witness, who Carol recognised the instant he walked in. It was the polite policeman who'd started to search her bag at Leominster Railway Station. He looked at Carol and gave her a smile before realising who and where he was and killing it dead.

It sounded to Carol's ear like Bellinger was going through the motions with this one, like he was more interested in his dinner than the case. Maybe he was wearying of chucking out sacrifices for Sonia to savage. Or maybe he was playing a different game. She couldn't tell.

"Constable Edrich," began Bellinger, "you came face to face with the defendant at Leominster Railway Station, correct?"

"Yes, sir," replied the constable.

"As you had been instructed to look out for a person who had, only minutes before, committed an armed robbery at Bowlands Bank in the centre of town, correct?"

"Yes, sir."

"And you duly spotted the defendant and very politely asked if you could have a look inside her bag, correct again?"

"Yes, sir."

"And what, pray, did you see inside the defendant's bag?"

"A pair of black plimsolls and a Sainsbury's shopping bag, sir."

"So," said Bellinger, staring straight at the jury, moving his head up and along the line to make eye contact with each member in turn, "plimsolls as identified in CCTV film of the robber leaving *every* crime scene along with a shopping bag of the *exact* type used to carry away the stolen money. Thank you, Constable. Oh and one last thing. Did you happen to notice anything unusual, unexpected, shall we say, about the bag the defendant was carrying?"

"It was very heavy, sir."

"Did you enquire as to why that was, Constable? And if you did, what was the reply given to you by the defendant?"

"I did ask, sir, and she said the abnormal weight was a gun."

"Your witness," said Bellinger, slumping down theatrically into his seat, job done.

"In your statement to the investigating detective, Constable Edrich," began Sonia, "you were unable to give any description of the woman whose bag you searched beyond that she was, and I quote here from your statement, 'a little old lady. They all look the same to me.' So the particular little old lady you encountered that afternoon could in fact have been just about anybody in that broad demographic. Correct?"

"Yes, ma'am."

"Before asking my second and final question of this witness, Your Honour," said Sonia, addressing the judge directly, "may I beg a brief indulgence regarding the items reported as having been seen?"

"Go ahead, Ms Patel, but make it mighty brief."

"For the record, an admittedly fast-and-dirty piece of research tells me that in the last year alone there were over twelve thousand pairs of black plimsolls sold in the UK, while Sainsbury's issued just shy of three million plastic bags. So the presence of either of these items in anybody's bag is hardly worthy of being called evidence."

"Point made and duly noted," snapped the judge. "Move it along, Ms Patel."

“One last question, as promised, Constable Edrich. At what point did you suspect that the ‘little old lady’ you searched that afternoon, *whomever she might have been*, could possibly have been telling *the truth* about her bag being abnormally heavy by virtue of a concealed gun?”

Constable Edrich shook his head before giving his one-word answer. “Never.”

# Chapter 36

"You were brilliant," gushed Carol when Sonia came into the holding cell to check on her before the afternoon session kicked off.

"He was toying with me," said Sonia, not needing to say who. "He was tossing up easy balls for me to smash out of the ground."

"I have no idea at all what that actually means," said Carol, "although I think I get the sense of what you're saying. But you're making him earn his corn, that's for sure," she added with an encouraging wink.

"What about you?" asked Sonia. "How are you bearing up? And I meant to ask – do you have family in the gallery?"

"Oh, I'm right as rain," said Carol. "But as for the other, I'm not sure. My daughter isn't talking to me and my husband doesn't drive, so he's a bit stuck. For sure he's here with me in spirit, which is probably a bit better than sitting watching it. Shame, though, 'cause he's missing out on seeing how good you are."

The two women hugged briefly before going their separate ways into the courtroom: Sonia out front of house and Carol back to the dock. This time she scanned the gallery more carefully and broke into an uncontrollable smile when she spotted Roy smiling down at her and giving a thumbs-up. She gave a small, surreptitious wave back.

Witness four was a tiny bespectacled man in an oversized moss-green corduroy jacket that had most definitely seen better days. His voice, though, was strong and assured as he introduced himself as Kenneth Yates, forensic accountant. Carol had never heard of such a thing, and found herself looking forward to what he had to say.

He'd tracked down all six of her money-laundering building society accounts, and had analysed in detail the transactions, placing all the deposits to within days of robberies three to six inclusive, and in each case the sum total deposited was equal to the sum stolen from the bank. He had also logged the withdrawals, all timed on the same day and again totalling the sum stolen. It was, in his expert opinion, a clear-cut case of low-level money laundering.

"Do you normally work on this sort of amount, Mr Yates?" asked Sonia, when it was her turn. "I mean, tracking, tracing, reporting and now testifying for a matter of some twenty-nine thousand pounds sum total."

"No," replied Yates succinctly.

"So what would be your typical threshold of involvement?"

"Ten million would be my normal cut-off. Pounds, dollars or euros."

"Not wanting to sound impolite here, Mr Yates, but can you please explain why you are here working on this case and its paltry amount?"

"I have no idea," said Yates. "I was instructed to do so, end of story."

Sonia gave a quick look to the jury to make sure they'd picked up on her unspoken suggestion of high-level involvement in a low-level case, and moved on. "In your lengthy experience of investigating money laundering, how common is it for a criminal to use their own name and address? Rare, would you say?"

"I would not use the term 'rare'," said Yates. "'Unique' is the only word I could find to describe it. I have never, ever, in eighteen years seen it before this case."

Sonia nodded her thanks at the witness. "One final thing while you're here, Mr Yates. How would you, using your profound professional judgement, rate the level of sophistication of this alleged money-laundering exercise, assuming that this is indeed what we are seeing here?"

"It would not even register on any sophistication scale," replied Yates, shaking his head, presumably at the pitiable effort. "It is crude, simplistic, and quite frankly embarrassing for me to investigate, and for whoever ran it to own up to."

Carol sat in the dock and flatly refused to be embarrassed. She thought she'd done rather well considering she'd had no idea at all how to do it when she'd started. And it had worked – the pompous little so-and-so hadn't mentioned that, had he?

She was still thinking that one over when the chatty lady from one of the Nantwich building societies was ushered in. Carol could never recall which was which by name, but she definitely remembered this woman. Lovely teeth.

"So, tell me, Mrs Quinn." Bellinger was already into his stride. "You recognise the defendant?" He paused to point at Carol.

Mrs Quinn looked at Carol and gave a tiny wave. "Yes, of course."

"And what did she tell you about how she came into the money she was about to deposit with you?"

"The first time," said the witness, "she told me she'd sold some of her late mother's jewellery. She couldn't believe how much it had been worth, sitting there all those years in her—"

"And on subsequent occasions?" cut in Bellinger.

"The horses," said Mrs Quinn in a stage whisper, as if she was letting on about a client's haemorrhoids. "Bet big money on long odds, so she told me."

"And the withdrawals?"

"Household projects, helping the kids out, the usual. And covering betting losses. She looked a little ashamed when she told me that one."

"And did she confide in you as to why she was opening and subsequently operating an account in Nantwich when there are perfectly acceptable and comparable options in her home town?"

Mrs Quinn looked furtively this way and that, not wanting to betray a confidence, but knowing she was about to. "She said she didn't want her husband to find out. She said if he knew she had money he'd have it away."

Carol snapped her eyes up to where Roy was sitting. He was looking straight at her. She gave the tiniest 'Not true' shake of her head and offered a weak smile. He grinned back and winked an 'I know it's not'.

"The horses, Mrs Quinn," said Sonia, already up and at it. "Did the defendant ever share with you what horse it was she had bet on so successfully?"

"Yes, she did."

"And did you check, incidentally of course, to see if what she was telling you was actually true, a reality?"

"I did," replied Mrs Quinn, smiling and shaking her head in a show of incredulity. "It was a horse called Cuppa-Cha. Came in at thirty to one in a race at Newmarket. To tell the truth, I *didn't* believe it – the name sounded too silly to me, too made up, which was why I checked."

The way Bellinger sat, hunched and yet relaxed, his robe accentuating the curve of his shoulders whilst concealing all below, made Carol think now more of a vulture than a raven. The little white wig made it even more obvious. And something deep in her stomach told her playtime was over, that the first phase that Sonia had told her about was now done and the real weapons were about to be deployed. So it came as no surprise when she heard Detective Inspector Templeton being called to the stand. The little blond runt strutted in and made a great show of theatrically reading the oath before sitting himself down, tugging at the knees of his trousers and flicking his jacket tail out behind him like a blasted concert pianist.

Bellinger went straight for it. "The defendant signed a written confession – that is correct, Detective Inspector?"

"It is," snapped Templeton.

"And yet she pleaded not guilty."

"She did."

"How do you reconcile this paradox, Detective Inspector?"

"I cannot. She confessed in full, signed the statement, and then presumably either changed her mind or had it changed for her."

"By whom?"

"I could only guess," said Templeton, glowering directly at Sonia. "But I could not say for fear of consequences."

Bellinger turned to face the judge. "The signed confession statement has been duly entered as an exhibit for the prosecution, Your Honour."

"Noted," said the judge.

"Moving on, Detective Inspector, please list for the court the fruits of your search of the defendant's property."

"We recovered several key items of evidence. The false moustache as identified by all the bank witnesses, the gun, again as identified by Lester Sweet, and the reversible hoodie coat that the defendant wore to evade recognition and capture."

"Kindly explain the reversible hoodie coat," said Bellinger.

"On every occasion the robber would seemingly disappear from CCTV surveillance soon after leaving the bank. I noticed that an elderly woman of a similar shape always emerged from the robber's last seen location very soon after. From this I deduced that the robber was effecting a change of identity, adopting a disguise."

"And you could, I presume, share this CCTV footage and sketches of the transformation with the court, should they so wish to view them first-hand?"

"I could."

"So we have hard evidence collected from the defendant's house," said Bellinger, "an effective inventory of damnation. We have multiple films of the robber leaving the robbed banks and transforming into an elderly lady, and we have a signed confession from the defendant. Is there anything more, Detective Inspector?"

"I had earlier worked out that the Leominster robber had taken the train to Whitchurch. I therefore had one of my officers collect CCTV footage from said town, from which I managed to piece together the precise route the robber took home. I was thus able to categorically demonstrate, without any doubt, that the robber was indeed the defendant, Carol Jackson."

Bellinger turned to face the jury and did a 'Well, there you have it' gesture with arms held out. "Thank you, Detective Inspector."

Sonia didn't move. Carol looked on. Oh no, she'd frozen! Bellinger had hit her with the big one and she'd had the wind knocked out of her. What a crying shame. All that work and effort, only to... No, wait a minute. Sonia was oh so very slowly unfurling herself from her chair. This wasn't a mouse under the cat's claw – this was a cobra preparing to strike.

"The arrest made interesting television," said Sonia. "Is it usual to have a television crew tagging along when arresting an armed robber, Detective Inspector Templeton?"

"It was a low-risk situation. And the public have a right to see good, successful police work in action."

"Low risk?" asked Sonia. "So why did you have an armed response team present? And why were you yourself wearing a bulletproof vest?"

"I said *low* risk," said Templeton, running a finger around the inside of his shirt collar. "Not zero risk. These things are always a matter of judgement."

"And then you led the defendant away in handcuffs, live on television," said Sonia, speaking slowly and softly for maximum effect. "Was this another element of risk assessment, Detective Inspector? An assessment that a diminutive sixty-nine-year-old woman might suddenly overpower you and your armed response team?"

"It's protocol," said Templeton, trying to sound superior. "Standard practice."

"I'm glad you mentioned that, Detective Inspector – standard practice." She hung the pause, waiting for Templeton to ask.

"Why?"

"At what point did you read your suspect her rights?"

"W-what?" Templeton looked shocked by the question.

"I asked," said Sonia, "at what point in the proceedings did you formally read my client her rights? On the doorstep? In the hall? In your car on the drive to Ternbury Police Station? Where? Come on now, this is important – standard practice."

"My DS did it," blurted Templeton.

Sonia made a big play of checking the notepad on her desk, flicking through a few pages before asking, "Detective Sergeant Roberts, is that correct?"

"Yes," said Templeton, fighting to retain his composure.

"Can we ask him?"

"Of course you can."

"Now?"

"Your Honour," Bellinger was on his feet, "counsel is attacking the witness and requesting an excursion beyond the bounds of legal process. She cannot simply ask the prosecution to interject a secondary witness within the testimony of a—"

"It is important, Your Honour," said Sonia. "Important for establishing the validity of the entire—"

"No, Your Honour," howled Bellinger in protest. "This cannot—"

"Mr Bellinger." Judge Dickens fixed him with a withering glare. "I fully understand and accept your protestations regarding legal procedure. However, we have reached a point of extreme jeopardy here. If due process was not followed, as is being alluded to by Ms Patel, we need to know and we need to know now. If, on the other hand, this is some sort of ruse on Ms Patel's part, it will be dealt with in the harshest possible manner. A simple yes or no from DS Roberts will clear it up. I am therefore inclined to do as Ms Patel suggests. So get him in here now."

# Chapter 37

Lovely Danny looked super nervous as he walked into the courtroom, thought Carol, like he couldn't understand why he was there. He'd been really nice to her right from the beginning and she was pleased to see him again, but also worried for him in case what was about to happen got him into trouble. He glanced across at her and gave the tiniest of acknowledging nods before taking his place on the stand.

Judge Dickens took control of the situation, reminding the court that what was happening right now was essentially a breach of practice but was, she felt, necessary and hence justified as a means to an end. In precise terms, this witness was here solely to verify the juncture at which the defendant had been read her rights. "Take the lead, Mr Bellinger," instructed the judge. "I want you to assume you have before you a witness for the prosecution, here to clarify a key point. So just the one question, and mind very carefully to *not* lead the witness."

Bellinger was clearly very unhappy about what was going on, although Carol couldn't work out if it was simply the so-called busted procedure he didn't like, or what might happen to his case as a result of the answer. She was also still trying to work out why Sonia had seemingly made such a big fuss about it, and even more so, why the judge had apparently supported her.

Bellinger rotated his shoulders and asked, "Detective Sergeant Roberts, at what point on the evening of the arrest did you formally read the suspect her rights?"

Danny cocked his head slightly to one side, like a deaf dog searching to hear his master's whistle. But he'd heard the question, right enough. He just couldn't seem to understand why he was being asked.

"Detective Sergeant?" prompted Bellinger.

"I didn't," said Danny.

"You did not read the suspect her rights?" repeated Bellinger.

"No, I didn't," repeated Danny.

"Why not?" barked Bellinger, for the first time appearing to lose his hitherto ice-cool demeanour. "Is it not the most basic of basic principles?"

"It is," replied Danny, not in any way rising to the attack. "But..."

"But what, Detective Sergeant?" demanded Bellinger.

Danny sighed. Carol guessed he was about to offer what they called a 'career-limiting' answer, and she was probably right.

"I wasn't the arresting officer. DI Templeton instructed me to hang back out of the way while he made the arrest. I only went into the property, after Mrs Jackson had been taken away, to conduct the search."

"Thank you, Detective Sergeant," said the judge, taking over before Bellinger burst a blood vessel. "And thank you for your candour. You may go now, but please don't stray too far in case we need to call you in again."

Danny stood up and twitched his back and neck as if still expecting something really bad to happen. But then again, maybe it had. It certainly looked that way as Templeton was recalled to the stand and Danny had to pass him on the way out. The glare from Templeton suggested Danny might be in for a rough time a little later on.

Before Sonia could continue her questioning of Templeton, Judge Dickens cut in, fixing the witness with her trademark death stare. "'Disappointment' doesn't even come near to what I am currently thinking, Detective Inspector Templeton. 'Perjury' is currently closer to the top of my word pile. So let me say this. I will just about accept a misremembering of what happened that evening, but be aware you are now skating on very thin ice. Continue, Ms Patel!"

Sonia maintained a blank expression: this was pure business and she didn't want anybody accusing her of becoming emotional about it. She didn't even build up to her question by saying it was a repeat. She simply asked it again. "At what point did you read the suspect her rights, Detective Inspector Templeton?"

The sides of his neck were visibly purple and sweat was glistening on his top lip. "It must have been when I entered the property."

"And if I told you that I have in my possession written eyewitness accounts of those few critical moments, albeit from family members, who are both willing to testify that you did not, what then?"

Templeton swallowed so hard he nearly choked as the blush spread up from his collar and across his cheeks. "I, I, must have, must have done it..."

"Thin...ice, Detective Inspector," growled the judge.

"You never did, did you, Detective Inspector?" said Sonia, sticking the dagger in to the hilt. "You forgot. You were so busy playing to the camera that you completely forgot one of the critical staples: the reading of the rights." She stopped and looked at Templeton, sweat running down his cheeks. "You can say yes or you can simply nod when I repeat, 'I forgot to read the suspect her rights.'"

Templeton gave a single small nod and stared down at his feet.

"In that case, Your Honour," said Sonia, turning to face the judge, "I request that my client's written confession is considered invalid and struck from the record."

Somebody in the public gallery gave a suppressed whoop, while a few others clapped.

Judge Dickens glowered up at them. "One more sound from up there and I will have you cleared out!" She looked back at Sonia, then at Bellinger. "There is no other option. The written confession is hereby declared inadmissible. Carry on, Ms Patel. And to think I considered you out of your depth."

Sonia took it as a compliment and turned her attention back to the melting and deflated Templeton. "You didn't really need that confession anyway, did you?" she said, not expecting any comment. "I mean, you've got all that evidence. All those CCTV tapes, right?"

Templeton nodded warily. Where was she going to stab him next?

"I've seen them," continued Sonia, "and your team's technical officer has done an excellent editing job on them. Now, I am not going to suggest there is anything wrong with them, anything fiddled or fixed, unlike certain witness statements that were updated after the—"

"Ms Patel!" barked the judge. "Behave yourself."

"I apologise, Your Honour, unreservedly."

"I doubt that very much, but watch yourself anyway."

"The problem for me," continued Sonia, "is that the CCTV images are all just blob people, like in a badly defined fuzzy L. S. Lowry painting. At no point, at least not that I can see from what you have submitted as evidence, do they show a face or even close. In fact there is nothing there beyond a vague shape to suggest that my client is actually in any of them. Yes, we have the wonderful full-face picture from the Whitchurch butcher's shop, but that was taken some hours later and many miles distant from Leominster."

"Is there a question coming, Ms Patel?" asked the judge.

"Detective Inspector, do you have in your possession, anywhere, hard forensic evidence that puts the defendant at the scene of the crime in any one of the six cases you listed on the charge sheet?"

Templeton almost choked the word out. "No."

"So what *do* you have, apart from films of persons unknown who may or may not have a passing resemblance to the basic morphology of the defendant?"

Templeton put his shoulders back. At last this hyena had given him an opening to get in a punch of his own. "We have the reversible coat that you can see in the videos and which was identified by the cashiers, we have the fake moustache that was also identified by all seven cashiers, and we have the gun that was identified by at least one of them. And all of these items were found hidden in the defendant's house."

Sonia leaned back as if the retaliation had floored her. She pretended to shake it off and asked her next question. "Did you have a search warrant, Detective Inspector?"

This time he laughed. Not a lot. Just enough to show that he was about to play a winning card at long last. "I didn't need one. Under section eighteen of the 1984 Police and Criminal Evidence Act, an officer at or above the rank of Inspector can authorise a search without a warrant." He finished with a 'Take that, bitch' smirk.

"Remind me," said Sonia, clearly undeterred by the detective's law lesson. "We have already established that you did not read the suspect her rights, but at what point did you officially arrest her?"

"Your Honour," Bellinger was on his feet, whining, "this is becoming tedious."

"Sit down, Mr Bellinger. Carry on, Ms Patel."

"At the doorstep," replied Templeton. "When the suspect opened the door."

Sonia sifted another sheet free from her table. "'You're nicked'," she read, looking up at Templeton to repeat it. "'You're nicked.' Is that how you arrest somebody these days, Detective Inspector?" In a flash, Sonia had put down the sheet of paper and picked up a small booklet, folded back at a particular page. It looked to Carol like a guidebook or some such thing. Sonia was looking down at the booklet as she spoke. "Are you telling me that you do not have to go through the five key points of making an arrest any more? Identifying yourself as a police officer, telling the subject that they're being arrested, telling them the crime they are being arrested on suspicion of having committed, explaining why it is necessary to arrest them, and, finally, explaining that they are not free to leave? All of that can now be reduced to 'You're nicked'?"

Templeton had the look of a man wanting the ground to open up and swallow him. He started to try to offer an answer, stumbled a few times, and finally gave up.

"I put it to you, Detective Inspector Templeton, that you did not formally arrest Mrs Jackson. That you were so busy playing Inspector Morse that you once again, as with the reading of the rights, omitted to follow the set process."

"What difference does it make?" snapped a deeply wounded Templeton. "I can still authorise a search. The Act says so. It's probably in that little book you're quoting from, if you read a bit more of—"

"It matters a great deal," said Sonia, calmly cutting across Templeton's mini rant. "Because, Detective Inspector, if you had cared to study the 1984 Police and Criminal Evidence Act a little more assiduously, you would have seen that you, as an Inspector, can *only* authorise a search *after* an arrest. And, as you did not arrest the suspect until you were all at Ternbury Police Station, the search of the defendant's house was unlawful, and, as such, all and any items thus collected cannot be entered as evidence."

The noise from the public gallery was unmistakably suppressed cheering poorly disguised as rapid chatter.

"Last chance!" shouted the judge, pointing an angry finger towards the noise. "And I mean it!" She turned her head to scowl down at the humbled Templeton. "Well, well, well, Detective Inspector. It appears you have single-handedly destroyed your own case. Failure after cock-up after bodge after heaven knows what. And as you so forcibly referred to the entire investigative decision-making in the first person, I suspect there is no other door at which to lay the blame. It is not for me to influence your superiors in how they might approach this, but I know what I would do, and it would not make pretty viewing. You may now leave us, Detective Inspector Templeton."

# Chapter 38

As Templeton slunk out with his tail between his legs, Judge Dickens called the day to a close. Bellinger still had one witness left to call in the hope of salvaging his case, and then it would be the turn of the defence, should they so wish.

Carol was feeling cock-a-hoop at how things had gone. She still couldn't help but feel bad about escaping justice – if that was what did happen – but there was a real chance now, with just about every bit of evidence having been either thrown out or undermined. Best of all, the nasty Templeton had been ripped to shreds. Carol had never before enjoyed somebody else's pain, but this was different: the little blighter deserved it.

When Sonia came to see her in the holding area the 'legal eagle' was far more reserved and restrained than Carol had expected.

"You were totally amazing, pet," gushed Carol. "Brilliant. It was like *Perry Mason* – even though you've probably never heard of him – rolled in with *Rumpole of the Bailey* and a bit of *Legally Blonde* to boot. Are you not over the moon?"

Sonia shook her head. "It's not over yet, not by a long chalk. Remember what I told you: Bellinger always has a trump card up his sleeve just in case the win looks like it's slipping away. Problem is, I cannot for the life of me..."

She stopped short, interrupted by a soft but firm double knock on the door. "Come in," she called warily, clearly not able to guess who it might be. The door opened and a familiar but unwelcome figure appeared. He looked different without the wig: less scary, but still imposing with his short steel-grey hair, and, close up, his pale grey eyes were like a shark's.

"Having fun?" crooned Bellinger, addressing his question directly to Sonia. "Thought I'd just pop down to the dungeons to say how impressed I was today. Honestly. Something of a shock, the proficiency of your performance, to say the least, but, heigh-ho, there's still tomorrow." He winked. "Leeds, wasn't it?" he said, using a musing sort of tone. "I only found out they had a law faculty last week. Is it as dour as the rest of that godforsaken city?"

Sonia looked the man straight in the eye. "You should never judge a book by its cover. And as for the law faculty, well, it's actually a lot like your beloved Oxford, but without the sodomy. Enjoy your evening."

"What was all that about?" asked Carol, once Bellinger had left them and whistled his merry way off along the corridor.

"I studied law at Leeds. Pompous twerps like Bellinger don't even recognise it as worthy of existence. But my qualifications are just as valid as his."

"Don't fret about it. And don't you worry about tomorrow. We have had an excellent day today and—"

"The day's not over just yet," interrupted Sonia. "I have a surprise for you." She grinned widely. "I've persuaded them to let you see Roy in here, now. Yes, I spotted him up in the gallery, waving down at you like a fourteen-year-old to his girlfriend. Anyway, they've said you can have half an hour before they take you back. Plus, I've arranged a taxi to get Roy home, and don't you dare ask who's paying."

She'd barely finished talking when the door opened and a uniformed security guard showed Roy inside.

"I'll leave you two to catch up," said Sonia. "Half an hour, remember, so make the most of it. I'll come back when the time's up."

The little room felt so quiet when Sonia closed the door. Neither of them wanted to disturb it, standing in silence two yards apart, looking at each other like it was the first time they'd met.

"That went well," said Roy eventually. "I didn't understand a lot of it, but your brief is a feisty one."

The only furniture in the room was a fixed bench along the wall opposite the door, doubling as a sofa and a bed. Carol suggested they sit there to talk and Roy agreed, sitting down beside her and taking her hand in his.

"Do you think she stands a chance of getting you off?" asked Roy, giving her hand a squeeze.

"If you'd asked me that first thing this morning I'd have said, 'Not a cat in hell's chance.' But after that performance today, I'm not so sure."

"That copper took a pasting," said Roy with a chuckle.

"He deserved it," said Carol. "Nobody likes him, the jumped-up little squirt."

"Wouldn't trust the prosecution fellow as far as I could throw him," said Roy. "Nasty, arrogant piece of work, if you ask me."

"How are you, love?" asked Carol, realising they could waste their entire half-hour talking about nothing important. "Are you coping?"

"Surprisingly well," he said. "The microwave's been taking a bashing." He laughed, knowing it had always been one of his wife's bugbears. "Sarah brings me frozen meals and they each have a handwritten sticker on telling me how long to 'nuke' them for. Every now and again I get one right and it's edible."

"How is she?"

"Still cross. Still won't talk about it."

"I miss her," said Carol.

"I know you do, love, and I think she's missing you. She's just being stubborn. I told her so and she said she gets it from me. How about that, eh? Talking of which, she's bludgeoned me into having a laptop computer in the house."

"You what?"

"Oh, I'm not doing computing stuff on it. She's just set it up so I can talk to Paul. And it's amazing. It's like he's in the next room, looking at me through a window. When you come home I'll be able to show you."

"What about our girlies?" asked Carol, glossing over the hole in her heart.

Roy snorted a laugh. "They think you are a-mazing," he said, trying to imitate Lauren's pronunciation. "Having a grandma who's *allegedly* a notorious bank robber is apparently nearly as good as having Justin the Beaver as a brother, whoever he might be. Apparently they've both got over a hundred followers on whatever-it's-called now, when they used to have half a dozen. They'd both like to come and see you, and they told me that if their mum is 'still being a tit' – their word, not mine – they'll hitch-hike down to see you by themselves."

"They couldn't do that," began Carol, alarmed. "They're only—"

"It's just a childish threat," said Roy. "Sarah *will* come round, but if not, then I'll arrange something. Maybe get Rainy to bring us all down in his garage van."

"Janice came to see me," said Carol. "She was funny. Turned up all in black like she was going to a funeral. Said she didn't think it was right to wear bright colours on a prison visit. And she's bought a place in Cyprus. It's on one of her Eddy's developments. A colonial bungalow with a shared pool. By the way, did you know her Eddy was gay?"

"From when he was about four years old," said Roy. "Remember that works Christmas party when he would only play with the Barbie dolls?"

"You're right," said Carol, "now I come to think of it."

"You sound sad," said Roy. "About Janice. What is it? Her going gallivanting off to the sun, or you being stuck in here?" He paused to think. "Or is it that we never went anywhere like that?"

"Don't be daft," said Carol, elbowing her husband gently in the ribs. "You wouldn't get me over there. Too ruddy hot for my liking. And too many cockroaches."

"Talking of cockroaches," said Roy, "the press have all buggered off from outside the house, thank goodness. I guess they might be back when you come home." Another squeeze of the hand. "Anyway, *they've* all gone, but I had another visitor. Or let's put it this way: I was visited at the bowling club."

"A spirit?" asked Carol, chuckling at her feeble joke.

"No, a visit as in somebody who just happened to be there – and who, incidentally, had never been there before – and wanted a little chat."

"Get on with it!"

"Have you ever heard of Percy Walsh?"

Carol shook her head. "I don't think so." A faint bell was ringing somewhere deep down, but she couldn't remember.

"*Midwestern Echo*?" prompted Roy.

"Got it," snapped Carol. "Janice keeps banging on about him. Says she's in love with the bloke 'cause of how he keeps kicking the rozzers – as she calls them – over the whole Red Fox thing. So he—"

"She," corrected Roy. "Percy Walsh is a woman. A stunningly attractive woman who caused multiple seizures and dislocated necks when she pitched up at the bowls club amongst all those geriatrics. And she wanted to talk to me about you."

"Me?"

"Well, not you exactly, but your alter ego, the Red Fox."

"Blow me down," said Carol, swivelling her hips on the makeshift sofa so she could turn to look directly at her husband. "This is a wind-up, right?"

"Not at all. She had ID and everything. Lovely young girl, she is, nice as pie."

"So tell me," pressed Carol, "what exactly did she want?"

"When the trial is finished, whichever way it goes, she says she would like to sit with you and hear your story. Do you know, she said you were an inspiration to women."

"In that I robbed a few banks and got caught and will probably go to prison?"

"In that you have demonstrated that a woman of whatever age or background can achieve whatever she dreams. Or something like that."

Carol was glowing. "And she'll put my story in the paper?"

Roy shook his head. "She wants to write a book about you. And not only that, she wants to pay for the privilege of writing your story. Twenty thousand pounds to start with, and then a percentage of the royalties from sales of..." He stopped. "The royalties from the..." Again his words were cut short.

Carol suddenly realised Roy's grip on her hand had weakened and slipped. He was fighting for breath, panting in short bursts as his free hand pawed at his throat.

"I'm sorry, love," he gasped. "I am so very..." Yet again he couldn't finish. He turned his head and looked at her, staring deep into her eyes with a look of love and regret. "I should have told... I should have..." His eyes turned up as he slumped backwards onto the bed.

"Roy! Roy! Somebody help! Please, somebody help!"

# Chapter 39

A paramedic had been in the building quite by chance, and was called down by the guard. He was at Roy's side within minutes of him collapsing and Carol screaming for help. All the medic could do was make sure the patient's airways were clear and then sit with him until the ambulance arrived a half-hour or so later. Carol spent the time holding her stricken husband's hand and crying floods of tears as she muttered pleas to all and any gods that might exist to help her love.

Not surprisingly, they wouldn't let her go with Roy to the hospital, but understanding the reason why didn't make it any easier for Carol to handle, collapsing to her knees in a wailing convulsion of anguish as they wheeled him away. And it was Sonia who knelt with her, arms wrapped around her favourite-ever client, whispering over and over again that it would be alright, he'd be fine, he'd be fine, he'd be fine.

At least they gave Carol the time to recover to a small extent before insisting she be transported back to prison. There was no provision for an overnight stay in the holding cells beneath the courthouse, so it had to be. But, again, knowing why didn't in any way help Carol process what was going on. And, of course, she was already into the phase of blaming herself for bringing on whatever it was that had hit Roy.

Sonia promised Carol that she'd contact Sarah and tell her what had happened. She would also do what she could, not being a relative, to find out how Roy was, where he was, and what had happened to him. She suggested maybe it was nothing more than a panic attack. Carol knew in her heart of hearts that it was something more.

She barely slept a wink that night, alternating between tossing and turning on her bed and pacing manically up and down the short length of her cell, all the time her head swimming and violently churning through a repeat cycle of blame and self-recrimination. It had to have been her, it had to have been. Her selfish, stupid, idiotic games. It has to have been that. No doubt. You did this to him, Carol!

Sonia was there just after six the next morning. She too looked like she hadn't slept, but waved away Carol's concern for her. "How could I sleep," she asked softly, "knowing what you must be going through?"

The good news, if you could call it such, was that Roy was stable and conscious and being very well looked after at the Princess Royal Hospital, where he had been admitted to the cardiac department. Sarah was with him, as she had been since the previous evening, having dropped the granddaughters at a friend's house for the night.

"Any idea what it was?" asked Carol. "A heart attack? A...?"

"I don't know," said Sonia. "Obviously, they wouldn't tell me even if I asked. You'll have to ask Sarah."

"But she's refusing to talk to me," said Carol, tears now streaming down her cheeks. "I've done this. I've destroyed our family, lost my daughter, and now—"

"Shh," cooed Sonia. "You did nothing of the sort. Your daughter will understand eventually, and your husband is comfortable and in excellent hands."

"Can *I* call the hospital?" asked Carol, pleading in her eyes.

"Probably," said Sonia. "But do you remember how you were so adamant that you needed to talk to Roy face to face to explain your situation? Well, I would like to propose that you give Roy the same opportunity. As I understand it, he is awake, and Sarah tells me he is desperate to talk to you."

"But how?" asked Carol. "With me stuck in here and him stuck—"

"I talked with Sarah," said Sonia. "We can set up a WhatsApp video call."

"A what?"

"Don't worry about the methodology. Just say yes and I'll set it up for this afternoon. I've asked Judge Dickens for a half-day today on the grounds of your trauma and, believe it or believe it not, she agreed to it. So you just have to get through this morning and then you can see and talk to Roy. What do you say?"

"What *could* I say?" asked Carol, not expecting or getting an answer.

It was a few minutes after ten when Judge Dickens brought the court to order and shocked Carol by offering her heartfelt best wishes that the defendant's husband would quickly recover. She could have left it there, but for some reason had to say that the events of the previous evening would not in any way, barring that afternoon's recess, influence the trial process or its outcome. With all that out of the way, she pressed on. "Mr Bellinger, your final witness, as I understand it."

Sonia looked around at Carol and gave the tiniest grimace. They both knew that whatever this witness was about to bring, it would be Bellinger's ace in the hole, his trump card, his sucker punch.

"Dr Sanderson," began Bellinger, "would you kindly share with the court your job title?"

Sanderson was a cadaverous man with a violently receding hairline, sallow cheeks, and deeply sunken eyes ringed in purple. The eyes themselves, though, were darting this way and that and glinting – like a predatory ferret's, thought Carol.

"Forensic Chief Scientist," replied the man in a voice as dry as sandpaper.

"Could you please be a little more specific?" cajoled Bellinger. "As in, your area of specialism and the department that you oversee?"

"Fingerprints," replied Sanderson succinctly.

"And recently you were requested to effect a sizeable and, as I understand it, very costly piece of work, am I correct?"

"Yes."

"And on whose behalf was this—"

"This is not twenty questions, Mr Bellinger," snapped the judge. "Can you kindly get to the point."

"Apologies, Your Honour. Dr Sanderson, you explain."

Sanderson sat himself upright, got his tie knot dead centre, and began. "Detective Sergeant Roberts from Ternbury Police Station contacted me about requiring an extensive and exhaustive fingerprint analysis of a number of banknotes recently recovered from a specific bank robbery. He was of the belief that the perpetrator of said robbery might possibly not have been as careful about wearing gloves *after* the robbery as he might have been during. Detective Sergeant Roberts' idea was that the thief may have counted the money prior to passing it on and, should a suspect eventually come into the frame, this evidence could be crucial."

"And so?" pressed Bellinger.

"So we fingerprinted and recorded every print from every single note, both sides."

"How many notes?"

"Three hundred and sixty-seven."

"And how many prints did you lift?"

"That we could term an 'evidential partial', one hundred and sixty-five thousand one hundred and fifty-nine."

"A very large number, Dr Sanderson," crooned Bellinger, very clearly enjoying himself – far too much for Carol's liking.

"Indeed, yes," agreed Sanderson with a double nod of the head. "Many hours on the 'lifting' and many more on the recording and cross-referencing. It's probably why DS Roberts' boss was so angry and formally reprimanded him for having authorised it."

Bellinger raised his eyebrows before going in for the kill. "And now to the results, if you please, Doctor. What did you find that could be of interest to this court?"

"The great majority of prints we lifted appeared in the collated list once or twice, which would be consistent with general circulation, so we concentrated only on those prints appearing on multiple notes. Not surprisingly, we found a number of these but managed to eliminate most of them by cross-checking against employees at the bank in question."

"The cream, please, Dr Sanderson," prompted Bellinger. "The clincher."

"Only one print appeared on all of the notes. From a middle finger and a full to three-quarter partial, always in approximately the same position on each note, exactly consistent with its owner counting said notes."

"And the owner of this *damning* fingerprint?" asked Bellinger.

Carol couldn't listen. She didn't need to. She knew the answer all too well. They'd been so very close to popping Bellinger's balloon and she'd gone and messed it up. One stupid little mistake and one act of – she had to admit – investigative brilliance from her new friend Detective Danny. She let her head fall forward and closed her eyes.

"Dr Sanderson?" asked Sonia, on her feet and sounding like she was trying hard not to cry. "These banknotes were in general circulation for some time, correct?"

"I presume so. That is not my area of expertise."

"But it *is* possible that a member of the public *could* have handled any one of these notes or, over time, many of them, correct?"

"Statistically so, of course."

"In which case, is it not possible that the defendant could have incidentally handled these notes in the course of normal public circulation?"

"Again, this is not my field of expertise," said Sanderson, "which is why I engaged our statistical evaluations department."

"And they told you what, exactly, Dr Sanderson?"

"The probability of a single person leaving a print on this number of notes in general circulation – even leaving aside the identical positioning of the print – is somewhere in the region of one in fourteen million. To put that into perspective, the chance of being struck by lightning in the UK is a little over one fourteenth of that."

The gasp and sigh of disbelief and maybe even disappointment from the public gallery drowned out Sonia's "No further questions", whilst bringing the customary angry rebuke from Judge Dickens. Carol watched on as her darling Sonia slumped down into her seat, shoulders sagging under the weight of imminent defeat as Bellinger stood tall, the matador before the crowd, the slain bull bloodied at his feet.

# Chapter 40

There was no escaping the reality. They had lost. Their glorious adventure had ended in crushing defeat as the fates would dictate; right victorious over wrong. Sonia tried to apologise for not having seen it coming but Carol would have none of it; she'd made the mistake and, anyway, she really had done the robberies so she should be punished. Besides which, her situation now paled into tiny insignificance when stood against the starkness of her husband's ill health.

On the short ride back to prison she again went through the endless loop of blaming and absolving herself. It must have been her that had brought on the attack, whatever it was. It couldn't have been anything to do with her. It had to be her who... Round and round it went, making her head hurt and her chest ache. If she didn't stop she'd be in the next bed to him before long. She'd just have to wait the few hours until the video call when Roy could tell her for himself and she could look into his eyes while he did.

Sonia had travelled to the prison in her own car, so was already waiting for Carol when she arrived at her cell. They hugged and cried together as one, Sonia yet again trying to say how sorry she was for failing her absolute favourite-ever defendant.

"Hang on a minute," said Carol, standing back from the embrace. "Up until now you told me you've only represented – let me get this straight – bike thieves and shoplifters, so being your favourite isn't like I've won a tough competition."

Sonia wiped away her tears and laughed. "You missed out vandals."

Carol laughed. Sonia joined her. But it was hollow and didn't last long.

"Have you heard anything more from Sarah?" asked Carol.

"Only to say that we're still on for two o'clock. She'll be there to make sure everything works properly at that end but – I am so sorry, Carol – she still doesn't want to talk to you."

Carol nodded and fought to make sure she didn't start blubbing again. She'd done more than enough of that over the last few hours and she didn't want to look all blotchy when Roy saw her. She needed to be strong for him, to help him through. Whatever it was, she needed to make sure he could see her resilience and match it.

The two women took a light snack together in Carol's cell, and a cup of tea to wash it down. And then, at around ten minutes before the agreed time, Sonia took out her laptop and made sure everything was ready.

"I'd like to have a chance to say something tomorrow," said Carol suddenly.

"What?" asked a surprised Sonia.

"We're going to lose, I know that," said Carol. "But that pompous stuffed shirt Bellinger and the ruddy nasty little runt Shirley Templeton have spent two whole days calling me ignorant, saying I'm not clever enough to have done it myself, and – quite honestly, Sonia – I have had enough."

"Meaning?"

"I want the chance to have a pop back!"

"Carol," said Sonia, her voice trying to soothe the anger she was seeing in Carol's eyes, "if I put you up there, Bellinger gets to have his turn at you."

"That's what I want," said Carol emphatically. "I want to go toe to toe with that – pardon my language – prick and tell him how it is."

"No, I'm sorry, I cannot allow you to—"

"Hey, Chubby, who are you working for, eh?"

Sonia laughed. "You remembered."

"I may be old and a bit wobbly on my pins – oh, and soon to be a convicted criminal – but I don't forget much."

"Alright then," said Sonia, shaking her head. "If that is what you want, Carol, then that is what you will get. Tomorrow morning I will call you as my one and only witness, and then it will be up to you. Now, shall we call Roy?"

Carol nodded and took a huge breath to calm her shakes, watching as Sonia typed the number into her computer to make the connection. In what seemed like an instant there was her Roy on screen, clear as day, just like – what was it he'd said about talking with their Paul in Canada? Oh yes – like he was in the next room and chatting through a window. The difference here was that Roy was lying in a bed with wires and tubes seemingly everywhere. He was still managing a smile, though.

Sonia leaned close to Carol's ear and whispered, "The little box in the bottom right corner is what Roy can see at his end."

Carol nodded her understanding and smiled at her man. She tried to speak but nothing would come free, so she just kept on smiling and nodding.

"Hello, love," he said.

"You old fool," she replied. "What *have* you gone and done?"

"I'm sorry," he said. "I really am."

"For what?"

"For not telling you."

"Telling me what?"

Roy was momentarily distracted by something going on at his end. A nurse, maybe. Or...no, it was Sarah. Carol waited, hoping her daughter would speak, but she didn't. She was saying something to her dad.

"Sorry about that, love," said Roy. "I'm being 'managed'."

"Is that Sarah with you?" she asked, knowing it was.

"Yes, she's been here since last night, bossing me about."

"So come on, then, tell me what's going on," said Carol, quickly distancing herself from her daughter's frostiness.

"I, I, I've been..."

"Was it me?" asked Carol. "Was it what I—"

"Stop!" instructed Roy, the force of his interruption causing him to lean back into the pillow and gasp a few short breaths. "I need to speak."

"I'm listening," said Carol.

"I've not been well for some time," he began. "A long time, actually, and way before you started having your little adventures, so don't you *ever* think different."

"But you...you never..."

"I kept trying to tell you, love, but I could never get it out. I got close a couple of times, like the other night when we were talking about Janice Worthington and how she and us workers had kept that secret for years and years. And when I found out about your special secret I thought I could... But I couldn't."

"Tell me now," said Carol. "Please."

A hand passed Roy a glass of water from off-screen. Sarah's hand. He took a sip and handed it back. "Remember my old man had that thing with his heart?" he said, his eyes fixed on Carol through the screen. "Well, seems like he passed it on down to me. I never even suspected until around six or seven years back when I had a couple of dizzy spells at the club. Cliff told me I needed to see a doctor, but I felt fine the rest of the time, so I kept putting it off. Eventually I did go, but even then, when the first set of results came through, I convinced myself it was all a big mistake. Thought they must have mixed up some other bugger's tests with mine. But the consultant told me there was no mistake. My heart muscles weren't working properly. Or, to be blunt, they were falling apart. The doctors in here have a name for it as long as your arm, which, of course, I can't remember, but basically, I'd left it too late and there was nothing they could do apart from give me pills to help me cope with the symptoms until such a time as the decay became too advanced."

It was all too much to take in, and Carol's brain was aching from working to understand what her husband was saying, whilst all the time trying to think of a suitable response. The result was a mental gridlock that left her incapable of anything beyond merely smiling at the screen.

"I've been secretly taking those pills ever since," said Roy, breaking into the silence. "But they don't fix anything. As I said, they just mask the symptoms. The decay is still happening, and..."

"And what?" asked Carol, finally managing to shake some words free.

"It's probably weeks rather than months," said Roy, adding a resigned smile.

Carol's tears flowed like a dam had burst. It couldn't be true. It simply could not be bloody true. How could it? How could he? He'd never had a day off work in his entire life. He went bowling twice a week. He was hers. Nobody and nothing had the right to take him away from her. Nobody!

"Carol? Carol!"

"I'm sorry, love," she said, sniffing back the nose run. "I just can't..."

"Nor me, at first. But now I..."

"Why didn't you tell me?"

Roy took his time to answer. "I thought about it. In fact I didn't think about much else. But..."

"But what, love?"

"At first I hoped it would just go away, somehow suddenly fix itself."

"And then?"

"Then I was embarrassed. Yes, embarrassed. I was the man of the house, the strong one, the breadwinner, the one whose job it was to look after you and our children. How could I be so weak and bloody feeble? And worse than that, I was going to leave you with nothing: no big pension, no life insurance pay-out, not even a house that we own. I shouldn't be doing that. It was wrong. Wrong, wrong, wrong, and I was ashamed."

"You can't—"

"And then," he said, cutting across her, "then I was scared. Scared about how you would react. And the longer I left it, the more scared I became. Do you remember what I said the other day about secrets and how difficult they are to keep, and yet more difficult to share? Well, that was exactly where I'd got myself to. Scared of sharing and yet scared of not sharing."

"Sarah knew, didn't she," said Carol, speaking it as a statement of fact.

"I bumped into her coming out of the doctors after picking up my pills," said Roy. "Oh, I tried to fib my way around it, but you know what she's like."

"She kept telling me we needed to talk," said Carol. "I thought she was nagging me to talk to you. I never for one minute thought it was the other way around."

"Maybe she was doing both," said Roy, adding a small chuckle. "Let's face it, we were both packing a whopper of a secret, eh?"

"You silly sod," said Carol, unable to think of anything else to say.

Roy gave a short laugh. "I love you, Carol Jackson. As I told you the other night, I always have and I always will, right to the end. And if it hadn't been for that mucky fling I had with Raquel Welch back in the early '80s, you would have been my one and only true love in my entire life." He laughed at his feeble joke.

"And I love you too, Roy Jackson. I always have and always will."

"How's the trial going?" he asked.

Carol was taken aback by the sudden change of direction, and took a second or three to answer. "We lost," she said.

"What?"

"Okay, we're going to lose. I'm going to lose. They found my fingerprints on the money they recovered from that hospice. It proves I did it, so..."

"I am so very proud of you, my love," he said. "You did something most people only dream about, let alone a sixty-nine-year-old woman. And what a send-off for—"

"Stop it," she commanded. "Please, Roy, stop it."

"Why should I?" he asked. "What's coming is a fact."

"I should be there with you, not stuck in this place. I want to hold you, hug you, whisper in your ear like I used to when we were courting. I want to—"

"Do you think they would let you come and see me?" he asked, his voice so ridiculously calm and businesslike. "One last visit?"

"I… I don't know," stammered Carol, glancing across at Sonia sitting silently in the corner and using only her eyes to pose the question.

Sonia shrugged as if to say something like 'I don't know, but it's worth asking.'

"The trouble is," said Carol, addressing the screen again, "they're absolutely convinced I've got some mastermind criminal accomplice on the outside just waiting to spirit me away first chance he gets. It's why they wouldn't give me bail. I haven't, of course, but no matter how many times I tell them they won't believe me. Anyway, I promise you, my love, I will do everything I can to come and see you."

"Hey, love," he said, "if you can't, don't worry, we can do this again. And in the meantime, you give them hell tomorrow, before they send you down."

# Chapter 41

After only three days the courtroom had become very familiar, as had the security company transport and the holding cells. And today everybody along the way had wished Carol well and told her how they hoped she could still "get away with it". There'd been a small crowd outside as she'd been driven in, and she couldn't help but giggle as she'd peered out of the van window to see a few dozen people of both sexes all wearing droopy ginger stick-on moustaches and chanting, "Red Fox." How strange, she'd thought, that a couple of weeks ago these folk would have passed her in the street without a second glance. Now here she was, a pin-up at sixty-nine.

Sonia had met her at the entrance and walked with her down to the holding cell. "We missed this," she said, thrusting a newspaper into Carol's hand. "It's from yesterday."

Carol held it out and read the front page. It was the *Midwestern Echo*, its banner headline screaming, 'Calamity Templeton'. Carol couldn't help but smile as she quickly scanned the first few lines as they ripped into Detective Inspector Shirley Templeton's catalogue of fundamental policing errors. Such a shame she herself had made that one fatal mistake. Just lucky it hadn't come to light in time for the *Echo*'s print run. "She wants to write my story," said Carol, tapping a finger on Percy Walsh's by-line whilst showing the page to Sonia. "In a book."

"It's a woman?" asked Sonia. "*Percy*?"

"Apparently, yes," said Carol. "Is she allowed to do that? Write my story?"

"Once the case has passed through the court she can pretty much do what she wants. But if you're found guilty you personally won't be able to receive any money from it. You're not supposed to profit from criminality."

"But she could pay any money she makes to charity, couldn't she?"

"Like carrying on the Red Fox's good works?" asked Sonia with a grin.

"In a way, yes," confirmed Carol. "At least then *some* good would come of it."

"I can't see why not," replied Sonia. "Hey, would you like me to represent you legally in the negotiations? And setting up the Red Fox legacy fund?" She winked.

"I would like that very much," said Carol. "Apparently she's already offered to cough up a few thousand quid, and then more when..." She stopped suddenly as she remembered that this was the message Roy was conveying when he'd collapsed.

"Are you really sure about today?" asked Sonia, spotting Carol's sudden upset and deftly moving the conversation on and away.

"I'm sure," said Carol without a moment's hesitation. "I may get a bloody nose out there but I need to feel like I've got the chance to land at least one decent punch on that preening popinjay."

"That what?" asked Sonia.

Carol laughed. "I don't actually know what one is, but I remember my mum used to say it when she was talking about the town mayor. She didn't like him."

"Okay then," said Sonia, "let's get this show on the road. Oh, and I've submitted a written request for you to be allowed to visit Roy in hospital. I can't see any reason why they would refuse, but who knows?"

"Thank you," said Carol. "You're a star."

As usual they'd gone their separate routes to the courtroom, and now here they both were: the finale, the end, the wrap-up. No fanfares, no drumbeats, just the last act before Carol was officially found guilty and sent to prison. Judge Dickens swept in like she always did, and Bellinger stood tall and victorious like he always had, even before he was formally declared the winner. And up there in the gallery it was yet again jam-packed. No Roy, of course, but a highly conspicuous primrose-yellow clad Janice waving both hands wildly and blowing multiple kisses at her superstar best friend. Her Tuesday hair appointment had been worth it, thought Carol with a chuckle. Very Bardot-esque.

"Ms Patel," began the judge. "I suspect we are nearing the end. Do you wish to prolong the agony or leave it here?"

"I have just the one witness, Your Honour. I call Carol Jackson."

The gasp from the gallery was instantly cut through by the judge. "I sincerely hope this is not some sort of Wagnerian Valhalla theatrics, Ms Patel."

"No, Your Honour. Sincerely not," said Sonia, bowing her head in supplication. "I am merely acting upon my client's direct instruction. I have counselled against it, but she is adamant."

"Very well, then," said the judge. "You may proceed."

The usher strode across to chaperone Carol from her perch in the dock down and across to the witness box, where the formalities were quickly dispatched. Sonia stood and looked at Carol, and there were tears in the corners of the young solicitor's eyes as she asked the single question they had agreed on beforehand.

"Mrs Jackson – Carol – did you steal that money?"

"No," said Carol, "I did not. I merely relocated it to a more worthy cause."

"No further questions," said Sonia, sitting herself down.

"Ms Patel," growled the judge, "I warned you. And so far I am not happy."

Sonia looked up at the judge and held her stare, blank-faced and unapologetic.

"Mr Bellinger," barked the judge, "finish this!"

"Mrs Jackson," he purred. He knew he'd won, but he was clearly perturbed by what was going on here as he very obviously could not understand it. "Did you just admit to the robberies with which you are charged?"

"You tell me," said Carol.

"I believe you did."

"Then you may be right."

"You seem unconcerned by your guilt and the consequent substantial time you will be spending behind bars. Is that a fair assumption on my part?"

"I'm only guilty when *they* say so," said Carol, nodding in the direction of the jury.

"And they will," crooned Bellinger. "Oh, they will."

"We'll have to see," said Carol. "Now, don't you want to take this opportunity to ask me about my accomplice? That other bloke, the one before you, he used it as a reason to keep me locked up without bail. And little Shirley Templeton, he kept banging on about it over and over. So isn't it about time you had a pop?"

Bellinger tried to pretend he wasn't unsettled by being put on the back foot by a little old lady, and wiggled his shoulders to buy himself time. "In that case," he said at last, "tell me about your accomplice. Who is he and where can we find him?"

"Or her," said Carol with a wink.

A titter from the gallery died under a hostile stare from Judge Dickens.

"Or her," said Bellinger.

"Tell me," said Carol, looking straight at her would-be tormentor. "Why are you lot so convinced I had an accomplice? Assuming, of course, I did it."

"Mrs Jackson," said Bellinger, stretching the name out like elastic. "Let us face facts here. You are an uneducated woman, and as—"

"Who said?" snapped Carol. "Who said I was uneducated?"

Bellinger sighed wearily as if the contest wasn't worthy of him. "You achieved," he said, sorting through a few loose papers on his table and retrieving one to read, "two CSEs at marginal pass level. Need I say more?"

"And you?" she challenged.

Bellinger clearly couldn't resist the chance to crow. "I have achieved multiple degrees from Oxford and a doctorate from Harvard in addition to my—"

"Bits of paper," snapped Carol. "That proves nothing more than you can swallow a load of stuff and regurgitate it later. We had a cat once that could do that."

This time the gallery laughed openly until a swift rebuke from the judge brought them to heel.

"Certificates and diplomas are the internationally accepted currency of learning achievement, Mrs Jackson."

"But learning and intelligence are not the same thing, are they?"

"Semantics," scoffed Bellinger.

"I don't know what that means," said Carol with a shrug, "but how about we do a little test?"

Bellinger looked to the judge for an escape route but she simply made a face to say, 'You started this, so get on with it.'

"As you will," offered a clearly reluctant Bellinger.

"You keep telling me I am an uneducated woman, right?"

A single wary nod from Bellinger.

"So tell me, what temperature oven do you need for the perfect Yorkshire pudding?"

"I have no idea."

"And what stitch would you use on a sewing machine to patch-repair denim jeans?"

"I..."

"Okay, let's try an easy one, shall we? What common cooking ingredient would you use to get bloodstains out of a white cotton shirt?"

"I have no idea! What the...?"

"Last chance," said Carol, on a roll and going for it. "What condiment would you use if you or a loved one got stung by a wasp?" She sat back in her chair, crossed her arms, and scowled at Bellinger.

"Your Honour," he implored, "this is intolerable. The witness cannot interrogate me. I am supposed to ask the questions of—"

"Do you know, Mr Bellinger?" asked the judge. "Any of them?"

"No, I do not," he snapped back.

"Then I would suggest," interrupted Carol before anybody else could speak, "that it is you who are uneducated. Not me."

This time it was a cheer from the gallery, and Carol was sure she could hear Janice whooping above the lot of them.

"One more!" boomed the judge. "Just one more peep out of you lot and I will have the gallery emptied and closed forthwith. This is not vaudeville." She pointed an unwavering bony finger at the naughty people. "Be warned!" She turned to look down at Carol and held the stare for a few seconds before asking, "What *do* you use for a wasp sting, Mrs Jackson?"

"Vinegar, Your Honour."

"Thank you, Mrs Jackson. Proceed, Mr Bellinger. And make it civil."

"Mrs Jackson," he continued, seemingly having recovered his composure during the interlude, "homespun remedies aside, and leaving behind the disagreement between you and the wider world regarding authentications of academic prowess, I note that you are evidently an unworldly person."

"Meaning what?"

"Meaning you have a limited view of the world."

"On a clear day I can see all the way to the horizon," said Carol. "Same as you, although, you being a fair bit taller, for you it has to be further away."

The gallery stifled its latest laugh almost before it had started.

"What I meant was, you have no passport or—"

"Don't like foreign food," said Carol. "Roy, my husband, gets a gyppy tummy just thinking about it."

Bellinger refused to allow himself to be caught again, swiftly changing his point of attack. "You do not even have a driving licence."

"Do you have a pilot's licence?" she snapped back. "For an aeroplane?"

"Of course not," replied Bellinger.

"Why not?" pressed Carol.

"It would be pointless," replied Bellinger. "I am not in possession of an airplane."

"And I haven't got a car, so we're level, then."

The gallery couldn't keep it together any more, and broke out into a mix of raucous laughter, clapping, and the odd cheer, all topped off by the unmistakable Janice cackle.

"Clear the gallery, now!" commanded the judge. "Get that rabble out of my court!"

It took several minutes to do the judge's bidding, the members of the public leaving reluctantly and with the odd isolated shout of encouragement to Carol. She didn't respond. She just sat there and waited. The end was near now. Once all was calm again, the judge nodded at Bellinger to get on and finish it, but it was Carol who spoke first.

"What is it with you, Mr Bellinger?" she asked, softly but firmly. "With you and Templeton? What is it that you simply cannot stomach about me having done this alone, on my own, all by myself? Why do you need to invent an accomplice? Is it because I didn't go to a fancy college or university and get bits of paper for being able to remember stuff? Or is it because I'm a working-class housewife whose sole focus in life has been to make a good home and bring up a loving, happy family? Or is it perhaps because I'm old, past my use-by date, worthless, a husk? Or is it simply because I am a woman?" Carol all but spat the last words at the man, revelling in the silence that followed whilst fixing him with the most hostile stare she could manage.

To his credit, Bellinger didn't respond. He merely stood and nodded at Carol a few times, like a hunter might in recognition of a worthy adversary he'd tracked and cornered prior to delivering the coup de grâce. "Mrs Jackson, did you...?" He didn't finish. He just left it there, the question, incomplete but explicit, hanging free and loose in the space between them.

"I did."

# Chapter 42

"Talk about going down in a blaze of glory!" squealed Sonia excitedly as she hurtled down the underground corridor to embrace Carol. "OMG, you were brilliant!" she continued, speaking the words like a machine gun as she hugged and hugged her favourite-ever client. "Bellinger just stood there at the end and took it. I never, ever expected him to do that. You showed him, Carol, you stuck it to him, you knocked him about like he's never been knocked about before. You are so—"

"Tired," said Carol, cutting across the tumbling avalanche of praise. "I need to go back to...you know...and lie down."

"I'm sorry," said Sonia, looking down and to the side in embarrassment. "I got a little carried away, didn't I?"

"A little," said Carol.

"It's just...oh, wow, gosh, Carol, I have never seen anybody do that before. And Judge Dickens just sat there and let it happen. You know, I'm pretty sure she was grinning under that witch face."

"Sorry to be a wet blanket," said Carol, "but what happens now?"

Sonia stood back and adopted a solemn face. "Now that you have formally confessed before the court, the jury will be dismissed and we'll move straight to sentencing. Dickens wants this all wrapped up in double-quick time, so she's booked it in for tomorrow morning. And that means she's already decided."

"Is that a good thing or a bad thing?" asked Carol, some way past the point of caring.

"I have no idea," said Sonia. "But my guess would be it's not going to be great."

"Have a stab," said Carol.

"Four, maybe five."

Carol nodded her resignation. "How often will I be allowed to see Roy?" she asked.

"If he can get to you, then—"

"He can't. Or let's just say, he most probably won't be able to leave the hospital."

"Then a couple of times a month, maybe," said Sonia, eyes downcast. "But you could probably get permission to video-chat a lot more frequently than..." She stopped as she saw the tears flowing.

Carol dabbed them away angrily. "It shouldn't be like this. I shouldn't have done what I did and made it so I can't be with him. I *need* to be with him. If he has only got weeks left like he told me, I should be there with him every day to the end. Every day, Sonia. In fact, night and day, every hour, every..."

The racking sobs completely took over, and she crumbled into her young solicitor's outstretched arms. They stood like that, entwined and silent apart from the muffled sniffs, for minute after minute until Carol pulled herself together and eased herself free.

"Did you get an answer about me being allowed to see Roy today?"

"Still waiting to hear," said Sonia. "But there is something else, although I think maybe now is not the time to share." She spoke the sentence like she was cripplingly embarrassed by it.

"Tell me," said Carol. "And tell me straight, or I warn you, I won't be making you that steamed spotted dick when I get out."

"Bellinger offered me a job. In London. It's very junior, but a big step up from here."

"Are you going to take it?"

Sonia nodded.

"Well done, you," said Carol. "I am so happy for you. Honestly."

"Thank you, Carol. Thank you for giving me this opportunity, and thank you for being such a truly wonderfully lovely—"

Sonia's mobile ringing cut her off. She heaved it out and listened, nodding and offering the occasional "Yes" and "I understand." Eventually she rang off and looked across at Carol.

"Judge Dickens has approved your visit to see Roy. Bellinger wasn't happy about it, so she imposed conditions. You have to be accompanied at all times and wear a tracker band on your ankle."

"Is that all?" asked Carol. "Come on, let's get going!"

# Chapter 43

Sonia didn't go with her to the hospital. It was Carol's time with her husband. Sonia was adamant she didn't want to intrude and, besides, she did have other work that she'd neglected of late. Plus, she wanted to make sure she had a good mitigation argument prepared in case she got the chance prior to sentencing.

Carol thanked her again and told her not to work too hard or too late, adding, "You don't want bags under those beautiful eyes, now, do you, pet?"

She watched Sonia all the way to the end of the corridor, where her Cheltenham Angel turned and gave a little wave before disappearing up the stairs. Almost immediately a pair of uniformed guards from the same transfer security firm appeared. One was barely out of his teens, and so spotty it looked like his entire face was about to erupt. The other, older and clearly more senior, did all the talking through a thick, unkempt beard.

"You gotta put this on," he said in a wholly charmless voice, holding out the tracker anklet. "What leg you want it on?"

Carol raised her left leg and presented the ankle to the beard.

He clumsily attached the loop and activated the tracker. "Let's go," he instructed, nodding his head towards the door, beyond which Carol knew their stinky van would be waiting.

The journey from the court building to the hospital couldn't have been any more than half an hour, probably less, and just as well, because Carol's insides were in chaos. Her heart was racing and her stomach was churning at the thought of seeing her Roy. Maybe it had all been a mistake, the diagnosis, like he'd told her he'd first thought or wished for. Maybe they'd found a miracle cure overnight and he'd be sent home in the morning, right as rain. Or maybe somebody high up would intervene and permit her to stay with him. Maybe, maybe, maybe...

At the hospital the two guards escorted her into the entrance lobby, one of them on each side, and the beard brusquely explained to the receptionist who they were, who they were there to see, and that they were to accompany "the prisoner" at all times. It was plain to see that they'd been expected, as the man on reception explained that Roy Jackson had been moved to a single-occupancy room, number 637, on the sixth floor. They'd made the arrangements specifically for the "special visit" so as to not upset hospital routines or other patients.

The guards seemed wholly disinterested in the whys and wherefores, with the beard merely grunting, "Where's the lift?"

The corridor to Roy's room looked to Carol like it stretched to the end of the world as the lift doors opened. Maybe that was where she was, in a dream, a nightmare, destined to walk and walk for all eternity and never reach her husband's side. Don't be daft, Carol, she scolded herself. And pull yourself together. You have to be strong. His room was about two thirds of the way along the corridor, fronting onto a small waiting area with a pair of well-worn benches and an illuminated drinks vending machine. Carol moved towards the door, only to realise the two goons were close behind. She turned to face the one who could talk, standing close and so having to crane her neck to look up at him.

"You are joking, aren't you?"

"My instructions are to keep you in sight at all times," he growled.

"We're on the sixth floor," hissed Carol. "I'm the Red Fox, not ruddy Spider-Man!"

"But—" he began to argue.

"Bugger off," said Carol. "I am going in here alone and you can sit there." She pointed at the benches. "And if I do make a run for it – ha!"

The beard growled and plonked himself down onto the bench, with Spotty-Boy following suit. Carol turned her back on them and stood for a moment in front of the door to where Roy would be. She took hold of the door handle and counted slowly to three before taking a deep breath and going in.

Inside, the room was gloomy, the lighting low-level and indirect, the only thing of any brightness being the screen above the bedhead displaying rows of jagged lines dancing across it to the tune of gentle rhythmic beeping. And slowly, at last, the person she'd come to see came into focus, propped up on a mound of huge white pillows and smiling directly at her. Through her tears, she could see the mass of wires connected to him here, there and everywhere, and a breathing tube disappearing up his nose and taped to his cheek.

"Hello, love," he said. "Thanks for making the effort."

Something moved in her peripheral vision, a shape stepping out from the corner shadows.

"Hello, Mum," said Sarah.

"Hello, darling girl," said Carol. "It's good to see you."

"Good to see you too, Mum."

Carol brushed away the tears still streaming down her cheeks and dripping from her jawline. "I'm sorry."

"Me too," said Sarah, now joining in with the tears. "I've been a brat."

"Aw, come here," said Carol, opening her arms wide for her daughter to come to her.

They hugged, tighter than they had for many years, and sobbed onto each other's shoulders.

"What about me?" asked Roy from his bed. "Don't I get a look-in?"

The two women broke apart and moved across to their special man, one on either side of the bed, Carol carefully lifting and holding his hand in both of hers, making sure not to disturb the tube thing sticking into the back of it.

"No miracle cure, then, since we last spoke," she said, forcing the words out from around the lump in her throat.

"No," said Roy, shaking his head. "Not gonna happen."

"And you said..." She couldn't speak the words.

"A few weeks, they reckon," said Roy, in a tone like he was telling her about a minor delay on the delivery of a new bowling bag.

"And there's nothing...?" Again she stalled.

"Nothing," he whispered. "They could up the doses of what I've been taking but it only suppresses the symptoms. What's going on underneath still happens. So, putting it straight, I won't be going home."

Sarah was checking her watch. "Dad, we need to get a move on."

"What's going on?" asked Carol. "Somebody got a train to catch?"

"Love," said Roy, waiting for Carol to completely lock eyes with him before continuing, "this is my *Titanic* moment."

"What the heck does that mean?" asked Carol, starting to feel like she was in the middle of something she didn't understand.

"The movie," said Roy, "*Titanic*. The bit at the end where that girl's on the raft and the lad is in the icy water dying of the cold. He tells her he loves her and makes her promise to never give up, to carry on and live out a long and beautiful life for both of them."

Carol shook her head in incomprehension as she stared at her man through tear-blurred eyes.

"I love you, Carol, and I want you to do the same for me as that girl on the raft," he said. "You must carry on. Live your life. And I want to spend my final few days in here imagining you laying under a warm sun and enjoying a well-earned rest."

"I'm going to prison, love. There's no warm sunshine in—"

"No you're not," he said, cutting across her.

"Mum," said Sarah, handing across two small pieces of folded card, each one covered with a beautiful brightly painted illustration of an azure sea lapping against a golden sandy beach lined with palm trees. "These are from the girls."

Carol looked at the fronts then opened each one in turn. The first said, 'Have a nice trip, Grandma', and the other, 'Bon voyage, Grandma'. Both finished with 'I love you' and the individual granddaughter's signature.

"What the...?"

"You're not going back to prison," said Roy. "You're going to Cyprus."

"Like heck I am!"

"You...are!" He almost shouted the words, spacing them wide apart, before finishing with a whispered, "Love."

"But what about you?"

He laughed. "Do I look like I'm packed and ready?" he asked.

"But..." Carol's head was spinning. She was lost.

"Your friend Janice Worthington bought a place out there. You know that. She said she'd already told you. And now she wants you to use it as a hideout, as she calls it. Said she'll be over to join you in a few months once the dust has settled here."

"But—"

"Sarah bought the air ticket. You fly out of Birmingham in about four hours from now, which is why we can't muck about here for too much longer."

"I've got no passport," said Carol, her brain automatically latching onto something hard and real to avoid the swirling mass of uncertainty.

"Trevor wants you to use his Alice's passport. Said she never got to use it and it's a shame for it to go to waste. He said Alice would want you to have it."

"Your tickets are all booked as 'Alice Knight' as well, Mum," said Sarah. "You're the same age, near enough, and you always said all old women look the same."

"Trevor's going to drive you to the airport," said Roy, taking over. "I'd keep your eyes closed if I was you: he's a terrible driver. And he'll help you through check-in and get you to the airport security entrance. After that, you just need to ask for help to get yourself on the right plane."

"And I'm flying to Cyprus?"

"No," said Sarah. "That would be too easy to trace. You're flying to Athens tonight, but don't worry about what to do when you get there. Janice has arranged for somebody called Robbie the Parrot Smuggler to meet you there and travel with you the rest of the way."

Carol couldn't help a short snort of laughter at her proposed escort's title. "But what about this thing?" she asked, lifting her leg to show the tracker tag.

"Rainy's in his van down in the car park," continued Roy. "He's got a set of bolt croppers in the back. We thought you might come in handcuffs but it'll cope with that thing just as easily. And then he's going to drive you to his yard, where..."

"I've left you a small bag of clothes and things for the journey," said Sarah, taking over. "And Trevor will be there waiting for you."

Carol's head was spinning like a top, but even then she could see the one big hole in this magnificent plan. "What about them?" she asked, jabbing a thumb in the direction of her two-man security detail just outside the door. "Or are you expecting me to shinny down six storeys on knotted bed sheets?"

Sarah checked her watch again. "That bit of the puzzle should be falling into place any minute now," she said.

Right on cue, Carol could hear a commotion going on outside the door. It was muffled, but clear enough to recognise it as Janice berating the security guards. Carol cocked her head to hear better, catching only one side of the argument.

"Out of my way, you beast. I'm a good friend of the family and I demand you let me in. If you lay a finger on me, fungus-face, I'll have your bollocks for earrings."

At last the racket died down, the door pushed slowly open, and in stepped Janice. Even in the dimmed interior lighting, her tangerine coat, hat and matching boots ensemble was eye-poppingly bright. "All set?" she hissed.

Roy and Sarah both gave the new arrival a silent thumbs-up as Janice struggled out of her coat at the same time as kicking off her boots. She looked at Carol.

"Say, 'What the hell are you doing here, Janice?'" she instructed.

"What the hell are you doing here, Janice?" said Carol in a bewildered murmur.

"No, no, no," groaned Janice. "Do it loud and aggressive."

"What the hell are you doing here, Janice?" yelled Carol.

"I want to see Roy!" Janice shouted back, following it up with a whisper to Carol, "Now shout, 'Get out of here, Janice. We don't want you in here.'"

"Get out of here, Janice!" shouted Carol. "We don't want you in here!"

All the time the pantomime had been going on, Janice had been strong-arming her best friend into the tangerine overcoat. "Get your shoes off," she whispered, "and now shout, 'Get out of here, Janice, and don't come back.'"

Carol had finally cottoned on, shoving her feet into Janice's boots and shouting, "Get out of here, Janice, and don't come back!" as Janice roughly forced the hat down low over her head before giving her friend a big hug.

"Now get going," hissed Janice into Carol's ear. "I'll see you in a few weeks. Oh, and shout something rude in my voice at 'you' before you slam the door and bugger off."

Carol hugged her friend and then turned to quickly hug her daughter, telling her how much she loved her.

Sarah wished her well, told her she and the girls loved her too, and promised she'd find a way to come and see her one day. "And Paul said to tell you all of the same," she added.

The tears were streaming now, but Carol still had one last thing to do before making her escape. She knelt at her husband's bedside and kissed his hand. Then she stood, stared into his eyes for the very last time, bent, kissed him lightly on the lips, and whispered, "My darling, darling man. I will always, always, *always* love you."

Fighting back the choking sobs, she forced herself to stiffen her back and stride across to the door where she paused momentarily before yanking it open, immediately turning around so as to back out. "And you, Carol fucking Jackson," she shouted into the room as the door swung slowly shut, "can go and fucking-well fuck yourself!" Then it was merely a play-acted angry little old lady scuttle along the corridor and down in the lift to freedom.

# Chapter 44

## *Somewhere Around a Year Later*

"Good morning, Detective *Inspector* Roberts," said Jacquie as she wandered into Danny's office carrying two mugs of coffee.

"And good morning to you too, Detective *Sergeant* Napier," he replied. It had become their customary morning banter of late.

"Sounds good, doesn't it?" she chuckled. "And after all those myriad times bloody Shirley told you that you would never, *ever* get promoted."

"Lucky I did, so there was a sergeant's job waiting vacant for somebody half capable to come along and fill it."

"And I thank you, boss," said Jacquie, doing a little curtsy as she placed Danny's coffee on his desk. "What did you think?" she asked, pointing down at the thumbed paperback on his desk. "*The Red Fox Diaries* – neat title, eh? Good old Percy Walsh."

"I enjoyed it," said Danny. "A bit slow in parts, but overall a good read."

"Any idea how she got all the inside info and stuff?" asked Jacquie. "I mean, our Carol had skipped before Walsh even got to talk to her."

"I'm guessing they managed to set up some sort of communication channel. Quite how is beyond me, but there are ways. And Walsh won't ever tell, that's for sure."

"Talking of Percy," said Jacquie, again pointing at the paperback, "she does not like Shirley one little bit, does she? Never misses the chance to put the boot in, not that he doesn't deserve it. I reckon he must have really upset her in that first meeting."

Danny chuckled. "I like the way she makes it sound like he's now working as a supermarket security guard, nabbing skanky shoplifters."

"Not far off," snorted Jacquie. "'Director of Security' sounds a mighty fine title, but not when it's for a chain of cheap-as-chips discount stores in Essex."

"So what did *you* think of the book?" asked Danny.

"I thought it was great. And the whole theme running through it about female empowerment was a really strong message. As was the underlying thread about perceptions of social class, and from there to social immobility. And then there's—"

"You're losing me now," said Danny. "I just read it as a good story."

"Typical," scoffed Jacquie. "But you come out of it very nicely," she added. "I mean, she makes you sound like some sort of sainted being. And a crack top-notch super-sleuth detective to boot. Bangs on pretty hard that if it hadn't been for you taking a punt on those fingerprints, we'd have almost certainly lost the case."

"I know," said Danny, nodding. "That defence lawyer was right on it."

"I still can't work out, though, how Walsh got to know about the memo in the supposedly confidential police file where Shirley recorded that you took the fingerprint initiative in direct contradiction to his express order. Any idea?"

Danny shook his head, but smirked mischievously. "None at all," he replied. "Not an inkling. But it didn't half help with securing my promotion."

"And hence mine," added Jacquie. "And then so on down the line, all the way to... Aye aye, speak of the devil."

Detective Constable Kevin Marsh had appeared in the doorway, a single sheet of paper in his hand. "Am I interrupting something?" he asked.

"Just chewing the fat before another day of detectiving," said Danny. He picked up his copy of *The Red Fox Diaries* and waved it at Kevin. "Have you read it?" he asked.

"I'm going to wait for the movie," said Kevin. "Want to see who gets to play me. But that aside," he said quickly, before either of his colleagues could make a rude suggestion, "it's a bit of a coincidence, you chatting about Foxy, because this just came in on the fax." He waved the sheet of paper. "It's a CFS report from Interpol."

"A what?" asked Jacquie.

"A credible fugitive sighting," said Danny. "It means some bunch of coppers somewhere in the world has spotted, or think they've spotted, a person on the international wanted list."

"It's her," said Kevin. "Carol Jackson, the Red Fox."

"What?" exclaimed Danny. "Where?"

"Larnaca, Cyprus," said Kevin, reading the sheet. "English woman, right age, right build, going under the name Alice Knight. Seems she's living in a private bungalow complex in a property owned by another English woman," he paused to read the name, "Janice Worthington."

"Wasn't that the best friend who helped her escape?" asked Jacquie.

"*Allegedly*," replied Danny. "Yes, it was her, but she said her coat was stolen while she was chatting to poor old Roy Jackson, God rest his soul, and nobody could be bothered to prove otherwise."

"Bit of a coincidence, though, isn't it?" pressed Jacquie.

"Have they got a picture, Kev?" asked Danny, holding out a hand for his DC to pass him the sheet. He took it and looked. It was a colour thumbnail embedded into the text. An elderly lady lounging on a wooden steamer-chair by a small swimming pool. Danny peered closely at the picture and, try as he might, he simply could not stop himself from purring, "Clever girl" under his breath. It was her, no doubt about it. The wily old, cunning old Whitchurch Red Fox relaxing under the Cypriot sun.

"So what do you want me to do, boss?" asked Kevin, looking awkwardly from Danny to Jacquie and back again.

"Send them back a message," said Danny. "Say, 'Thank you very much, but we have studied the information and concluded categorically that this woman is *not* Carol Jackson.' Then add a bit of flim-flam about how we've got the real one in our sights and expect to be making an arrest soon in... what shall we say, Malaga?"

"Will do," said Kevin, adding a knowing wink. "And what about that?" he asked, pointing at the CFS report.

"This," said Danny, waving the sheet gently in the air, "is going in the shredder."

www.ingramcontent.com/pod-product-compliance
Lightning Source LLC
LaVergne TN
LVHW091117080826
845145LV00008B/1956
*9781800423220*